OECUMENE

Tales of Ancient Greece & Egypt

IVAN EFREMOV

Paperback ISBN: 978-1-947228-04-7
ePub ISBN: 978-1-947228-03-0

Written by Ivan Efremov
Published by Royal Hawaiian Press
Cover art by Tyrone Roshantha
Translated by Rafal Stachowski
Localized/Edited by Carol Barker
Publishing Assistance by Cheeky Kea Printworks

Translated and published in English with permission.

First Edition

PROLOGUE

A fresh autumn breeze swept over the ruffled surface of the Neva. In the bright sunshine the tall, slim spire on the Fortress of Peter and Paul as a streak of gold piercing the blue canopy of the sky. Below it, the Palace Bridge gracefully curved its broad back over rising and falling waves that sparkled and splashed against the granite steps of the embankment.

A young sailor sitting on a bench glanced at his watch, jumped up and walked off rapidly along the embankment, past the Admiralty building whose yellow walls reared their crown of white columns high into the transparent autumn air. He walked quickly, paying no attention to the holiday atmosphere that surrounded him. He strode along with a light and confident step. The exercise warmed him, and he pushed his sailor cap on to the back of his head. He crossed a garden whose trees were aflame with autumn tints, passed along one side of an open space, and for a moment stood before the entrance to the Hermitage Museum where two polished granite giants supported a massive balcony raised over a humped pavement. Scars made by German bombs were still seen on the giant bodies.

The young man entered the heavy doors, took off his greatcoat and hurried towards a white marble staircase leading from the semi-gloom of the vestibule to a brightly lit colonnade surrounded by a row of marble statues. A tall, slim girl, smiling with pleasure, came to meet him. Her attentive eyes, set wide apart, seemed to grow darker and warmer. The sailor looked at the girl in some embarrassment, but when he saw that she was just putting her cloakroom check into her open bag, he knew that he was not late. His face lit up, and he confidently proposed starting their tour of the museum with the Gallery of Antiquities. The young people passed through the crowd of visitors, making their way along rows of columns supporting a brightly painted ceiling. After looking at the remains of vases and stone slabs bearing inscriptions in unknown languages, dismal, black statues from ancient Egypt, sarcophagi, mummies, and other funereal appurtenances that seemed even more depressing in the gloomy galleries of the lower story, they felt the need for bright colors and sunshine.

The youth and the girl hurried to reach the upper rooms. Passing through two more rooms, they made their way to a side staircase that led to the galleries from a small room with tall, narrow windows through which gleamed a pale sky. A number of conical octagonal showcases stood between the white columns, but the small items of ancient art exhibited in them did not seem to attract the attention of visitors.

Suddenly the girl's eyes caught a patch of marvelous blue-green light in the third showcase; it was so brilliant that it seemed to be a source of light in itself. The girl led her companion to the showcase. A flat stone with round edges lay on a sloping bed of silver-colored velvet. The stone was extraordinarily pure and translucent. Its glowing blue-green color was unexpectedly joyous, brilliant, and deep. On the upper surface, obviously polished by the hand of man, cleanly cut human figures, no bigger than one's little finger, stood out in sharp relief. The color, brilliance, and light emanating from the clear tone formed a striking contrast to the gloomy severity of the gallery and the pale tones of the autumn sky. The girl heard her companion heave a deep sigh and noticed a dreamy look in his eyes that spoke of memories evoked by the stone.

"That's just like the southern sea on a fine afternoon," said the young sailor slowly, with the absolute confidence of one who has seen things resounded in his words.

"That's something I've never seen before," replied the girl. "I feel some sort of depth in that stone, some sort of light and joy... I can't exactly explain... Where do people find stones like this?"

The general heading over the four showcases: Antae Burials: 7th Century, Middle Dnieper, River Ros, nor the label on the showcase itself: Grebenets Burial Mound, Ancient Clan Shrine, told the young people nothing. The other objects that surrounded the beautiful stone were equally incomprehensible: broken knives and spearheads so ugly and damaged by rust as to be unrecognizable, flat bowls, and some sort of pendants of blackened bronze and silver in the form of a trapezium.

"All this was dug up in Kiev Region," the young man hazarded a guess, "but I've never heard that stones like that are found anywhere in Ukraine. Who could we ask?" The young man looked around the big gallery. It was just their bad luck that there was not a single museum guide anywhere within sight; nobody but the woman caretaker sitting on her chair near the staircase.

From the staircase came the sound of footsteps and a tall man in a carefully pressed black suit came down into the gallery. From the way the caretaker got up and greeted him with deference, the girl guessed rightly that he was a man of importance in the museum. She gave her companion a quiet nudge, but he was already on his way to meet the newcomer. Standing to attention, sailor-fashion, he began:

"May I ask you something?"

"Certainly. What is it you want to know?" said the scientist, screwing up his near-sighted eyes to examine the young couple.

The sailor told him what had interested them. The scientist laughed. "You have a nose for good things, young man!" he exclaimed approvingly. "You've lighted on one of the most interesting exhibits in our museum! Did you examine the carving closely? No? Too small? And what do you think this thing is for? Look!" He reached up and took hold of a wooden frame hinged to the upper edge of the showcase and lowered it over the glass. A big magnifying glass came into position precisely opposite the stone. He pressed a switch, and a bright light illuminated its surface.

More interested than ever the young couple peered through the magnifying glass. The enlarged carving seemed to come to life. On one edge of the transparent, blue-green stone, fine but scanty lines traced the nude figure of a girl standing with her right hand raised to her cheek. Rolls of thick, curly hair lay on her delicately molded shoulders. The face had been carved with great attention to detail.

The remaining part of the stone was filled by three male figures, their arms around each other's shoulders; these figures were drawn with far greater skill than that of the girl. The shapely muscular figures had been caught in motion. There was something dynamic in the turn of the bodies, strong, urgent and at the same time restrained. The big man in the center, taller than those on either side of him, had thrown his mighty arms around their shoulders.

The side figures, armed with spears, stood with their heads bent attentively. The poses expressed the tense vigilance of warriors ready at any moment to repulse the attack of an enemy.

The three tiny figures were the work of a great artist. The basic idea - fraternity, friendship, and the universal struggle - was expressed with extraordinary force.

The charm of the bright, transparent stone, which served both as material and as background, greatly enhanced the beauty of the cameo. A limpid, warm tint that seemed to emanate from the depths of the cold transparent stone tinged the bodies of the three embracing men with the golden joy of sunshine. Under the figures and on the smooth, lower edge, some incomprehensible marks had been hurriedly and irregularly scratched.

"Have you had a good look? I can see you're thrilled with it." The voice of the archaeologist gave the young people a start. "Good. If you like, I'll tell you something about that stone. This is one of the riddles that we sometimes come across in historical documents from the past. Listen while I tell you just what the puzzle is. That stone is a beryl. In general, it is not a particularly rare mineral, although blue-green beryls of such pure water are rare enough. South Africa is the only place in the world where they can be found. That's the first point.

"The carving on the stone is a cameo and ornaments of this type were greatly admired in Greece when ancient Hellenic art was at its best. Now the beryl is a very hard stone, and such a carving could only have been made with a diamond that the Greek sculptors did not have. That's the second point.

"Next, take the three male figures. The central one is undoubtedly a Kemtiu – that's the name the Ancient Egyptians called coal-coated or black people – the one on the right a Hellene, and that on the left, one of the Mediterranean peoples, probably a Cretan or an Etruscan. Lastly, the quality and technique indicate that the work belongs to the most flourishing period in the history of Greece. Nevertheless, there are a number of features that show that it was made at a much earlier date. Then, the spears are of a peculiar shape unknown in either Greece or Egypt. So, you see there are several contradictions and a number of incompatible indicants, but despite them, the cameo exists, it's before your eyes."

The archaeologist paused and then continued in the same abrupt way:

"There are many more historical riddles. All of them tell us one thing - how little we know. We have very little knowledge of how the ancient peoples lived. Amongst the Scythian works of art in our gold repository, for example, we have a gold buckle. It is two thousand six hundred years old and carries the image of the extinct saber-toothed tiger in all its details. Yes, yes, and the paleontologists will tell you that the saber-toothed tiger became extinct three hundred thousand years ago. Ha! And in Egyptian tombs, you will see frescoes on which every kind of animal found in Egypt is drawn with amazing accuracy. Amongst them is an unknown animal of tremendous size that looks like a giant hyena-such an animal is unknown in Egypt, in all Africa, in fact. Then, in the Cairo Museum, there is a statue of a girl found in the ruins of the city of Akhetaton, built in the 14th century B.C. She is not an Egyptian and the work is not Egyptian, it is like something from another world. My colleagues will tell you that it is con-ven-tion-al-ized," drawled the archaeologist with a touch of sarcasm.

"In connection with this, I always like to recall another story. On those same Egyptian wall paintings, you often come across a little fish. Just a tiny fish with nothing special about it except that it is always drawn upside down, belly upwards. How could the Egyptians, whose drawings are always so precise, draw such an unnatural fish? Explanations, of course, were forthcoming: it was explained away by conventionalism, by religion, by the influence of the cult of the god Amon. The conclusions were quite convincing, and everybody was satisfied. Then it was discovered that there is a fish in the Nile today exactly like the one in the paintings. It swims belly upwards! Very instructive. But I'm running away with myself! Good-bye, you'll find the riddles of history interesting."

"Just a minute, Professor!" exclaimed the girl. "Excuse me, but can't you explain this riddle yourself. Tell us what you think about the stone" The girl stopped in embarrassment.

The archaeologist smiled.

"There's no getting away from you. All that I can tell you is sheer guesswork, that's all. One thing is certain: real art reflects life. Art itself is living and can only rise to new heights in the struggle against the old.

"In the distant past, when that cameo was carved, slavery, oppression, and lawlessness reigned supreme. Many people lived out their lives in perpetual misery. There were slaves, however, who fought for their emancipation, and oppressed people who rose up in arms against their oppressors. When one looks at this cameo one feels that the friendship of the three warriors arose out of the fight for liberty. Perhaps they fled from slavery to their own countries.

"I think that cameo is further evidence of a struggle waged in a distant epoch and hidden from us by time. It is even possible that the unknown artist also took part in the fight. Yes, he must certainly have been there; otherwise, his work could not have been so perfect. And look how both of you fixed your attention on the cameo."

The young man and woman, overwhelmed by the mass of information given to them, again pressed close to the magnifying glass. The stone seemed even more mysterious and incomprehensible to them. The pure, clear, and deep color of the sea... and on it the figures of three men linked in a fraternal embrace. The brilliant, scintillating stone and the golden tinge on the perfect, undraped bodies stood out with even greater force in the cold, dull gallery of the museum. The young girl, full of life and feminine charm, seemed to be standing on the seashore. With a sigh, the young sailor straightened his aching back. The girl still kept her eyes on the stone. The shuffling of feet and the noise of an approaching excursion group resounded down the corridors. Only then did the girl tear herself away from the case. The switch clicked, the frame lifted, and the blue-green crystal lay sparkling on its velvet bed.

"We'll come here again, won't we?" asked the sailor.

"Of course, we shall," answered the girl. The young man took her gently by the arm, and they walked down the white marble staircase deep in thought.

CHAPTER ONE.

The Sculptor's Apprentice

The flat rock jutted far out into the sea. It had retained the warmth of the day and the youth sitting there was not in the least disturbed by the fresh gusts of wind that found their way between the cliffs. The sea, invisible in the darkness of night, splashed faintly against the foot of the rock. The young man stared into the distance, contemplating the point at which the end of that silver band called the Milky Way disappeared into the darkness.

He was watching the falling stars; a cluster of them had flashed by to pierce the sky with their fiery needles, and then disappear behind the horizon, fading like burning arrows falling into the water. Again, the flaming arrows flashed across the heavens, flying into the unknown, to the fabled lands that lay beyond the sea on the very borders of Oecumene. (Oecumene: the name given by the ancient Greeks to the inhabited world surrounded by water, Oceanos.)

"I will ask grandad where they fall," decided the youth and thought how wonderful it would be to fly like that through the sky direct to some unknown destination.

But then he was no longer a youth. A few more days and he would attain the age of a warrior. He would never be a warrior, however, but would become a famous artist, a sculptor of renown.

His innate ability to see right forms in nature, to sense and remember them, made him different from most people. Or so his teacher, the sculptor Agenor, had told him. And so it was, for where others passed indifferently by, he would halt in sheer amazement, seeing that which he could neither comprehend nor explain. The myriad of manifestations of nature charmed him by their constant mutations.

Later his vision grew clearer, and he learned to distinguish the beautiful and retain it in his memory. There was elusive beauty in all things; in the curve of the crest of a running wave, in the locks of Thessa's hair when the wind played in them, in the stately columns of the pine trunks and in the menacing rocks that rose proudly over the seashore.

From the moment he first became conscious of this he had made the creation of beautiful forms his aim in life. He wanted to show beauty to those unable to perceive it for themselves. What could be more beautiful than the human body! To mold it, however, was the most difficult of all the arts. This told him why the living features he retained in his memory were not to be found in the statues of the gods and heroes he saw all around him and which he was being taught to make. Even the most skilled sculptors of Oeniadae (Oeniadae-Pandion's birthplace, at the south-western tip of Northern Greece the story belongs to the early period in Greek history, before the classical era) could not mold a moving image of the living human body.

The youth instinctively felt that certain features expressing joy will power, wrath or tenderness were crudely exaggerated, and to give this artificial prominence to certain forcefully expressed features the artist had sacrificed all else. But he must learn to depict life! Only then, would he become the most celebrated sculptor in his country and people would acclaim him and admire the things he would create. His would be the first works of art to perpetuate the beauty of life in bronze or stone!

The youth had been carried far away into the land of

dreams when he was aroused by a bigger wave crashing against the rock. A few drops of water fell on the youth's face. He shivered, opened his eyes and smiled, embarrassed, in the darkness. Oh, Gods! That dream was probably still far away in the future. In the meantime, his teacher Agenor was constantly upbraiding him for his clumsy work and for some reason or another, the teacher was always right. There was his grandfather. Grandad showed little interest in Pandion's progress as an artist, for he was training his grandson with a view to making him a famous wrestler. As though an artist needed strength! Still, it was a good thing grandad had taught him like that, had made him more than ordinarily strong and hardy; Pandion liked to show his strength and prowess at the evening contests in the village, when Thessa, his teacher's daughter, was present, and to note the gleam of approbation in the girl's eyes.

With burning cheeks, the youth jumped to his feet, every muscle in his body tensed. He thrust out his chest as if to challenge the wind and raised his face to the stars; suddenly he laughed softly. He ambled to the edge, peered into the seemingly bottomless gloom, gave a loud cry and sprang from the rock. The calm, silent night immediately came to life. Below the cliff there was the sea whose waters wrapped his hot skin in a cooling embrace, sparkling with tiny dots of fire around his arms and shoulders. The waves, in their play, forced the youth upwards, striving to throw him back. As he swam in the darkness, he estimated the undulations of the waves and confidently threw himself at the high crests that appeared suddenly before him. It seemed to Pandion that the sea was bottomless and boundless; that it merged with the dark sky in a single whole.

A big wave lifted the youth high above the sea, and he saw a red light far away along the coast. A smooth stroke and the wave obediently carried the youth to the shore, towards a scarcely visible grey patch of sand. Shivering slightly from the cold he again climbed on to the flat rock, took up his coarse woolen cloak, rolled it up, and set off at a run along the beach towards the light of the fire.

The aromatic smoke of burning brushwood curled through the adjacent thickets. The feeble light of the flames lit up the wall of a small hut built of rough-hewn stones with the eaves of a thatched roof projecting over it. The wide-spreading branches of a single plane tree protected the shelter from inclement weather. An old man in a grey cloak sat by the fire, deep in thought. On hearing the approaching footsteps, he turned towards them, his smiling, wrinkled face, the tan of which showed darker in the frame of a grey curling beard.

"Where have you been so long, Pandion?" asked the old man reproachfully. "I've been back a long time and wanted to talk to you."

"I didn't think you'd come so soon," answered the youth. "I went to bathe. And now I'm ready to listen to you all night if you like."

The old man shook his head in refusal. "No, the talk will be a long one, and you have to be up early in the morning. I want to give you a trial tomorrow, and you will need all your strength. Here are some fresh cakes. I brought a new stock of them with me and here is the honey. It's a festive supper tonight: you may eat as becomes a warrior - little and without greed."

The young man contentedly broke a cake and dipped

the white, torn edge into an earthen pot of honey. As he ate, he kept his eyes fixed on his grandfather who sat silently watching his grandson with a fond look. The eyes of both, the old man, and the youth, were alike and unusual; they gleamed golden, like the concentrated light of a sunray. There was a widespread belief that people with such eyes were descended from the earthly lovers of the "Son of the Heights," - Hyperion, the sun god.

"I thought about you after you'd gone today, Grandad," said the youth.

"Why is it that other bards live in good houses and eat their fill although they know nothing but their songs? But you, Grandad, who know so much, who make such wonderful songs, have to toil on the sea. The boat's too heavy for you now, and I'm your only helper. We haven't got a single slave."

The old man smiled and placed his gnarled hand on Pandion's curly head.

"That's what I wanted to talk to you about tomorrow. Only one thing will I say tonight: many different songs may be composed of the gods and about people. If you are honest with yourself, if your eyes are open, your songs will not sound pleasant to the lordly owners of the land and the warrior chiefs. And you will have neither rich gifts, nor slaves, nor fame, you will not be known in the great houses, and you will not gain a livelihood from your songs. Time for bed," the old man broke off. "Look, the Chariot of the Night (Chariot of the Night - the Great Bear constellation. Cf. Charles's Wain. -Tr.), is already turning to the other side of the heavens. Its black horses travel fast, and a man who wants to be strong must rest. Come on." The old man moved off towards the narrow doorway of his miserable hut.

The old man awakened Pandion early next morning. The cold autumn was drawing near; the sky was overcast with heavy clouds, a biting wind rustled in the dry reeds and in the few remaining leaves of the plane tree. Under his grandfather's stern and exacting guidance, Pandion went through his gymnastic exercises. Thousands and thousands of times, from early boyhood, he had repeated them every day at sunrise and sunset, but today grandad selected the most difficult exercises and increased their number. Pandion hurled a heavy javelin, threw stones, and jumped over obstacles with a sack of sand on his shoulders.

At last, grandad fastened a heavy piece of walnut wood to his left hand, placed a gnarled wooden club in his right and tied a piece of a broken stone vase to his head. Restraining his laughter for fear of wasting his breath, Pandion awaited a sign from his grandfather and then set out at a run northwards, where the path from the littoral ran round a steep, stony slope. He raced along the way like lightning, scrambled up to the first ledge of a cliff, turned and came down even faster.

The old man met his grandson at the hut, relieved him of his burden and then pressed his cheek to the lad's face to determine the degree of tiredness from the rate of his breathing. After a few seconds, the youth said:

"I could run there and back many times before I would ask for a rest."

"Yes, I think you could," answered the old man slowly, and proudly straightened his back. "You're fit to be a warrior, capable of fighting tirelessly in battle and carrying heavy bronze accouterments. My son, your father gave you your health and strength, and I have developed them in you and made you bold and enduring."

The old man cast a glance over the youth's figure, allowing his eyes to rest on his broad, powerful chest and on the powerful muscles that rippled under the skin without a single blemish.

"I'm the only relative you have," he continued, "and I'm old and weak; we've neither wealth nor servants, and our entire phralry (phratry - a union of several Clans; tribes grew out of several phratries when the gentile social system still predominated) consists of three villages on a stony seashore.

The world is vast, and many dangers beset a lonely man. The greatest of them is the loss of liberty, the possibility of being taken captive and sent to slavery. This is why I have devoted so much time and effort to make a warrior of you. You are a man of courage who is competent in all matters of war. Now you are free to serve your people. Come; let us make a sacrifice to Hyperion, our patron, in honor of your attaining man's estate."

Grandfather and grandson made their way along the patches of sedge grass and reeds towards a narrow spit of land that reached far out into the sea like a long wall. Two thick oaks with wide-spreading branches grew at the end of the spit. Between them stood an altar built of rough limestone blocks behind which was a blackened wooden post, crudely carved in the shape of a human figure. This was an ancient temple dedicated to the local deity, the River Achelous, which joined the sea there.

The mouth of the river was hidden in the green reeds and bushes swarming with migratory birds from the north. Before them stretched the mist-covered sea. Waves raced with a crash against the point of a spit resembling the neck of some gigantic animal holding its head under water. The solemn roar of the waves, the shrill cries of the birds, the whistling of the wind in the reeds and the rustling foliage of the oaks; all these sounds merged into an uneasy, rumbling melody.

The old man lit a fire on the rude altar and threw a piece of meat and a cake into the flames. When the sacrifice had been made, the old man led Pandion to a big stone at the foot of a steep mossy cliff and bade him push the boulder aside. The youth did so with ease and then, following his grandfather's instructions, thrust his hand into a deep crevice between two strata of limestone. There was a rattle of metal and Pandion drew out a bronze sword, a helmet and a broad belt of square copper plates serving as armor for the lower part of the body- all of them dulled with patches of verdigris.

"These are the arms of your father, who died young," said the grandfather in a low voice. "A shield and bow you must acquire yourself."

The youth bent excitedly over the accouterments and began carefully cleaning off the verdigris. The old man sat down on the stone, leaned his back against the cliff and fell to watching his grandson and trying to hide his sorrow from him. Pandion left his armor and, in a burst of ecstasy, threw himself on the old man, embraced him. The old man placed an arm around the youth, feeling the knots of his mighty muscles. It seemed to the grandfather that his long-dead son was reborn in this youthful body, designed to overcome obstacles. The old man turned the youth's face towards himself and stared long into the open, golden eyes.

"Now you have to decide, Pandion: will you go at once to the chief of our phratry to serve him as a warrior, or will you remain Agenor's apprentice?"

"I shall remain with Agenor," answered Pandion without giving the matter a second thought. "If I go now to the chief in the village, I shall have to stay there to live and eat in the company of the men, and you will be left here alone. I don't want to be parted from you and shall stay and help you."

"No, Pandion, we must part company," said the old man, firmly but with an effort.

The youth jumped back in astonishment, but the old man's hand held him.

"I have fulfilled the promise I made my son, your father, Pandion," continued the old man. "Now you must make your own way in life. You must start on your life's road free, not burdened by the care of a helpless old man. I am leaving our Oeniadae for fertile Elis, where my daughters live with their husbands. When you become a famous sculptor, you will be able to find me."

The youth's heated protests only made the old man shake his head. Pandion had said many caring, imploring and discontented words before he finally realized that the old man had for years carried in his mind this unalterable decision and that his experience of life made him implacable. With a sad and heavy heart, the youth spent the whole day with his grandfather helping him prepare for his journey.

In the evening, they sat down together on an upturned, newly caulked boat, and the grandfather got out a lyre that had seen much in its time. The robust and youthful voice of the aged bard carried along the beach, dying out in the distance. He sang a song filled with sadness, one that recalled the regular beating of the waves against the shore.

At Pandion's request, the old man sang him the lays of the origin of their race, and about neighboring lands and peoples. Aware of the fact that he was hearing the words for the last time, the youth tried to catch every single one of them, striving to remember songs that from earliest childhood had been tightly bound up with the image of his grandfather. Pandion pictured in his mind the ancient heroes who had united the tribes. The old bard sang of the stern beauties of his native land where all things in nature are gods incarnate; he sang of the greatness of those who loved life and conquered nature, instead of hiding from her in the temples and turning their backs on the present day, and the youth's heart beat furiously. It was as though he stood at the beginning of roads leading into the unknown distance where every turn opened up new and unexpected vistas.

That morning it seemed that the hot summer had returned. The clear blue of the sky breathed heat, the still air was filled with the song of the grasshoppers, and the white cliffs and boulders gave off a dazzling reflection of the sun. The sea had turned transparent and rippled idly along the shore, for all the world like old wine in a giant cup.

When his grandfather's boat was lost to sight in the distance, sorrow gripped Pandion's breast like an iron band. He fell to the ground, resting his head on his crossed arms. He felt himself a small boy, alone and abandoned, who with the departure of his grandfather had lost part of his own heart. Tears poured over Pandion's arms, but these were not the tears of a child; they came in huge, separate drops that brought no relief.

His dreams of great deeds had receded far into the background. Nothing could console him. He wanted to stay with his grandfather. Slowly but surely came the realization that the loss was irreparable, and Pandion made an effort to set his feelings under control. Ashamed of his tears, he bit his lip, raised his head, and gazed for a long time into the distant sea, until his confused thoughts again began to flow smoothly and consistently. He rose to his feet, his eyes swept over the sun-warmed shore and the hut under the plane tree, and again unutterable sorrow overcame him. He realized that the carefree days of his youth were past, never again to return with their semi-childish dreams.

Pandion plodded his way slowly to the hut. Here he buckled on his sword and wrapped his other possessions in his cloak. He fastened the door securely so that storms might not enter the shelter and went off along a stony path swept clean by the sea winds, the harsh dry grass swishing mournfully under his feet. The path led to a hill covered with dark green bushes whose sun-warmed leaves gave off the strong odor of pressed olives. At the foot of the hill, the path branched into two - the right-hand path leading to a group of fishermen's huts on the seashore, the other continuing along the riverbank to the town.

Pandion took the left-hand path and passed the hill. His feet sank into hot white dust, and the singing of myriads of grasshoppers drowned the noise of the sea. The stony slope of the hill disappeared in a wealth of trees where its foot reached the river. The long narrow leaves of the oleanders and the dense green of the bay trees were overshadowed by the dense foliage of huge walnut trees, the whole merging into a curling mass that seemed almost black against the white background of limestone.

Pandion's path led him through the forest shade and after a few turns brought him to an open glade on which stood some small houses clustered at the foot of the gently sloping terraces of the vineyards. The youth quickened his pace and hastened towards a low, white house visible behind the angular trunks of an olive grove. He entered an open shed, and a middle-aged, black-bearded man of medium height rose to meet him; this was Agenor, the master sculptor.

"So, you've come at last," exclaimed the sculptor in some elation. "I was thinking of sending for you. And what's this?" Agenor noticed that Pandion was armed. "Let me embrace you, my boy. Thessa, Thessa!" he shouted, "come and look at our warrior!"

Pandion turned quickly round. Out of the inner door peeped a girl in a dark red himation thrown carelessly over a chiton of fine, but faded pale blue cloth. (Himation - woman's outer garment consisting of a rectangular piece of material in the form of a shawl, usually thrown over the shoulder but in bad weather could be used to cover the head. The chiton is a long, sleeveless garment of thin material, worn without the himation in the house.) A smile of pleasure revealed her lovely teeth but an instant later the smile vanished, the girl frowned and gave Pandion a cold stare.

"See. Thessa's angry with you. For two whole days you haven't been able to find time to come here and tell us you were not going to work," said the sculptor, reproachfully.

The youth stood silently with drooping head, and his eyes shifted stealthily from the girl to his master.

"What's wrong with you, boy? No, not boy but warrior," said Agenor. "Why this sadness and what's that bundle you have brought with you?"

Hesitantly, incoherently, again afflicted by the sorrow of parting, he told of his grandfather's departure.

Agenor's wife, the mother of Thessa, approached

them. The sculptor laid his hands on the youth's shoulders. "You have long since earned our love, Pandion. I am glad you have chosen the life of an artist in preference to that of a warrior. The fighting will come. You won't be able to avoid it, but in the meantime, you have much to achieve by hard, persevering labor and meditation."

Pandion, following the custom, bowed low to Agenor's wife and she covered his head with the corner of her mantle and then pressed him fondly to her bosom.

The girl gave a little shout of joy and then, with signs of embarrassment, disappeared into the house, followed by her father's smile.

Agenor sat down by the entrance to his workshop for a quiet rest. A grove of ancient olive trees grew right outside the house; their huge, angular trunks were intertwined most fantastically that to the contemplative eye of the artist, resembled people, and animals. One of the trees was like a kneeling giant whose arms were held wide apart above his head. The rugged irregularities of another tree-trunk formed an ugly body, distorted by suffering. It seemed as though all the trees were bent under the effort to raise upward the heavy weight of their many branches covered with tiny silvery leaves.

The figure of a woman in a bright blue holiday himation with gold ornaments slipped out of the other side of the house. As she disappeared behind the slope of the hill, the sculptor recognized his daughter. Treading softly with her bare feet, Agenor's wife came and sat down beside her husband.

"Thessa has gone to Pandion in the pine grove again," said the sculptor and then added, "The children think we don't know their little secret!"

His wife laughed gaily but turned suddenly serious as she asked:

"What do you think of Pandion now that he's been with us a year?"

"I like him more than ever," answered Agenor and his wife nodded her head in agreement. "But..." The artist paused before choosing his next words.

"He wants too much," his wife finished the sentence for him.

"Yes, he wants a lot, and much has been granted him by the gods. There is nobody to teach him. I cannot give him what he's seeking," said the old artist with a note of sorrow in his voice.

"It seems to me that he's too uncertain, he can't find his own vocation; he's not like other lads," the woman said in a low voice. "I can't imagine what he wants, and sometimes I feel sorry for him."

"You're right, my dear. No happiness will be Pandion's if he strives to achieve that which nobody else has ever been able to. You are worried, and I know why. You're afraid for Thessa, aren't you?"

"No, I'm not afraid. My daughter is proud and brave. Still, I feel that her love for Pandion may bring her sorrow. It's a bad thing for a man to be afflicted, like Pandion, with the passion of the seeker - not even love will heal his eternal yearning."

"As it healed me." The sculptor smiled fondly at his wife. "I suppose I was like Pandion, once."

"Oh, no, you were always stronger and more balanced," said his wife, stroking Agenor's greying head.

The artist gazed into the distance beyond the pines amidst which Thessa had disappeared. The girl hurried on to the sea, frequently glancing back, although she knew that so early on the morning of a holiday nobody would go to the sacred grove.

Waves of heat were already surging from the white stones of the barren hills. At first, the path led across flat land covered with thorn bushes and Thessa walked warily so as not to tear the skirts of her best chiton made of fine, almost transparent material brought from overseas. Farther on, the ground rose in a low, rounded hill covered with brilliant red flowers, blazing in the bright sunlight like a mass of dark flames. Here there were no thorns, and the girl took up the folds of her chiton, lifted it high and ran on.

Thessa passed quickly by the isolated trees and soon found herself in the grove. The straight trunks of the pines shone like purple wax, their broad crowns rustled noisily in the wind and their spreading branches, bristling with needles as long as a man's hand, were turned to golden dust in the sun's rays. An odor of heated resin and pine needles, mingled with the breath of the sea, filled the whole grove.

The girl slackened her pace, unconsciously submitting to the solemn calm of the woods. To her right, a grey rock sprinkled with fallen pine needles rose up amongst the trees. A shaft of sunlight slanted down into a small glade turning the surrounding trees into columns of red gold. Here the rumbling roar of the sea was heard more clearly; although it could not be seen, the sea made its presence felt by the low, measured chords of its music.

Pandion ran out from behind the rock to meet Thessa, caught her by her outstretched arms and pulled her towards him, then, pushing her a little way back, gazed intently at her as though he were trying to absorb her image to the full.

Locks of her shining black hair quivered on her smooth forehead, her thin eyebrows, slightly arched, rose towards her temples; the shape of her brows gave her big dark blue eyes an elusive expression of mocking pride. With a gentle movement, Thessa escaped the youth.

"Make haste, people will be coming here soon!" she said, looking fondly at Pandion.

"I'm ready," he said, going towards the rock in which was a narrow vertical crevice. On a block of limestone stood an unfinished statue of kneaded clay about three feet high. Beside it, the sculptor's wooden tools were laid out - curved saws, knives, and trowels.

The girl threw off her himation and slowly raised her hands to the brooch, which fastened the folds of the flimsy chiton on her shoulder.

Smiling, Pandion watched her, and selecting his tools, but when he turned towards the statue, the triumphant smile gradually vanished. That crude figure was still far from possessing Thessa's ravishing beauty. Again, the clay had already assumed the proportions of her body. Today must decide everything. Finally, he would give the piece of dead earth the charm of living lines.

With a frown of determination, Pandion turned towards Thessa. She glanced sideways at him and nodded her head. With downcast eyes, the girl leaned against the trunk of a pine tree with one arm behind her head. Immersed in his work Pandion did not speak. The youth's penetrating gaze shifted from the body of his model to the clay and back again, changing, measuring, comparing. This struggle between the dead clay, indifferent to the form it was given, and the creative hands of the artist who strove to provide it with the beauty of the living girl, had been going on for many days. Time passed, and the youth's attentive ear had on several occasions, caught the suppressed sighs of the tired girl.

Pandion stopped work, stepped back from the statue and Thessa gave an involuntary shudder as she heard the bitter groan of disappointment that escaped him. The clay figure had grown much worse. There had been life in it, hinted at by scarcely perceptible lines, but now that these had been made prominent, the statue was dead. It had become nothing more than a crude semblance of Thessa's tawny body standing before the trunk of a huge pine tree the color of old gold.

Biting his lips, the youth compared the statue with Thessa, making a desperate effort to find out what was wrong. Actually, there was nothing that could be called wrong; it was merely his failure to breathe life into his work, to catch the changing forms of the living body. He had thought that the strength of his love, his frank admiration of Thessa's beauty would enable him to rise to great heights, to a tremendous feat of creation that would give the world a statue such as it had never before seen. He had thought so yesterday, half an hour ago, even! But he could not, he had not the ability, it was beyond his powers. Not even for Thessa, whom he loved so well!

What should he do? The whole world had grown dark to Pandion, the tools fell from his hands, the blood rushed to his head. In despair at the realization of his impotence, the youth rushed to the girl and fell on his knees before her. The girl, embarrassed and perplexed, placed her hands-on Pandion's hot, upturned face.

With the intuition of a woman, she suddenly realized the struggle that was going on in the soul of the artist. With maternal love, she bent over the youth, whispered consoling words to him, pressed his head to her bosom and ran her fingers through his short curls. The youth's burst of despair was slowly ebbing away.

Voices came from the distance. Pandion looked round; his passion had gone and with it went his proud hopes. He felt that his youthful dreams would never come true. The sculptor went up to his statue and stood before it wrapped in thought. Thessa laid her tiny hand on the crook of his arm.

"Don't you dare, you foolish boy," whispered the girl.

"I can't, I dare not, Thessa," Pandion agreed, never once taking his eyes off the statue. "If that..." the youth stammered, "if that had not been modeled from you - if it were not you, I would destroy it on the spot. The thing is so crude and ugly that it has no right to exist and somehow resemble you."

With those words, the youth pushed the block of stone together with the statue back into the crevice in the rock and closed the narrow entrance with rocks and a few handfuls of dry pine needles.

Pandion and Thessa set off in the direction of the sea. For a long time, they walked on in silence. Then Pandion spoke, he wanted his beloved to share his grief and disappointment. The girl tried to persuade Pandion not to give up trying. She told him how confident she was of him and of his ability to carry out his plans. Pandion, however, was implacable. For the first time that day he had realized how far he was from real virtuosity, that the road to real art lay through many years of dogged toil.

"No, Thessa, only now have I, at last, understood that I can't embody you in a statue!'" he exclaimed passionately. "I'm too poor here and here," he touched his heart and his eyes, "to be able to depict your beauty."

"Is it not all yours, Pandion?" The girl threw her arms impetuously round the artist's neck.

"Yes, Thessa, but how I sometimes suffer on account of it! I'll never cease to adore you, Thessa, and at the same time, I can't make a statue of you. I must embody you in clay, in stone. I must understand why it's so difficult to depict life; if I cannot understand this myself how can I ever hope to make my creations live?"

Thessa was all attention as she listened to the youth, feeling that now Pandion was opening up his heart to her in full, although the realization that she was unable to help him made her sad. The artist's grief was hers too and there arose in her heart a still unformed alarm.

Pandion suddenly smiled, and before Thessa realized what was happening, his strong arms lifted her off her feet. Pandion ran lightly to the beach, sat the girl down on the sand and disappeared behind a round hill. A second later, the girl saw Pandion's head rise above the crest of an incoming wave. Soon the youth returned to her. Muscles that played and flexed shook the drops of water from his skin and not a trace of his recent sorrow was left. It seemed to Thessa that nothing serious had happened in the grove. She laughed softly as she recalled her pitiful clay image and the woeful countenance of its creator. Pandion also made fun of himself and boasted boyishly of his strength and prowess before the girl. Then slowly and with frequent halts on the way, they returned to the house. But deep down at the bottom of Thessa's heart, the faint alarm still made itself felt.

Agenor placed his hand on Pandion's knee.

"Our people are still young and poor, my son. Hundreds of years must we live in plenty before a few hundred people will be able to devote themselves to the noble calling of the artist, before hundreds of people are able to devote themselves to the study of the beauty of man and of the world. The time is not long past when we depicted our gods by hewing them from a stone or a tree trunk. However, I can tell you as one who is striving to penetrate the laws of beauty, that our people will go further and will transcend all others in depicting the beautiful. Today, however, the artists of the older and richer lands are more skilled than ours."

The old artist got up and brought from the corner of the room a box of yellow wood from which he took something wrapped in red cloth. He removed the wrapper and with great care placed before Pandion a statuette of ivory, about a cubit in height. (Cubit: the length of the arm from the elbow to the tip of the middle finger – approximately 18 inches.) Time had given the ivory a pink tinge, and its polished surface was covered with a network of tiny black cracks.

The carving depicted a woman holding snakes in her outstretched hands, with the reptiles coiled around her arms as far as the elbow joints. A tight belt with raised edges encircled her slender waist, supporting a long skirt that reached to her heels and was ornamented by five transverse stripes of gold. Her back, shoulders, sides and a light veil, leaving the breast undraped, covered upper parts of the arms. The heavy tresses of waving hair were not caught up in a knot on the nape of the neck as was the custom with the women of Hellas but were gathered on the crown. From this knot, heavy locks fell on the neck and back of the woman.

Pandion had never seen anything like it. He could feel that the statuette was the work of a great master. His attention focused on the strangely listless face; it was flat and broad, the cheekbones very well defined with the lower jaw slightly protruding. The straight, thick brows augmented the impression of listlessness on the woman's face, but the bosom was heaving as though with a sigh of impatience. Pandion was dumbfounded. If only he had the skill of the unknown artist! If only his chisel could depict with such precision and beauty the form that lived under the rosy-yellow surface of that old ivory!

Agenor was pleased with the impression he had produced; he watched the youth closely, stroking his cheek with the tips of his fingers.

At last, Pandion broke off his silent meditation and placed the carving at some distance from him. He did not take his eyes off the dully-gleaming work of the old master.

"Is that from the ancient eastern cities?" the youth asked his teacher in a low, sad voice. (The eastern cities: Pandion is referring to the cities of Eastern Greece (Hellas) where the Mycenaean civilization flourished from 1600-1200 B.C. This civilization was the direct descendant of the Aegean or Cretan civilization, a pre-Hellenic culture that is still little known. Mycenae, Tirinthus and Orchomenus were the cultural centers of the Mycenaean period.)

"Oh, no," answered Agenor. "That statuette is older than the ancient towns of Mycenae, Tirinthus, and Orchomenus with all their gold. I took it from Chrisaor to show you. When his father was a young man, he sailed to Crete with a raiding party. He found this statuette amidst the remains of an ancient palace some twenty stadia – an ancient measure of length where one stadia, 607 feet, equals the length of a stadium – from the ruins of Cnossus, the City of the Sea Kings that was destroyed by terrible earthquakes."

"Father," said the youth with suppressed excitement, touching the beard of his master as a sign of request, "you know so much. Could you not, if you wanted to, copy the art of the old masters, teach us and take us to those places where these wonderful creations are still stored? Is it possible that you have never seen the palaces that the legends tell of? When I listened to my grandfather's songs, I often thought of them!"

Agenor lowered his eyes, and a dark shadow marred his calm and pleasant face.

"I can't explain it to you," he began after a moment's thought, "but soon you'll feel it yourself: that which is dead and gone cannot be brought back. It doesn't belong to our world, to our souls... it is beautiful but hopeless... it charms, but it doesn't live."

"I understand, father!" the youth exclaimed passionately. "We should only be slaves to dead wisdom, even though we imitate it to perfection. We have to become the equals of the old masters or even better than they, and then... oh, then...." Pandion stopped, unable to find words to express his thoughts.

Agenor's eyes gleamed as he looked at his apprentice and his hard, old hand pressed the lad's elbow in approbation.

"You said that well, Pandion. I could not express it so well myself. The art of the ancients must be a measure and an example for us but certainly nothing more. We must go our own way. To make that way shorter, we must learn from the ancients and from life. You are clever, Pandion."

Pandion suddenly dropped to the earthen floor and embraced the knees of the artist.

"My father and teacher let me go to see the ancient cities. I must, by all the gods, I must see it all for myself. I feel that I have the power to achieve great things. I must learn to know the countries that gave birth to those rare things which are met with amongst our people and which amaze them. Perhaps I..." The youth stopped, he blushed to his very ears, but still, his bold, direct glance sought that of Agenor.

With knitted brows, the latter stared away from him in concentration but did not speak.

"Get up, Pandion," said the old man at last. "I've been expecting this for a long time. You are no longer a boy, and I can't detain you even though I should like to. You're free to go wherever you will, but I tell you, as a son and as an apprentice, more than that, I tell you as my friend and equal, that your wish is fatal. It promises you nothing but terrible catastrophe."

"Father, I fear nothing!" Pandion threw back his head, his nostrils dilated.

"Then I was mistaken - you are still a boy," objected Agenor in calm tones. "Listen to me with an open heart if you really love me."

Agenor began to tell Pandion his story in a loud, tense voice:

"In the eastern cities the old customs are still observed and there are many ancient works of art there. Women dress today as they did a thousand years ago in Crete, in long stiff skirts extremely richly ornamented, with bared breasts and the shoulders and back covered. The men wear short, sleeveless tunics, have long hair, and are armed with short bronze swords. A gigantic wall surrounds the city of Tirinthus, fifty cubits in height. The wall is built of huge blocks of dressed stone decorated with bronze and gold ornaments that reflect the sunlight so that from a distance they look like fires dotting the wall.

"Mycenae is still more magnificent. The city is built on the summit of a high hill, gateways made of huge blocks of stone are closed with bronze grilles. The city's buildings can be seen from a great distance on the surrounding plain.

"Although the colors of the frescoes are still bright and fresh in the palaces of Mycenae, Tirinthus, and Orchomenus, and the chariots of the wealthy landowners again race along smooth roads paved with huge white stones as they did in former times. The grass of oblivion is gaining headway on the roads, in the courtyards of the empty houses and even on the sides of the mighty walls.

"Gone were the days of great wealth," Agenor told his pupil, "the days of long journeys to fabulous Aigyptos. (Aigyptos-the Greek name from which the modern word Egypt is derived. It is a Greek distortion of the Egyptian Het-Ka-Ptah, the Palace of the Spirit of Ptah, another name for Memphis, the City of the White Walls.) The environs of these cities were now inhabited by strong phratries with large numbers of warriors. Their chiefs had subordinated vast territories, had made the cities part of their domains, had subjugated the weaker clans and declared themselves the rulers of the lands and the peoples.

"In Oeniadae, where they lived, there were no mighty

chiefs, just as there were no cities and beautiful temples. Then, in the east, there were more slaves. More men, and women who had lost their liberty. Amongst them, apart from the captives seized in foreign lands, were members of poorer clans, the fellow-countrymen of their masters. What then would be the fate of a stranger in these lands? If he was not backed by a powerful phratry with whom it was dangerous for even a strong chief to quarrel, or if he were not to be accompanied by a strong-armed escort of his own, there were only two ways open to him - slavery or death."

"Remember, Pandion," the artist took the youth by both hands, "we live in a troubled and dangerous time- clans and phratries are at enmity with each other, there are no common laws and the threat of slavery hangs over the head of all travelers. This beautiful country is no place to travel in.

"Remember that if you leave us, you will be without hearth or rights; anybody can humiliate or kill you without fear of invoking a blood feud or paying blood money. You're alone and poor, I can't help you in any way. You can't gather even a small band of fighting men! Alone you must surely perish unless the gods make you invisible! You see Pandion, although it seems the simplest thing in the world to you to sail a thousand stadia across the bay from our Cape Achelous to Corinth. You think that it is but a half day's journey to Mycenae, a day's to Tirinthus and three days to Orchomenus when in reality, it would be the same to you as a journey beyond the bounds of Oecumene!" Agenor got up and went to the door, drawing the boy with him.

"You're like a son to my wife and me, but I'm not thinking of us. Try to imagine the sufferings of my Thessa if you were to languish in slavery in some foreign land!"

Pandion flushed a deep red but did not answer.

Agenor felt that he had not convinced Pandion and that the youth was floundering in a sea of indecision between two strong affections, one that chained him to the house and the other that beckoned him from afar, despite the certainty of danger.

Thessa did not know what to do for the best. First, she would oppose the journey and then, with noble pride, would tell Pandion to go.

Several months passed, and when the winds of spring blowing across the Gulf of Corinth, brought with them the faint aroma of the flowering hills and mountains of Peloponnesus, Pandion, at last, chose his life's road. He was determined to enter into single combat with a strange and distant world.

The half-year that he intended to spend in foreign parts seemed like an eternity to him. At times Pandion was dismayed by the thought that he was leaving his native shores forever. Agenor and other wise men of their clan advised Pandion to go to Crete, the home of the descendants of the Sea People, the birthplace of an ancient civilization. Although the large island was much farther than the ancient cities of Boeotia and Argolis, the journey would be safer for a single traveler. The island lay at the junction of several sea routes and was now inhabited by different tribes. Foreigners - merchants, sailors, and porters - were continually met on its shores. The multilingual population of Crete engaged in commerce and were more peaceful than the inhabitants of Hellas and, in general, were kinder to strangers. In the interior of the island, behind the mountain barriers, however, there still lived the descendants of ancient tribes who were hostile to all strangers.

Pandion was to cross the Gulf of Calydon to a sharp promontory opposite Lower Achaia where he would hire himself out as a rower on one of the boats carrying wool to Crete after winter storms during which the frail boats of the Greeks avoided long journeys.

On the night of the full moon, the youth of the district gathered for dances on the large glade of the sacred grove. In the little courtyard of Agenor's house, Pandion sat in deep thought, oppressed by his sorrow. The inevitable must come on the morrow. He must thrust out of his heart everything that was near and dear to him and face an unknown destiny. He must part with his beloved, and an uncertain future and loneliness awaited him.

Thessa's clothing rustled inside the silent house, and then she appeared in the dark opening of the doorway, adjusting the folds of a mantle thrown over her shoulders. The girl called softly to Pandion who immediately jumped up and went to meet her. Thessa's hair was folded into a heavy knot on the nape of her neck, and three ribbons crossed the top of her head, coming together under the knot.

"You've done your hair like an Attic girl today," exclaimed Pandion. "It's very beautiful."

Thessa smiled and asked him somewhat sadly:

"Aren't you going to dance for the last time, Pandion?"

"Do you want to go?"

"Yes," answered Thessa firmly. "I'm going to dance for Aphrodite and also do the crane dance."

"You're going to dance the Attic crane dance, so that's

why your hair is done that way! I don't think we've ever danced the crane dance before."

"Today everything is for you, Pandion!"

"Why is it for me?" asked the astonished youth.

"Surely you haven't forgotten that in Attica they dance the crane dance in memory," Thessa's voice quivered, "of the successful return of Theseus from Crete and in honor of his victory. (Theseus - the hero of Greek mythology who went to Crete and defeated the monster, Minotaur, in its underground labyrinth; the most handsome girls and youths of Attica had been sacrificed annually to the monster, and Theseus freed his country of this bloody tribute to the ruler of Crete). Come on, dearest." Thessa stretched out both hands to Pandion and, pressing close to each other, the two young people disappeared under the trees of the sacred grove beyond the houses.

The sea met them noisily, beckoning and opening up its endless waters. In the rays of the early morning sun, the distant surface of the sea bulged in the curved lines of a gigantic bridge. The slow, rolling waves, tinged pink in the dawning sun, carried tatters of golden foam from some distant shore, perhaps even from fabled Aigyptos itself. The sun's rays danced, broke, and rocked on the tireless, ever-moving waters, giving a faint, flickering radiance to the air.

The path, from which the group of houses and Agenor's family waving their last greetings could still be seen, disappeared behind a hill. The coastal plain was deserted, and Pandion was alone with Thessa before the sea and the sky. In front of them, a tiny boat loomed black on the beach, in which Pandion was to sail around the spit at the mouth of the Achelous and cross the Gulf of Calydon.

The youth and the girl walked on in silence. Their slow steps were uncertain. Thessa looked straight at Pandion who could not take his eyes off her face.

Soon, far too soon, they came to the boat. Pandion straightened his back and with a deep sigh expanded his cramped chest. The moment that had lain heavily on him for days and nights had come at last. In that final moment, there was so much he wanted to say to Thessa, but the words would not come. Pandion stood still in 'embarrassment, his head filled with incomplete thoughts, inconsequent and incoherent.

With a sudden, impetuous movement, Thessa threw her arms around his neck and whispered to him hurriedly and brokenly, as though she were afraid, they might be overheard:

"Swear to me, Pandion, swear by Hyperion, and swear by the awful Hecate, goddess of the moon and sorcery... no, swear by your love and mine that you will not go farther than Crete, that you will not go to distant Aigyptos where you'll be made a slave and be lost to me forever. Swear that you will return soon." Thessa's whispering broke off in a suppressed sob.

Pandion pressed the girl tightly to him and pronounced the oath; before his eyes there passed expanses of sea, rocks, groves, houses and the ruins of unknown cities, everything that was to keep him away from Thessa for six long months, months in which he would know nothing of his beloved or she of him. Pandion closed his eyes, and he could feel Thessa's heart beating. The minutes passed, the inevitable parting drew ever nearer, and further anticipation had become unbearable.

"On your way, Pandion, hurry... good-bye..." whispered the girl.

Pandion shuddered, released the girl, and ran to the boat. The boat lay deep in the sand, but his strong arms moved it and the keel grated over the sand. Pandion went knee-deep into the water and then turned to look round. The boat, rocked by a wave, struck him on the leg. Thessa, motionless as a statue, stood with her eyes fixed on the spot behind which Pandion's boat would soon disappear.

Something snapped in the youth's breast. Pandion pushed the boat off the sandbank, jumped into it and seized the oars. Thessa turned her head sharply, and the westerly breeze caught her hair that she had loosened as a sign of mourning. Under powerful strokes of the oars, the boat drew rapidly away from the shore, but Pandion never once took his eyes off the girl, standing with her face lifted high above her bare shoulder.

The wind blew Thessa's shining black tresses over her face, but the girl made no move to brush them back. Through the hair, Pandion could see her luminous eyes, her dilated nostrils, and the bright red lips of her half-open mouth. Her hair, fluttering in the wind, fell in dense masses on her neck, its curling ends lying in countless ringlets on her cheeks, temples, and high bosom.

The girl stood motionless until the boat was far from the shore and had turned its bows to the southeast. It seemed to Thessa that the boat was not turning around the spit but that the spit, dark and forbidding in the shadow of the sun's low rays, was moving out into the sea, gradually drawing nearer to the boat. Now it had reached a tiny black spot in the glistening sea - now the dot was concealed behind it.

Thessa, conscious of nothing more, sank on to the damp sand.

Pandion's boat was lost amidst the countless waves. Cape Achelous had long since been lost to view, but Pandion continued to row with all his strength as though he were afraid that sorrow would force him to return. He thought of nothing at all, he only tried to tire himself out by hard work. The sun was soon astern of the boat, and the slow-moving waves took on the color of dark honey. Pandion dropped his oars on to the bottom of the boat and, balancing on one leg so as not to overturn the boat, sprang into the sea. The water refreshed him, and he swam for a while pushing the boat before him; then he climbed back and stood up at full height.

Ahead of him lay a sharp-pointed cape, while away to the left he could see the longish island that closed the harbor of Calydon - the object of his journey from the south. Pandion again set to work with his oars, and the island began to grow in size as it rose from the sea. Soon the line of its summit broke up into separate pointed treetops that in turn became rows of stately cypress trees looking like gigantic, dark spearheads.

The curved, rocky end of a promontory protected the cypresses from the wind, and on its southern side, they grew in profusion, striving ever upwards into the clear blue sky. The youth steered his boat carefully between rocks fringed with rust-colored seaweed. Through the greenish gold of the water, the clean sandy seabed could be clearly seen.

Pandion went ashore, found a glade of soft young grass in the vicinity of an old, moss-grown altar, and there drank up the last of the fresh water he had brought with him. He did not feel like eating. The harbor that lay on the far side of the island was no more than twenty stadia away. Pandion decided that he would approach the ship's master fresh and in full strength and so lay down to rest awhile.

A picture of yesterday's festival dances arose with extraordinary clarity before Pandion's closed eyes.

Pandion and the other youths from the district were lying on the grass waiting until the girls had finished their dance in honor of Aphrodite. The girls, dressed in light garments caught in at the waist with ribbons of many colors, were dancing in pairs, back to back. Linking their hands each of them looked back over her shoulder as though she were admiring the beauty of her partner. The wide folds of the white tunics rose and fell like waves of silver in the moonlight, the golden, sun-tanned bodies of the dancers bent like slender reeds to the strains of the flutes-at the same time soft and attenuated, doleful and joyful.

Then the youths mingled with the girls in the crane dance, rising on to the tips of their toes and extending their arms like wings. Pandion danced beside Thessa, whose worried eyes never left his face. The youth of the district were more attentive to Pandion than usual.

There was only one young man, Eurymachus, who was in love with Thessa, whose face showed that he was glad of his rival's departure; and there was the tantalizing Aenoia who could not help teasing him. Pandion noticed that the others did not joke with him in their usual way; there were fewer sarcastic remarks at his expense. It seemed as though a line had been drawn between the one who was leaving and those who were to remain.

The moon sank slowly behind the trees. A heavy curtain of darkness fell over the glade.

The dances were over. Thessa and her friends sang the Hirasiona – the song of the swallow and spring-a song that Pandion loved to hear. At last, the young people made their way in pairs to their houses. Pandion and Thessa were the final couple to depart, deliberately slowing down to be alone. No sooner had they reached the ridge of the hill overlooking the village than Thessa shuddered, stopped, and pressed close to Pandion.

The sheer wall of white limestone behind the vineyards reflected the moon like a mirror. A transparent curtain of silver light veiled the houses, the littoral, and the dark sea - a light that was permeated with deadly charm and silent sorrow.

"I'm terribly afraid, Pandion," whispered Thessa. "Oh, how great is the power of Hecate, goddess of the moonlight, and you are going to the country where she rules."

Pandion, too, caught Thessa's excitement.

"No, no, Thessa, Hecate rules in Caria, but I am not going there, my way lies towards Crete," exclaimed the youth, urging the girl towards their house.

Pandion awoke from his dream. It was time to eat and continue his journey. He made a sacrifice to the God of the Sea, walked down to the beach, measured his shadow to judge the time, found that it measured nineteen feet and realized that he would have to hurry to reach the ship before evening.

Rounding the island, Pandion saw a white post standing in the sea - the sign of a harbor-and redoubled his efforts at the oars.

CHAPTER TWO

The Land of Foam

The wind raised clouds of coarse sand as it howled mournfully through the dry bushes. Like a road built by some giants unknown, the ridge ran away eastwards, curving around a broad, green valley. On the seaward side, the mountains descended to the water's edge in a gentle, flower-covered slope, which, from a distance, gave it the appearance of a massive piece of gold rising out of the shimmering blue of the sea.

Pandion increased his pace. Today he was more homesick than ever for Oeniadae. He remembered that he had been advised not to penetrate into that distant, mountain-encircled part of Crete where the descendants of the Sea People were unkind to strangers. Pandion had a need to hurry. He had already spent five months in various parts of the island that stretched in a chain of mountains rising out of the sea. The young sculptor had seen many strange and marvelous things that the ancients had left in the empty temples and almost unpopulated cities.

He had spent many days in the gigantic Palace of Cnossus, the older parts of which went back to times beyond the memory of man. As he wandered up and down the countless staircases of the palace, the youth saw, for the first time in his life, columns of red stone narrowing at the base, and he marveled at the cornices brightly painted with black and white rectangles or decorated with black and light blue whorls resembling a series of moving waves. Brightly colored pictures covered the walls.

Pandion gazed in breathless amazement at the images of the sacred games with the bulls, the processions of women bearing vessels in their arms, girls dancing within an enclosure, outside which stood a crowd of men, unknown, sinuous" animals amongst the mountains, and strange plants.

Pandion thought the outlines of the figures unnatural, and the plants rose up on exceedingly long and almost leafless stems. At the same time, he realized that the artists of ancient days had deliberately distorted natural proportions to express some idea, but the idea was incomprehensible to the youth who had grown up at liberty in the lap of nature, beautiful even when stern.

In Cnossus, Tylissos, and Aelira, and in the mysterious ruins of the ancient harbor of the "slate city" whose name had long been forgotten, all the houses were built of slabs of smooth, grey, stratified stone instead of the usual blocks. Pandion saw many female statuettes of ivory, bronze and faience, marvelous vessels and dishes and cups made of an amalgam of gold and silver, and covered with the most delicate drawings.

These works of art astounded the young Hellene, but they were as little understood by him as the mysterious inscriptions in the forgotten symbols of a dead language were that he came across amongst the ruins. The magnificent craftsmanship to be seen in the tiniest detail of any of these things did not satisfy Pandion; he wanted something more. He did not want to limit himself to abstract depiction. He strove for an incarnation of the living beauty of the human body he worshipped.

Quite unexpectedly, Pandion discovered realistic

images of people and animals in the works of art brought from distant Aigyptos. The people of Cnossus, Tylissos, and Aelira, who showed Pandion these things, told him that many more of them were still to be found near Phaestos, where the descendants of the Sea People still lived.

Despite warnings of the danger involved, Pandion decided to penetrate the ring of mountains on the southern coast of Crete. In a few more days he would have seen everything there was to see and would sail back home to Thessa.

Pandion was now confident of his own ability. Much as he would have liked to learn from the craftsmen of Aigyptos, his love for his own country and for Thessa was stronger, and the oath he had sworn to the girl held him tightly bound.

How wonderful it would be to sail home with the last ship in autumn. He would be able to look into the bright, blue eyes of his beloved, and to see the quiet joy of Agenor, the teacher who had replaced his father and grandfather.

Pandion screwed up his eyes and gazed out at the boundless expanse of the sea. No, it was not for him; there, ahead of him, lay distant, strange lands, Aigyptos, but his own native land was behind him, beyond the mountain ridge, and he was still moving onwards, away from his own country. He had to see the ancient temples of Phaestos, of which he had heard so much in the coastal towns.

With a sigh, he increased his pace until he was almost running. A spur led down from the mountain in broad terraces covered with boulders like tufts of grass, with dark patches of bush between them. Amongst the trees at the foot of the slope, he could see the faint outlines of the ruins of a vast building, walls half collapsed, the remains of arches, and gates still standing in their framework of black and white columns.

Silence reigned in the ruins, and the curves of the broken walls stretched out towards Pandion like giant hands ready to seize their victim. The surfaces of the walls were furrowed with fresh cracks, the aftermath of a recent earthquake.

The young sculptor trod quietly amongst the ruins, trying not to disturb the silence there, peering into dark corners beneath columns that still stood in their places.

Pandion turned a projecting corner and found himself in a rectangular, roofless hall, the walls of which were covered with the well-known brightly colored frescoes. As he looked at the black and brown figures that followed each other in quick succession, figures of men carrying shields, swords, and bows amongst strange animals and ships. Pandion remembered the tales of his grandfather and realized that before him was a picture of a band of soldiers on a raid into the land of the blacks, situated, according to ancient legend, on the very borders of Oecumene.

Pandion was astounded at this evidence of the tremendous journeys made by the ancients and gazed long at the frescoes until, turning away from them at last, he saw a marble cube standing in the middle of the hall. The cube was ornamented with blue rosettes and whorls of glass and at its base lay heaps of freshly picked flowers. Somebody had been there! There must be people living amongst those ruins!

Anxiously, the youth made his way to the exit, a portico

overgrown with grass. The entrance, consisting of two square white and two round red columns, stood on the edge of a low cliff that rose just above the dense foliage of the trees.

A dusty, well-trodden path led down the cliff side. Descending into the valley, Pandion came to a smooth, metaled road. He made his way eastwards, striving to step silently on the hot stones. The broad leaves of the plane trees on the right-hand side of the road, scarcely stirring in the hot air, cast a line of shadow.

Pandion sighed with relief as he sought refuge from the blazing sun. He had long wanted to drink, but in his own country, where water was scarce, he had been taught abstinence.

After walking along for some two stadia, he saw a long low building at the foot of a hill where the road turned to the north. Some small rooms, like a row of similar boxes, were open on the side that faced the road and were quite empty. Pandion recognized the building as an old travelers' rest house; he had seen many of them in the northern part of the island and hurried into the main entrance, brightly painted, and divided into two by a single column. The faint murmur of running water called to the youth, exhausted as he was by the heat and the long journey.

Pandion entered the bathhouse where the water ran from a spring, the ground around which was paved with heavy slabs of stone, poured through a wide pipe and then through the rims of three successive basins into a big funnel built into the wall.

Pandion threw off his clothes and sandals, washed in the pure cold water, drank his fill and lay down on a stone bench to rest. The babbling of the running water, the gentle whispering of the leaves had a soothing effect on him, and eyes inflamed from the sun and wind in the mountain passes refused to keep open. Pandion slept.

He did not sleep long. When he awoke the shadow from the column intersecting the sunlit floor, had scarcely changed its position. He jumped up and hurriedly donned his simple clothing. He felt fresh and rested. He ate some dry cheese, took another drink, and made for the doorway. There he came to a sudden halt. From a distance came the sound of voices. He went out on to the road to look round. There could be no doubt about it. From the dense growth of bushes to one side of the road came laughter, snatches of an unknown language and the sounds of stringed instruments.

Pandion's sensations mingled with joy and fear, his muscles tensed, and he involuntarily grasped the hilt of his father's sword. With a few whispered words of prayer to his patron and ancestor Hyperion, the youth plunged into the thicket, making straight for the voices. It was stifling in the thicket, and the strong scents made it difficult for him to breathe. With the greatest of care, he made his way round tall bushes with long thorns, slipped between the trunks of the strawberry trees with their thin, smooth, light grey bark and found his way barred by a grove of myrtles that stood before him in a solid wall. Bunches of white flowers hung down from the dense foliage.

For a second Pandion thought of Thessa. In his country, the myrtle tree was sacred to youthful virginity. The voices now sounded quite close to him - the people were talking in hushed voices for some reason, or another and Pandion realized that he had misjudged the distance. The decisive moment had come. Bending low, Pandion dived under the nether branches, carefully pushing them aside with his hands. On a glade covered with young grass, an unusual sight met his eyes.

In the center of the glade lay a snow-white bull with long horns. Little black patches were sprinkled on the beast's well-groomed flanks and face. Some distance away in the shade stood a group of youths, girls and elderly people. A tall, straight-backed man with a wavy beard and a gold band on his head, wearing a short tunic encircled by a bronze belt, stepped forward and made a sign.

A young girl dressed in a long, heavy mantle immediately left the group. She raised both arms above her head; the movement caused the mantle to fall to the ground, leaving her standing in a loincloth held in place by a wide white belt ornamented with a fluffy black cord. Her blue-black hair hung loosely about her shoulders and on both arms, she wore slim gold bangles above the elbow. With light, rapid steps, almost dancing, she approached the bull, then stopped suddenly and emitted a guttural cry.

The bull's sleepy eyes opened wide and flashed fire; he bent his forelegs under him and began to raise his heavy head. Like an arrow, the girl darted forward and pressed herself against the bull. For a second or two, the girl and the beast were motionless.

A cold shiver ran down Pandion's back. The bull straightened his forelegs while his hind-legs still lay on the ground, and lifted his head high. The beast formed a sort of heavy pyramid of menacing muscle. The girl's brown body pressed close to the steep slope of the animal's back, created a sharp contrast to its white skin. With one hand, she clung to a horn, and the other arm encircled the bull's great neck. One of the girl's strong legs stretched along the back of the monster, and the upper part of her body was sprung forward like a drawn bow. The contrast between the lines of the bull, beautiful but monstrous in their strength and weight, and the graceful human body held Pandion spellbound.

For a fraction of a second, he saw the austere face of the girl with its tightly pressed lips. With a dull roar, the bull rose to its feet and leaped with a facility astonishing in such a tremendous body. The girl was thrown into the air, pressed her hands into the bull's mighty withers, threw her legs up and turned a somersault between the high horns. She landed on her feet some three paces from the bull's head. Stretching out her arms the girl clapped her hands and again emitted a short, sharp cry. The infuriated bull lowered its horns and rushed at her. Pandion was horrified: it seemed that that beautiful and courageous girl must surely be killed.

Throwing all caution to the winds the youth seized his sword and was about to dash on to the glade when the girl, with incredible agility, again sprang towards the bull, escaped the lowered, death-dealing horns, and was once more on the bull's back. In its fury, the beast raced around the glade tearing up the earth with its hoofs and roaring threateningly. The young bullfighter sat calmly on the enraged animal's back, her knees pressed tightly into its broad flanks, now working like bellows from the animal's rapid breathing. The bull flew towards the group of people who greeted it with cries of joy. There was a loud handclap as the girl somersaulted backward and landed on the ground behind the bull. Breathing rapidly in joyous excitement, she rejoined the crowd of onlookers.

The bull made a straight run to the edge of the glade, then turned and raced towards the people. Five of them immediately stepped forward, three youths and two girls, and the game began again with even higher speed. The gasping bull turned towards the young people who were calling him on with cries and handclapping, and they jumped over him, sprang on to his back, pressed close against his sides for a moment, avoiding the terrible horns with great agility.

One of the girls managed to sit directly on the bull's neck, immediately in front of the hump of his withers. The bull's eyes popped out of their sockets and foam came from his mouth. With his head lowered, his muzzle almost touching the ground, the bull did his utmost to throw the fearless girl from his back. She leaned backward, her two hands grasping the withers behind her back and her feet propped firmly against the base of the animal's ears. She kept her position for a few seconds and then sprang lightly to the ground.

The youths and girls spread out in a single line some distance from each other and played leapfrog over the animal's back in succession. The game went on for a long time - the bull dashed back and forth with awe-inspiring roars, threatening death, but the gracefully lithesome human figures darted unharmed around him.

The bull's roar turned to a hoarse groan, his skin became dark with sweat and foam flew from his mouth together with his irregular breath. A few moments more and the bull came to a standstill, lowered his massive head and glared from side to side. The air was filled with the joyous cries of the onlookers.

The man with the gold band on his head gave a sign,

and the youthful participants in the games left the animal in peace. People who had been standing and sitting on the grass drew together, and before Pandion realized what was happening, they had disappeared into the bushes.

The bull remained alone on the empty glade with nothing to show for the recent combat but its stertorous breathing and the trampled grass. Only then did the excited Pandion realize his great good fortune. He had been a witness of the ancient bull games that, hundreds of years before his time, had been so common on Crete, in Mycenae and other ancient Greek cities.

The agile, enterprising man had conquered in a bloodless battle with a bull, an animal sacred to the peoples of antiquity as the incarnation of military power, of intense, menacing strength. The lightning speed of the animal was counteracted by still higher speed, while the precision of movement was the only guarantee of safety for the players.

Pandion had been trained in feats of strength and agility since childhood and, therefore, could well imagine what degree of training was required to develop the human body for participation in such dangerous amusements.

He did not risk following the players and returned to the road. He decided that it would be better to seek hospitality from these people in their own homes.

For a distance of several stadia, the road continued dead straight and then turned suddenly southwards, to the sea, and the trees along the verge gave way to dusty bushes. By the time Pandion reached the bend in the road, his shadow had noticeably lengthened. He heard rustling noises in the bushes and stopped to listen. A bird, he could not say what kind, as the sun was in his eyes, flew up and again dived into the bushes. Pandion's fears were allayed, and he continued on his way, paying no further attention to the sounds. From a distance a came the soft, melodious cooing of a wild dove. Another two birds answered the call, and then all was silent again.

Now Pandion turned the bend in the road the cries of the dove were repeated very near him. The youth stood still, trying to get a glimpse of the bird. Suddenly he heard the beating of wings behind him, and a pair of wood pigeons sailed into the air.

Pandion turned around and saw three men with heavy cudgels in their hands. With deafening cries, the three newcomers threw themselves on Pandion. In a second, he had unsheathed his sword but received a blow on the head. Everything went dark, and he staggered from the weight of other men jumping on him. Another four men had appeared from the bushes behind him.

Pandion was almost unconscious but realized that he was lost. He defended himself desperately, but a blow on his arm caused him to drop his sword. The youth fell on his knees and threw the man who clung to him over his head; a second man fell from a blow of his fist while a third flew away with a groan from a kick of Pandion's foot.

The attackers, apparently, did not intend to kill the stranger. They dropped their cudgels and again fell on Pandion. Under the weight of five bodies, he collapsed face down in the dust that filled his mouth and nose and irritated his eyes. Panting from the strain Pandion rose on to all fours to throw off the attackers. They threw themselves under his feet and pressed his neck downwards. Again, the bodies writhed in a heap on the ground raising clouds of dust that turned red in the sun's rays.

The attackers realized the unusual strength and

endurance of the youth and ceased their shout. The silence of the deserted road was broken only by the sounds of the struggle, the groans and hoarse breathing of the combatants. Their bodies were covered with dust and their clothes dirty and torn to shreds, but still the struggle went on.

Several times Pandion threw off his assailants and struggled to his feet, but again they fell on him, grasping him by the legs. Suddenly cries of victory rent the air: reinforcements had arrived, and another four men joined the struggle. The youth's arms and legs were bound with strong thongs. More dead than alive from exhaustion and despair, Pandion closed his eyes. His conquerors, speaking in lively tones in an unknown language, lay down in the shade beside him to rest after the strenuous struggle.

When they were rested, they made signs to the youth to go with them. Pandion realized the uselessness of further resistance; he decided to reserve his strength for a more, opportune moment and nodded. They unbound his legs and Pandion, surrounded by his enemies, staggered along the road.

Soon they came to a group of wretched houses built of undressed stone. The people came out of them to meet them - an old man with a bronze band on his head, some women and children. The old man went up to Pandion, looked him over approvingly, felt his muscles and said something to Pandion's captors in merry voices.

The youth was taken to a small house. The door opened with a piercing shriek. Inside there was a small furnace, an anvil with tools thrown down around it and a heap of charcoal. Two large, light wheels hung from the walls. An evil-looking old man of small stature, but with long arms, ordered one of Pandion's escort to blow up the furnace while he took a metal hoop from a nail in the wall and went over to the captive.

The smithy struck Pandion roughly under the chin and began measuring the hoop for his neck. He muttered something in dissatisfaction and then went to the far corner of the smithy and with a loud rattle dragged out a metal chain. He put the end link in the fire and set about bending the bronze hoop on the anvil, adjusting it to the required size by frequent blows of his hammer. Only then did the youth realize the full extent of the disaster that had overtaken him.

Images of all that was dear to him flashed through his mind one after another. Thessa was waiting there on his native shore, she believed in him, in his love and in his return. In a moment, they would fasten the bronze slave's collar on his neck, and he would be riveted to a sturdy chain without any hope of early deliverance. He had counted the last days of his stay in Crete. Soon he would be able to set sail for the harbor of Calydon whence his fatal journey had begun.

"O Hyperion, my ancestor, and thou, O Aphrodite, send me death or deliverance," whispered the youth in a low voice.

The smithy calmly and methodically continued his work; he measured the hoop a second time, flattened out the ends, bent them over and made holes in them. He had only to rivet the chain to the collar. The old man grunted a short order and Pandion was seized, then told by signs to lie on the ground beside the anvil. The youth mustered all his strength for the last attempt at escape. Blood spattered from under the thongs that bound his elbows, but Pandion forgot all pain when he felt his bonds weakening. In another second, they had burst. With his head, he butted the chin of the man who was trying to make him lie down, and the man fell to the ground. The youth knocked down two more of them and dashed off along the road. With howls of fury, his enemies gave chase.

The cries of the pursuers brought more men armed with spears, knives, and swords; the number of the pursuers continued to grow.

Pandion turned off the road and, leaping over the bushes, made for the sea, his angrily screaming pursuers hot on his heels. The bushes grew scantier, and the ground rose in a short slope. Reaching the top Pandion halted-far below, under a wall of steep cliffs, lay the sea, sparkling in the sunlight. A red ship, sailing along slowly some ten stadia from the shore, could be clearly seen.

The youth ran along the edge of the cliff, trying to find a path leading downwards, but the vertical wall of the cliffs extended far in both directions. There was no way to escape. His pursuers were already clear of the bushes, extending as they ran into a long crescent to cut off Pandion on three sides. He looked towards his pursuers and then down at the cliff.

Death is before me and slavery behind, was the thought that ran through his head. *Forgive me, Thessa, if you ever find out...* No further time was to be lost.

The rock on which Pandion was standing extended beyond the cliff face. Some twenty cubits below him, there was another ledge on which a low pine tree was growing. Sweeping his beloved sea with a glance of farewell, the youth sprang into the thick branches of the lone tree. For a second the infuriated cries of his enemies reached his ears. Pandion crashed through the tree, breaking its branches and lacerating his body. He flew past the rocky ledge on to the soft resilient ground of the lower slope. The youth rolled some twenty cubits farther down the hill and came to rest on a ledge damp from the spray that reached it at high tide.

Stunned and still unaware that he had escaped, the youth rose to his knees. The pursuers above him were trying to hit him with stones and javelins. The sea splashed at his feet. The ship drew nearer as though the mariners were interested in what was happening on shore. There were noises in Pandion's head; his whole body ached dreadfully, bringing tears to his eyes. Dimly he realized that when his pursuers carried bows and arrows, he would most certainly be killed.

The sea drew him on. The approaching ship seemed like salvation sent by the gods. Pandion forgot that it might be a foreign ship or might belong to his enemies - he felt that his native sea could not deceive him. He stood up on his feet, assured himself that his arms were intact, jumped into the sea and swam for the ship. The waves swept over his head, his battered body did not want to submit to his will, his wounds burned painfully, and his throat was parched.

The vessel drew nearer to Pandion, and those on board gave him cries of encouragement. He could hear the creaking of the oars; the hull of the ship rose over his head and strong hands seized him and pulled him on to the deck.

Unconscious and seemingly lifeless, the youth lay stretched out on the warm planks of the deck. They brought Pandion around and gave him water. He drank long and avidly. Pandion felt himself being carried to one side and covered over with something; then he sank into a deep sleep.

The mountains of Crete could be faintly distinguished on the horizon. Pandion stirred, gave an involuntary groan, and opened his eyes. He was on board a ship that was nothing like those of his own country, with their low gunwales protected at the sides by wattles of plaited withies and with the oars above the hold. This vessel had high sides, the rowers sat below the deck on either side of a gangway that widened in the depths of the hold. The single sail on the mast in the center of the ship was higher and narrower than those on the ships of Hellas. Piles of hides lying on the deck gave off a foul odor.

Pandion was lying on the narrow triangular deck in the prow of the vessel. A bearded man with an aquiline nose approached him wearing thick woolen clothing, who offered him a bowl of warm water mixed with wine. He spoke to Pandion in an unknown language with sharp, metallic intonations. Pandion shook his head. The man touched him on the shoulder and with an authoritative gesture pointed to the stern sheets of the vessel. Pandion gathered his bloodstained rags around his loins and made his way along the gunwale towards the awning in the stern. Here sat a thin man, aquiline-nosed, like the one who had brought Pandion. His lips, framed in a thick beard that stuck out in front of him, parted in a smile. His wind-dried, rapacious face, like a bronze casting, had a cruel look about it.

Pandion gathered that he was on board a Phoenician merchant ship and that the man before him was either the captain or the owner.

He did not understand the first two questions the man asked him. Then the merchant spoke in a broken Ionian dialect that Pandion could understand although there were Carian and Etruscan words mixed in his speech. He asked Pandion about his adventures, learned who he was and where he had come from and, thrusting his eagle-nosed face with its unblinking eyes close to Pandion, said to him;

"I saw your escape - that was a deed of valor worthy of one of the heroes of old. I'm in need of such strong and fearless warriors in these waters, and on the coasts, many pirates who plunder our merchants. If you serve me faithfully, you'll have an easy life, and I shall reward you."

Pandion shook his head in refusal saying that he must return to his own country as soon as possible and imploring the merchant to put him ashore on the nearest island.

The merchant's eyes flashed evilly.

"My ship is sailing straight to Tyre. There is nothing but sea on that route. I'm king aboard my ship, and you're in my power. I could order you to be killed immediately if I wanted to. Take your choice - either there," the Phoenician pointed below the deck where the oars moved rhythmically to the plaintive singing of the rowers, "where you'll be a slave chained to the oars, or join them," the merchant's finger swept round and pointed below the awning: there sat five husky, half-naked men with stupid and brutal faces.

"Don't keep me waiting too long," he said.

Pandion looked helplessly around him. The vessel was fast drawing away from Crete. The distance between him and his own country was rapidly increasing. There was no help to be expected from anywhere. Pandion decided that he would have more chance of escape as a soldier.

The Phoenician, however, who was well acquainted

with the habits of the Hellenes, made him swear three awful oaths of loyalty. The merchant then treated his wounds with soothing ointments and led him to the group of fighting men, telling them to feed him.

"Keep an eye on him," he warned them. "Remember that all of you are responsible to me for the actions of every single one."

The senior soldier laughed approvingly, patted Pandion on the shoulder, felt his muscles and said something to the others. The soldiers roared with laughter. Pandion looked at them in perplexity, for now, his deep sorrow made him not as other men.

In the four days that he had spent on board ship, Pandion had become used to his new position. The wounds and bruises proved but slight, and they soon healed. Another two days sailing would bring them to Tyre.

The master of the vessel recognized the intellect and varied knowledge possessed by Pandion and was very satisfied with him. He had several long talks with Pandion, who learned from him that they were following the ancient sea route established by the people of Crete in their journeys to the southern lands of the black people.

The way lay along the shores of mighty and hostile Aigyptos, and farther along the gigantic deserts as far as the Gates of the Mists. (The Gates of the Mists-the Strait of Gibraltar. The Sea of Mists-the Atlantic Ocean.)

At the Gates of the Mists, where the rocks of north and south drew close together forming a narrow strait, the world ended.

Beyond them lay the vast Sea of Mists. Here the ships turned south and soon reached the hot shores of the land of the black people, rich in ivory, gold, oils, and skins, Pandion knew that the ancient inhabitants of Crete had used this route, for he had seen pictures of such a journey on the day that had proved fatal to him. The Sea People's ships reached lands farther to the south than any visited by emissaries from Aigyptos.

In Pandion's time, however, Phoenician ships sailed along the northern and southern shores in search of cheap merchandise and strong slaves, but they rarely passed beyond the Gates of the Mists.

The Phoenician sensed unusual talents in Pandion and wanted to keep him in his service. He tempted the youth with the pleasures of distant journeys, drew for him pictures of his future advancement and prophesied that after ten, or fifteen-years good service he could himself become a merchant or master of a ship.

Pandion listened with interest to the Phoenician's stories, but he knew full well that the life of a merchant was not for him, that he would never exchange his native land, Thessa and the free life of the artist for wealth in a foreign country.

As the days passed, his longing to see Thessa, even if only for a moment, became more and more unbearable, as did his desire to hear the mighty noises of the sacred pine grove in which he had spent so many happy hours.

Lying beside his snoring companions, Pandion could get

no sleep, with difficulty stilled his fast-beating heart, and stifled groans of despair. The ship's master ordered him to learn the work of helmsman. The time hung heavily, when Pandion stood at the stern oar, calculating the direction of the ship by the movement of the sun, or following the instructions of an experienced helmsman, steering his way by the stars at night.

So, it was on that night. Pandion stood with his hip pressed against the gunwale, his hands firmly grasping the stern oar to overcome the resistance of the rising wind. On the other side of the vessel, which, as was the custom in those days, had a stern oar or rudder on either side, stood a helmsman and a soldier. The stars flitted through gaps in the clouds and then disappeared in the gloom of the threatening sky, and the mournful voice of the wind, growing deeper in tone, rose to an ominous howl. The vessel was tossed on the waves, the oars slapped dully on the water, and the voice of the overseer could be more frequently heard as he drove the slaves on with curses and blows of his whip.

The master, who had been sleeping under the awning, came out on deck. He studied the sea attentively and, obviously troubled, went to the chief helmsman. They talked together for a long time. Then the master awakened the sleeping soldiers and sent them to the stern oars, himself taking his place beside Pandion. The wind veered sharply round and started beating furiously at the ship. The waves rose higher and higher, sweeping over the deck.

The mast had to be unstopped, and as it lay on the piles of hides, it projected beyond the bow, striking dully against the ship's high prow.

The struggle against wind and waves was becoming more and more desperate. The master, muttering either prayers or curses under his breath, ordered the helmsmen to turn the vessel to the south. With the wind behind her, the ship raced forward into the black, unknown sea.

The night passed quickly in heavy work at the rudder. In the grey light of dawn, the gigantic waves looked even more threatening. The storm had not subsided, the wind, unabated, lashed the frail ship.

Shouts of alarm swept across the deck-all hands called the master's attention to something to the starboard of the vessel. There, in the dull light of the dawning day, a long line of foam broke the sea. The waves slowed down in their mad race as they approached the blue-grey line.

The entire crew of the vessel clustered round the master, even the helmsman handing over his oar to a soldier.

Shouts of alarm gave way to rapid and excited speech. Pandion noticed that all eyes were fixed on him, fingers pointed in his direction and fists threatened him. He could understand nothing of what was going on but saw the master making angry gestures of protest. The old helmsman, seizing the master by the arm, spoke to him for a long time, his lips near the master's ear. The master shook his head in refusal, and shouted some sharp words but, at last, he apparently had to give way. In an instant, the people threw themselves on the astounded youth, binding his hands behind him.

"They say you have brought misfortune upon us," said the master to Pandion, waving his hands disdainfully in the direction of his crew. "You're the herald of calamity. It's your presence on board that has drawn our ship towards Tha-Quem, (Tha-Quem-the Black Land, or simply Quemt, the Black, the name given by the ancient Egyptians to their country.) in your language Aigyptos. To placate the gods, you must be killed and thrown overboard. My people demand this, and I cannot protect you."

Pandion still did not understand and stared hard at the Phoenician.

"You do not know that it means death or slavery to land on the shores of Tha-Quem," the master muttered despondently. "In days of old, there was a war between Tha-Quem and the Sea People. Since then everybody who lands anywhere in that country, except the three ports open to foreigners, is either killed or sent into slavery and his property goes to the King of Tha-Quem. Do you understand now?" The Phoenician broke off abruptly and, turning away from Pandion, gazed at the fast-approaching line of foam.

Pandion realized that he was again being threatened with death. Ready to fight to the very last minute for a life that was dear to him he cast a helpless glance full of hatred at the infuriated crowd on the deck. The hopelessness of the situation caused him to take a rapid decision.

"Master!" exclaimed the youth. "Tell your people to release m. I will jump into the sea myself!"

"That's what I thought," said the Phoenician, turning towards him. "Let these cowards learn from you!"

In answer to an imperious gesture from the master, the crew released Pandion. Without looking at anybody, the youth walked towards the ship's gunwale. The people made way for him in silence as they would for a man going to his death.

Pandion stared fixedly at the line of foam that hid the low shore, instinctively comparing his strength with the speed of the vicious waves. Fragments of thoughts flashed through his mind: *the land beyond the foam line, the Land of Foam... Africa...* (Africa-from the Greek aphros- foam.

Hence also Aphrodite - the foam-born.)

So. This was the dreaded Aigyptos, and I'd vowed to Thessa by all the gods and my love for her that I would not even think of journeying so far! O, Gods! What game was fate playing with me? However, I will most likely perish, and that would be for the best.

Pandion dived head first into the noisy depths and, using his strong arms, swam away from the ship. The waves seized hold of him; it seemed that they took delight in the death of a man. They threw him high on their crests, and then cast him down into the troughs, they crushed and battered him, they filled his nose and mouth with water, they slashed his eyes with foaming spray. Pandion no longer thought of anything - he was struggling desperately for his life, for every breath of air, working furiously with his hands and feet. The Hellene, born by the sea, was an excellent swimmer.

Time passed, and the waves carried him on and on towards the shore. He did not look back at the ship. He had forgotten its existence in the face of almost certain death. The rocking of the waves grew less. They swept on more slowly than before in long rollers that rose and fell in a roaring swirl of seething foam. Every fresh wave carried Pandion a hundred cubits nearer the shore. Sometimes he sank into the trough of a wave; then a terrific weight of water crashed down on him, driving him down and down into the dark depths until his heart was ready to burst.

Thus, he swam on for several stadia, much time passed in this struggle against the waves until at last his strength failed him and he felt that it was becoming impossible for him to continue the battle against the giant waters that were trying to embrace him.

As he grew weaker, the will to live died out in him, it became more and more difficult to strain his aching muscles and his desire to continue the struggle weakened. With jerky movements of arms that worked almost outside his will he rose on the crest of a wave, turned his face towards his distant country and shouted at the top of his voice:

"Thessa, Thessa!"

The name of the one he loved, hurled twice in the face of fate, in the face of the monstrous and indifferent might of the sea, was immediately drowned by the howl of the stormy waves. One of them closed over Pandion's motionless body. The youth sank down into the water and suddenly struck the seabed in a whirl of churned-up sand.

Two soldiers in short green kilts, an outpost of the Great Green Sea coast watchers (Great Green Sea was the name given by the Egyptians to the Mediterranean.), leaned on their long spears and stared at the horizon.

"Captain Seneb sent us here for nothing," said the elder of them in a lazy voice.

"But the Phoenician ship was quite close to the shore," objected the other. "If the storm hadn't died down, we'd have got easy booty, and right close to the fortress, too."

"Look over there," said the older soldier, pointing along the beach.

"May I remain unburied when I die if that isn't a man from the ship!"

For a long time, the two soldiers gazed at the black speck on the beach.

"Let's go back," said the younger soldier. "We've been trudging through the sand long enough already. Who wants the body of a despised foreigner instead of rich booty-the merchandise and slaves that were on that ship?"

"You talk without thinking," the older man interrupted him again. "Those merchants are sometimes richly dressed and wear jewelry. A gold ring wouldn't do you any harm. Why should we report every drowned man to Seneb?"

The soldiers marched along the damp sand of a beach beaten hard by the storm.

"Where's your jewelry?" the young soldier asked mockingly. "He's stark naked."

The older man uttered a disgruntled curse because indeed, the man lying face down on the sand was completely unclothed, his arms bent helplessly under his torso and his short curly half full of sea-sand.

"Look," exclaimed the older soldier. "He isn't a Phoenician." What a strong and beautiful body! It's a pity he's dead, he would have made a fine slave, and Seneb would have rewarded us."

"What country is he from?" asked the younger.

"I don't know. Perhaps he's a Turusha or a Kefti, or maybe one of those Sea Peoples, the Hanebu. (Turusha-Etruscan. Kefti or Keftiu-the Egyptian name for Crete and its inhabitants. Hanebu-northerner.) They are rarely found in our blessed land and are valued for their endurance, strength, and intellect. Three years ago... wait a minute, he's alive, and praise be to Amon!"

The body lying on the sand twitched almost imperceptibly. The soldiers threw down their spears, turned the unconscious man over and began massaging his stomach and legs. Their efforts were successful. The unconscious man - it was Pandion - opened his eyes and coughed painfully. His sound constitution had stood up to the test, and before an hour had passed, the soldiers led him, supporting him under the arms, to the fortress. They made frequent halts on their way, but before the hottest part of the day, Pandion was brought to a tiny fort standing on one of the countless sleeves of the Nile Delta, to the west of a big lake.

The soldiers gave Pandion water to drink; fed him a few pieces of bread dipped in beer, and laid him down on the floor of a small earthen shed. The terrific strain had left its mark on Pandion. A sharp pain racked his chest, and his heart's action was weak. An endless procession of waves passed before his closed eyes. As he lay in a heavy torpor, he heard someone open the frail door, made from fragments of ship's timbers. The captain of the outpost, a young man with a sickly and unpleasant face, bent over him.

The captain removed the mantle that had been thrown over Pandion's legs. He made a close examination of his captive. Little did Pandion imagine that the decision that was then ripening in the captain's mind was to bring him further tribulation? The captain, satisfied with what he had seen, covered Pandion over and left the shed.

"Two rings of copper and a jug of beer each," he snapped at the soldiers.

The coast watchers bowed humbly before him, but at his back, they sent looks that might kill.

"O Mighty Sekhmet, look what price we've been given for such a slave," whispered the younger soldier as soon as the captain had withdrawn. "You'll see, he'll send him to the city and sell him for no less than ten rings of gold..."'

The captain suddenly turned back.

"Hi, Senni!" he shouted. The older soldier ran

obediently to him. "Keep an eye on him. I make you responsible for him. Tell my cook to give him the best of food, but take great care, for this captive is a mighty warrior. Tomorrow make ready the light boat, and I'll send the captive as a gift to the Great House." (The Great House - a euphemism for the King of Egypt whose name it was forbidden to pronounce. In Egyptian - Per-o, whence the ancient Hebrew, Pharaoh.)

"We'll give him a sleeping-draught in his beer so that there will be no trouble with him."

Slowly Pandion raised his heavy eyelids. He had been sleeping so long that he had no conception of time or of his whereabouts. He had vague, fragmentary memories of a bitter struggle in the stormy sea, of being taken somewhere after that and then of lying in some quiet, dark place. He tried to move but felt that his body was bound. Turning his head with difficulty, he saw a wall of green reeds topped with star-like brushes. Above him spread the clear sky; from somewhere nearby, quite close to his ear, came the faint gurgle and splashing of water. It gradually dawned upon Pandion that he was lying, bound hand and foot, in a long, narrow boat. By raising his head, he could see the bare legs of the men punting the boat along with long poles. They were well-built men with skin the color of bronze, and they were dressed in white loincloths.

"Who are you? Where are you taking me?" shouted Pandion, trying to catch a glimpse of the people standing in the stern of the boat.

One of them, a man with a clean-shaven face, bent over Pandion and said something in rapid tones. The strange language, with its melodious tongue clicks and strongly accented vowels, was quite incomprehensible.

Pandion strained all his muscles to break his bonds, continually repeating the same questions. It gradually sank into the mind of the unfortunate captive that these people could not possibly understand him. Pandion managed to rock the boat, but one of his escorts immediately brought a bronze dagger close to his eyes.

Disgusted with people, with himself and with the world at large, Pandion ceased his attempts at resistance and did not renew them again during his long journey through the labyrinth of swamp rushes. By the time the boat reached a stone wharf, the sun had long passed the horizon, and the moon hung high in the sky.

Here his legs were unbound and quickly and skillfully massaged to restore circulation. The soldiers lit two torches and made their way to a high rammed earth wall in which was a heavy, bronze-bound door.

After a lengthy altercation with the soldiers of the watch, Pandion's escort handed a tiny scroll over to a sleepy-eyed, bearded man who had suddenly appeared, and received in return a piece of black leather.

The heavy door groaned on its hinges. Pandion's hands were unbound, and he was thrust into the prison. The warders, armed with spears and bows, pushed back a massive wooden beam and Pandion found himself in a small square room packed with human bodies lying pell-mell on the floor. The people were breathing heavily and groaning in their unquiet sleep. Pandion, choking from the foul stench that seemed to ooze from the very walls, looked for an empty space on the floor and sat carefully down. He could not sleep; he pondered over the events of the last few days and his heart grew heavy within him.

The hours of his solitary, nocturnal meditation dragged slowly by. Pandion thought of nothing but liberty although now he could see no way of escape from bondage. He was far into the interior of an entirely unknown country and alone. An unarmed captive, who knew nothing of the language of the hostile people that surrounded him, he could not understand anything. He realized that they did not intend to kill him and resolved to wait. Later, when he knew something about the country, but what, then, awaited him in that 'later?'

As never before Pandion felt the urgent need of a companion who would help him overcome his terrible desolation. He pondered over the fact that there was no worse state for a man to be in, alone amongst strange and hostile people in an unknown and unknowable country, a slave, cut off from the whole world by virtue of his status. Loneliness would be much easier to bear if he were alone with nature - such solitude would strengthen rather than weaken his spirit.

Pandion bowed to his fate and fell into a strange lethargy. He awaited dawn and looked indifferently upon his companions in misfortune, captives from different Asian tribes unknown to him. They were better off than he was. They could talk to one another; they could share their grief, recall the past and discuss the future. The other prisoners cast equally curious glances on the silent Hellene.

The warders threw Pandion a piece of coarse linen for a loin-cloth and then four black-skinned men brought in a big earthen vessel of water, barley cakes and the stalks of some green vegetable.

Pandion was astounded at the sight of entirely black faces in which the teeth, the whites of the eyes and the brownish-red lips stood out so brightly. He guessed that they were slaves and was surprised at their jolly and kindly countenances. The Kemtiues laughed, showing their white teeth, as they made fun of the prisoners and of each other.

Was it possible, that, with the passage of time, I too, would be capable of finding joy in anything, of forgetting the pitiful role of a man deprived of his liberty? Could the constant ache that gnawed at my heart possibly pass away?

And Thessa? O Gods, if Thessa should know where I am! No, Thessa must never know. I will return to her or die; there was no other way.

Pandion's thoughts were disturbed by a long, drawn-out cry. The door opened. Before his eyes sparkled a wide river. His place of imprisonment was quite close to the water's edge.

A strong detachment of soldiers surrounded the captives with a phalanx of spears and drove them into the hold of a big ship. The ship sailed away upstream, and the captives were given no opportunity to look round them. It was stiflingly hot in the hold; the sun, standing high in the heavens, scorched the prisoners, and it was difficult to breathe in an atmosphere befouled by their exhalations.

Towards evening it grew cooler. The exhausted captives began to recover and started talking. The vessel sailed on all night. There was a short halt in the morning when the prisoners were fed, and the wearying journey continued. Several days passed in this way but Pandion, stupefied and apathetic, lost count of them.

At last, a livelier note could be heard in the voices of the rowers and soldiers, and there were sounds of bustle on the deck. The long journey was over. The captives were left in the hold all night, and in the morning, Pandion heard orders given in a loud, drawling voice.

The escort stood in a half-circle, spears thrust out in front of them, on a dusty sun-baked square. The captives left the ship one by one and immediately fell into the hands of two giant soldiers beside whom lay a heap of short ropes. The Egyptians bound the prisoners' arms so tightly that their shoulders were bent back, and their elbows met behind them. The groans and cries of the victims had no effect on the giants who gloried in their own strength and in the helplessness of their victims.

Pandion's turn came. One of the soldiers seized him by the arm immediately the youth, blinded by the glaring sun, set foot on land. The pain drove away all Pandion's apathy. He had been trained in fist fighting and easily escaped the hands of the soldier. He struck him a deadly blow on the ear; the giant fell face down in the dust and the other, momentarily losing his presence of mind, jumped away. Thirty enemy soldiers surrounded Pandion with their spears pointed at him.

In unspeakable fury, the youth leaped forward hoping to die in battle, for death seemed like deliverance to him. He did not know the Egyptians; however, whose methods of handling recalcitrant slaves were the accumulated result of thousands of years' experience. The soldiers immediately gave way and closed in behind Pandion who was thus left outside the circle. The bold youth was knocked off his feet and borne to the ground under the weight of several attackers. The end of a spear-shaft caught him a sharp blow in the ribs. The breath was knocked out of him, and a fiery-red haze floated before his eyes. In an instant, the Egyptians brought his hands together above his head and fastened them to a wooden instrument shaped like a toy boat. The soldiers then left the youth in peace.

The remaining captives were quickly bound, and all of them were driven off along a narrow road between the river and the fields. The young sculptor suffered intense pain: his arms were stretched at full length above his head with the wrists gripped in a wooden clamp that squeezed the bones. This instrument of torture did not permit him to bend his elbows or lower his hands on to his head.

The second party of slaves joined Pandion's group from a side road; then came the third party until there were altogether two hundred slaves in the group. All of them were bound most cruelly, and a number were wearing stocks like Pandion's. The captives' faces were twisted in pain; they were pallid and dripping with perspiration. Pandion walked along in a daze, scarcely taking note of his surroundings.

The country through which they marched was a rich one. The air was clean and fresh, silence reigned on the narrow roads, and the mighty river carried its waters slowly towards the Great Green Sea. The palms nodded their heads very slightly in the light breeze from the north and green fields of ripening wheat were interspersed with vineyards and orchards. The entire country was a vast garden, carefully tended for thousands of years.

Pandion could not look from side to side. He stumbled along, his teeth clenched in pain; past the high walls that surrounded the houses of the wealthy. The houses were light and airy two-storied structures with tall, narrow windows over the columned entrances. The snow-white walls, decorated with an intricate pattern in pure, bright colors, stood out sharply in the blinding sunlight.

Quite suddenly, the captives were confronted by a colossal stone edifice with straight, enormously thick-walls built of huge blocks of stone dressed with amazing skill. The dark and mysterious building seemed spread-eagled on the earth, crushed under its terrific weight. Pandion passed a row of massive columns, gloomily grey against the bright green background of the gardens that covered the plain. Palms, fig, and other fruit trees alternated in seemingly endless straight rows.

The hills were covered with a dense tangle of grape vines. In a garden by the river stood a high, light structure painted in the same bright colors as the other buildings of that city. Before the façade that opened on to the river, and beyond wide gates, stood tall mast-like poles with bunches of waving ribbons on top of them.

Over the wide entrance was a substantial snow-white balcony with two columns supporting a perfectly flat roof. The cornice of the roof was painted with an ornament in which bright blue and gold designs alternated. The bright blue and gold zigzags also ornamented the capitals of the columns. At the back of the balcony, in the shade cast by carpets and curtains, could be seen people dressed in long white garments of some finely pleated material.

The personage seated in the center inclined over the rail, his head heavy with the red and white double crown of the ruler of the two Kingdoms, Upper and Lower Egypt.

The escort, together with the commander, who had marched so importantly at their head, prostrated themselves face downwards on the ground. On a motion from the hand of Pharaoh, the living God and supreme ruler of the land of Tha-Quem, the captives were drawn into a single line, and then marched slowly past the balcony. The courtiers who crowded the balcony exchanged whispered remarks and laughed merrily.

The beauty of the palace, the rich raiment of Pharaoh and his courtiers, their haughty, free and easy postures made a sharp contrast to the pain-racked faces of the tormented slaves-and this aroused fierce indignation in Pandion's heart. He was beside himself from the pain in his arms; his body trembled as though with ague, his badly bitten lips were caked with dried blood, but the youth straightened his back, heaved a deep sigh, and turned a wrathful face towards the balcony.

Pharaoh turned and said something to his courtiers, and all of them nodded their heads in approval. The procession of slaves moved slowly on.

Soon Pandion found himself behind the house, in the shade of a high wall. Gradually the whole party of slaves gathered there, still surrounded by the silent soldiers. From around the corner appeared a corpulent, hook-nosed man carrying a long ebony staff inlaid with gold and accompanied by a scribe carrying a wooden tablet and a roll of papyrus. The man said something to the commander of the escort in haughty tones. The commander immediately doubled up in a low bow and transmitted the order to his soldiers. Obeying the aristocratic finger, the soldiers pushed their way into the crowd of prisoners and brought out those indicated to them.

Pandion was one of the first selected. Altogether about thirty of the strongest and bravest-looking were chosen. Immediately they were marched back along the same narrow road to the edge of the garden. From there the soldiers drove their captives along a low wall. The path grew steeper and led to a square of windowless walls standing in a hollow between the wheat-fields. Soldiers armed with bows walked freely up and down thick, brick-built walls some ten cubits in height. On the corners, there were shelters of matting. The entrance was in the wall facing the river and nowhere else were there either doors or windows; the blank, greenish-grey walls breathed fiery heat.

The escort led the prisoners through the doorway, and then withdrew rapidly, and Pandion found himself in a narrow courtyard between two walls. The second or inner wall was lower than the outer and had only one door, on its right-hand side. Some crude benches occupied the vacant space in the courtyard although most of it was taken up by a low building with a black hole of an entrance.

Soldiers with lighter colored skin than those who had escorted them on their journey surrounded the group of captives. They were all tall, with lithe, well-developed bodies and many of them had blue eyes and reddish hair. Pandion had never seen such people before, any more than he had seen the real inhabitants of Aigyptos, and did not know that they were Libyans.

Two men came out of the building; one of them carried something made of polished wood and the other, a grey faience pot. The Libyans seized Pandion and turned him around with his back towards the newcomers. The youth felt a slight pricking sensation on his left shoulder blade, on which a polished wooden board, bristling with short needles, had been placed. The man then struck the board sharply with his hand. The blood spurted out, and Pandion gave an involuntary cry of pain. The Libyan wiped away the blood and began rubbing the wound with a rag soaked in some liquid from the faience pot. The blood ceased flowing immediately, but he dipped the rag in the liquid several times and continued to rub the wound. Only then did Pandion notice the bright red mark of some little figures in an oval frame (The hieroglyphs of Pharaoh's name were written in an oval frame or cartouche.) on the left shoulders of the Libyans that surrounded him and realized that he had been branded.

The wooden frame was removed from Pandion's wrists, and he was unable to stifle the groan caused by the pain in his stiffened joints. With the greatest difficulty, he lowered his arms. Then, bending low, he entered the doorway in the inner wall and there, in a dusty courtyard, sank exhausted to the ground.

Pandion took a drink of stale water from the sizeable earthen jar that stood by the door and began to examine the place that was, in the opinion of those in authority, to be his home to the end of his days.

High, impenetrable walls, guarded by sentries who walked up and down them, surrounded the vast square of land with a side of about two stadia. The entire right-hand half of the enclosure was occupied by tiny rammed earth cells built one against the other, the rows of them separated by long narrow gangways.

There were similar small cells in the left-hand corner. A low wall surrounded the anterior left-hand corner, and a strong smell of ammonia came from there. Vessels for water stood near the door. Here a long strip of ground had been plastered with clay and was swept clean: this was the place allotted for eating, as Pandion learned later. All the free space in the square was trampled hard and smooth, with not a single blade of grass to relieve its dusty grey-surface. The air was heavy and stifling, it seemed as though all the fiery heat of the day poured into that sunken square, cut off by high walls and open to the sky. This was the shehne, the slave compound, one of the hundreds scattered throughout the land of Tha-Quem.

Slaves of all nations were crowded in these compounds. They constituted the labor power that was the foundation of the wealth and beauty of Aigyptos.

The compound was silent and deserted. The slaves were out at work, and only a few sick men were left lying listlessly in the shade of the wall.

This particular shehne was designed for newly arrived captives who had but recently fallen victims to the land of slavery and had not established families to increase the number of hands toiling in the Black Land.

Pandion had now become a mere hereditary slave of Pharaoh and was one of the eight thousand who served in gardens, canals, and buildings of the palace domains.

Other captives from amongst those who had been through the royal inspection with Pandion were distributed amongst the higher officials as Sahu-slaves who, on the death of their masters, would be transferred to the shehne of Pharaoh.

An oppressive silence filled the stifling atmosphere, broken only by occasional sighs and groans from the new slaves driven here together with Pandion. The brand burned like red-hot coals on Pandion's back. The youth could find no place for himself. A patch of dusty earth, hemmed in by high walls, replaced the open sea and shady groves on the wave-washed shores of his native land.

Instead of a free life together with his beloved, slavery in a foreign land infinitely far from all that was near and dear to him was to be his future. It was only the hope of liberation that kept the young Hellene from smashing his head against the wall that cut him off from the widespread and beautiful world.

CHAPTER THREE

The Slave of Pharaoh

As in previous years, the bushes covering the hilly slopes burst into a carpet of flaming flowers, as spring came again to the shores of Oeniadae. The bright constellation of the Archer (the early setting of the Archer constellation was regarded as heralding the end of the winter storms) had begun to set early, and the regular west wind announced the beginning of the seafaring season. Five ships had returned to Calydon, having left for Crete in early spring, and then two Cretan ships had arrived. However, Pandion was on none of them.

Agenor was frequently lost in silent meditation, but he strove to keep his feelings of alarm hidden from his family. The lone traveler had disappeared in Crete and had been lost somewhere in the mountains of that huge island, amidst large communities of people whose languages he did not know. The old artist had decided to go to Calydon, and from there, if an opportunity presented itself, leave for Crete to find out what he could of Pandion's fate.

Thessa had lately got into the habit of wandering off alone. Even the silent sympathy of her family lay heavy on her. In profound grief, the girl stood before the calm, eternally moving sea. Sometimes she ran down to the shore in the hope that Pandion would return to the place where they had parted. However, these days of faith had long since passed. Thessa was now sure that far beyond the line that divides the sky from the sea, some misfortune had occurred. Only captivity or death could have prevented Pandion from returning to her. Thessa implored the waves that came rolling in from afar; perhaps from that place where her beloved Pandion was now - to tell her what had happened. She was sure that she had to wait, but a little while and the waves would give her a sign to tell her where Pandion was. But the waves the sea cast at her feet were all alike, and their rhythmic noise told her no more than silence would have done.

How could she discover what had become of her lover? How could she, a woman whose lot in life is to be with her man, the mistress, and protector of his home, his companion when traveling and the healer of his wounds - how could she overcome the distance that separated them?

There was but one road for the woman who refused to obey a man, be it her father, husband, or brother, and that was to become a hetaera in the city or the harbor. She was a woman. She could not set out for another country. She could not even attempt to search for Pandion. There was nothing left for her to do but wander up and down the shores of the mighty sea. There was nothing she could do! No way in which she could help! Even if Pandion had perished, she would never, never know where he had died.

A deluge of silver-blue moonlight inundated the entire valley. It was cut off by deep black shadows from crevices in the steep cliffs, but it streamed along the river, following its course from south to north. Darkness filled the square well of the slave compound near Nut-Amon, or Waset, the great capital city of Aigyptos. The brightly illuminated rough surface of the wall, cast a dull reflection.

Pandion lay on a bundle of coarse grass on the floor of his narrow cell. With great caution, he thrust his head out of the low entrance that looked like a rat-hole. At the risk of attracting the sentries' attention, the young Hellene got up on his knees to admire the pale disc of the moon floating high in the heavens over the edge of the dark wall. It was painful to think that the same moon was shining over distant Oeniadae. Perhaps Thessa, his Thessa, was asking Hecate where he was, little suspecting that from his stinking hole; his eyes too, were fixed on that silver disc. Pandion drew his head back into the darkness that was filled with the dusty smell of heated clay and turned his face to the wall.

The raging despair of the first days, the fits of terrible grief, had long since passed. Pandion had changed considerably. His thick, clean-cut brows were knit in a permanent frown, the golden eyes of the descendant of Hyperion were dark with the fires of wrath that secretly but stubbornly burned in them, and his lips were now kept tightly pressed together. His powerful body, however, was still filled with inexhaustible energy; his intellect was unimpaired. The youth had not lost heart; he dreamed of liberty.

Pandion was gradually developing into a feared fighting man, not only because of his courage, strength, and boundless determination, but also because of the urge to maintain his spirits, even in the hell that surrounded him, and to carry his dreams, desires, and love through all trials and tribulations.

That which had been impossible to a lonely man ignorant of the language and the country had become possible - Pandion had a companion, a comrade. A comrade! Only he who has had to stand alone in the face of menacingly superior forces; only he who has been alone in a distant foreign land, can appreciate the full the meaning of that word. A comrade means friendly help, understanding, protection, common thoughts and dreams, wise counsel, timely reproach, support, and comfort.

During the seven months, he had been employed on jobs near the capital, Pandion had learned something of the strange language of Aigyptos, and began to understand his fellow-slaves despite their many tongues. He began to distinguish those who had clear-cut, distinct individuality from amongst the five hundred slaves confined in the shehne and daily driven out to work.

On their part, the other slaves gradually learned to trust one another, and some of them became friendly with Pandion. The terrible privations that they shared, the collective longing for liberty, united them in a common struggle to win their emancipation, strike a blow at the blind, oppressive forces of the rulers of the Black Land and return to their long-lost native lands.

Home - they could all understand the word. To some, it meant land that lay beyond the mysterious swamps in the south, to others somewhere beyond the sands to the east or west and to the rest, like Pandion, a land beyond the seas in the north.

There were but few in the shehne, however, who had strength enough to prepare for the combat. The others, exhausted by their heavy drudgery and constant undernourishment, were slowly fading away without a murmur. These were mostly people of advanced age, who had no interest in what was going on around them. There was not a spark of resolution in their dull eyes. They showed no desire to communicate with their companions. They worked, ate slowly, and sank into a heavy sleep and next morning shuddered at the cries of the warders who awakened them to trudge along in the column of slaves, sluggish and indifferent.

Pandion soon realized why there were so many separate cells in the slave compound. They kept people apart. After supper, it was forbidden to communicate with one another. The sentries on the wall watched for infringements of this rule and the next morning an arrow or a stick fell to the lot of the disobedient. Not every slave possessed either the strength or the courage to take advantage of the darkness and crawl to the cells of his companions, but some of Pandion's comrades did.

Three men became Pandion's closest companions. The first of them was Kidogo, a huge Kemtiu almost four cubits in height, who came from a very distant part of Africa to the south-west of Aigyptos. Kindly, jolly and exuberant, Kidogo was also a skilled artist and sculptor. His expressive face, with its broad nose and thick lips, immediately attracted Pandion's attention by its intellect and energy.

Pandion was used to well-built Kemtiues, but this giant immediately drew the attention of the sculptor by the beauty of his well-proportioned body. Muscles seemingly forged from iron, suited Kidogo's light and lithe figure. His enormous eyes seemed all attention and were astounding in their animation against the background of a black face.

At first, Pandion and Kidogo communicated with each other using drawings made with a pointed stick on the earth or on walls. Later, the young Hellene began to talk to the Kemtiu in a mixture of the language of Quemt and the simple, easily remembered language of Kidogo's people. In the pitch darkness of moonless nights, Pandion and Kidogo crawled to each other's cells, and, talking in whispers, gained fresh strength and courage in the discussion of plans for escape.

One evening, after Pandion had been there for a month, a group of new slaves was driven into the shehne. The newcomers sat or lay near the door gazing hopelessly around them, their tormented faces bearing the seal of grief and despair so well known to every one of the captives. On returning from work in the evening, Pandion was going to the big water vessels to get a drink when suddenly he almost let his bowl drop. Two of the newcomers were murmuring softly in Etruscan, a language with which Pandion was familiar. The Etruscans were a strange, rough and ancient people who frequently visited the shores of Oeniadae, where they enjoyed the reputation of sorcerers knowing the secrets of nature.

So overwhelming was the power of memories his home evoked, that Pandion's whole body trembled; he spoke to the Etruscans, and they understood him. When he asked them how they fell captive to the Egyptians, both of them sat silently as though they were not at all pleased with the meeting.

The two Etruscans were of medium height, very muscular, and had broad shoulders. Their dark hair, matted with dirt, hung in uneven strands on both sides of their faces. The older of the two was apparently about forty years old, and the younger was approximately the same age as Pandion. The likeness between them was immediately apparent - their sunken cheeks stressed the protruding cheekbones, and their stern hazel eyes flashed with a stubbornness that nothing could break.

Pandion was both puzzled and annoyed by the indifference of the Etruscans and hurried back to his own cell. For several days after this, Pandion deliberately paid no attention to them, although he knew they were watching him.

Some ten days after the arrival of the Etruscans, Pandion and Kidogo were sitting side by side over a supper of papyrus stalks. The two friends ate their food quickly and then lingered a while to talk while the others were finishing their meal. Pandion's neighbor on the other side was the older Etruscan. Unexpectedly he laid his heavy hand on the youth's shoulder and looked mockingly into Pandion's eyes when he turned towards him.

"A poor comrade will never gain his liberty," said the Etruscan slowly, with a note of challenge in his words; he did not fear that the warders would understand him, for the inhabitants of Tha-Quem did not understand the languages of their captives and despised all foreigners.

Pandion jerked his shoulder impatiently, not having understood the import of the Etruscan's words, but the latter squeezed hard with his fingers that dug into Pandion's muscles like bronze talons.

"You despise them, and you shouldn't." The Etruscan nodded his head towards the other slaves who were busily eating. "The others are no worse than you, and they also dream of liberty."

"They are worse," exclaimed Pandion arrogantly. "They've been here a long time, and I haven't heard of any attempts at escape!"

The Etruscan pressed his lips together contemptuously.

"If youth doesn't possess sufficient intelligence, then youth must learn from age. You're strong and healthy, there's still strength left in your body after a day's heavy toil, and lack of food hasn't yet undermined your strength. They have lost their strength; that's the only difference between you and them, and that's your good luck. But, remember that you can't escape from here alone. You have to know the road and breakthrough by force, and the only force we have is all of us together. When you are a good comrade to all of them, there'll be a better chance of your dreams coming true."

Amazed at the shrewdness of the Etruscan, who had fathomed his most secret thoughts, Pandion could find no answer and only hung his head in silence.

"What's he saying? What's he saying?" Kidogo kept asking him.

Pandion wanted to explain but at that moment, the overseer beat on the table. The slaves who had finished their meal had to make way for the next party and go to their cells for their night's rest.

During the night, Pandion and Kidogo discussed the Etruscan's words for a long time. They had to admit that the newcomer understood the position of the slaves better than anybody else did. Those who bore the brand of Pharaoh had to know the way out of the country if their escape was to be successful. This was not all: they had to fight their way through a land with a hostile population who believed that the "savages" were created to work for the people chosen by the gods. The two friends were despondent at this, but they had a feeling of trust in the clever Etruscan.

A few more days passed, and there were four friends in Pharaoh's shehne. Gradually they acquired greater authority amongst the other slaves. Many of the slaves regarded the older Etruscan, bearing the awe-inspiring name of Cavius, the god of death, as their senior. The three others, the young Etruscan, whose name was Remdus,

Kidogo and Pandion, three robust, hardy and bold men, became his most reliable assistants.

By degrees from amongst the five hundred slaves, more and more fighters appeared who were willing to risk their lives in the faint hope of returning to their native lands. Just as slowly, the remainder, the cowed, the tormented and oppressed, regained confidence in their strength and hope grew stronger that by uniting, they could resist the organized might of a vast state.

But the days passed, empty and aimless. Bitter days of captivity, days of heavy drudgery that they hated if only because it contributed towards the prosperity of the cruel taskmasters who had thousands of human lives at their disposal. At sunrise each day, columns of worn-out men under armed escort left the shehne for work in different places.

The inhabitants of Aigyptos despised all foreigners and did not take the trouble to learn the languages of their captives. For this reason, fresh slaves were at first employed on the simplest tasks. Later, as they learned the Quemt language, they were given more complicated instructions and learned handicrafts. The overseers did not bother about the names of their slaves and called them by the names of the peoples to which they belonged.

Thus, Pandion was called Ekwesha - Egyptian for all the peoples of the Aegean Sea; the Etruscans were Turu-sha, while Kidogo and all other black slaves were merely called Nehsu - Kemtiu.

For the first two months in the shehne, Pandion and forty other fresh slaves did repair work on the canals in the

Gardens of Amon, (a temple at Karnak, near Luxor) rebuilt dykes washed away by the previous year's floods, loosened the earth around fruit trees, pumped water and carried it to the flower-beds.

The overseers took note of the hardiness, strength, and ability of the newcomers, and gradually selected a new detachment that was sent for building work. It happened that the four friends and thirty other strong slaves - the leaders of the mass of slaves in the shehne - were all in the same group. When they were transferred to building work, their regular contact with the others was interrupted, since they remained away from the shehne for weeks on end.

The first work given to Pandion away from Pharaoh's gardens was the dismantling of an old temple and tomb on the west bank of the river some fifty stadia from the shehne. The slaves were loaded on to a boat and ferried across the river, under the supervision of an overseer and five soldiers. They were marched along a path northward, to a ridge of vertical cliffs that formed a large ledge. The path led them past tilled fields on to a metaled road.

Suddenly a picture unfolded before Pandion's eyes that forever impressed itself on his memory. The slaves had been halted on a wide-open space sloping down to the river, and the overseer had gone away, bidding them await his return.

This was the first opportunity Pandion had of studying his surroundings more or less leisurely. Directly in front of him, rose a vertical wall of copper-colored rock, three hundred cubits high, dotted with patches of blue-black shadow. From the foot of the cliff, the white colonnade of a temple spread out over three terraces. A path of smooth grey stone rose from the riverside plain. On either side were rows of strangely carved sphinxes-monsters in the form of recumbent lions with human heads.

Further, a broad white staircase between walls on which twining yellow snakes were carved - one on either side - led to the second terraced building supported by low columns, twice the height of a man, of dazzlingly white limestone. In the central part of the temple, he noticed the second row of similar columns. On each of them was the representation of a human figure in a royal crown with the hands folded over the breast.

Flanked by a colonnade, the second terraced temple had a big open space with a lane of recumbent sphinxes. Some thirty cubits higher was the third or upper terrace of the temple, surrounded by a colonnade and filling a natural indenture in the cliff face.

The lower terrace of the temple extended in width over a distance of some one and a half stadia. At the extremes, there were simple cylindrical columns. In the center, they were square, and higher up they had six or sixteen faces. The central columns, the capitals of the side columns, the cornices of the porticos and the human figures, were all painted in bright blue and red colors which made the glaring white of the stone still more dazzling.

This temple, brightly lit up by the sun, formed a striking contrast to other gloomy, oppressive temple buildings that Pandion had seen. The young Hellene could not imagine anything more beautiful than those rows of snow-white columns in a framework of colored patterns.

On the terraces grew trees such as Pandion had never seen before - low trees with a dense cluster of branches covered with tiny leaves growing close to each other. These trees gave off a very potent aroma, and their golden-green foliage gave them a very gay appearance, backed by snow-white columns accentuated by the red cliffs.

In a burst of wild admiration, Kidogo nudged Pandion, smacked his lips and emitted inarticulate sounds expressing approbation. None of the slaves knew that the architect Sennemut built the temple, before which they stood, about five hundred years earlier for his mistress Queen Hatshepsut, Queen of the 18th Dynasty from 1500-1457 B.C. The temple is at Deir-el-Bahri and was called Zesher-Zesheru - the most magnificent of the magnificent. The Temple of Montuhotep 4th, a Pharaoh of the Middle Kingdom, 11th Dynasty, about 2050 B.C.

The strange trees growing on the terraces had been brought from the Land of Punt, to which Queen Hatshepsut had sent a big expedition by sea. Since that time, it had been the custom for every new expedition to Punt to bring back young trees for the temple and renew the old plantation, which was thus seemingly preserved from ancient days.

The voice of the overseer came from the distance. The slaves hurried away from the temple and passing round it to the left, found yet another temple, also built on a ledge on the cliff, this time in the form of a small pyramid resting on rows of closely placed columns.

Higher up the river, there were two other temples of polished grey granite. The overseer led his party to the nearest of them, where they joined another party of about two hundred slaves busy dismantling the temple. The white plaster on the interior walls was decorated with brightly colored drawings executed with great mastery.

The building officials and technicians of Aigyptos, who had charge of the work, were only interested in the polished granite blocks with which the portico and the colonnade were faced. The interior walls were ruthlessly destroyed.

Pandion was shocked at this wanton destruction of ancient works of art and managed to get into the group of slaves employed in piling the stones on to wooden sleds and dragging them down to the river to be loaded on a low-lying boat. He did not know that the Pharaohs of Aigyptos had long been dismantling ancient temples, mostly those of the Middle Kingdom (2160-1580 B.C.) which contained a large quantity of beautifully dressed stone; they had no respect for monuments of the past and hastened to perpetuate their own names by building temples and tombs from ready materials.

Neither the Hyksos, the barbaric Shepherd Kings who had conquered Tha-Quem many centuries before, nor the slaves who revolted and ruled the country for a short period some two hundred years before Pandion was born, had touched these magnificent edifices. Now, following the secret instructions of the new Pharaohs of Aigyptos, the temples and tombs of the ancient kings were being dismantled and gold poured into the treasury of the rulers from the plundered tombs hidden under the ancient sand-covered pyramids and from the magnificent underground tombs of the great kings of the 18th, 19th and 20th dynasties.

Pandion spent three months altogether on this work of dismantling the temple. He and Kidogo worked hard, doing their utmost to lighten the labor of their comrades. This was exactly what their taskmasters wanted: the labor system in Tha-Quem was organized in such a way that the weak had to keep pace with the strong. The unusual strength and shrewdness of Kidogo and Pandion attracted the attention of the overseers, and they were sent to the workshop of the stonemasons to learn the craft.

One of Pharaoh's sculptors took them away from this workshop and thus cut them off completely from their comrades in the shahne. Pandion and Kidogo were housed in a long, uncomfortable shed with a number of other slaves who had already mastered the simple craft. Native inhabitants of Aigyptos, free craftsmen, occupied a few huts in one corner of the big workshop yard where there were piles of undressed stone and rubble. The Egyptians kept markedly clear of the slaves as though they might be punished for any connections with them; later Pandion learned that this actually was the case.

The master of the workshop, a royal sculptor, did not suspect that Pandion and Kidogo were real sculptors and was astonished at the progress they made.

The young men longed for some creative activity and gave themselves up whole-heartedly to their work, forgetting for a time that they were working for the hated Pharaoh and the vile land of slavery.

Kidogo waxed enthusiastic over his models of animals: hippopotamuses, crocodiles, antelopes, and other strange beasts Pandion had never seen; other slaves to make faience statuettes used his models.

The Egyptian sculptor noticed Pandion's fondness for modeling people and undertook to teach this promising young Ekwesha; he insisted on the utmost thoroughness in work done to order.

"The slightest negligence is the ruin of perfection," the Egyptian sculptor would constantly repeat-this was the watchword of the ancient masters of the Black Land.

The Hellene studied assiduously, and at times, his nostalgia was forgotten. He made great progress in the precise work of finishing off statues and bas-reliefs from hard stone and in the embossing of gold ornaments. Pandion accompanied the sculptor to Pharaoh's palace and saw apartments of unbelievable luxury.

On the colored floors of the royal quarters, there were representations of the thickets of the Great River with their plants and animals, all drawn wonderfully lifelike and framed with wavy lines or spirals of many colors. The faience tiles on the walls of the rooms were covered with a transparent blue glaze through which shone fantastic designs in gold leaf, works of art that were nothing less than magic.

Amidst all this magnificence, the young Hellene looked with hatred on the haughty, immobile courtiers. He examined their white garments, ironed in tiny pleats, their heavy necklaces, rings and lockets of cast gold, their wigs of curled hair falling to the shoulders and their embroidered slippers with upturned toes.

Like a silent shadow Pandion followed the hurrying master sculptor; on his way, he took note of valuable thin-walled vessels cut from rock-crystal and hard stone, glass vases and pots of grey faience decorated with pale blue designs. He was fully aware of the tremendous amount of labor that had gone into the production of these works of art.

The greatest impression was produced by a gigantic temple near the Gardens of Amon where Pandion began his life as a slave, languishing behind the high walls of the she-fine. This was a temple of many gods built in the course of more than a thousand years. Each of the kings of Tha-Quem had added something new to an already colossal structure more than eight hundred cubits in length.

On the right bank of the river, within the bounds of the capital city Nut-Amon, or simply Nut-the city-as the Egyptians called it, lay magnificent gardens with straight rows of high palms at both ends of which were a number of temples.

These temple buildings were connected by long avenues of statues of strange animals with the riverbanks and the sacred lake in front of the Temple of Mut, a goddess that Pandion could not understand. Granite beasts, three times the height of a man, with the bodies of lions and the heads of rams and men, gave him a sensation of oppressiveness. Mysterious, frozen into immobility, they lay on their pedestals, close together, bordering an avenue lit up by the blinding sun, their heads hanging over passers-by.

The towering obelisks, fifty cubits high, covered in bright yellow sheets of an amalgam of gold and silver, gleamed like incandescent needles thrust through the coarse, dark foliage of the palms. In the daytime the silver-covered slabs of stone with which the avenues were paved blinded the astonished eyes; by night, in the light of the moon and stars, they were like the flowing stream of an unearthly river of light. Enormous pylons flanked the entrance to the temple. The huge surfaces of these pylons were covered with enormous sculptures of the gods and Pharaohs, and with inscriptions in the mysterious language of Tha-Quem. Colossal doors, covered with sheets of bronze inlaid with ornaments in the gold-silver amalgam, closed the passage between the pylons; their cast bronze hinges, each the weight of several bulls, were imposing in their massiveness.

The interior of the temple was a forest of thick columns fifty cubits high carrying heavy bas-reliefs that filled the upper part of the temple. The huge blocks of stone in the walls, roof, and columns were polished and fitted to each other with miraculous precision. Drawings and bas-reliefs, painted in bright colors, covered the walls, columns, and cornices in several tiers. Sun discs, hawks and animal-headed gods gazed down morosely from the mysterious semi-darkness of the distant parts of the temple.

Outside there were the same bright colors, gold, and silver; the monstrously massive buildings and sculptures stunned, blinded, and oppressed all who saw them.

Everywhere Pandion saw statues of pink and black granite, red sandstone and yellow limestone-the deified rulers of Tha-Quem sitting in inhuman serenity and arrogant poses. In some cases, these were colossal, up to forty cubits in height cut from the living rock, angular and crude; others, awe-inspiring in their dreadful gloom, were carefully painted, well-finished sculptures, much more than human height.

Pandion had grown up amongst simple people who were in constant communion with nature and was at first overcome with awe. Everything in this vast, rich country produced a most profound impression on him. The giant structures built by some means beyond the ken of mortal man, the awful gods that hid in the gloom of the temples, the incomprehensible religion with its elaborate rites, the mark of antiquity on the sand-embedded buildings - all this at first gave Pandion a sense of oppressiveness. He believed that the haughty and inscrutable inhabitants of Aigyptos were the masters of profound truths, of some powerful science that was hidden in the writings of the Black Land which no foreigner could understand.

The country itself, squeezed by death-dealing, lifeless deserts into a narrow strip of a valley watered by a huge river carrying its waters from some distant and unknown place in the far south, was a world unto itself, in no way related to the other parts of Oecumene.

The sober mind of the young Hellene, however, gradually sifted this mass of impressions in the search for simple and natural truths. Pandion now had time for meditation; the young sculptor's spirit, with its constant striving for the beautiful, began to revolt against the life and art of Aigyptos, a protest that later became conscious.

The fertile land, in which inclement weather was unknown, the bright, clear, and almost permanently cloudless sky, the amazingly transparent and invigorating air, all seemed to have been specially created for a healthy and happy life.

Little as the young Hellene knew of the country, he could not but help but notice the poverty and crowded conditions of the Nemhu, the poorest and most numerous inhabitants of Aigyptos. The colossal temples and statues, the beautiful gardens could not hide the endless rows of mud hovels that housed tens of thousands of craftsmen working for those palaces and temples.

As far as the slaves languishing in hundreds of compounds were concerned, Pandion knew about these from his own experience. It gradually became clear to him that the art of Aigyptos, subordinated to the rulers of the country, the Pharaohs, and priests, and controlled by them, was the exact opposite of that which he sought - the reflection of life in art.

It was only when he caught sight of the temple Zesher-Zesheru, open and designed to merge with the surrounding landscape, that he felt that there was something close and pleasing to him here. All other giant temples and tombs were, as a rule, hidden behind high walls. Behind those walls, the craftsmen of Aigyptos working at the bidding of the priests had made use of all the artifice at their disposal to take man away from life, to humiliate him and crush his spirit, force him to realize his own insignificance in the face of the majesty of the gods and the Pharaohs.

The enormous size of the structures, the colossal amount of labor and material involved did crush the spirit of man. The constantly repeated succession of identical, monotonous forms, piled one on the other, created the impression of infinite distance. Identical sphinxes, identical columns, walls, and pylons-all with a careful scantiness of detail-were solid and immobile. Gigantic statues, all similar, lined the passages within the temples, gloomy and ominous.

The rulers of Aigyptos and arbiters of her art were afraid of space; they fenced themselves off from the world of nature and then filled the interiors of their temples with massive stone columns, thick walls and stone beams that often occupied more space than did the room between them. The greater the distance from the entrance, the thicker grew the forest of columns in the temple, and the rooms, insufficiently lit, grew progressively darker. The huge number of narrow doorways made the temple mysteriously inaccessible, and the permanent semi-darkness served to increase the fear of the gods.

Pandion gradually fathomed the secret of this deliberate effect on the spirit of man, an effect achieved through many centuries of building experience. If Pandion could have seen the enormous pyramids, whose perfect geometrical form stood out so sharply above the wavy lines of the surrounding sand, he would have sensed more fully the imperious manner of setting off man against nature. This was the method adopted by the rulers of Tha-Quem to conceal their fear of the unknown, a fear reflected in the sullen, mysterious religion of the Egyptians. The craftsmen of the Tha-Quem glorified their gods and their rulers, striving to express their strength in colossal statues of the Pharaohs and in the symmetrical immobility of their massive bodies.

On the walls, the Pharaohs themselves were depicted in pictures more than life-size. Dwarfs swarmed around their feet-the other inhabitants of the Black Land. In this way, the kings of Egypt used every means at their disposal to emphasize their greatness. They believed that by humiliating the people in every way, they were exalting themselves, that in this way their influence would be augmented.

Pandion still knew very little of the beautiful native art, the real art of the people of the Black Land, that was not held in bondage by courtiers and priests but was expressed in articles of everyday use amongst the common people. He felt that real art lay in a simple and joyful coalescence with life itself. It should be as different from everything created in Aigyptos as his native land. His homeland had a variety of rivers, fields, forests, sea, and mountains. Colorful changes of seasons at home differed from this country, where the terraced cliffs rose so monotonously from one single river valley, everywhere alike, that was surrounded on all sides by burning- sands and filled with carefully tilled gardens.

Thousands of years before the inhabitants of Aigyptos had hidden from the hostile world in the valley of the Nile. Today their descendants were trying to turn their faces away from life by hiding in their palaces and temples.

Pandion felt that the majesty of the art of Aigyptos was, to a considerable extent, the fruit of the natural abilities of slaves of different races; the most talented were selected from millions, and these involuntarily devoted all their creative effort to the glorification of the country that oppressed them.

When he had freed himself of his submission to the might of Aigyptos, Pandion resolved to escape as soon as possible and to convince his friend Kidogo of the necessity of this step. His head was filled with these ideas when he, with Kidogo and ten other slaves, made a long trip to the ruins of the ancient town of Akhetaton. (Akhetaton (Tel el-Amarna) - the capital of Pharaoh Amenhotep 44th, 1375-1358 B.C.)

The young sculptor ruffled the smooth surface of the river with his oars, the fast movement of the boat downstream giving him a sensation of joy. The journey was a long one, almost three thousand stadia, a distance virtually equal to that which separated his native land from Crete, and which had once seemed to him to be immeasurably great.

During this voyage, Pandion learned that the Great Green Sea, as the people of Aigyptos, called it, and on the northern shores of which Thessa was awaiting his return, was twice as far away as Akhetaton.

Pandion's happy mood passed very quickly: for the first time, he realized how far inland he was in the depths of Aigyptos and how great a distance separated him from the seacoast where there might be a possibility of returning home. He bent moodily over his oars, and the boat slipped over the smooth surface of the endless river, past thickets of green shrubs, tilled fields, reed jungles, and white-hot cliffs.

The royal sculptor lay under a striped awning in the stern sheets and was fanned by a servile slave. Rows of tiny huts stretched along the banks-the fertile land fed a tremendous number of people.

Thousands of people swarmed the fields, gardens, and papyrus thickets, toiling to earn a scanty livelihood. Thousands of people packed the narrow streets of the countless villages on the outskirts of which towered huge ungainly temples, firmly shut off from the sun.

It suddenly struck Pandion that not only he and his comrades were doomed to a pitiful existence in Tha-Quem, but the inhabitants of those miserable huts were also enslaved by their joyless drudgery, that they, too, were the slaves of the ruler and his courtiers despite the fact that they despised him, Pandion, as a branded savage. Lost in thought, Pandion struck his neighbor's oar with his own.

"Hi, Ekwesha, wake up, look out for yourself!"

At night, the slaves were shut up in the prisons that stood in the vicinity of each township or temple. Pharaoh's sculptor was treated with respect everywhere by the local authorities, and he went away to his rest accompanied by two trusted servants.

On the fifth day, the boat turned a bend formed by out jutting river-washed rocks. Beyond the bend lay an extensive plain cut off from the river by rows of tall palms and sycamores. The boat approached a stone-paved embankment with two wide staircases leading down to the water. A massive tower rose behind a crenelated wall on the riverbank. The heavy gates stood half-open and through them could be seen a garden with ponds and flower-dotted lawns, beyond which stood a white building decorated with colorful designs. This was the house of the High Priest of the local temples.

The royal sculptor, before whom the sentries bowed in servile humility, entered the gates while the slaves remained outside under the surveillance of two soldiers. They did not have to wait long, for the sculptor soon returned with another man who carried a scroll of papyrus and led the slaves past the temples and dwelling houses to a big site occupied by ruined walls and a forest of columns, the roof over which had collapsed.

Amongst the ruins of this dead town, there were, here and there, small buildings in a better state of preservation. An occasional tree stump indicated the site of former gardens; dried up ponds, basins and canals were filled with sand, a thick layer of sand covered the stone-paved roads and piled up against walls eroded by time. Not a living soul was to be seen anywhere. Deadly silence reigned in the blazing heat.

The sculptor explained in a few words to Pandion that these were the ruins of the once beautiful capital of the Heretic Pharaoh (The Heretic Pharaoh-Amenhotep IV who tried to introduce into Egypt a new religion with only one god-the sun disc Aton) whom the gods had cursed. No true son of the Black Land dares pronounce his name. Pandion could not discover what this Pharaoh, who had reigned four centuries earlier, had done and why he had built a new capital.

The newcomer unrolled his papyrus, and the two Egyptians studied the drawing on it to discover the whereabouts of a long building with the columns at its entrance lying on the ground. The interior walls of this building were faced with azure-blue stones with veins of gold in them. Pandion and the other slaves were given the job of removing these thin stone slabs that had been firmly cemented to the walls. The job took them several days to complete. They spent the night there amidst the ruins, food, and water was brought to them from the neighboring dwellings.

When they had finished their job Pandion, Kidogo and four other slaves were ordered to search the ruins in any direction they liked, and look for any works of art that might have been left there which could be taken as gifts for Pharaoh's palace.

The Kemtiu and Pandion set out together, the first time without escort and away from the keen eye of the overseer. The two friends climbed on to the gate turret of some large building to get a view of their surroundings. From the east sand crept up to and into the ruins and stretched away in a desert of rolling dunes and piles of stone as far as the eye could reach. Pandion looked over the silent ruins and, in his excitement, grasped Kidogo's arm tightly.

"Let's run, we won't be missed for a long time, nobody can see us," he whispered.

The Kemtiu's good-natured face spread in a smile.

"Don't you know what the desert is?" he asked in astonishment. "At this hour tomorrow, the soldiers of the search party would find our dead bodies already dried up by the sun. They," Kidogo meant the Egyptians, "know what they are doing. There is only one road to the east, it follows the water holes, and they are guarded. In this place, the desert holds us tighter than any chains."

Pandion nodded his head gloomily - his momentary

excitement had passed.

In silence, the two friends left the turret and set out in different directions, looking through holes in the walls and entering rooms through their dark doorways. Inside a small, well-preserved, two-storied palace, where there were the remains of the wooden latticework on the windows, Kidogo had the good fortune to find a small statue of an Egyptian girl carved from hard yellow limestone. He called Pandion, and together they examined the work of some unknown master. The girl's pretty face was typically Egyptian, such as Pandion already knew - the low forehead, narrow eyes slanting upwards towards the temples, protruding cheekbones, and thick lips with dimples at the corners of the mouth.

Kidogo took his find to the master of the workshops while Pandion penetrated farther into the ruins. He wandered on, stepping mechanically over wreckage and heaps of stones, taking no note of his direction, and soon he found himself in the shade of a length of wall that was still standing. Right in front of him, he saw a tightly closed door leading to underground premises. Pandion pressed on the bronze door handle. The rotten boards collapsed under his weight, and he entered a room whose only light came from a narrow chink in the ceiling.

It was a small room built in a thick wall of excellently dressed stone. Two light armchairs of ebony inlaid with ivory were covered with a layer of dust. In one corner lay a half-rotten casket.

Against the opposite wall, a grey stone statue stood on a block of rose-hued granite. It was a full-size female figure, the lower part of which had been left unfinished. Two lithe panthers of black stone, one on either side of the statue, stood as though on guard. Pandion carefully brushed the dust from the statue and stepped back in silent admiration. The skill of the craftsman had reproduced, in stone, the transparent material that enveloped the girl's body. With her left hand, she pressed a lotus bloom firmly to her breast. Her thick hair, braided in a number of thin plaits, framed her face in a heavy coiffure divided by a straight parting and falling over her shoulders. The charming girl did not resemble an Egyptian. Her face was rounder, her nose small and straight and she had a high forehead, and big eyes set wide apart.

Pandion glanced at the statue from one side and was amazed at the strange and subtle mockery that the sculptor had given to the girl's face. Never had he seen such an expression of verve and intellect in a statue; the artists of Aigyptos loved majestic and indifferent immobility more than anything else. The girl was more like the women of Oeniadae, or even more like the beautiful inhabitants of the islands of his native sea. The bright, intelligent face of the statue was far removed from the sullen beauty of Egyptian works of art and was carved with such great skill that Pandion once again felt the torture of nostalgia.

The young Hellene wrung his hands and tried to imagine the model from which the statue had been carved, a girl that somehow seemed near to him, a girl that had found her way to Aigyptos by unknown roads four centuries ago. Had she been a captive like himself or had she come from some distant country of her own free will?

A ray of sunlight, falling through the crack in the ceiling, cast a dusty light on the statue. It seemed to Pandion that the expression on the girl's face had changed - the eyes blazed, the lips trembled as though a flutter of mysterious, hidden life had reached the stone surface of the statue. Yes, that was the way to carve a statue. Here was the master from whom he could learn to depict living beauty one who had long been dead!

Reverently Pandion laid careful fingers on the face of the statue, feeling for the tiny and elusive è details that made the statue a living thing. For a long time, he remained standing before the statue of the beautiful maiden who smiled at him in mocking friendliness. It seemed to him that he had found a new friend, whose smile lightened the burden of the endless succession of joyless days. Unconsciously the youth's thoughts turned to Thessa, and her living image rose before him again.

Pandion's eyes wandered over the ornament on the ceiling and walls where stars, bunches of lotus flowers and curving lilies were intermingled with bull's heads. Suddenly Pandion shuddered: the vision of Thessa disappeared and before him, on the wall, stood a picture of captives tied back to back, being dragged to the feet of Pharaoh.

Pandion remembered that it was late and that he must hurry back. He had to take something with him to justify his long absence. He looked again at the statue and realized that he could not place it in the hands of the master sculptor. He regarded such an act as tantamount to treachery. It would be like delivering the girl into slavery for a second time.

Looking around, he suddenly remembered the casket he had seen in the corner. Pandion knelt down and removed from it four faience drinking cups, shaped like lotus blossoms, and covered with bright blue enamel. That would be enough. Pandion took his last look at the statue of the girl, trying to fix in his memory every detail of her face, and with a deep sigh carried the four cups outside. He looked round to make sure that he was not observed and hurriedly covered the entrance to the room with big boulders and then filled all the spaces between them with rubble so that it looked like part of the damaged wall. He wrapped the cups up carefully in his loincloth, made an involuntary gesture of farewell in the direction of the statue, safe in its asylum, and hurried off to join the others.

The shouts of the slaves showed him the direction, loudest amongst them being the strong, resonant voice of Kidogo. The royal sculptor met Pandion at first with threats but calmed down the moment he saw the treasure Pandion had brought him.

The return journey took three days longer as the rowers had to fight against the current of the river. Pandion told Kidogo about the statue, and the Kemtiu approved his action, adding that the girl had probably come from the Mashuashi, a people living on the northern edge of the Great Western Desert.

Pandion tried to persuade Kidogo to flee, but his friend only shook his head in reply, rejecting all the plans suggested by the Hellene. During the seven days of the journey, Pandion failed to convince his friend but he, himself, was unable to remain inactive; it seemed that he would not be able to hold out much longer and must inevitably perish. He longed for his companions who had stayed on the building jobs and in the shehne. He felt that these men were the force that could bring liberation, and which gave him hopes for the future. Here there was no hope of freedom and that made Pandion pant in helpless fury.

Two days after their return to the workshops, the royal sculptor took Pandion to the palace of the Chief Builder, where a festival was being prepared. Pandion was ordered to fashion clay statuettes and from them make molds for the shaping of sweet biscuits. When Pandion had finished his work, he was told to remain at the palace to carry home the palanquin of the royal sculptor when the feast was over.

Pandion did not pay any attention to the other slaves, men, and women that filled the palace, but went off by himself in the garden.

It had grown dark, bright stars lit up the sky, but still, the feast went on. Sheaves of yellow light piercing the darkness of the garden from the open windows illuminated the trunks of trees, the foliage, and flowers of the shrubs and were reflected in patches of glowing red from the mirror-like surfaces of the ponds.

The guests were assembled in a big hall on the ground floor decorated with pillars of polished cedar wood. From the hall came sounds of music. For a long time, Pandion had heard nothing in the way of music except mournful and unknown songs, and he gradually drew closer to the big, low window, hid in the bushes, and watched what was going on.

A heavy aroma of sweet oils came from the crowded room. The walls, pillars, and window-frames were hung with garlands of fresh flowers, mostly lotus blossoms, Pandion noticed. Brightly-colored jugs of wine, baskets, and bowls of fruit stood on low tables near the seats.

The guests, excited by the wine they had drunk and anointed with perfumed unguents, were crowded along the walls, while in the space between the columns girls in long garments were dancing. Their black hair, braided into numerous thin plaits, swung about the shoulders of the dancers. Wide bracelets of colored beads covered their wrists, and girdles of similar design shone through the thin material of their raiment.

Pandion could not help noticing a certain angularity in the bodies of the Egyptian dancing girls who differed very significantly from the strong women of his own country. At one end of the room, young Egyptian girls played on a variety of musical instruments: two girls played flutes, another played on a harp of many strings, and still two others extracted harsh rattling notes from long two-stringed instruments.

The dancing girls carried thin leaves of gleaming bronze in their hands and from time to time interrupted the rhythm of the dance melody with sharp, ringing blows on them. Pandion's ear was unaccustomed to the sudden changes from high tones to low, to the poignantly moaning notes with a constantly changing tempo. The dances ended, and the tired dancing girls gave up the floor to the singers. Pandion listened attentively, trying to understand the words, and found that when the melody was slow and low in the tone, he could understand the purport of the song.

The first song glorified a journey to the southern part of Quemt.

"There you will meet a pretty girl who will offer you the flowers of her bosom," Pandion understood.

Another song exalted the military valor of the sons of Quemt with loud shouts and expressions so tortuous they seemed meaningless to Pandion. He left the window with feelings of irritation.

"The names of the brave will never die." The last words of the song drifted towards him as the singing ended and was followed by sounds of laughter and bustle; Pandion again looked into the window.

Slaves had brought in a fair-skinned girl with closely cut, wavy hair and pushed her into the middle of the room. She stood there confused and afraid amidst flowers trodden underfoot by the dancers. A man came out of the crowd and said a few angry words to the girl. Obediently she took the ivory lute that was offered her, and the fingers of her tiny hands ran over the strings. Silence fell as the girl's low clear voice rang out through the room. It was not the jerky, suddenly rising and falling melody of the Egyptians, but a song that flowed freely and sadly.

At first, the sounds fell slowly, like the splashing of separate drops of water, then they merged into regularly rising and falling waves, that rolled and whispered like the waves of the sea and carried with them such unrestrained sorrow that Pandion stood stock-still. He could hear the free, open sea rolling through the song and in the incomprehensible sounds of that magic voice.

The sea, unknown and unloved here in Aigyptos, was so near and dear to Pandion that at first, he stood aghast as all that was hidden deep in his soul burst suddenly out. That longing for freedom that Pandion knew so well was weeping and wailing in the song. He put his fingers to his ears, clenched his teeth to keep from screaming, and ran away to the far end of the garden. Throwing himself on to the ground in the shadow of the trees, Pandion gave way to a fit of uncontrollable sobbing.

"Hi, Ekwesha. Come here! Ekwesha!" shouted

Pandion's master.

The young Hellene had not noticed that the feast was over. Pharaoh's sculptor was very obviously drunk. Leaning on Pandion's arm and supported on the other side by his own slave, born in bondage, the Master of the Royal Workshops refused to enter his palanquin and expressed the desire to walk home.

Halfway home, occasionally stumbling over irregularities in the road, he began to praise Pandion, prophesying a great future for him. Pandion was still under the magic created by the song and did not hear what his master was saying. In this way, they walked to the brightly colored portico of the Egyptian's house. His wife and two slave girls, bearing lamps, appeared in the doorway. The royal sculptor stumbled up the steps and slapped Pandion on the shoulder. The latter went down again as no slave from the workshops was allowed to enter the house.

"Wait a minute, Ekwesha!" said the master gleefully, trying to bend his face into the semblance of a cunning smile.

"Give that to me!" He almost snatched the lamp out of the hand of one of the slave girls and whispered something to her. The girl disappeared into the darkness. The Egyptian pushed Pandion through the door and led him into the reception-room. On the left, between the windows, stood a beautiful vase with an elegant, dark red design. Pandion had seen such vases in Crete, and once more the youth's heart pained him.

"His Majesty, life, health, strength," the sculptor pronounced in solemn tones, "has ordered me to make seven vases like the one brought from the islands of your seas. (Life, health, strength - these three words always had to be added to any mention of Pharaoh) Only we must change those barbaric colors for the blue color favored in Tha-Quem. If you earn distinction in this work, I'll mention your name in the Great House. And now..." The master raised his voice and turned towards two dark figures that were approaching them. They were the slave girl who had left at his behest and another girl wrapped in a long-striped cloak.

"Come closer," ordered the Egyptian impatiently, lifting the lamp to the face of the girl in the cloak.

Her big, bulging black eyes looked fearfully at Pandion, her puffed, childish lips opened in a fluttering sigh. Pandion saw wavy locks protruding from under the cloak, a delicate nose with nervously twitching nostrils – the slave girl was undoubted Asiatic origin, from one of the tribes in the east.

"Look, Ekwesha," said the Egyptian, with an unsteady but strong movement pulling the cloak off the girl. She gave a faint cry and covered her face with her hands as she stood there stark naked. "Take her as your wife."

The royal sculptor pushed the girl towards Pandion and she, trembling all over, pressed herself close to the young Hellene. Pandion moved slightly back and stroked the tangled hair of the young captive, submitting to a mixed feeling of pity and tenderness for this pretty, scared creature. The royal sculptor smiled and snapped his fingers in approval.

"She will be your wife, Ekwesha, and you will have handsome children that I can leave to my children as a legacy."

It was as though a steel spring had suddenly uncoiled inside Pandion. The revolt that had long been seething within him and that had been further excited by the song he had heard that evening, reached its highest point. A red haze stood before his eyes.

Pandion stepped away from the girl, looked around the room and raised his hand. The Egyptian, growing immediately sober, ran into the house calling loudly to his servants for help.

Pandion did not even look at the coward and with a laugh of disdain kicked the expensive Cretan vase so hard that its earthenware fragments flew to the floor with a dull clatter. The house was filled with cries and the sound of running feet. A few minutes later Pandion lay at the feet of his master who bent over him, spat on him, shouting curses and threats.

"The scoundrel deserves death. The broken vase is of greater value than his worthless life, but he can make many beautiful things... and I don't want to lose a good worker," said the sculptor to his wife an hour later.

"I'll spare his life and won't send him to prison because from there they'll send him to the gold mines, and he'll die. I'll send him back to the shehne, let him think things over, and by the time of the next sowing I'll bring him back."

And so, Pandion, badly beaten but still unbowed, returned to the shehne and, to his great joy, met his old friends, the Etruscans. The whole building gang had been employed on watering the Gardens of Amon since they had finished dismantling the temple. Towards evening, the next day the shehne door opened with its usual creak to admit the smiling Kidogo, whose arrival was greeted by the shouts of the other slaves. The Kemtiu's back was puffed and swollen from the blows of a whip, but his teeth shone as he smiled and there was a merry twinkle in his eyes.

"I heard they'd sent you back here," he informed the astonished Pandion, "and I began to stagger about the workshop knocking down and breaking everything that came my way. They beat me and sent me here, which is what I wanted," said Kidogo.

"But you wanted to become a sculptor, didn't you?" asked Pandion mockingly.

The Kemtiu waved a carefree hand and, rolling his eyes terrifyingly, spat in the direction of the great capital city of Aigyptos.

CHAPTER FOUR

The Fight for Freedom

The stones, heated by the blazing sun, burned the arms and shoulders of the slaves. The gentle breeze brought no coolness to them but instead aggravated their plight by covering them in the fine dust from the stones that ate into their eyes. Thirty slaves, already at the end of their strength, were pulling on thick ropes to raise on to the wall a heavy stone slab bearing a bas-relief of some sort. The slab had to be placed in a prepared nest at the height of some eight cubits from the ground. Four experienced and nimble slaves were steadying the slab from below.

Among them was Pandion who stood next to an Egyptian, the only inhabitant of Aigyptos amongst the many nations in their slave compound. This Egyptian, condemned to eternal slavery for some unknown, awful crime he had committed, occupied the end cell in the privileged southeastern corner of the shehne. Two purple brands in the shape of a broad cross covered his chest and back while on his cheek a red snake was branded. Morose, never smiling, he did not talk to anybody and, despite the horror of his own position, despised the foreign slaves in the same way as his free fellow-countrymen did. At the present moment, he was not paying any attention to anybody and, with his shaven head lowered, was pressing with his hands against the heavy stone to prevent it from swaying.

Suddenly Pandion noticed that the strands of a rope holding the stone were beginning to snap, and shouted to warn the others. Two of the slaves jumped to one side, but the Egyptian paid no attention to Pandion and could not see what was going on above his head-he remained standing under the heavy stone. With a wide sweep of his right arm, Pandion gave the Egyptian a shove in the chest that sent him flying clear of the danger spot.

At that very moment, the rope snapped, and the stone crashed down, grazing Pandion's hand as it fell. A yellowish pallor spread over the Egyptian's face. The stone struck against the foot of the wall, and a big piece was broken off the corner of the bas-relief.

The overseer came running towards Pandion with a shout of rage and lashed at him with his whip. The square hippopotamus-hide lash, two fingers thick, cut deeply into the small of Pandion's back. The pain was so great that everything went misty before his eyes.

"You wastrel, why did you save that carrion?" howled the overseer, slashing at Pandion a second time. "The stone would have remained whole if it had fallen on a soft body. That carving is worth more than the lives of hundreds of creatures like you," he added as the second blow struck home.

Pandion would have rushed at the overseer, but the soldiers who hurried to the scene brutally thrashed and seized him. That night Pandion lay face downwards in his cell. He was in a high fever, the deep whip cuts on his back, shoulders, and legs were inflamed. Kidogo came crawling to him and brought him water to drink, from time to time pouring water over his aching head. A slight rustling sound came from outside the door, followed by a whisper:

"Ekwesha, are you there?"

Pandion answered and felt somebody's hands laid on him in the darkness. It was the Egyptian. He took a tiny jar out of his belt and spent a long time rubbing something into the palms of his hands. Then he began to pass his hands carefully over Pandion's wales, spreading some liquid unguent with a pungent, unpleasant smell. The pain made the Hellene shudder, but the confident hands of the Egyptian continued their work. By the time the Egyptian began to massage the legs, the pain in Pandion's back had died away; a few minutes later Pandion had dropped quietly off to sleep.

"What did you do to him?" whispered Kidogo who was quite invisible in his corner. After a short pause, the Egyptian answered him:

"This is kiphi. It's the finest ointment, and the secret is known only to our priesthood. My mother brought it here by paying a big bribe to a soldier."

"You're a good fellow. Excuse me if I thought you were trash!" exclaimed the Kemtiu.

The Egyptian muttered something between his teeth and disappeared silently into the darkness.

From that day onwards, the Egyptian made friends with the young Hellene, although he still ignored his companions. After that, Pandion often heard a rustling sound near his cell, and if he were alone the lean, bony body of the Egyptian would come crawling in. The lonely, embittered son of Tha-Quem was outspoken and talkative when he was alone with the sympathetic Pandion, who soon learned the Egyptian's story.

Yakhmos, the son of the moon, came from an old family of nedshes, faithful servants of former Pharaohs who had lost their position and their wealth with a change of dynasty.

Yakhmos had had good schooling and had been employed as a scribe by the Governor of the Province of the Hare. He chanced to fall in love with the daughter of a builder who demanded that his son-in-law be a man of means. Yakhmos lost his head for love of the girl, determined to get the money, come what may, and turned to the robbery of the royal tombs as a means to speedy enrichment. His knowledge of the hieroglyphs was a great advantage to him in the commission of a horrible crime that was always cruelly punished. Yakhmos soon had large quantities of gold in his hands, but in the meantime, the girl had been given in marriage to an official in the far south.

Yakhmos tried to drown his sorrows in merry feasting and the purchase of concubines, and the money soon melted away. He already knew the dark road to wealth, and he again set out to do nefarious deeds and was eventually caught and brutally tortured. His companions were either executed or died under torture. Yakhmos was sentenced to exile in the gold mines. Every year a new party was sent there at the time of the floods and to await his dispatch Yakhmos, was put into a shehne since there was a shortage of labor for the building of the new wall of the Temple of Ptah.

As Pandion listened with interest to Yakhmos' story, he was amazed at the valor of a man who in appearance was far from brave.

Yakhmos told of his adventures in the fearful underground labyrinths, where death awaited the intruder at every step from traps cunningly designed by the builders.

In the oldest tombs that lay deep below the huge pyramids. Huge, thick slabs of stone that closed the gangways protected the treasures and the royal sarcophagi. The later tombs were in a labyrinth of false corridors that ended in deep wells with smooth walls. Huge blocks of stone fell from above when the intruders tried to move the stones that protected the tombs, heaps of sand shot down through wells from above and barred their way forward.

If the bold intruders tried to pass the sand and penetrated deeper into the tombs, more earth showered down on them from the wells and buried the robbers in a narrow passage between the sand-heaps and the newly fallen earth. In the newer tombs, stone jaws closed noiselessly in the darkness of the narrow tunnels or a frame studded with sharp spears crashed down from the columns immediately the intruder set his foot on a certain fatal stone in the floor.

Yakhmos knew the many horrors that had lain buried for thousands of years, awaiting their victim in silence. He gained his experience at the expense of many others who had perished in the performance of their horrible profession. On many occasions, the Egyptian had come across the decaying remains of unknown people who had perished in the traps in the distant past.

Yakhmos and his companions had spent many nights on the verge of the Western Desert where the Cities of the Dead stretched for thousands of cubits. Hiding in the darkness, not daring to speak or strike a light, feeling their way to the howl of the jackals, the laughing of the hyenas, and the menacing roar of the lions, the plunderers, dug their way through stifling passages or cut through whole cliffs in an effort to find the direction in which the deeply hidden tomb lay.

This was a horrible profession, fully worthy of a people who thought more of death than of life, who strove to preserve for all eternity the glory of the dead rather than living deeds.

Pandion listened in amazement and horror to the tales of adventure told by this thin, insignificant man who had so often risked his life for the sake of a few moments' pleasure and could not understand him.

"Why did you continue living like that?" Pandion asked him one night. "Why couldn't you go away?"

The Egyptian smiled a silent, mirthless smile.

"The Land of Quemt is a strange land. You, a foreigner, cannot understand her. We are all imprisoned here, not merely the slaves, but also the free sons of the Black Land. Long, long ago, the deserts protected us. Today Tha-Quem is squeezed in between the deserts - it is a big prison for all those who are unable to make long journeys with a strong band of warriors.

"In the west is the desert-the kingdom of death. The desert in the east is passable only to large caravans with a good supply of water. In the south, there are savage tribes hostile to us. All our neighbors burn with hatred against our country whose well-being is founded on the misfortunes of weaker peoples.

"You're not a son of Tha-Quem and can't understand how we fear to die in a strange land. In this valley of the Hapi, everywhere alike, where our ancestors have lived for thousands of years and tilled the soil, dug canals, and made fertile the land, we, too, must live and die. Tha-Quem is shut off from the world, and that lies like a curse upon us. When there are too many people their lives are of no value, and there is nowhere for us to migrate to, the people chosen by the gods are not loved by the peoples of foreign lands."

"But would it not be better for you to flee now that you're a slave?" asked Pandion.

"Alone and branded?" came the Egyptian's ejaculation of astonishment. "I'm now worse than a foreigner. Remember, Ekwesha, there's no escaping from here! The only hope is to turn the whole of the Black Land upside down by force. But who can do that? It's true there have been such things in the days of long ago." Yakhmos sighed regretfully.

These last words aroused Pandion's curiosity, and he began to question Yakhmos. He learned about the great slave rebellions that had, from time to time, shaken the whole country. He also learned that the slaves had been joined by the poorer sections of the population whose lives differed little from those of the slaves. He learned, too, that the common people were forbidden to have any contact with the slaves since "a poor man could infuriate the mob in the slave compound." Such were the Pharaohs' injunctions to their sons. The poorer sons of Quemt, the tillers of the soil and the craftsmen, lived in the narrow world of their own street. They made as few acquaintances as possible, they humbled themselves before the soldiers, the "heralds" who brought them the commands of the officials. Pharaoh demanded humility and drudging toil, and for the slightest act of disobedience, the offender was mercilessly beaten. The considerable body of officials was a tremendous burden on the country, freedom to leave the country and travel was the prerogative of the priests and nobility alone.

At Pandion's request, Yakhmos drew a plan of the Land of Quemt in a patch of moonlight on the floor. The young Hellene was horrified: he was in the very middle of the valley of a great river thousands of stadia in length. There were water and life to the north and south, but to get there through a densely populated land with countless military fortifications, was impossible. In the empty deserts on either side, there was no population nor was there any means of subsistence. The few caravan roads along which there were wells were strongly guarded.

After the Egyptian had left him, Pandion spent a sleepless night trying to think out a plan of escape. Instinctively, the youth realized that hopes of a successful flight would grow weaker as time went on and he became more and more exhausted from the unbearable slave labor. Only people possessing extraordinary strength and endurance could expect fortune to smile on them if they attempted to escape.

The next night Pandion crawled to the cell of the Etruscan, Cavius, told him all he had learned from the Egyptian and tried to persuade him to try to arouse the slaves to rebellion. Cavius did not answer him but sat stroking his beard, deep in thought. Pandion was well aware that preparations for rebellion had long been underway and that the various tribal groups had chosen their leaders.

"I can't stand it any longer, why should we wait?" exclaimed Pandion passionately. Cavius hurriedly put his hand over his mouth.

"Better death," added the Hellene, somewhat more

calmly. "What is there to wait for? What will change? If changes come in ten years, then we shan't be able to fight or flee. Are you afraid of death or what?"

Cavius raised his hand.

"I'm not afraid, and you know it," he said brusquely, "but we have five hundred lives dependent on us. Do you propose to sacrifice them? You'll get your death at a high price."

Pandion struck his head against the low ceiling as he sat up suddenly in his impatience.

"I'll think it over and talk to people." Cavius hastened to add, "But still, it's a pity there are only two other shehne near us and that we have no access to them. We'll talk tomorrow night, and I'll let you know. Tell Kidogo to come."

Pandion left Cavius' cell, crawled hurriedly along the wall to get there before the moon rose, and made for Yakhmos' cell. Yakhmos was still awake.

"I went to see you," whispered the Egyptian in excited tones, "but you weren't there. I wanted to tell..." he stammered. "I've been told that I'm being taken away from here tomorrow; they are sending three hundred men to the gold mines in the desert. That's how matters stand - nobody ever comes back from there."

"Why?" asked Pandion.

"Slaves sent to work there rarely live more than a year. There's nothing worse than the work down there amidst the sunbaked rocks, with no air to breathe. They give them very little water, as there isn't enough to go around. The work consists of breaking hard stones and carrying the ore in baskets. The strongest of the slaves drop exhausted at the end of the day's work, and blood runs from their ears and throats.

"Farewell, Ekwesha, you're a fine fellow although you

did me a wrong turn by saving my life. It's not the rescue that I value, but the sympathy you showed me. Long, long ago, a life of bitterness made one of our bards compose a song in praise of death. That song I repeat today.

"Death lies before me like convalescence before a sick man, like relief from sickness," intoned the Egyptian in a whisper, "like sailing before the wind in fine weather, like the perfume of the lotus, like a road washed by the rain, like the return home after a campaign..." Yakhmos' voice broke off in a groan. Overcome by pity, the young Hellene drew nearer to the Egyptian.

"But you can take your own..." Pandion stopped short. Yakhmos staggered back from him.

"What are you saying, foreigner. Do you imagine I can allow my Ka to torment my Ba for all eternity in never-ending sufferings?" (Ka - the soul of the intellect. Ba-the corporeal soul, the spirit of the body.)

Pandion understood nothing of what the Egyptian was saying. He sincerely believed that suffering ended with death but did not say so out of tolerance for the faith of the Egyptian. Yakhmos pushed aside the straw on which he slept at night and began digging in the corner of his cell.

"Here, take this dagger, if ever you dare... and this will remind you of me if a miracle happens and you gain your liberty." Yakhmos placed a smooth, cold object in Pandion's hand.

"What's that? What do I want it for?"

"It's a stone I found in the underground rooms of an old temple hidden amongst the rocks."

Yakhmos, glad of an opportunity to forget the present in reminiscences of the past, told Pandion of a mysterious old temple that he had come across during his search for rich tombs, at a bend in the Great River many thousands of cubits below the "City," the capital, Waset.

Yakhmos had noticed traces of an old path that led to steep cliffs from the shore of a small cove densely overgrown with rushes. The place was far from any village and was never visited by anybody since there was nothing to interest the farmer or the shepherd in those barren, rocky cliffs. There was no danger in continuing his search and Yakhmos immediately plunged into a narrow canyon strewn with huge boulders. The boulders that covered the path had apparently fallen after it had ceased to serve as a means of communication with the riverbank.

For a long time, Yakhmos roamed amongst the rocks, hollows washed out by water, and thorn bushes. The canyon was swarming with spiders and their webs, stretching across the path, clung to the perspiring face of the plunderer of royal tombs. At last, the canyon widened to form an enclosed valley amidst the high hills. In the middle there was a small eminence surrounded by double rows of irrigation ditches - apparently, there had formerly been a spring there that was used to water the gardens. Silence reigned in the gloom of that stifling, windless valley around which gleaming black cliffs rose in a solid wall. At the far end, there was another narrow canyon similar to that by which Yakhmos had entered a place forgotten by all.

The tomb robber climbed up a hill and from there noticed an entry cut in the cliffside that had been hidden before by the eminence. Fallen stones blocked the entry, and Yakhmos had to work for a long time before he could get inside.

At last, he found himself in the cool darkness of a cave.

After he had rested a little, he lit the lamp that he always carried with him and made his way along a high corridor, carefully examining the statues on either side, afraid of cunning traps that threatened him with a tormenting death. His fears, however, were unfounded: either the old-time builders had not prepared any traps, relying on the remoteness of the temple to keep it from the eyes of strangers, or the thousands of years that had elapsed had rendered the traps ineffective.

Without any hindrance, Yakhmos entered a big, round underground chamber in the center of which was a statue of the god Thoth, his long beak stretching down from the height of his pedestal. In the walls, Yakhmos found ten narrow slits of doorways, arranged at equal distances around the chamber. They led to rooms filled with half-rotted objects: scrolls, papyri, and wooden tablets covered with drawings and inscriptions. One of the rooms was filled with dried grasses that turned to dust the moment he touched them; in another lay a pile of stones.

In this way, Yakhmos inspected eight of the rooms, all of them square, without finding anything that interested him. The ninth doorway leads Yakhmos into a long room surrounded by granite columns. Between the columns were slabs of black diabase covered with writing in the ancient language of Tha-Quem.

In the middle of this room stood another statue of the long-beaked, ibis-headed god Thoth; in a flat bronze bowl on the pedestal of the idol lay a precious stone that glittered in the light of the lamp. Yakhmos seized it avariciously, brought it close to the light and could not restrain an exclamation of disappointment. The stone was not of those that were valued in Tha-Quem. The experienced eye of the tomb robber immediately told him that the stone would be of no value to the merchants. The strange thing was, however, that the more he looked at the stone, the more it pleased him. It was a blue-green fragment of crystal about the size of a spearhead, flat, polished, and unusually transparent.

Yakhmos grew interested and resolved to read the writing on the walls hoping to find an explanation of the stone's origin. He still had not forgotten the ancient language of Tha-Quem that he had learned in the school for chief scribes and set about deciphering hieroglyphs that were in a splendid state of preservation on the hard diabase.

The ventilation channels in the underground chamber had long since collapsed. The lamp began to burn low, but still, Yakhmos read stubbornly on. Gradually the story of a great deed of valor, performed shortly after the building of the Great Pyramid of Cheops, was unfolded before this professional tomb robber.

Pharaoh Jedephra (Jedephra - a Pharaoh of the 4th Dynasty (2877-2869 B.C.)) sent his treasurer Baurjed, on an expedition far to the south, to Tha-Nuter, the Land of Spirits, to discover the bounds of the earth and of the Great Arc, the ocean. Baurjed left from the harbor of Suu, on the Blue Waters, (Blue Waters - the Red Sea. Suu-the modern El-Quseir) on seven of the biggest ships.

For seven years, the sons of the Black Land were absent. Half of the men and four of the ships were lost in terrible storms on the Great Arc, but the others sailed on and on to the south, along unknown coasts, until they eventually reached the fabulous Land of Punt. Pharaoh's orders, however, drove them still farther south. They had to find the end of the earth.

The sons of the Black Land left their ships and continued their way south overland.

For more than two years, they continued their journey through dark forests, crossed vast plains and high mountains - the home of the lightning-and, by the time their strength was almost exhausted, reached a big river on which lived a powerful people, builders of stone temples. Here they discovered that the end of the earth was still immeasurably distant - far, far away to the south, across plains of blue colored grass and through forests of silver-leaved trees. It was there, beyond the ends of the earth, that the Great Arc flowed, the ocean, whose bounds were known to no man.

The travelers, realizing that they were helpless to carry out Pharaoh's orders to the letter, returned to the Land of Punt, and built, and equipped a new ship in place of their old ones that were worm-eaten and battered by storms on the Great Arc.

There were scarcely enough survivors to man one ship. The bold adventurers, however, loaded the vessel with gifts from Punt and set out on their unbelievably difficult journey. The urge to return to their native land lent them strength. They conquered wind and waves, sandstorms and submerged rocks, hunger, and thirst, and returned to the harbor of Sun in the Blue Waters seven years after their departure.

Much had changed in the Black Land: the new Pharaoh, the ruthless Khafre, made the country forget everything except the building of a second gigantic pyramid that was to exalt his name for thousands of years. The return of the travelers was entirely unexpected, and Pharaoh was disappointed to learn that the earth and the ocean were immeasurable and that the peoples inhabiting the regions to the south were numerous and strong.

Baurjed showed Pharaoh, who considered himself the ruler of the world that the Land of Quemt was nothing but a tiny corner of a vast world, abounding in forests and rivers, fruits, and animals, and inhabited by numerous peoples skilled in all manner of work and hunting.

The wrath of Pharaoh descended upon the travelers, and Baurjed's companions were exiled to distant provinces. It was forbidden, on pain of death, to make any mention of the journey; passages in the writings left by Jedephra where the dispatch of the expedition southwards to the Land of Spirits was mentioned were all expunged.

Baurjed himself would have been a victim of the wrath of Pharaoh, and all memory of his journey would have disappeared for all time, had it not been for a wise old priest of Thoth, the god of learning, art, and writing. This priest had inspired the dead Pharaoh to investigate the bounds of the earth and seek new sources of wealth for a country that had become impoverished by the building of a colossal pyramid. He was forced to leave the court of the new Pharaoh by the priests of Ra (Ra-the sun god, chief deity of the Egyptians in the Pyramid period) and helped the traveler by offering him asylum in a hidden Temple of Thoth where secret books, plans, and samples of stones and plants from distant lands were stored. On the orders of the priest, Baurjed's great journey was recorded on stone slabs so that it might be preserved in an unapproachable underground chamber until such times as the country stood in need of that knowledge.

Baurjed brought a blue-green transparent stone, unknown to the people of Tha-Quem, from the most distant land he reached beyond the great southern river. Such stones were obtained in the Land of the Blue Plains, three months journey south of the great river. Baurjed offered this symbol of the extreme ends of the earth to the god Thoth. This was the stone Yakhmos had taken from the pedestal of the statue.

Yakhmos was unable to read the story of the journey to the end. He had just come to a description of the beautiful submarine gardens seen by the travelers in the Blue Waters when the lamp went out, and the plunderer had the greatest difficulty in getting out of the underground chamber, taking with him only the unusual stone.

In the light of day, the crystal from the distant land seemed even more beautiful; Yakhmos would not part with the stone, but it did not bring him good luck.

Pandion had a great journey to his native land ahead of him, and Yakhmos hoped that the stone with which Baurjed had returned from an unheard-of distance would help the Hellene, too.

"Didn't you know anything about that journey before?" asked Pandion.

"No, it has remained hidden from the sons of Quemt," answered Yakhmos. "Punt has long been known to us, the ships of Quemt have made many journeys there at various times, but the lands farther south still remain, for us, the mysterious Land of the Spirits."

"Can it be possible that there have been no other attempts to reach those countries? Could not somebody else have read those inscriptions, as you did, and have told others about them?"

Yakhmos thought for a while; he did not know how to answer the foreigner.

"The princes of the south, the governors of the southern provinces of Tha-Quem, have often penetrated into the interior of the southern countries, but they only wrote about their spoils, about the ivory, gold, and fish they brought to Pharaoh, so the road remains unknown. Since then, nobody has tried to sail farther south than Punt. It is too dangerous - there are no such brave people today as there were in ancient times."

"But why hasn't anybody read those inscriptions?" insisted Pandion.

"I don't know, I can't answer that question," admitted the Egyptian.

Yakhmos, of course, could not know that the priests, whom the people believed to be great scholars, the holders of ancient secrets, had long since ceased to be any such thing. Learning had degenerated into religious ceremony, and magic formulas, the papyri that contained the wisdom of past ages were rotting away in the tombs. The temples were deserted, and in ruins, nobody was interested in the history of the country as told by countless inscriptions on hard stone. Yakhmos could not know that such is the inevitable fate of all science that alienates itself from the invigorating strength of the people and becomes the property of a narrow circle of the initiated.

Dawn was drawing nigh. With a feeling of despondency, Pandion bade farewell to the unfortunate Egyptian to whom no hope of salvation remained. The young Hellene wanted to take the dagger and leave the stone to Yakhmos.

"Can't you understand that I need nothing anymore?" said the Egyptian.

"Why do you want to throw away such a beautiful

stone in this foul hole of a shehne?"

Pandion took the dagger between his teeth, grasped the stone in his hand and, crawling in the shadows, reached his own cell in safety. Until daylight broke, he lay sleepless. His cheeks burned, and shudders ran over his whole body. He lay thinking of the significant change that was to enter his life, of the imminent end of the monotonous stream of weary days of sorrow and despair.

The hole that formed the entrance to his cell turned grey, and the pitiful objects that constituted his entire possessions gradually emerged from the darkness. Pandion held the dagger in the morning light. The broad blade of black bronze (Black bronze - an especially hard alloy of copper and one of the rare metals. The metallurgists of antiquity were able to obtain alloys of exceptional hardness by adding zinc, cadmium, and other metals to the bronze.) with a high rib down the middle, was sharpened to a fine edge. The massive hilt was carved in the form of a lioness, the savage goddess Sekhrnet.

Using the dagger, Pandion dug a hole under the wall. He was hiding the Egyptian's gift in it when suddenly he remembered the stone.

Fumbling in the straw, he found it and took it to the light to examine it more thoroughly. The flat fragment of crystal with rounded edges was about the size of a spearhead. It was hard, extremely clear, and transparent and its color seemed to be a greyish blue in the darkness that precedes the dawn.

As Pandion laid the stone on the palm of his hand, the rays of the rising sun suddenly struck it. The stone was transformed. It lay on Pandion's hand in all its brilliance. Its blue-green color was unexpectedly joyous, bright, and deep, with a warm tinge of a transparent, golden wine color. The hand of man had apparently polished the mirror-like surface of the stone.

The coloring of the stone reminded Pandion of something that was very familiar to him, its reflection brought warmth to the youth's heavy heart. Thalassa! The sea. It was exactly that color, far from the shore, at the time when the sun hung high in the blue heavens. Natura'e, the divine stone, is what the unfortunate Yakhmos had called it!

The miraculous sparkle of the crystal on the morning of a joyless day was a good omen to Pandion.

Yakhmos' farewell gifts were a magnificent dagger and a stone of unknown properties. Pandion believed that the stone portended his return to the sea, to the sea that would not betray him, that would bring him back to liberty and his native land. The young Hellene peered intently into the stone out of whose transparent depths rolled the waves of his native shores.

The menacing roll of the big drum thundered over the cells. This was the signal arousing the slaves for their day's work.

Pandion made a quick decision - he would not part with that unusual stone, he would not leave that symbol of the free sea in the dusty earth of the shehne. Let the stone remain with him always.

After a few futile attempts, he eventually found a way to hide the stone in his loincloth and, although he lost no time in burying the dagger, was almost late for the morning meal.

On the journey and during their work in the gardens, Pandion observed Cavius and noticed that the latter was constantly exchanging short phrases first with one, and then with another, of the shehne leaders known to Pandion. These immediately went away from the Etruscan and talked to their followers. Pandion chose a safe moment and drew near Cavius. The Etruscan did not raise his head from the stone he was dressing but spoke softly and quickly, without even taking a breath.

"Tonight, before the moon rises, in the end gallery of the northern wall..."

Pandion returned to his work. On the way back to the shehne, he passed Cavius' message on to Kidogo. Pandion spent the evening in anticipation. For a long time, he had not been in such high spirits and so well prepared to fight.

As soon as the compound had quietened down and the sentries on the wall were dozing, Kidogo appeared in the darkness of Pandion's cell. The two friends crawled quickly to the wall and turned into the narrow corridor between the cells. They reached the north wall where the shadows in the corridor were deepest of all. The sentries rarely walked along this wall. They could observe the compound more easily from the western and eastern walls, looking along the corridors between the cells. There was, therefore, no danger that the sentries above would hear their whispered conversation.

No less than sixty slaves lay in two rows in the corridor, their feet pressed against the walls and their heads together. Cavius and Remdus were in the middle.

The elder Etruscan called Pandion and Kidogo to him in a whisper. Feeling for the Etruscan's hand, Pandion passed to him the dagger he had brought with him. Cavius felt the cold metal in some perplexity, cut his hand on the sharp blade, and then avidly gripped the weapon, whispering his thanks.

The experienced old soldier had yearned for weapons, and the dagger brought joy to his heart. He also realized that by handing the precious dagger over to him the Hellene recognized his seniority and had elected him the leader, without words.

He did not stop to ask Pandion where he had got the dagger but began to talk in whispers, making long pauses so that those near him could pass his words on to their more distant comrades who were out of hearing. The conference of the leaders had begun. The question of the life and liberty of five hundred slaves, imprisoned in the shehne, was to be decided. Cavius said that the rebellion could not be put off any longer, that there was no hope in the future, and the situation would only get worse if the slaves were again broken up into groups and sent in different directions.

"The strength that is our only guarantee of success in the struggle is being undermined by the heavy drudgery required by our taskmasters; every month in captivity means loss of health and vitality. Death in battle is honorable and joyful. It is a thousand times easier to die in battle than to die under the blows of a whip."

A unanimous whisper of approval passed along the rows of invisible listeners.

"We must not delay the revolt," continued Cavius, "but

there is one condition that must be fulfilled: we must find a way out of this accursed country. Even if we are joined by two or three other shehne, even if we are able to get weapons, our forces will still be small, and we shall not be able to hold out for long.

"Ever since the Great Revolt of the slaves, the rulers of Quemt have done everything possible to keep the slaves divided in separate compounds. We have no contact with the others, and we shall not be able to arouse a large number of people simultaneously. We are right in the capital, where there are many soldiers, and we shall not be able to fight our way through the country. The archers of Aigyptos are a te-rri-ble force; we shall not have many bows, and not everybody will be able to use them.

"Let us think whether we can make our way through the desert to the east or the west. We may find ourselves in the desert shortly after leaving the shehne. If we are unable to cross the desert, then I think we must drop the idea of a revolt. It will be a useless waste of effort and a tormenting death. Then let only those of us flee that are prepared to make an attempt to pass through certain death with a faint hope of liberty. I, for example, will try."

Excited whispers filled the air around the now silent Etruscan. His words, passed from end to end of the rows of slaves, had at first aroused militant ardor in the listeners, but now doubt was spreading amongst those bold leaders.

His words took away all hope of a successful outcome. They removed even the ghost of a chance so that the bravest of the warriors wavered. Whispers in many languages carried down the coal-black tunnel of the corridor.

An Amu, a Semite from the land beyond the Blue

Waters, crawled to the center of the group where the four friends lay. Men of the Amu tribe constituted a large proportion of the inhabitants of the shehne.

"I insist on a revolt. Let death be our lot, but we shall be revenged on the accursed people of this accursed land! We will be an example to be followed by others! Too long has Quemt been living in peace, the brutal art of oppression has robbed millions of slaves of the will to fight. We will light the flames of revolt."

"It's good that you think like that, you're a brave man," Cavius interrupted him. "But what will you say to those whom you will lead?"

"I will say the same to them," answered the Semite fervently.

"Are you sure they'll follow you?" whispered the Etruscan. "The truth is too painful... and lies are useless under such circumstances. The people will easily sense the truth. To them, the truth is that which each carries in his own heart."

The Semite did not answer him.

In the meantime, the lean, lithe body of the Libyan Akhmi squeezed through the rows of recumbent men. Pandion knew that this young slave, captured during a battle at the Horns of the Earth, came from a noble family. He assured them that near the tombs of the most ancient kings of Quemt, near the cities of Tinis and Abydos, a road led to the southwest as far as Wahet-Wer, a large oasis in the desert. It was a road with good wells, plenty of water and was unguarded by troops.

They had to plunge into the desert immediately behind the temple Zesher-Zesheru, turn southwest and cross the road at a point a hundred and twenty thousand cubits from the river.

The Libyan undertook to lead them to the road and farther. There were but few troops at the oasis, and the insurgents could easily seize it. The next stage was a mere twenty-five thousand cubits across the desert to the next oasis, Pasht, that stretched westward in a long, narrow strip. Farther still, they would find the Oasis of Mut, whence a route with wells led to the hills of the Dead Serpent. From this latter place, there was a road leading southward to the Land of the Blacks, which the Libyan did not know.

"I know that road," Kidogo put in. "I traveled that road in the first year of my captivity. There's a good supply of dates at the oases, and we can rest there. There are no fortifications at any of them, and we can take pack animals with us. With their help, we can get as far as the Dead Serpent and from then on, beyond the Salt Lake, there's more water."

The Libyan's plan was generally approved. It seemed entirely possible of fulfillment.

The ever-cautious Cavius, however, asked the Libyan more questions.

"Are you certain that there are wells at a distance of a hundred and twenty thousand cubits from the river? It's a long journey to make."

"It may be a little more," answered the Libyan calmly. "A strong man can make that journey without water under one condition. We must start no later than midnight and march without a halt. You can't live more than twenty-four hours without water in the desert, nor can you march in the afternoon."

One of the Asians, a Heriusha, proposed attacking the fortress on the road to the harbor of Suu, but, despite the fact that this plan was very attractive to the slaves, most of whom were Asians, and to the Amu, it was dropped since it was agreed that it would be impossible to fight their way to the east.

The Libyan's plan was more promising, although there was disagreement between the Kemtiues and the Asians: the road to the south-west took the Asians still farther from their native land, but it was advantageous to the Kemtiues and the Libyans. The Libyans hoped to travel northwards from the Oasis of Mut and reach that part of their country that was not under the rule of the Egyptians. Pandion and the Etruscans intended going with the Libyans.

An elderly Nubian pacified them all when he said he knew a road to the south, that by-passed the fortresses of the Black Land, and went through the plains of Nubia to the Blue Waters.

The narrow crescent of the moon rose above the terraced hills of the desert, and still the insurgent slaves continued to plan their flight. They were now discussing the details of the revolt and gave a task to each group under a specific leader. The revolt was timed to begin on the night after the next, immediately it became completely dark.

Sixty men crawled silently back to various parts of the compound while above them, silhouetted against the moonlit sky, stood the sentries, little suspecting what was going on below them and full of contempt for those who slept in the dark hole beneath their feet.

Cautiously and unnoticed, the plans for the revolt continued all next day and night, and all through the second day. The leaders, for fear of traitors, spoke only to those with whom they were well acquainted, expecting that the others would join the general mass of the insurgents once the sentries had been removed.

The night of the revolt came. Groups of people assembled in the darkness, one for each of the three walls - the northern, western, and southern. On the eastern side, two groups gathered under the inner wall. The movement of the men had been carried out so speedily that by the time Cavius struck an upturned water jug with a stone, giving the signal for attack, they had already formed living pyramids. The bodies of seventy men formed a slope against the vertical wall. There were five such living bridges over which men, intoxicated with the coming battle, swarmed from all sides.

Cavius, Pandion, Remdus, and Kidogo were amongst the first to mount the inner wall. The Hellene, without pausing to think, leaped down into the darkness, and was followed by dozens of others. Pandion knocked down a soldier who appeared from the guard-house, jumped on his back and twisted his neck. The Egyptian's backbone cracked softly, and his body went limp in Pandion's hands.

All around him, in the darkness, the slaves hunted and seized their hated enemies. In their fury men attacked armed soldiers with their bare hands. Before any of the soldiers could defend himself against an attacker from the front, others jumped on him from the sides and from behind. Unarmed, but strong in their wrathful fury, the slaves dug their teeth into the hands that held weapons and stuck their fingers into the soldiers' eyes.

Weapons, weapons at any cost - this was the one idea of the attackers. Those who succeeded in seizing a dagger or spear were still more furious in their attacks, feeling death-dealing strength in their hands.

Pandion struck right and left with the sword he had taken from a dead enemy. Kidogo fought with a huge pole used for carrying water. Cavius mounted the living bridge and threw himself at four soldiers on guard over the inner door.

The astounded Egyptians put up a poor resistance as they were literally crushed by the avalanche of silent men that fell on them from above.

With a shout of triumph, Cavius pushed open the heavy bolt on the doors, and soon the crowd of liberated slaves occupied the entire area between the walls, broke into the house of Commandant of the shehne and killed the soldiers resting there after the guard had been changed.

On the walls above, the struggle was even more desperate. The nine sentries on the wall had noticed the attacking slaves in good time. Arrows whistled through the air and the silence of the night was broken by the moans of the wounded and the thud of bodies falling from above. Nine Egyptians, however, could not long resist a hundred of infuriated slaves, who flew directly on to the spears of the soldiers and rolled down from the wall together with them.

In the meantime, the soldiers and officials had been dealt with in the narrow confines between the two walls: the keys of the outer gates had been found on the dead Commandant, and the screech of the rusty hinges as the gates opened was like a cry of victory in the night. Spears, shields, daggers, bows - everything was taken from the soldiers, down to the last arrow.

The armed slaves headed the crowd of runaways and

all of them, in deep silence, made their way to the river. Every boat, barge or raft they could get hold of was used to begin the river crossing. Several men perished in the river, falling victims to the huge crocodiles that guarded the waters of Tha-Quem.

Before two hours had elapsed, the vanguard of the column reached a shehne situated on the other bank of the river on the road to Zesher-Zesheru. Cavius, Pandion and two Libyans went openly to the gates and knocked, while about a hundred other slaves pressed close against the wall near the gates.

A soldier shouted down from the wall, asking them what they wanted. A Libyan, who spoke the language of Tha-Quem, fluently demanded the Commandant of the shehne, saying that he had a letter from the Director of Royal Works. Several voices were heard behind the door; a torch was lighted, and the door opened, showing them a courtyard between two walls similar to that they had just left.

The Captain of the Guard stepped forward from a group of soldiers and demanded the letter. Cavius rushed at him with a howl of fury and plunged Yakhmos' dagger into his breast while Pandion and the Libyans rushed at the other soldiers. The other armed slaves, who were standing prepared for action, took advantage of the confusion and burst into the shehne with terrifying cries.

The torches went out, and the darkness was filled with suppressed groans, howls, and martial shouts. Pandion made short work of two opponents and opened the inner door. The call to revolt resounded throughout the shehne, now awakened by the noise of battle, as slaves darted here and there calling to their astounded fellow-countrymen in their native language.

The compound hummed like a beehive; the howls grew in volume until they merged into a deep roar. The soldiers on the walls dashed back and forth, afraid to descend. They shouted threats at the slaves and from time to time let fly arrows at random. The fight in the corridor between the walls died down. Well-aimed arrows flew from the courtyard at the clearly visible soldiers on the walls and the second shehne was liberated.

The crowd of liberated slaves puzzled and inebriated by their sudden liberty, streamed through the doors, and spread in all directions, paying no attention to the shouts of their liberators. In a short time, savage howls came from the direction of the houses and fires broke out in several places. Cavius advised the other leaders to assemble those of their shehne companions who were already acquainted with discipline.

The Etruscan stood deep in thought, running his fingers through his beard. In his eyes, turned westwards in the direction to be followed, there was a red glint - the reflection of the fires.

Cavius was thinking that they had most probably made a mistake in liberating the slaves from the second shehne without any preparatory work amongst them. His own followers were already familiar with the conception of a common, purposeful struggle, and it was possible that more harm than good would come of joining them to a mass of people who were unprepared, who acted as individuals and were intoxicated by the possibility of vengeance and liberty. Such proved to be the case. A large number of slaves from the first shehne were also attracted by the idea of plunder and destruction. Apart from that, the time had been lost, every minute of which was of the utmost importance.

The smaller column moved on towards the third shehne situated some eight thousand cubits from the second, in the immediate vicinity of the Temple of Zesher-Zesheru. There was no time to change the plan of the revolt, and Cavius foresaw very great difficulties. And as they approached the shehne, the Etruscan noticed the silhouettes of soldiers drawn up on the walls and heard shouts of "A'atu, a'atu!" (insurgents) followed by the whistle of the arrows with which the Egyptians greeted the approaching column from a long distance.

The insurgents halted to discuss a plan of attack. The shehne, prepared for defense, was a good fortress, and its capture would occupy considerable time. The insurgents raised a tremendous noise to awaken the slaves in the shehne and encourage them to attack the guards on the wall from within.

Cavius, who was already hoarse, shouted at the top of his voice to the other leaders, trying to persuade them to abandon the attack. They would not agree; the easily obtained victory had given them confidence, and it seemed to them that it would be possible to liberate all the slaves in Quemt and conquer the country.

Suddenly the Libyan, Akhmi, let out a penetrating howl and hundreds of heads turned in his direction. The Libyan waved his arms, pointing in the direction of the river.

From the high bank that rose steeply towards the cliffs, the river that washed the numerous landing places of the capital could be seen over a long distance. Everywhere the lights of torches flared up, merging into a dully flickering line; flickering points of lights appeared in the middle of the river and were gathering in two places on the bank on the side of the insurgents.

There could be no doubt - large detachments of soldiers were crossing the river, hurrying to surround the place where there were fires and the escaped slaves were concentrated. Here, the insurgents were still dashing from place to place, seeking a means of attacking the shehne. Some tried to approach the enemy by following the bed of an irrigation canal. Others were expending valuable arrows.

A glance cast over the vague outlines of the dark mass of people told Cavius that there were not more than three hundred men in the column capable of giving battle. Of these, less than a half, had knives or spears, while only about thirty bows had been captured. Only a short time would elapse before hundreds of the terrible archers of the Black Land would send clouds of long arrows into them from a great distance, and thousands of well-trained troops would draw a tight ring around slaves who had only just tasted liberty.

Akhmi, his eyes flashing in anger, shouted that it was already past midnight and that if they did not start immediately it would be too late.

It cost the Akhmi, Cavius, and Pandion many precious minutes to explain to the crowd, inflamed and eager for battle, the uselessness of any attempt to stand up against the troops of the capital. The leaders insisted on an immediate march into the desert and, in case of necessity, were prepared to start out themselves, leaving behind those who were distracted by the search for weapons, by plunder and revenge.

Some slaves who did not agree left the column and set

off along the river towards the wealthy estate of some aristocrat whence loud noises and the light of torches came. The remainder, a little more than two hundred men, agreed to go.

Soon the long dark column, winding like a snake through a narrow canyon between steep cliffs still hot from the daytime sun, made their way to the flat edge of the valley. The runaways were confronted with an endless plain of sand and stones. Pandion looked back for the last time at the huge river gleaming faintly below them. How many days of sorrow, despair, hope, and wrath he had spent beside that calmly flowing waterway! Joy and infinite gratitude to his trusty comrades filled the heart of the young Hellene. In triumph, he turned his back on the land of slavery and increased his already fast pace.

The band of insurgents had marched some twenty thousand cubits from the rim of the valley when the Libyan halted the column. Behind them, in the east, the sky had begun to grow light. The contours of the rounded sand-dunes, some of them as much as a hundred and fifty cubits high, stretching far away to the vague, scarcely visible line of the horizon, were but faintly perceptible in the dull leaden light of early morning. At the hour of dawn, the desert was silent, and the air was motionless. The jackals and hyenas had ceased their howls.

"You've been hurrying us all the time, why do you linger now? What do you want?" impatient slaves in the back rows asked the Libyan. He explained that the most challenging part of the journey was about to begin - endless ridges of sand-dunes, one after the other, each ridge higher than the last until they reached a height of three hundred cubits.

The slaves were re-formed into a column two deep and were told that they would have to keep going without halt, without dropping back, paying no attention to fatigue. Those who fell behind would never reach their destination. The Libyan would go ahead and seek a path between the dunes.

It turned out that hardly anybody had found an opportunity to drink before leaving and many of them were already tormented by thirst after the heat of battle. Not everybody had a mantle, cloth or even rags with which to cover his head and shoulders from the sun, but there was nothing they could do about it.

Strung out in a column two hundred cubits long, the slaves moved on in silence, their eyes fixed on their feet dragging through the soft sand. The leading files zigzagged right and left winding their way through the dunes to avoid slopes of shifting sand.

A wide purple strip glowed in the sky to the east. The crescent-shaped and sharply serrated ridges of the sand-hills turned to gold. In the sunlight, the desert appeared before Pandion's eyes like a sea with high frozen waves, whose smooth slopes reflected an orange-yellow light. The excitement of the night gradually died down, and the men grew calmer. Liberty, the expanse of the desert, the gold of the distant dawn, all served to revive men weary of captivity. Joy filled their hearts in place of malice and fear, sorrow, and despair.

The morning light grew brighter, and the sky seemed to recede into its bottomless blue depths. As the sun rose higher, its rays at first gave them friendly warmth, but soon began to burn and sear them. The slow, dragging, toilsome path through the labyrinth of deep gullies between high sand-hills became more and more difficult. The shadows of the hills grew shorter; it became painful to walk over the burning hot sand, but the men went on, never stopping, never looking back. Ahead of them lay endless ridges of sand-hills, all exactly the same, that cut off all view of their surroundings.

As time went on air, sunlight and sand merged into one huge sea of flame, that blinded, asphyxiated, and burned like molten metal.

The journey was especially difficult for those who came from the northern countries like Pandion and the two Etruscans. Pandion felt that his head was squeezed in an iron band, the blood throbbing furiously at the temples, causing him great pain. He was almost blinded. Before his eyes floated patches and stripes of the most astoundingly brilliant colors that flowed and whirled, changing their combinations in wonderful kaleidoscopic patterns. The unbearable strength of the sun turned the sand into golden dust permeated with light.

Pandion was in a delirium, hallucinations grew out of his maddened brain. The colossal statues of Aigyptos moved through flashes of crimson fire and sank into the waves of a purple sea. Then the sea fell back and packs of strange creatures, half-beast, and half-bird, flew down from the steep cliffs at amazing speed. And once more, the granite Pharaohs of the Black Land formed into battle order and advanced towards Pandion.

Staggering on, he rubbed his eyes and slapped his cheeks to see what was really there. The heat-breathing slopes of the sand dunes piled one on the other in the blinding, grey-gold light.

Again, the whirling vortices of colored fire appeared, and Pandion was lost in a heavy delirium. Nothing but the fervent desire for freedom could have made him keep moving in step with Kidogo, leaving thousands of sand dunes behind.

Fresh chains of hills confronted the runaways and between them were huge, smooth-sided craters at the bottom of which could be seen coal-black patches of soil. The hoarse, imploring moans that passed along the column grew more and more frequent. Here and there, exhausted men dropped to their knees or fell face down in the scorching sand, begging their comrades to put an end to their suffering.

The others turned morosely away from them and continued their way until the pleas died away behind them and beyond sand-hills so soft in their configuration. Sand, burning hot sand; monstrous quantities of sand, stretching to infinity; silent and evil sand that seemed to have drowned the whole universe in its stifling, treacherous flames.

Ahead of them, a patch of silver in the golden fire of the sun's rays appeared in the distance. The Libyan gave a brief shout of encouragement. Clearer and clearer, against the brownish background, appeared patches of ground covered with salt crystals that shone with an intolerably brilliant blue gleam.

The sand dunes grew smaller and soon gave way to hard, well-packed sand. The feet of the marchers moved more freely, liberated from the cloying embrace of the friable sand. The hard, yellow clay, furrowed with dark cracks, seemed to them like the stone-paved path of some palace garden.

The sun was still a hand's breadth from the zenith when

the insurgent slaves reached a low, cliff-like ledge of stratified brownstone, and from there turned sharply to the left, to the south-west. In a short re-entrant, that bit into the cliff at a wide angle so that from a distance it looked like the black entrance to a cave, was an ancient well, a spring with cool, fresh water.

To prevent disorder amongst people already mad with thirst, Cavius placed the strongest of the slaves to guard the entrance to the gully. The weakest were allowed to drink first. The sun had long passed the zenith, and the men kept on drinking as though they would never stop. They lay for a while in the shade of the cliff with distended bellies and then crawled back to the water again.

The runaways gradually regained their vitality, and soon the rapid speech of the hardy Kemtiues could be heard, accompanied by occasional laughter and jocular altercation.

No joy, however, came to the men with returning life. Too many of their faithful comrades had remained behind to die in the labyrinth of sand-dunes, comrades who had only just entered the path to freedom, who had fought bravely, with contempt for death, comrades whose efforts had merged in the supreme common effort with those who had been spared.

Pandion was astonished at the change that had taken place in those slaves with whom he had spent such a long time in the shehne. That dull indifference to their surroundings that gave the same expression to all their tired, worn-out faces was gone. Eyes that had been dull and listless were now looking around, full of life and interest, and the features of the somber faces seemed to be more sharply defined.

They were already people and not slaves, and Pandion

remembered how right Cavius had been in his wisdom when he reproached Pandion with contempt for his companions. Pandion had had too little experience of life to be able to understand people. He had the mistaken view that the inhibition born of long captivity was natural in them.

The men crowded on to the small patches of life-giving shade in the gully. In a short time, they were all overcome by deep sleep; there was no fear of the pursuit overtaking them on that day. Who but people prepared to face death for the sake of liberty could pass through the fiery hell of that sea of sand in the daytime? The runaways rested until sunset, by which time their tired feet were again ready for the journey. The small quantity of food that the strongest had managed to carry through the desert was carefully shared out amongst all of them.

There was a long journey to be made to the next well. The Libyan said that they would have to keep on all night, but that at dawn before the day grew hot, they would find water. After that, the road again lay through sand-hills, the last between them and the big oasis.

Fortunately, the stretch of sand-hills was not of great width, no more than that they had already passed, and if they set out in the evening when the sun was in the south-west, they would reach the big oasis during the night and find food there. They would only have to go twenty-four hours without food. Not all this seemed so very terrible to people who had suffered so much. The chief thing that encouraged them and gave them strength was the fact that they were free, and were moving farther and farther away from the hated Land of Quemt, and that the possibility of their being overtaken was diminishing.

The sunset died away, grey ash covered its flaming red

embers. Drinking their fill for the last time, the runaways moved on. The depressing heat had gone, scattered by the black wings of night, and the darkness tenderly caressed skin that had been burned by the flames of the desert.

Their way lay across a low, level plateau covered with sharp-edged stones that cut the feet of the less cautious. By midnight, the runaways dropped down into a wide valley sprinkled with grey, round boulders. These strange stones, between one and three cubits in diameter, lay about like stone balls with which some unknown gods had been playing. The men were no longer in a column but walked on without any formation, cutting diagonally across the valley towards a rise that could be seen some distance in front of them.

After a terrible stupefying day that had shown the weakness of man with such ruthlessness, the quiet calm of the night gave rise to profound meditation. It seemed to Pandion that the endless desert rose up to meet the bowl of the sky. The stars seemed quite near in the clear air and permeated with a kind of glow. The moon rose, and a silver carpet of light lay on the dark earth.

The party of runaway slaves reached the rise. The gentle slope consisted of blocks of limestone, polished by the fine sand until they shone and reflected the light of the moon in what looked like a blue glass staircase. When Pandion set foot on their cold, slippery surface, it seemed to him that he had only to go a little higher and he would reach the dark blue bowl of the sky.

The rise ended, the staircase vanished, and the long descent began into the dark valley, covered with coarse sand that lay black below them. The valley was encircled with a chain of serrated crags that jutted out of the sand at all angles, like the stumps of gigantic tree-trunks.

By dawn, the party had reached the cliff and for a long time wandered through a labyrinth of crevasses until their Libyan leader found the well. From the cliff could be seen the serried ranks of a new army of sand dunes that formed a hostile ring around the rocks amongst which the runaways had taken refuge. Shadows of deep violet lay between the rosy slopes of the sand hills. While they were close to water, there was nothing terrible about the sea of sand.

Kidogo found a place protected from the sun by an enormous stone cube that hung-over walls of sandstone cutaway on the northern side by a deep, dry watercourse. There was sufficient shade for the whole party between the rocks, and they lay down to rest until sunset. The tired men immediately dropped off to sleep.

There was nothing to do but wait until the sun, raging in the high heavens, became more amenable. The sky that had seemed so close to them during the night had now receded to an unfathomable distance and from that great height blinded and burned the men as though in revenge for the breathing space given them during the hours of darkness.

Time went on. The peacefully sleeping people were surrounded by a sea of fiery sunlight that cut them off from their native lands where the sun did not destroy all living things.

Cavius was suddenly awakened by faint, plaintive groans. The puzzled Etruscan raised his heavy head and listened. From time to time he heard sharp cracks coming from different directions and then long, drawn-out plaintive moans filled with sorrow. The sounds grew louder, and he looked around him in fear. There was no sign of movement anywhere amongst the sunbaked rocks; all his comrades occupied their former places and were either sleeping or listening. Cavius roused the calmly sleeping Akhmi. The Libyan sat up, yawned, and then laughed right in the face of the astounded and alarmed Etruscan.

"The stones are crying out from the heat of the sun," explained the Libyan, "and that's a sign that the heat is subsiding."

The cracking of the stones greatly disturbed the other runaway slaves. The Libyan climbed on to a high rock, looked through the crack between his folded hands and announced that soon they could set out on the last march to the oasis; they must drink their fill for the march.

Although the sun had sunk far to the west, the sandhills still radiated heat. It seemed an impossible feat to leave the shade and go out into that sea of fire and sunlight. Nevertheless, the men formed a column, two by two, and without a single protest followed the Libyan - so strong was the call of freedom. Pandion and Kidogo formed the third pair behind the Libyan, Akhmi.

The inexhaustible endurance and joviality of the Kemtiu were a frequent encouragement to the Hellene who felt little confidence in himself when confronted with the might of the desert. The fiery, hostile breath of the desert again forced the men to bow their heads low before its savage face.

They had journeyed no less than fifteen thousand cubits when Pandion noticed that their Libyan guide seemed somewhat distressed. Akhmi had halted the column twice while he mounted a sand-hill, sinking up to his knees in the soft sand, to examine the horizon. The Libyan, however, did not answer any questions. The sand-hills grew lower, and Pandion asked Akhmi in a glad voice whether the sand was coming to an end.

"We've still a long way to go; there's a lot more sand yet," snapped the guide gloomily and turned his head towards the north-west.

Pandion and Kidogo looked in the same direction and saw that the burning sky was covered with a leaden haze. A dark wall that rose straight up had conquered the fearful might of the sun and the glow of the sky. Suddenly they heard resonant, pleasant sounds-high, singing, purely metallic notes, like silver trumpets playing an enchanting melody behind the sand dunes. The sounds were repeated, grew more frequent and louder, and hearts beat more rapidly, affected by some unconscious fear brought by those silver notes that were like nothing on earth and far removed from all that was mortal.

The Libyan stopped and fell on to his knees with a plaintive cry. Raising his hands towards the heavens, he prayed to his gods to protect them from an awful calamity. The frightened runaways cowered together in a crowd between three sand-hills.

Pandion looked inquiringly at Kidogo and staggered back -the Kemtiu's black skin had turned grey. Pandion had seen his friend frightened for the first time and did not know that a Kemtiu's skin turns grey with pallor.

Cavius seized the guide by the shoulders, lifted him to his feet without an effort and asked him angrily what had happened. Akhmi turned towards him, his face distorted with fear and covered with beads of perspiration.

"The sands of the desert are singing; they call to the wind, and with the wind, death will come flying - there will be a sand-storm."

An oppressive silence hung over the party broken only by the sounds of the singing sand. Cavius stood still in bewilderment - he did not know what to do, and those who realized the degree of danger that threatened them kept silent.

At last, Akhmi came to himself.

"Forward, forward, as quickly as possible! I saw a stony place where there's no sand: we must get there before the storm reaches us. If we stay here death is certain, we'll all be buried in the sand, but over there, maybe some of us will be saved."

The frightened men ran after the Libyan guide. The leaden haze had changed to a ruddy gloom that spread over the whole sky. Menacing wisps of sand whirled around the hilltops like smoke; the hot breath of the tiny windswept particles of sand into the men's inflamed faces. There was no air to breathe; it was as though the atmosphere were filled with some corrosive poison.

The sand-hills opened out, and the runaways found themselves on a small patch of stony ground, black and smooth. All around them the rumble and roar of the oncoming wind increased in fury, the ruddy cloud darkened on its lower side as though a black curtain were being drawn across the sky. Its upper side remained a dark red, and the disc of the sun was hidden by that awful cloud.

Imitating their more experienced comrades the men tore off their loincloths and rags that covered their heads and shoulders, wrapped them around their faces and dropped on to the stony ground, pressing close against each other.

Pandion was slow in making his preparations. The last thing he saw filled him with horror. Everything around him was in motion. Stones as big as his fist rolled over the black ground like dry leaves in an autumn wind. The sand-hills threw out long tentacles in the direction of the party; the sand was moving and was soon flowing all around them like water thrown up by a storm on to a low beach.

A whirling mass of sand rushed at Pandion; the youth fell face down and saw nothing more. His heart beat furiously and its every beat resounded in his head. His mouth and throat seemed coated with a hard crust that prevented his panting breath from escaping.

The whistling of the wind reached a high note, but that, too, was drowned by the roar of the moving sand; the desert howled and rumbled around him. Pandion's head went dizzy, he struggled against unconsciousness towards which the stifling, withering storm was driving him. Coughing desperately, he freed his throat of sand and again began his rapid breathing. Pandion's bursts of resistance were repeated at ever-growing intervals until at last, he lost consciousness.

The thunder of the storm grew ever more insistent and menacing, it rumbled in peals across the desert like huge bronze wheels. The stony ground gave forth an answering rumble like a sheet of metal, and clouds of sand swept over it. Grains of sand, charged with electricity, burst into blue sparks giving the whole mass of moving sand a bluish glow as it rolled over the desert. It seemed that at any moment, rain would fall, and fresh water would save the people, dried up by the overheated air and lying unconscious. But there was no rain, and the storm raged on.

An ever-thickening layer of sand that hid the weak movement and stifled the rare moans covered the dark pile of human bodies.

Pandion opened his eyes and saw Kidogo's black head outlined against the stars. Later Pandion learned that the Kemtiu had been working over the motionless bodies of his friends, Pandion, and the Etruscans, for a long time.

People were busy in the darkness, digging out their comrades from under the sand, listening to the feeble signs of life in their bodies and laying aside those who would breathe no more.

The Libyan, Akhmi, with some of his fellow-countrymen, who were accustomed to the desert, and a few Kemtiues had gone back to the well amongst the rocks for water. Kidogo had remained with Pandion, unable to leave his friend who was scarcely breathing.

At last fifty-five half-dead men, led by Kidogo, finding the road with difficulty, and supporting each other as they walked along, followed in the tracks of those who had left earlier. Nobody gave a thought to the fact that they were going back, that they would meet with a possible pursuit; the mind of every one of them was concentrated on one thing - water. The craving for water swept aside all will to struggle; it was stronger than any other urge - water was a lodestone in the dull fever of their inflamed brains.

Pandion had lost all conception of time; he had forgotten that they had journeyed not more than twenty thousand cubits from the well; he had forgotten everything except that he must hold on to the shoulders of the man in front and keep step with those plodding ahead.

About halfway to the well, they heard voices in front of

them that sounded unusually loud: Akhmi and the twenty-seven men who had gone with him were hurrying to meet them, carrying rags steeped in water and two old gourd bottles they had found at the well. The men mustered strength enough to refuse the water and propose to Akhmi that he go back to those who had remained at the scene of the catastrophe.

Superhuman efforts were needed to keep going as far as the well; their strength grew less with every step, nevertheless the men allowed the water-carriers to pass in silence and continued to plod on. A wavering black haze spread before the eyes of the stumbling people; some of them fell, but encouraged by the others and supported by their stronger comrades they continued on their way.

The fifty-five men could not remember the last hour of their journey - they walked on almost unconsciously, their legs continuing their slow, stumbling movements. But reach the goal they did; the water revived them, refreshed their bodies, and enabled their congealed blood to soften their dried muscles.

No sooner had the travelers fully recovered than they remembered those left behind. Following the example of the first party, they went back, carrying rags dripping with water - the source of life - to those wandering in the desert. This help was invaluable because it came in time. The sun had risen. The last group of those still alive was given strength by the water brought by the Libyans.

The people had halted amidst the sand dunes and could not muster strength enough to continue their way despite all persuasion, urging and even threats. The wet rags enabled them to keep going for another hour, which proved sufficient to reach the well. In this way another thirty-one men reached the water; altogether a hundred and fourteen were saved, less than half the number that had set out into the desert two days before.

The weakest had perished during the first day's desert march. Now the awful catastrophe had taken toll of the best and strongest fighters. The future seemed more indefinite than before. The forced inactivity was depressing; there was no strength left to continue the planned journey; weapons had been abandoned in the place where the sandstorm had overtaken them. If the insurgents had had food they could have recuperated much more easily, but the last remnants had been distributed the night before, and there was nothing left.

The sun was blazing in the clear unclouded sky and those who had remained at the scene of the catastrophe, even if there had been a faint flicker of life in them, had by now, no doubt, perished. The survivors hid in the gully between the rocks where the day before they had lain together with those who were no longer amongst the living.

As on the previous day the people awaited sundown, but although the heat of the day had died down and night had already fallen, they still waited, hoping that the cool night air would enable the weaker men to continue their struggle with the desert that stood between them and their native land. This last hope, however, was fated never to be fulfilled.

As night drew on the runaways felt that they could continue their way slowly forward and were about to set out when suddenly they heard the distant braying of an ass and the barking of dogs. For a time, they hoped it might be a merchant caravan or the party of a tax collector, but soon horsemen appeared in the semi-darkness of the plain.

The well-known cry of "A'atu!" resounded over the desert. There was nowhere to flee to, they had no weapons to fight with and hiding was useless - the sharp-eared dogs would soon find them. Some of the insurgents sank to the ground, their last ounce of strength gone; others dashed about aimlessly amongst the rocks. Some of them tore their hair in desperation. One of the Libyans, still a young man, groaned plaintively and tears filled his eyes. The Amu and the Heriusha stood with bowed heads and clenched teeth. Several of the men began involuntarily to run away but were immediately halted by the dogs.

The more self-restrained stood still where they were, as though in a trance, their minds, however, actively seeking ways of salvation. The soldiers of the Black Land were fortunate in their chase - they had caught up with the runaways at a moment when they were very weak. If they had retained but half of their former energy many of them would have preferred death to second captivity.

Their vitality, however, had been sapped and the runaways did not offer any resistance to the soldiers approaching with drawn bows.

The struggle for freedom was over - those who slept their eternal sleep amidst the abandoned weapons were a thousand times more fortunate than the survivors. Worn out, all hope of liberty gone, the slaves became submissive and indifferent to their fate. Very soon the hundred and fourteen men, their hands bound behind their backs and chained together by their necks in parties of ten, straggled back across the desert to the east under the blows of whips. A few of the soldiers visited the scene of the catastrophe to make sure there were none left alive there.

The pursuers expected a reward for every slave they

brought back – only this saved the runaways from a horrible death. Not one of them died on the awful journey back when they dragged along tied together, lashed by whips and without food. The caravan moved slowly, keeping to the road, and avoiding the sands.

Pandion dragged along, never daring to look at his companions, and unreceptive to outside impressions. Even the blows of the whip could not arouse him from his state of torpor. The only thing he remembered of the journey back to slavery was the moment when they reached the Nile, near the city of Abydos. The Captain of the escort halted the party to examine the wharf where a barge should have awaited the captives. The prisoners were huddled together on the crest of the descent into the valley. Some of them sank to the ground. The morning breeze brought with it the smell of fresh water.

Pandion, who had remained on his feet, suddenly noticed pretty, delicately blue flowers on the very edge of the desert. They swayed on their long stems spreading a fine aroma all around, and Pandion felt that this was the last gift sent to him from his lost liberty. The young Hellene's lips cracked and bleeding, quivered and uncertain, weak sounds escaped his throat. Kidogo, who had been watching his friend with some alarm during halts - he was chained to a different group during the march - turned to listen.

"... Blue." He heard only the last word, and Pandion again sank into a coma.

The runaways were freed of their bonds, and driven on to the barge that was to take them to the suburbs of the capital. Here they were kept in prison as particularly dangerous and persistent rebels and would inevitably be sent to the gold mines. The prison was a huge hole dug in the hard, dry ground, faced with brick, and roofed by a number of steep vaults. Four narrow slits cut in the roof served as windows, and the entrance was a sloping trap-door in the roof through which food and water were lowered.

The constant gloom of the prison proved a mercy to the runaways: many of them had inflamed eyes caused by the terribly harsh light of the desert, and had they remained in the sunlight they would undoubtedly have lost their sight. But how tormenting was their captivity in a dark, stinking hole after a few days of liberty! The captives were wholly cut off from the world, and nobody cared what they felt or experienced.

Despite the hopelessness of their position, however, they again began to hope for something as soon as they had started to recover from the effects of their awful journey. Cavius, somewhat brusquely as usual, again began to outline ideas that all could understand. Kidogo's laughter was heard again as were the piercing cries of the Libyan Akhmi.

Pandion recovered more slowly, the collapse of his hopes had made a deeper impression on him. Many times, he had felt the stone hidden in his loincloth, but it seemed like sacrilege to him to take out Yakhmos' wonderful gift in that foul, dark hole. The stone, moreover, had deceived him, it possessed no magic; it had not helped him obtain his liberty and reach the sea.

At last, however, Pandion did take the blue-green crystal out of its hiding place and carry it stealthily to the pale ray that shone through the slit in the roof but did not reach the ground. With the first glance, he cast at the joyous iridescence of the stone, the desire to live and fight returned to him. He had been deprived of everything; he did not even dare to think of Thessa; he did not dare to evoke memories of his native shores. All that was left to him was the stone the stone that was like a dream of the sea, of another life, the real life he had known in the past. Pandion began to gaze frequently at the stone, finding in its transparent depths that joy without which it would have been impossible to live.

Pandion and his companions did not spend more than ten days in their underground prison. Without any sort of interrogation or trial, the authorities up there in the world above decided the fate of the runaway slaves. The trap door opened suddenly, and a wooden ladder was lowered into the prison. The slaves were led out and, blinded by the glaring sun, were immediately bound, and chained together in groups of six.

They were then driven down to the Nile and loaded on to a big barge sailing upstream. The rebels were being sent to the southern frontiers of the Black Land, to the Gates of the South, from where they would begin that last journey from which there was no return - to the terrible gold mines of the Land of Nub. (Gates of the South - the towns of Neb and Swan, the modern Syene and Aswan, on the islands of Elephantine and Philae. Nub (Egypt, gold) - the collective name for all the lands along the Nile south of the First Cataract; later Nubia).

A fortnight after the runaway slaves had exchanged their underground prison for a floating jail, at a distance of five hundred thousand cubits upstream to the south of the capital of Tha-Quem, the following scene was enacted in the luxurious palace of the Prince of the South on the Island of Neb.

The Prince of the South and Governor of the Province

of Neb, the cruel and imperious Kabuefta, who considered himself second only to Pharaoh in the Black Land, had summoned to his presence the Commander of the Host, the Lord of the Hunt, and the Chief Caravan Leader of the South. Kabuefta received his guests on the balcony of his palace where an abundant feast was spread; his Chief Scribe was also present. Kabuefta, a big muscular man, seated, in imitation of Pharaoh, on a high throne of ebony and ivory, towered arrogantly above his companions. He noticed the inquiring glances, which the assembled officials exchanged, and smiled to himself.

The palace stood on the highest part of the island, and the view from the balcony embraced the wide sleeves of the river sweeping round a group of temples built of white limestone and red granite.

Along the banks were dense growths of tall palms whose dark feathery foliage stretched along the foot of the steep, rocky cliff of the river bank. A vertical granite wall bordering a high plateau shut off the southern view; the First Cataract of the Nile was situated at the eastern point of this plateau. At this point, the valley of the river suddenly narrowed, and the expanse of calm, well-tilled fields was broken off abruptly by the immeasurably great expanses of the deserts of Nub, the land of gold.

From terraces on the cliffside, the tombs of past Princes of the South looked down upon the palace - these were the graves of bold explorers of the countries inhabited by the black people, beginning with the great Herkhuf who had led caravans into the countries of the south at the time of the 6th Dynasty. (2625-2475 B.C.)

An experienced desert traveler could discern the regular lines of hieroglyphs of a tremendously long inscription that from that distance had the appearance of the cuneiform inscriptions of the Asian countries. The ruler of the south, however, had no need to read the inscriptions. He knew by heart the proud words of Hemu relating his journey to the Land of Punt (Puoni): "In the eighth year... the keeper of the seal, the keeper of all that is and is not, the curator of the temples, granaries and the white house, the keeper of the Gates of the South, (Retranslated from Golenishchev's Russian version of the Egyptian original.) so all these titles belonged to Kabuefta as much as to his legendary ancestor."

The distance was lost in the greyish haze caused by the heat, but it was cool on the island-a north wind struggled against the heat encroaching from the south, driving it back to the wilderness of sunburnt plains.

The Prince of the South gazed long at the tombs of his ancestors and then with a gesture ordered a waiting slave to fill the glasses for the last time. The feast was over; the guests rose and followed their host into the inner rooms of the palace.

They entered a square, not very high room, beautifully decorated in the style of the great days of Tuthmosis the 3rd. (Pharaoh Tuthmosis the 3rd (1501-1447 B.C.) statesman and soldier who added to Egyptian conquests.) The smooth white walls were decorated at the bottom with a broad light blue border, containing an intricate straight-line design composed of white lines, while a narrow strip of wall around the ceiling bore a pattern of lotus flowers and symbolic figures, carried out in blue, green, black, and white tones on a background of dull gold.

The ceiling was divided by four wooden beams of a deep cherry color, and surrounded by a checkered border in black and gold. The spaces between the beams were painted in bright colors - gold spirals and white rosettes on a checkerboard background in red and blue. The wide doorposts of polished cedar-wood were bordered with narrow black stripes broken by numerous pairs of blue lines drawn across them. A carpet, a few folding chairs of ivory covered in leopard skin, two armchairs of gold-inlaid ebony, a few chests on legs which also served as tables, constituted the entire furniture of the big, bright, and airy room.

Without undue haste, Kabuefta took his seat in one of the armchairs, and his clear-cut profile stood out sharply against the white wall. The officials pulled their chairs closer to him, and the Chief Scribe stood by a tall table of ebony inlaid with gold and ivory. On the polished surface of the table lay a scroll of papyrus with a red and white seal.

At a sign from the Prince of the South, the Scribe unrolled the papyrus and stood for a moment in respectful silence. The Commander of the Host, a gaunt, bald-headed man without a wig, winked at the little, stubby Caravan Leader, giving him to understand that the talk for which they had been summoned would now begin. Sure enough, Kabuefta inclined his head and spoke to the assembled officials.

"His Majesty, the Ruler of the Upper and Lower Black Lands, life, health, strength, has sent me an express letter. In it His Majesty commands me to do something unheard of - to bring to the City a beast with a horned nose such as inhabits the land beyond Wawat (the stretch of the Nile between modern Aswan and Khartoum); these animals are distinguished for their monstrous strength and ferocity.

"In the past, many beasts from the southern lands have been brought alive to the Great House. The people of the City and the people of Tha-Meri-Heb have seen huge apes, giraffes, the beasts of Seth, (Beasts of Seth-okapi, an animal from the same group as the giraffe. They are now found only in the dense jungles of the Congo but were formerly widespread throughout Africa, being very numerous in the Nile Delta. The figure of the dread Seth, god of darkness, is modeled after this animal.) and the groundhogs; savage lions and leopards accompanied Ramses the Great, (Ramses the 2nd (1229-1225 B.C.), the great conqueror. Tame lions fought on the side of the Egyptians against the Hittites.) and even fought against the enemies of Tha-Quem, but never has a rhinoceros been caught alive.

"From time immemorial the Princes of the South have provided the Black Land with everything needed from the lands of the black people; nothing has ever been impossible for them to perform. I wish to continue this glorious tradition: Tha-Quem must see a live rhinoceros. I have summoned you that we may take counsel on the easiest way to bring at least one of these terrible monsters to Tha-Quem. What do you say, Nehzi, who have seen so many glorious hunts?" he asked, turning to The Lord of the Hunt, a morose, obese individual whose wavy hair, dark skin and humped nose betrayed in him a descendant of the Hyksos.

"The beast of the southern plains is indescribably fierce; his skin is impervious to our spears, his strength is that of the elephant," began Nehzi importantly. "He attacks first, smashing and crushing everything that stands in his way. He is not to be caught in a pit: the heavy animal would most certainly be injured. If we arrange a big hunt and seek a female with her young, we might kill the mother, capture the babe and take it to Quemt."

Kabuefta struck angrily on the arm of his chair.

"Seven times seven will I fall to the feet of the Great House, my ruler. Fie on you," the finger of the Prince of the South prodded the dumbfounded Lord of the Hunt, "who dares to sin against His Majesty. Not a half-dead babe must we bring him, but a great beast, nefer-neferu, the best of the best, an animal in the prime of life, capable of inspiring fear in full measure. Nor can we wait until a cub grows to maturity in captivity. The royal command must be fulfilled with all haste especially as the animal lives far from the Gates of the South."

Peheni, the Caravan Leader, suggested sending some three hundred of the bravest soldiers without arms but with ropes and nets to capture the monster. The Commander of the Host, Senofri, scowled at this and Kabuefta frowned at him.   Then the Caravan Leader hastened to add that it would not be necessary to send soldiers but that it would be better to force the Nubians themselves to capture the beast, Kabuefta shook his head, twisting his mouth into a derisive smile.

"The days of Tuthmosis and Ramses are long past - the despised inhabitants of the Land of Nub are no longer bowed in submission. Senofri knows with what efforts and cunning we are able to curb the lust of their hungry mouths. No, that will not do, we must capture the animal ourselves."

"And if, instead of soldiers, we were to sacrifice slaves," suggested Senofri with caution.

The worried Kabuefta was suddenly aroused.

"I swear by Ma'at, the all-seeing goddess of truth, that you're right, O wise commander! I'll take rebels and runaways from the prisons, these are the boldest of the slaves. They shall capture the monster."

The Lord of the Hunt smiled an unbelieving smile.

"You are wise, O Prince of the South, but might I make bold to ask, how are you going to compel the slaves to face certain, death from this fierce monster? Threats will not help, you can only threaten them with death instead of death. What difference will it make to them?"

"You understand animals better than you do men, Nehzi, so leave the men to me. I shall promise them liberty. Those who have already faced death for the sake of liberty will be willing to do EO again. That's exactly why I shall take only rebellious slaves."

"And will you fulfill your promise?" asked Nehzi again.

Kabuefta stuck out his lower lip haughtily.

"The majesty of the Prince of the South does not permit him to sink so low as to lie to slaves, but they will not return. Leave that to me. You would do better to tell me how many men you'll need to capture the animal and how far it is to the places where it is to be found."

"We'll need no less than two hundred men. The animal will crush half of them, and the remainder will overcome him by their numbers and tie him up. Two months from now begins the season of floods and the grass of the plains will spring up. At that time the animals will come north for the grass, and we shall then be able to seek them close to the river near the Sixth Cataract. The most important thing is to capture the animal in the vicinity of the river since the men will not be able to carry a live animal that weighs as much as seven bulls. Once on the river, we can take it by water in a big cage as far as the City."

The Prince of the South was thinking deeply, making

calculations, and his lips quivered.

"Het!" he said at last. "So, let it be. A hundred and fifty slaves will be enough if they fight well. A hundred soldiers, twenty hunters, and guides. You will take command of the whole party, Nehzi! Get busy making your arrangements at once. Senofri will select reliable soldiers and peaceful Kemtiues." (Peaceful Kemtiues -the name given by the Egyptians to Kemtiues who served in the army and police.)

The Lord of the Hunt bowed. The officials left the chamber, making merry over Nehzi's new appointment. Kabuefta seated the Scribe and began to dictate a letter to the governors of the prisons of the two towns at the Gates of the South, Neb, and Swan.

CHAPTER FIVE

The Golden Plain

At the foot of a staircase, leading down from a hill at the southern end of the Island of Neb, stood a crowd of slaves chained to huge bronze rings hanging from the granite pillars that rose above the lower terrace. All the hundred and fourteen survivors of the flight were there, and another forty Kemtiues and Nubians with savage faces and bodies crisscrossed with the scars of old wounds. The crowd languished long in the blazing sun waiting to learn their fate.

At last, a man in white raiment with the glitter of gold on his forehead, breast and on his black staff, appeared on the upper landing of the staircase. He walked slowly in the shade of two fans, carried by Nubian soldiers. Several other men, important officials, judging by their clothes, surrounded the Prince. This was Kabuefta, the Prince of the South. The soldiers quickly drew a cordon around the slaves; a prison scribe, who accompanied the captives, stepped forward and prostrated himself before the Prince.

Kabuefta, calmly, never changing the expression on his immobile face, came down the stairs and advanced right up to the slaves. He cast a rapid, contemptuous glance over all those present. Turning to one of the officials, he said something in careless tones, although there was a slight note of approval in his voice. The Prince of the South struck the ground with his staff; its bronze ferrule rang sharply on the stone pavement.

"All of you look at me and listen! Let those who do not understand the language of Quemt be led aside; they will get an explanation later."

The soldiers hurriedly obeyed the order, taking away fifteen Kemtiues who did not understand the language.

Kabuefta spoke loudly and slowly, in the language of the people, carefully selecting his words. It was obvious that the Prince of the South frequently had to talk to foreigners. The Prince explained to the slaves the matter in hand; he did not try to hide the fact that it meant death for many of them, but he promised liberty to the survivors. The majority of the captives expressed their agreement in exclamations of approval, the remainder kept a sullen silence, but nobody refused.

"Het!" continued Kabuefta, "so let it be." Again, his glance swept over the lean and dirty bodies. "I'll order that you be fed nourishing food and are given an opportunity to bathe. The journey through the five cataracts of the Hapi is a hard one; it will be easier to travel in light boats. I will give orders for you to be freed if you swear you will make no attempt to escape."

Cries of joy interrupted his speech. He waited until they subsided and then continued:

"In addition to the oath, I give the following order: for everyone that runs away ten of his best comrades will be flayed, sprinkled with salt and cast bound on to the sandy banks of the Land of Nub. Those who show cowardice when tackling the animal and run away will be subjected to horrible tortures; I have warned the inhabitants of the Land of Nub, and under threat of punishment they will track down all runaways."

The end of the Prince's speech met with morose

silence, which Kabuefta paid no attention to as he again, looked over the slaves. His experience helped him make a faultless choice.

"Come here, you," said the Prince to Cavius. "You will be in charge of the trappers and the mediator between my hunters and your companions."

Cavius made an unhurried bow to the Prince and his lips curved in a grim smile.

"You are selling us liberty at a high price, O Prince, but we are willing to buy It," said the Etruscan and turned to his comrades. "The savage beast is no worse than the gold mines, and we have greater hope."

Kabuefta left them, and the slaves were returned to their prison. The Prince of the South kept his promise: the rebels were well fed; they were released from their chains and collars, and twice a day were taken down to the Nile to bathe in coves fenced off to keep out the crocodiles.

Two days later, a hundred and fifty-four slaves were joined to a detachment of soldiers and hunters sailing upstream on light boats made of reeds. The journey was a long one. The inhabitants of the Black Land reckoned four million cubits from the Gates of the South to the Sixth Cataract of the Nile. The river flowed almost in a straight line through Wawat and Yer-thet, but in the Land of Kush, situated higher upstream, it made two wide bends, one to the west and the other to the east. (Kush-the name given by Egyptian geographers to the part of the Nile Valley between the Second and Fifth Cataracts; it included the ancient lands of Jam and Karoi. Yerthet was the province south of the Second Cataract, Wawat between the First and Second.)

The Lord of the Hunt was in a hurry: the journey would

take two months; in nine weeks the water would begin to rise, and it would be more difficult to work their way upstream when the speed of the current increased. Then again, it would only be possible to bring the huge animal in a heavy boat over the many cataracts when the floods were at their highest. There would be but little time for the return journey.

Throughout the long journey, the slaves were well fed, and they felt strong and healthy, despite the hard work they did every day rowing the boats against a current that was especially swift at the cataracts. They did not worry much about the hunt that was still before them since every man was confident that he would survive and gain his freedom.

The contrast between the unknown wild lands through which they passed and the period of waiting in a black hole in anticipation of brutal punishment, was too great for them. And the men now full of life and strong in mind and body worked with a will. The Lord of the Hunt was pleased with them and did not grudge them food - all the towns and villages that lay on their way provided it.

Immediately on leaving the Island of Neb, Pandion and his comrades saw the First Cataract of the Nile.

The river was squeezed between rocky cliffs, and its swift current broke into separate streams of seething white water, that roared and raged down the slope amongst a tangled mass of black rocks. Hundreds of years before Pandion's time many thousands of slaves, working under the guidance of Tha-Quem's most skilled engineers, had built canals through the granite rocks so that even the big warships could pass the cataract easily.

The light boats of the hunting expedition did not find any

great difficulty in passing the first or any of the other cataracts. The slaves stood up to the waist in water, pushing the light boats from one rock to another. Sometimes they had to carry the boats on their shoulders along convenient ledges cut on the banks by the floodwaters.

Day after day, the hunters made their way farther and farther southwards. They passed a temple hewn out of living rock on the left bank of the river. Pandion's attention was drawn to four gigantic figures, each about thirty cubits high, standing in a niche. These gigantic statues of the conqueror, Pharaoh Ramses II, seemed to guard the entrance to the temple.

The expedition passed the Second Cataract, which stretched the length of a whole day's journey.

Still higher up the river, they came to the Island of Uronartu with the rapids of Semne; a fortress had been built there nine centuries before on water-eroded granite cliffs by the Pharaoh who conquered Nubia and had been given the name of "Repulse of the Savages." (Senusret III (the legendary Sesostris) 1887-1849 B.C., a Pharaoh of the 12th Dynasty (2000-1788), famous for his colossal building works.) The thick walls, twenty cubits high and built of sunbaked brick, were still in an excellent state of preservation; they were thoroughly overhauled every thirty years.

On the cliffs, there were stone tablets with inscriptions forbidding the Kemtiues to enter the Land of Tha-Quem. The gloomy grey fortress with square turrets at the corners and several other turrets facing the river, with narrow staircases leading from the river through the rocks, rose high above the surrounding country, a symbol of the proud might of Quemt.

None of the slaves, however, suspected that the great

days of mighty Quemt were passed, that a country that had been built up by the labor of countless slaves was being rent asunder by constant rebellions and that she was threatened by the growing strength of new peoples.

On their way, they passed four other fortresses standing on rocky islands or cliffs on the riverbank.

The boats then rounded an ox-bow in the river in the center of which was situated the town of Hem-Aton, that had been built by the same heretic Pharaoh who had built the capital city amongst the ruins of which Pandion had found the statue of the mysterious girl. The inhabitants of the town were Egyptians who had either been exiled or had fled from the Black Land in times long past.

At the end of the ox-bow, the river turned at right angles, forced into its new course by high cliffs of dark sandstone. Here began the third narrow stretch of swift-flowing water almost a hundred thousand cubits in length, which took the hunters four days to pass.

The fourth stretch of the Nile, above the city of Napata, capital of the kings of Nub, was still longer - it took five days to navigate it. A further delay of two days was caused by negotiations between the Lord of the Hunt and the rulers of Kush.

At the Fourth Cataract, the hunters were overtaken by three boats carrying Nubians, who were sent ahead to locate the rhinoceros.

Riverside settlements were fewer and farther apart than in Tha-Quem. The valley itself was much narrower, and the cliffs that bounded the desert plateau could be clearly discerned through the heat haze.

Hundreds of crocodiles, some of them of enormous

size, hid in the reed thickets or lay on the sand-banks exposing their greenish-black backs to the blazing sun. Several careless slaves and soldiers fell victims to the cunning attacks of the silent reptiles right before the eyes of their comrades.

There were large numbers of hippopotamuses in these waters. Pandion, the Etruscans, and other slaves from the northern countries were already familiar with these ugly animals that bore in Egyptian the name of hie. The hippopotamuses did not show any fear of people nor did they attack them without cause, so that the slaves were able to pass quite close to them. A large number of blue patches in front of the green wall of rushes ahead of them showed the resting places of the hippopotamuses in the broader parts of the valley, where the river spread into an expansive, smooth-surfaced lake. The wet skin of the animals had a bluish tinge.

The ungainly monsters watched the boats pass, holding above the water their strange blunt heads, that looked as though the snouts had been chopped off. Very often, the animals held their square jowls under the water so that the yellow, muddy stream flowed over the dark mounds of foreheads surmounted by tiny protruding ears. The eyes of the hippopotamuses, situated on bumps on the head and giving them an expression of ferocity, gazed at the passing boats in stupid persistence.

In those places where the granite cliffs rose straight from the riverbed, forming cataracts and rapids, they came across deep holes between the crags filled with unruffled, transparent water.

On one occasion, when the men were carrying the

boats over a portage that ran along the edge of a granite cliff, they saw a huge hippopotamus walking along the bottom of one of these holes on his short stumpy legs. Under the water, the bluish skin of the animal turned a deeper blue. Experienced Kemtiues explained to their comrades that the Me often walk along the beds of rivers in search of the roots of water-plants.

The river valley changed its direction for the last time - at a big, densely populated, and fertile island it turned almost due south, and only a short distance divided them from their goal. The steep banks of the river grew lower. They were cut by wide, dry watercourses in which thick growths of thorny trees occurred.

On the journey between the Fourth and Fifth Cataracts two boats overturned and eleven men, all of them poor swimmers, were drowned.

After passing the Fifth Cataract, they met the first tributary of the Nile. The wide mouth of the River of Perfumes, a right tributary of the Nile, joined the main stream in an extensive jungle of reeds and papyri. An impenetrable green wall, up to twenty cubits in height, intersected by the zigzags of streams and backwaters, barred the entrance to the river. The banks of the Nile had now become separate, clearly defined ranges of hills, on which groves of trees were becoming more frequent; their thorny trunks were higher, and the long dark ribbons of the groves ran far into the interior of an unknown and unpopulated land. The slopes of the hills bristled with clumps of coarse grass that rustled in the wind.

The time was drawing near when they would have to pay for their journey in freedom, without chains and without prisons, and a suppressed alarm filled the hearts of the slaves. (River of Perfumes - the Atbara, falling into the Nile from the East.) Soon the terrible trial will begin – some will be saved at the cost of the blood and sufferings of their comrades, others will remain forever in this unknown land, having made the supreme sacrifice.

Such were Cavius' thoughts as he cast an involuntary glance over his companions, trying to imagine what the future held in store.

As they sailed farther upstream, the country took on the character of a plain. Marshy banks framed the smooth surface of the water in a sharply defined line of dark grass that stretched away inland as far as the eye could reach. The star-shaped brushes of the papyrus plants hung over the river, breaking the monotonous line of the level banks. Grass-covered islets broke the stream into a labyrinth of narrow passages, where the deep water lay dark and mysterious between the green walls.

In places where there was hard ground on the banks, the travelers saw large patches of cracked, sunbaked clay bearing the footprints of many animals. Birds that looked like storks but were the height of a man amazed the slaves by their large beaks. It looked to them as if the birds' heads were surmounted by huge chests with the edges of the lids turned upwards. The monsters' evil yellow eyes gleamed from under pendent orbits.

After passing the point where the River of Perfumes entered the Nile, they journeyed for two days along a stretch of the river straight as a spear-shaft until they saw the faint smoke of two signal fires on a ledge of the bank. Here they were awaited by the hunters and Nubian guides who had gone ahead; the signal told them that the beast had been found.

That night a hundred and forty slaves escorted by ninety soldiers marched westwards from the river. Warm, heavy rain poured down on the parched soil. The humidity made the men dizzy, for they had long forgotten what rain was like under the permanently cloudless sky of Tha-Quem.

The hunters marched through coarse grass that grew waist-high, occasionally passing the black silhouettes of trees. Hyenas and jackals howled and barked on all sides, wild cats rent the air with their loud mewing and the raucous voices of night birds, calling to each other, had a particularly ominous sound.

A new country, mysterious and indefinite in the darkness, opened up before the dwellers of Asia and the Northern Shores, a country teeming with life independent of man and unsubdued by him. Ahead of them appeared a huge tree whose large crown covered half the sky; its trunk was thicker than any of the big obelisks of the Black Land. The people made camp under this tree and there spent the night that was to be the last for many of them.

Pandion could not get to sleep for a long time. He was excited by thoughts of the coming fight and lay listening to the sounds of the African plain lands. Cavius sat by the camp-fire discussing plans of action for the next day with the hunters; then he, too, lay down with a heavy sigh as he looked over the restlessly dozing or sleepless figures of his comrades. He could not understand the carefree attitude of Kidogo, who was calmly sleeping between Pandion and Remdus. Throughout the journey, the four friends had kept together. The Kemtiu's unconcern seemed to him the very highest degree of bravery that even he, a soldier who had many times faced death, could not lay claim to.

Morning came, and the slaves were divided into three groups each headed by five hunters and two local guides. Every slave was provided with a long rope or thong with a noose at the end. Four men in each party carried a big net made of exceptionally strong ropes, the mesh of which was a cubit across. Their task was to catch the monster with the ropes, entangle him in the nets and then bind his feet.

In complete silence, they set out across the plain, each group at some distance from the others. The soldiers stretched out in a long line, arrows held to their bows as they did not trust the slaves. Before long Pandion and his comrades reached a level plain overgrown with grass more than waist high and dotted here and there by trees with umbrella-shaped crowns. (The African acacia and certain varieties of mimosa.) Their grey trunks spread out into branches almost from the roots, forming a huge funnel so that the trees looked like inverted cones while their transparent, dull green foliage seemed to be floating in the air.

Between the trees, there were dark patches of tall, small-leafed shrubs, at times stretching along the scarcely perceptible depression of a temporary watercourse and at other times visible from a distance as a shapeless dark mass.

Occasionally they came across trees with trunks of enormous thickness whose huge gnarled and knotted branches were covered with young leaves and bunches of white flowers. These massive trees stood out sharply in the plain, their far-spreading crowns casting huge patches of black shadow. Their fibrous bark had a metallic hue that looked like lead; their branches seemed to be cast from copper, and the aroma spread by their flowers resembled that of almonds.

The sun turned the scarcely moving, coarse grass to gold over which the green lacework of the trees seemed to be floating in the air. A row of thin black spears appeared above the grass. A group of antelopes - the oryx - showed their horns and disappeared behind a line of bushes. The grass was still rather scanty, patches of bare, cracked earth showed on all sides since the rains had only just begun.

On their left appeared a grove of trees whose feather-like leaves resembled palms, but their trunks opened out into two branches at the top, like the spread fingers of a hand, and on these, in turn, other branches grew. (The baobab-a tree typical of the African savanna.) It was here that the hunters had seen the rhinoceroses on the previous day and, making a sign to the slaves to stay where they were, the hunters crawled cautiously towards the grove, and peered amongst the trees where it was dark after the bright sunlight outside. There were no animals there, and the hunters led the slaves towards a dry watercourse densely overgrown with bushes. Here there was a spring which the rhinoceroses had turned into a mud-hole where they lay during the hottest hours of the day.

The hunters came to an open space around which were three of the big umbrella-headed acacias. They were still about two thousand cubits from the dry watercourse when one of the Nubian guides at the head of the party stopped and threw out his arms in a signal to halt. It became so silent that the humming of insects could be plainly heard.

Kidogo touched Pandion on the shoulder – he pointed to one side where Pandion saw something under the low, thorny trees that looked like two smooth blocks of stone. These were the awe-inspiring animals of the southern plains.

At first, the animals did not notice the hunters and

continued lying on the ground with their backs towards them. The animals did not seem very big to Pandion, and one of them, a female, was much smaller than the other.

The slaves did not know that the hunters, hoping for a generous reward, had picked out an exceptionally large male rhinoceros of the light-skinned variety (In former times, the white rhinoceros was considerably more common in Northern Sudan.) that was much bigger than its southern relatives were, higher in the shoulder, had a wide square jowl and light grey skin. The hunters decided to change the plan of attack so that the female would not intervene and spoil the hunt

The Lord of the Hunt and the Captain of the escort troops climbed up a tree, cursing the long thorns on its trunk. The soldiers hid behind bushes.

The slaves joined forces in a single group, spread out in several lines and, together with the hunters, rushed across the open plain with deafening shouts, waving their ropes and giving themselves courage by shouting their war cries. The two animals jumped to their feet with amazing speed. The huge male stood still for a second, his eyes fixed on the people approaching him, but the female, more frightened than he, ran away to one side. This was what the hunters had counted on, and they ran swiftly away to the right to cut her off from her companion.

From the treetop, the Lord of the Hunt could see the gigantic body of the immobile rhinoceros, the black curve of ears peeked forward and separated by the high hill-like crown of the animal's head. Behind his ears rose the high hump of its massive withers and in front of them gleamed the sharp end of its horn. It seemed to the Egyptian that the animal's tiny eyes were looking down at the ground with a stupid and even offended look in them.

A minute later the rhinoceros turned, and the Egyptian saw its long head, awkwardly curved in the middle, the steep slope of its withers, the ridge of bones protruding on its rump, its legs as thick as tree-trunks and its little tail sticking up in a warlike manner. The huge shining horn, no less than two cubits long, situated on the animal's nose, was very thick at the root and sharply pointed at the tip. Behind it was another horn, smaller than the first, also sharp, with a round, broad base.

The hearts of the people running towards the rhinoceros beat furiously - close at hand it seemed a most fearful monster. The enormous body was no less than eight cubits in length, and its powerful withers towered a good four cubits above the ground. The rhinoceros snorted so loudly that every man heard it and then hurled itself at the oncoming people. With agility unbelievable in so great a body, the massive animal was an instant later in the middle of the crowd. Nobody had time to lift a rope.

Pandion found himself some distance from the massive animal that rushed past like a whirlwind. He just had time to notice the animal's distended nostrils surrounded by folds of skin, a torn right ear, and flanks covered with little hillocks like growths of lichen. After that, everything was mixed up in Pandion's head. A shrill scream rang out across the plain; an awkwardly twisted human figure flew through the air.

The rhinoceros made a wide path through the crowd of slaves and dashed past them into the open plain, leaving several prostrated bodies behind him, turned, and again hurled himself at the unfortunate people. This time human figures hung on to the rapidly moving mass of flesh. But the monster was made up of solid muscles and thick bones and clothed in skin as hard as armor-plating and the men flew off in different directions.

Again, the rhinoceros began stamping the doomed slaves underfoot, crushing them and goring them with its horn. Pandion, who had run forward together with the others, was stopped by a dull, heavy blow, and found himself on all fours. Wailing groans and piercing shrieks swept across the field, and the air was filled with clouds of dust.

The Lord of the Hunt, who had been shouting from his treetop to encourage the slaves, was now silent as he looked in confusion at the battle. Not a single rope had been fastened to the animal, and already some thirty men lay dead or wounded. The soldiers, pale and trembling, took cover behind the trees, praying to the gods of Tha-Quem for salvation.

For the third time the rhinoceros attacked the people, and although they gave way before him, he managed to gore Remdus, the younger Etruscan, with his horn. With abrupt snorts, the animal dashed furiously amongst the people, goring them, and trampling them underfoot. Foam flew from the animal's nostrils; his tiny eyes gleamed with rage.

With a furious howl, Cavius hurled himself at the monster, but his rope slipped off the horn; the Etruscan himself flew aside, bleeding - the rough hide of the rhinoceros had torn the skin from his shoulder and chest. Cavius got to his feet with difficulty, roaring in helpless fury.

Scared by the strength of the rhinoceros the people staggered back from him, the less brave of them sliding behind the backs of their comrades. It seemed that little more was required to make them scatter in all directions, abandoning their hopes of liberty.

Again, the rhinoceros turned to attack the people. Again, the air was filled with howls. Kidogo stepped forward. The Kemtiu's nostrils were distended; he was filled with that fire of battle that is born of mortal danger when a man forgets everything except the necessity to fight, to fight for life. Leaping aside from the awful horn that threatened certain death, Kidogo ran after the animal and seized hold of its tail. Pandion, recovering from the terrible shaking he had received, picked up a net that was lying on the ground.

At that moment, he realized that he should be ahead of his comrades whose bodies had shielded him when he lay stupefied on the grass. Some faint memories flitted through his mind - the glade in Crete, the dangerous games with the bull. The rhinoceros was not much like a bull, but Pandion decided to use the same methods. Throwing the rolled-up net over his shoulder, he rushed at the rhinoceros.

The animal had come to a halt, was pawing the ground with its hind-legs, churning up clouds of dust, and had thrown Kidogo far away. Two Libyans, understanding Pandion's plan, attracted the animal's attention to one side and, with a single bound, he reached the animal and pressed tightly to its side. The rhinoceros turned like lightning, its rough hide tearing Pandion's skin. Pandion felt a terrible pain, but forgetting all else, hung on to the animal's ear. In the way he had seen it done in Crete, Pandion threw his body across that of the animal and landed on his broad back. The rhinoceros twisted and turned. Pandion hung on for all he was worth. *If I can only hold on!* was the one thought that repeated itself in his brain.

Pandion held on for the number of seconds necessary to throw the net over the animal's head. The horns protruded through the mesh of the net and Pandion was filled with wild joy, but instantly he became blind to his surroundings and lost consciousness. Something cracked, a heavy weight fell on him, and everything went dark before his eyes.

In the heat of battle, Pandion had not noticed that Kidogo had again caught hold of the animal's tail and that ten Libyans and six Amu had seized the net he had flung over the animal's head. In his effort to throw off the people, the rhinoceros had rolled over on to one side breaking the arm and collarbone of the young Hellene who fell heavily to the ground.

The people took immediate advantage of the monster's fall. With loud shouts the slaves fell on the rhinoceros, a second net enveloped its head, and two nooses were made fast on a hind-leg and one on a foreleg. The animal's snorting developed into a deep roar; it rolled over on to the left side, then on to its back, crushing people's bones under its heavy weight. It seemed that there was no limit to the animal's strength. Six times it rose to its feet, got mixed up in the ropes and rolled over on to its back again, killing more than fifty men. Still the ropes and thongs on its legs increased in number, and the hunters drew the strong nooses tight. Three nets enveloped the animal from head to foot.

Soon a crowd of people, bleeding, sweating and covered in dirt, lay on the madly struggling rhinoceros. The animal's hide, covered with human blood, had become slippery, the men's crooked fingers would not hold, but the ropes were drawn tighter and tighter. Even those who had been crushed by the animal's heavy weight in its last effort to free itself clung to the ropes with the rigid grip of death.

The hunters came up to the recumbent animal with fresh ropes, bound all four tree-like legs and tied its head to its forelegs by ropes passed behind the horn. The terrible battle was over. The panic-stricken people gradually came to their senses; the muscles of their lacerated bodies began to twitch as though they were feverish and black patches floated before their unseeing eyes.

At last, the frantically beating hearts grew calmer; here and there sighs of relief were to be heard, for the people had begun to realize that death had passed them by. Cavius, covered with bloody mud, rose staggering to his feet; Kidogo, trembling all over, but already smiling, came up to him. The smile, however, immediately left the Kemtiu's greying face when he found that Pandion was not amongst the living. Seventy-three men had survived. The remainder had either been killed or had received mortal wounds.

The Etruscan and Kidogo sought for Pandion amongst the dead in the downtrodden grass, found his body and carried it into the shade. Cavius scrutinized him but could not find any mortal injuries. Remdus was dead; the fiery leader of the Amu had also perished and the brave Libyan Akhmi, his chest crushed, lay dying.

While the slaves were counting their losses and carrying the dying to the shade of the trees, the soldiers brought a substantial wooden platform from the river - the bottom of the cage that had been prepared for the rhinoceros; they rolled the body of the bound monster on to it and dragged it to the river on rollers.

Cavius went up to the Lord of the Hunt.

"Order them to help us carry away the wounded," he said, pointing to the soldiers.

"What do you want to do with them?" asked the Lord of the Hunt, looking with involuntary admiration at the mighty Etruscan, smeared with blood and dust, whose face was all stern grief.

"We'll take them back down the river: perhaps some of them will live as far as Tha-Quem and its skilled physicians," answered Cavius, gloomily.

"Who told you that you will return to Tha-Quem?" the Lord of the Hunt interrupted him.

The Etruscan shuddered and stepped back a pace.

"Was the Prince of the South lying to us, then? Are we not free?" shouted Cavius.

"No, the Prince did not lie to you, despised one - you are free!" With these words, the Lord of the Hunt held but a small papyrus scroll to the Etruscan. "Here's his ordinance."

With great care, Cavius took the precious document that made freemen of the slaves.

"If that's so, then why..." he began.

"Be silent," snapped the Lord of the Hunt haughtily, "and listen to me. You're free here," the Lord of the Hunt stressed the last word. "You may go wherever you please - there, there and there," his hand pointed to the west, east and south, "but not to Tha-Quem or to Nub that is under our rule. If you disobey, you'll again become slaves. I presume," he added in brutal tones, "that when you've thought matters over, you'll return and fall to the feet of our ruler and suffer what fate has predestined for you as servants of the Chosen People of the Black Land."

Cavius took two steps forward. His eyes gleamed. He stretched out his hand to one of the soldiers who was looking in perplexity at the Lord of the Hunt, and with a bold gesture pulled the short sword from his belt. The Etruscan raised the flashing weapon point upwards, kissed it and spoke quickly in his own language, which nobody could understand.

"I swear by the Supreme God of Lightning, I swear by the God of Death whose name I bear, that despite all the evil deeds of this accursed people I will return alive to the land of my birth. I swear that from this hour I shall not rest until I sail to the shores of Tha-Quem with a strong army to take payment in full for all the evil that has been done."

Cavius waved his hand over the field where the bodies lay scattered and then with great force hurled the sword to his feet. The sword sank deep into the earth. The Etruscan turned sharply round and walked off towards his comrades but suddenly turned back.

"I ask you only one thing," he said to the Lord of the Hunt who was going off with the last of the soldiers.

"Order them to leave us a few spears, knives and bows. We have to protect our wounded."

The Lord of the Hunt nodded his head without speaking and disappeared behind the bushes, making his way to the river by the broad path created by the platform on which the rhinoceros had been dragged away.

Cavius told his comrades what had been said. Cries of wrath muttered curses and helpless threats mingled with the plaintive moans of the dying.

"We'll think about what we're going to do later on," shouted Cavius. "The first thing we have to decide is what to do with the wounded. It's a long way to the river, we're tired and can't carry them that far. Let us rest a little, and then fifty men can go to the river and twenty will remain here on guard - there are many wild beasts about."

Cavius pointed to the spotted backs of hyenas flashing through the long grass, attracted by the smell of blood. Huge birds with long, bare necks circled around the field, landed, and then flew off again. The dry earth, burned by the sun, gave off waves of heat, the network of sunspots under the trees trembled very slightly and the cries of wild doves sounded mournful in the hot silence.

The fever of battle had passed, wounds and knocks were beginning to ache, grazed skin started to burn and fester. The death of Remdus had been a heavy blow to Cavius - the youngster had been the one link with the Etruscan's distant homeland. Now that link was broken. Kidogo, forgetting his own wounds, sat over Pandion.

The young Hellene had apparently received some internal injury and did not return to consciousness. He was breathing; however, his breath coming through his parched lips in a scarcely audible whistle. Several times Kidogo looked at his comrades lying in the shade, then jumped to his feet and called for volunteers to go to the river for water for the wounded. Groaning involuntarily, the men rose to their feet. Immediately they felt an intolerable thirst that stung and burned their throats. If they, the survivors, were so much in need of water, what must be the sufferings of the wounded who were silent only because they had not the strength to groan?

It was no less than two hours fast walking to the river if they went in a straight line. Suddenly the sound of voices came from beyond the bushes - a party of soldiers, about fifty of them, carrying vessels with water and food, appeared in the glade. There were no Egyptians amongst them, only Nubians and Kemtiues had come, led by two guides.

The soldiers stopped talking as soon as they saw the battlefield. They made their way to the tree under which Cavius was standing and, without a word, placed at his feet earthen and wooden vessels, a dozen spears, six bows with full quivers, four heavy knives and four small hippopotamus-hide shields studded with brass plates.

The thirsty men threw themselves madly at the water jars. Kidogo seized one of the heavy knives and said he would kill anybody who touched the water. They began hurriedly pouring water from two of the vessels into the dry mouths of the wounded after which the others were allowed to drink. The soldiers went away without saying a single word.

Amongst the slaves, there were two men skilled in the treatment of wounds and they, together with Cavius, set about bandaging their comrades' injuries. Pandion's broken bones were set and put in splints of hard bark and bound with strips torn from his own loincloth.

When he removed Pandion's loincloth, Kidogo saw the brightly shining stone that was hidden in the folds of the cloth. The Kemtiu hid it carefully, believing it to be a magic amulet.

Two other wounded had to be put in splints, one of them a Libyan with a broken arm, and the other a slim, muscular Kemtiu, who lay helpless with his leg broken below the knee. The condition of the others was apparently hopeless since the terrible horn of the rhinoceros had gored them deeply, injuring them internally. Some of them had been crushed under the tremendous weight of the animal or under its tree-trunk legs.

Before Cavius had time enough to treat all the wounded, the dark silhouette of a man hurrying towards the scene of the battle appeared in the yellow grass. It was a local inhabitant who had guided the soldiers, returning of his own accord and bringing food and water.

Breathing heavily from the exertion of his rapid journey he approached Cavius with his hands outstretched, palms upwards. The Etruscan recognized this as a sign of friendship and answered with the same gesture. The guide then squatted on his heels in the shade of the tree and, leaning on his long spear, began to talk rapidly, pointing towards the river and to the south. His listeners, however, were at a loss: the Nubian did not know more than ten words of the language of Tha-Quem while Cavius did not understand a single word of what the Nubian was saying. Amongst the slaves, however, they found interpreters.

It turned out that the guide had dropped back from the party of soldiers and had returned to help the slaves find their way. The Nubian told them that the liberated slaves were driven out of the districts subordinate to Tha-Quem so that it would be dangerous for them to return to the river - they might be enslaved again. The guide advised Cavius to journey to the west where they would soon come to a big, dry valley. They must travel southwards through this valley for four days until they met peaceful nomad herdsmen.

"You will give them this," said the Nubian, taking off a sheet that was thrown across his shoulder, a kind of symbol made of red twigs, bent and plaited into a special shape, "then they will receive you hospitably and will give you asses to carry the wounded. Still farther to the south is the country of a rich and peaceful people, who hate Quemt. There the wounded can be healed. The farther you go to the south the more water you will find, and the rains will be more frequent. You will always find water in the dry watercourse that you will follow if you dig a hole two cubits deep."

The Nubian rose to his feet, in a hurry to go. Cavius wanted to thank him, but suddenly they were approached by one of the Asian slaves with a long, tangled, and dirty beard and a mass of uncombed hair on his head.

"Why do you advise us to go to the west and the south? Our home's there." The Asian pointed to the east, in the direction of the river.

The Nubian stared fixedly at the speaker and then answered slowly, pausing after each word:

"If you cross the river, you will find a waterless stony desert in the east. If you cross the desert and the high mountains, you will reach the shores of the sea where Tha-Quem rules. If you are able to cross the sea, on the other side, it is said, there is a desert still more terrible. In the mountains and along the River of Perfumes, there live tribes that provide slaves for Tha-Quem in exchange for weapons. Think it over for yourself!"

"Is there no road to the north?" asked one of the Libyans in wheedling tones.

"Two days journey to the north begins an endless desert: at first it is dry clay and stones, and beyond them there is sand. How will you go that way and for what? It may be that there are roads and sources of water there, but I do not know them. I have told you of the easiest road, the one I know well."

Indicating with a gesture that the talk was at an end the Nubian left the shade of the tree. Cavius followed him, placed his arm around his shoulders and began to thank him, mixing Egyptian and Etruscan words; then he called an interpreter.

"I have nothing I can give, I have nothing myself except..." the Etruscan touched his dirty loin-cloth, "... but I shall always keep you in my heart."

"I want no payment for my help, I, too, follow the dictates of my heart," answered the Nubian with a smile. "Who of us that have known the oppression of Tha-Quem would not help you brave men who have gained your liberty at such a terrible price! Look here, you take my advice and keep the symbol I gave you. I'll tell you something else: there's a water-hole to your right, about two thousand cubits from here, but you had better go away today, before nightfall. Good-bye, bold foreigner, my greetings to your comrades. I must hurry."

The guide disappeared, and Cavius, wrapped in thought, looked long after him. No, they could not leave today and abandon their dying comrades to be torn to pieces by the hyenas. If there were water nearby, that would be all the more reason for staying where they were.

Cavius returned to his comrades who were discussing what was to be done next. Since they had quenched their thirst and eaten, the men had become cooler in their judgment and were carefully weighing up the next move. It was clear to all of them that it would be impossible to go north - they had to get away from the river as quickly as possible, but opinions were divided on the question of whether to go south or east.

The Asians, who constituted almost a half of the survivors, did not want to go deeper into the Land of the Black People and insisted on traveling eastwards. The Nubians said that in three, weeks they could reach the shores of the narrow sea that divided Nubia from Asia and the Asians were ready to attempt another journey through the desert to get home more quickly.

Cavius had been taken captive during an armed expedition. He had a family in his native land, and he hesitated: the possibility of a quick return home was very tempting. His shortest way would be through Quemt, floating downstream in a boat until they reached the sea; but as an experienced soldier, who had spent much of his life wandering, he realized that a small group of people, lost in a strange land, especially in a desert, where every water-hole was known, could only survive by a miracle. So far, the Etruscan had not met with any miracles in his life and did not have much faith in them.

Kidogo, who had left Pandion to take part in the council, now put in his word. It turned out that Kidogo was the son of a potter and came from a rich and numerous tribe living on the seacoast that forms the western boundary of the Land of the Black People. Here the dry land was indented by a large bay called the Southern Horn. (The Gulf of Guinea.)

Kidogo did not know the road home from Nubia: he had been taken captive on the edge of the Great Desert when he was on his way to Quemt, impelled by a passionate desire to see for himself the miracles of craftsmanship performed in that country.

The Kemtiu, however, believed that his homeland could not be very far to the south-west from the scene of the recent battle. Kidogo assured the others that they could learn the right road from that tribe to which the Nubian guide had advised them to go. Kidogo promised hospitality to all his comrades if they reached the country where his people lived; he then told Cavius that in his childhood he had heard that people like him and Pandion had sailed from the northern seas to visit his country.

After Cavius had weighed everything up he advised his comrades to take the advice of the Nubian guide and journey to the south, for Kidogo's words made the unknown Land of the Black People seem less hostile to him. The sea there was free. It was not under the rule of the hated Tha-Quem, and would provide the road by which they could return to their homes. The Etruscan trusted the sea more than he did the desert. The Asians protested and would not agree but the Libyans supported Cavius, to say nothing of the Kemtiues-all of them were prepared to journey to the south and the west: there lay the road to their homes.

The Asians maintained that they did not know how the nomads would treat them, and especially how they would be received by that numerous tribe the guide had spoken of; they said that the symbol the guide had given Cavius might be a trap and that they would again be made slaves.

It was then that the Kemtiu who lay with a broken leg attracted attention to himself by snouts and gestures. Hurriedly, swallowing his words and spluttering, he said something, trying to smile, and frequently beating his breast. From that impassioned speech, from that flood of unknown words, Cavius understood that the Kemtiu came from that tribe the guide advised them to try to reach with the aid of the nomad herdsmen and that he was avowing the peacefulness of his people.

Then Cavius made his decision and took the side of the Kemtiues and Libyans; he spoke against the Asians who continued to insist on their plan. The sun was already sinking, and they had to think about water and a bivouac for the night, so Cavius advised them to wait until morning. Although they all wanted to get away from that terrible glade, strewn with their dead, they had to stay there in order not to cause the unnecessary dying suffering by moving them.

Ten men went to the water hole indicated by the Nubian and returned with jars full of warm, brackish water that smelled of clay. On the advice of the Kemtiues, a fence of thorn branches was built between the trees to ward off the attacks of the hyenas. On the side facing the glade, three fires were built. Three men remained to watch the wounded and ten men with spears sat by the fires.

In those parts, night falls quickly. The clouds were still visible in the west when, from the north and the east, there came rolling a wave of darkness that drowned the tops of the trees, lighting the many lamps of the stars above them.

Very soon Cavius, who was unacquainted with southern countries, understood why the guide had advised them to leave this place as soon as possible. The howling of the jackals filled the air and from all sides came the hysterical laughing of the hyenas. It seemed that hundreds of the animals had come running from all directions to devour not only the dead but the living as well. There was a fearful racket on the glade, grunting, the cracking of bones and sounds of gnawing. The sickly-sweet smell of bodies decomposing in the heat spread rapidly over the earth. The men shouted, threw clots of dirt and stones, ran out with flaming brands, but it was all in vain-the number of carrion seekers steadily increased.

Suddenly a dull rattling sound came from beyond the

thorn barrier followed by a thunderous roar that seemed to roll along the ground and shake the earth. The animals feeding on the glade fell silent. The men who had been sleeping awoke and jumped to their feet; in the silence that ensued the wounded groaned more loudly.

The roar drew nearer to them, a low sound of terrible strength that seemed to come from a large trumpet. An indistinct silhouette with a huge head appeared beside the end tree - an enormous lion was approaching the frightened men and behind it slunk the sinuous shape of a lioness. Spears were turned in the direction of the animals, their bronze tips shining faintly in the dull flames of the fires. At the risk of firing the dry grass, the men shouted and threw burning brands at the lions. The stupefied animals stopped in their tracks, then ran off to the glade. The men stood with their spears ready for a long time, but the lions did not attack.

Those whose turn it was to rest had not had time to fall asleep before the thunderous roar of a lion, followed by a second and a third, again rent the air. No less than three lions were wandering around the camp and the lioness, who had appeared earlier, made a fourth.

The men realized that the low, carelessly built barrier was unpardonable neglect on their part. Four men with spears stood ready to repel any possible attack from behind, while the six other spearmen remained standing by the fires.

Nobody slept anymore. The men armed themselves with whatever they could and sat or stood staring into the darkness. Another roar rent the air, and an enormous lion with a sand-colored mane appeared near the end fire. The flickering flames of the fire made the huge beast seem still bigger and his eyes, fixed on the people, radiated a green gleam.

By sheer bad luck one of the northern Asians, inexperienced in hunting, stood nearby with a bow. Frightened by the animal's roar, he sent an arrow straight into its face. The roar broke off with a drawn-out moan, which turned to a hoarse cough and then ceased.

"Look out!" came the desperate cry of one of the Nubians.

The lion's body whirled through the air; with a single bound, the animal crossed the line of fires and landed between the people. It was not easy to cause confusion amongst the conquerors of the white rhinoceros - spears stopped the lion, biting into his flanks and chest while four arrows pierced his sinuous body. Two spear-shafts broke with a dry crack under the heavy blows of the lion's paws and at that moment, three tall Kemtiues, projecting themselves with round shields, thrust their heavy knives into the beast's chest. The lion howled long and plaintively and the men, covered with his blood, jumped back. A momentary silence was broken by deafening shouts of victory that rolled across the plain.

The body of the dead lion was thrown down in front of the fires and the men set about binding the injuries of two freshly wounded, who still trembled with the fever of battle.

The lions wandered around the encampment until sunrise, roaring furiously from time to time, but they made no further attacks.

With the dawn of a new day that came with blinding suddenness, five of the badly wounded men died. Another seven were found to have died during the night - in the excitement of the scuffle with the lion nobody had noticed when it occurred.

Akhnii was still breathing, his grey lips moving faintly from time to time. Pandion lay with his eyes open, his breast rose and fell with calm, regular breathing. Kidogo bent over him and was horrified to discover that his friend could not see him. However, when he brought water, Pandion drank it immediately and slowly closed his eyes.

After breakfast from the remnants of yesterday's food, Cavius proposed to start out. The Asians had come to an agreement amongst themselves during the night and objected. They shouted that in a country where there were so many beasts of prey, they must inevitably perish; they must hurry to escape from this diabolical plain and the desert was safer and better known to them. No matter how much Cavius and the Kemtiues tried to persuade them, they remained resolute.

"Very well, do as you please," said the Etruscan with determination. "I'm going south with Kidogo. Let those who want to go with us come here, those who want to go east, over there to the left."

A group of black and bronze-colored bodies immediately formed around the Etruscan-the Kemtiues, Libyans and Nubians were with him, altogether thirty-seven men, not counting Pandion and the Kemtiu with the broken leg who had raised himself on one elbow and was listening intently to what was going on. Thirty-two men went to the left and stood with their heads stubbornly bowed.

The weapons and vessels for water were divided equally between the two groups so that the Asians would not be able to blame their comrades for a possible failure. As soon as the things had been shared out, the long-bearded leader of the Asians led his people away to the east, towards the river, as though their affection for their comrades might shake their determination. Those who remained stood for a long time looking after those who had parted from them on the threshold of liberty, then with sighs of sadness set about their own affairs.

Cavius and Kidogo examined Pandion and the wounded Kemtiu and carried them over to another thin-branched tree. When they tried to lift Akhmi, a howl escaped the Libyan's throat, and the last breath of life left the body of that brave fighter for freedom. Cavius advised the Libyans to lift the dead man on to a tree and tie him securely with ropes. This was immediately done although they knew that the body would be torn to pieces by carrion birds; nevertheless, it seemed less repulsive than leaving him as food for the foul hyenas.

In silence, without a single word, Cavius and Kidogo cut some branches.

"What are you doing?" asked one of the tall Kemtiues, approaching the Etruscan.

"Litters. Kidogo and I will carry him." Cavius pointed to Pandion. "And you will carry him," he pointed to the Kemtiu with his leg in splints. "The Libyan will be able to walk without help with his arm in a sling."

"We'll all carry the man who was the first to jump on to the rhinoceros," answered the Kemtiu, turning to his companions. "That brave man saved us all. How can we forget it? Wait a bit, we can make better litters."

Four Kemtiues set to work with great skill making litters. They were soon ready - the many ropes left lying on the scene of the battle with the rhinoceros were plaited between long poles which were kept rigid by double struts between them. In the center of the struts, they placed little cushions made of hard bark and covered with a piece of lion's skin.

The Kemtiu with the broken leg watched them at work, smiling joyously, his dark eyes filled with an expression of loyalty.

The wounded men were placed on the litters, and everything was ready for the departure. The Kemtiues stood in pairs by the litters, lifted them high to the full length of their arms, and fixed the little cushions firmly on their heads. The litter-bearers started out first, marching easily and in step with each other.

Thus, it was that Pandion set out on his journey without having recovered consciousness. Two Nubians and a Kemtiu, armed with spears and a bow, undertook to act as guides; they went ahead, and the other thirty men followed in single file behind the litters. The end of the procession was brought up by another three-armed men, two with spears and one with a bow.

The travelers passed around the edge of the open glade westwards, trying not to look at the remains of their comrades and carrying with them a bitter memory of guilt at not having been able to shield them from the nocturnal depredations of the carrion eaters.

Shortly after their midday halt, they reached a wide dry watercourse that even from a distance was visible on account of the lines of bushes that edged it and stood out clearly against the yellow grass of the plain.

The watercourse took them due south, and they continued without further halts until sundown. That day they did not have to dig for water - a small spring sent its waters to the surface through a crack between two blocks of coarse-grained, friable stone; but they had to work hard preparing their camp and encircling it with a wall of thorn-bushes. That night they all slept soundly, not in the least troubled by the distant roars of lions and hyenas prowling in the darkness.

The second and third days passed quietly. Only once did they see the black mass of a rhinoceros plodding through the grass with lowered head. In their confusion the men stood still - their recent experience was still fresh in their memories. The travelers lay down in the grass. The rhinoceros raised its head and again, as at that terrible moment, they saw its rounded ears set wide apart, with the tip of the horn rising between them. The folds of its thick skin encircled its shoulders and hung down in rolls to its heavy legs that were hidden by the grass. The massive animal stood still and then turned and continued on its way in the former direction.

They frequently came across small herds of yellowish-grey antelopes that the hunters brought down with their arrows; they made excellent and tasty food.

On the fourth day the watercourse widened out and then disappeared; the yellow clay earth gave way to unusual, bright red soil (Laterite - a red, ferrous soil, found in southern countries, the product of the erosion of igneous rocks) that covered the crushed granite in a thin layer. Rounded granite hills formed dark patches on that tiresome red plain. The grass had gone, its place was taken by thick leaves that stuck out of the ground like bunches of sharp, narrow sword-blades (Sansevieria - a strange plant found in dry laterite deposits). The guides made a wide detour of patches of this peculiar plant with leaves whose edges were as sharp as razors.

The red plain spread out in front of them, clouds of dust, all the same size, rose into pillars and shut out the glare of the sun. The heat was overwhelming, but the travelers kept going, fearing that this waterless plain might prove very extensive. The watercourse with its subterranean stream of water was far behind them. Who knew when they would find the water that is so essential to man in this country!

From the summit of one of the granite hills, they noticed that ahead of them lay a line of something golden - apparently, the red soil came to an end there, and the grassy plain began again. This proved to be true, and shadows had only lengthened by half after the midday halt when the travelers were already marching over rustling grass, shorter than before, but much thicker. To one side of their road, they saw a huge green cloud that seemed to be floating in the air over the blue-green patch of its own shadow - the mighty "guest tree" was inviting them to rest in the shade of its branches. The guides turned toward the tree. The tired travelers hastened their steps, and soon the litters were standing in the shadow beside a tree-trunk, that was divided by longitudinal depressions into separate rounded ribs.

A number of the Kemtiues formed a living ladder up which others climbed to reach the huge branches of the tree. Shouts of triumph from above told the others that they had not been mistaken in their assumptions: the tree-trunk, some fifteen cubits in diameter, was hollow and contained water from the recent rains. The jars were filled with cool dark-colored water.

The Kemtiues threw down some of the fruits of the

tree, long fruits, as big as a man's head and tapering to a point at each end. Under its thin, hard skin, the fruit contained a floury yellow substance, sour-sweet in taste, that was very refreshing to the dry mouths of the travelers. Kidogo broke open two of the fruits, took out some small seeds, crushed and mixed them with a small quantity of water and started feeding Pandion with them.

To the joy of the Kemtiu the young Hellene ate with a good appetite and for the first time that day, raised his head in an effort to look round (during the march, when he lay on the litter, Pandion's face was usually kept covered with big leaves plucked from bushes near the water-holes). With an effort, Pandion stretched out his hands to Kidogo, and his weak fingers pressed the Kemtiu's hand. But there was something dull and pitiful in the young Hellene's eyes. Kidogo was very excited and asked his young friend how he felt, but got no answer. The wounded man's eyes again closed as though the feeble spark of returning life had tired him beyond all measure.

Kidogo left his friend in peace and hurried to tell Cavius the excellent news. Cavius, who had grown still more morose since the day of the awful battle, went over to the litter and sat down, peering into his friend's face. By placing his hand on Pandion's breast, he tried to judge the strength of his heartbeats.

While he was sitting by Pandion, one of the Nubians, who had climbed to the top of the tree to survey the surrounding land, let out a loud shout. He called out that far ahead of them, almost on the horizon, he could see the dark lines of fences of thorn-bushes such as the nomad herdsmen build to protect their cattle from predatory animals. It was decided, to spend the night under the tree and set out at dawn to reach the nomad encampment early in the day.

By sundown, the whole sky was overcast with heavy clouds; the starless night was unusually quiet and dark; the velvet darkness was so intense that they could not see a handheld before the face. Very soon zigzag shafts of lightning made a ring round the whole sky, and peals of thunder came rolling from afar. The lightning flashes grew in number, hundreds of fiery snakes twisted across the sky like the huge dry branches of some gigantic tree. The roar of the thunder deafened them, and the lightning blinded those who sought to leave their refuge. From a great distance came a noise that steadily increased to a fierce roar. This was an approaching wall of violent rain.

The tree shook as an entire ocean of water poured down from the heavens. The cascades of cool rain beat on the earth with an awful noise and a lake formed around the tree that hid its thick roots. In the light of the solid walls of fire that alternated with absolute darkness, it seemed that the whole plain would be flooded by the great mass of rainwater that kept pouring down on it. The flashes of lightning, however, soon stopped, the rain died down, and a starlit sky spread over the plain; a slight breeze brought with it the odors of grasses and flowers invisible in the darkness.

The Libyans and the Etruscan were dumbfounded at a storm which seemed like a terrible catastrophe to them, but the Kemtiues laughed gleefully, telling them that it was an ordinary shower, such as are common in the rainy season, and not a very heavy one at that. Cavius could only shake his head, telling himself that if such rains were considered ordinary in these parts, they were likely to meet with many strange adventures in the Land of the Black People. And he guessed right.

Next day the barking of dogs suddenly interrupted their journey. Long thorn hedges appeared through the mist, caused by the evaporation of the previous day's rainwater, and behind the hedges, they saw the low huts of the herdsmen. A crowd of men wearing leather aprons surrounded the travelers. Their high-cheek boned faces were inscrutable; their narrow eyes looked with suspicion at the Egyptian weapons carried by the former slaves. The symbol they had received from the Nubian, however, produced a most favorable impression. Out of the crowd stepped five men wearing black and white feathers, their hair dressed high on their heads and held in place by plaited twigs with green leaves.

The Nubians could understand the language of the nomads, and soon the newcomers were seated sipping sour milk within a close circle of listeners. The Nubian slaves told their story. Interrupting each other, they jumped up and down in their excitement and a chorus of exclamations of astonishment greeted their tale. The feather-bedecked chieftains merely slapped their thighs.

The nomads provided six guides and ten asses to help the strangers on their way. The guides were to take the travelers some seven days journey to the south-west to the big village of a settled tribe that stood on the banks of a river that always contained water. The litters were remade and fixed to four asses; the other animals carried water, sour milk, and hard cheese in sturdy leather bags. As the men now had no loads to carry, they could make longer journeys, covering no less than a hundred and twenty thousand cubits a day.

Day followed day. The endless plain lay under the broiling sun, at times silent and languid in the heat, at others swept by winds that made the grass billow like the waves of the sea.

The travelers penetrated farther and farther into the wild lands of the south where there were countless herds of savage beasts. Their unaccustomed eyes did not at first notice herds of animals that flashed by in the tall grass - only their backs could be seen above the grass. Sometimes their horns were short and curved, long and straight, or twisted into a spiral.

Later they learned to distinguish the different kinds - the long-antlered Oryx, the reddish bull antelope, heavy and short in the body, the hairy gnu, with its ugly humped nose, and the long-eared antelopes, no bigger than a small calf, that danced on their hind-legs under the trees. (The gerenuk or Waller's antelope - a long-necked animal that stands on its hind-legs to reach the leaves of the trees on which it feeds.)

Coarse, hard-stemmed grass, the height of a man, waved around them on all sides like a boundless field of corn. This expanse of grass turned golden in the sunlight. Patches of fresh green along the wadies and holes that were now filled with water broke up the sunlight.

The blue and purple spurs of mountains piled up beyond the horizon cut deep into the grassy plain. At times the trees grew close together, forming a darker island in the yellow grass, then again, they would be scattered far from each other like a flock of frightened birds. They were mostly the umbrella-shaped trees that had so astonished Cavius when he first made the acquaintance of the golden plain - their thorny trunks spread upwards and outwards from the roots to form a funnel so that they looked like inverted cones.

Some of the trees had thicker and shorter trunks that also divided into a considerable number of branches - the dense, dark foliage of these latter looked like green domes. The palms were visible from a great distance on account of their double, forked branches with the disheveled, knife-like feathery leaves bunched at the ends of them.

As the days passed, Cavius noticed that the Kemtiues and the Nubians who had been so clumsy and slow-witted in Tha-Quem and on the Great River had now become stronger, more resolute, and confident in themselves. And although his authority as leader was still undisputed, he began to lose confidence I himself in this strange land with laws of life that he could not understand. The Libyans, who had shown themselves so well in the desert, were helpless here. They were afraid of the grassy plain, inhabited by thousands of animals; they imagined countless dangers in the grass and thought they were threatened with unknowable calamities at every step.

It was indeed no easy road to travel. They came across growths of grass with heads containing millions of needle-like thorns (the thorny heads of arcanite grass) that penetrated the skin, causing great pain and suppuration. During the hottest hours of the day, many of the beasts of prey lay hidden under the trees. The lithe spotted body of a leopard would sometimes appear out of a patch of black shadow that looked like a cave amongst the brightly sunlit tufts of grass.

With astonishing agility, the Kemtiues stalked the red antelopes, and there was always an abundance of their succulent and tasty meat so that former slaves grew strong from the +nourishing food. When a herd of huge grey-black bulls (the African buffalo) with long horns curving downwards appeared in the distance, the Kemtiues sounded the alarm, and the whole party sought cover amongst the trees to escape the most terrible animal that inhabits the African plains.

The guides had apparently misjudged the distance: the travelers had been on their way for nine days, and there was still no sign of any human habitation. The Libyan's arm had healed. The Kemtiu with the broken leg had so far recovered as to sit up in his litter, and at night, he hopped and crawled around the fire to the delight of his companions who shared the joy of his convalescence. Only Pandion still lay silent and indifferent, although Kidogo and Cavius forced him to take more nourishment.

This being the period of the rains, the abundant life of the plains was at its peak. Millions of insects sang and hummed noisily in the grass; brightly hued birds flashed like blue, yellow, emerald-green, and black-velvet apparitions through the tangle of gnarled grey branches. The loud cries of diminutive bustards became more and more frequent in the heat of the day - "mac-har, mac-har," they cried.

For the first time in his life, Cavius saw the giants of Africa close at hand. Noiselessly and serenely the huge grey bulk of the elephants was frequently to be seen sailing over the grass, their leathery ears extended like sails in the direction of the travelers and the brilliant white of their tusks contrasting sharply with the snaky black trunks that waved above them. Cavius liked the look of the elephants, the calm wisdom of their behavior made them so different from the fussy antelopes, the malicious rhinoceroses and the lithesome beasts of prey that seemed like coiled springs.

On several occasions the men had an opportunity to observe the majestic beasts at rest: the herd stood closely packed in the shade of the trees. The huge old bull elephants bowed their domed heads, heavy with great tusks, while the cows, whose heads were flatter, held them high as they stood asleep.

Once they came across a lonely old bull. The giant was standing fast asleep in the sun. He had apparently dozed off in the shade, but the sun had moved on in its course and the old elephant, deep in slumber, did not feel the heat. Cavius stood still for some time admiring the mighty giant of the plains. The elephant stood like a statue, its hind-legs somewhat apart. The lowered trunk was coiled, the tiny eyes closed, and the thin tail hung over the sloping rump. The thickly curved tusks projected menacingly in front of him, their points far apart on either side.

In places where trees were scanty, they saw animals of strange shape. Their long legs carried short bodies with steeply sloping backs, the forelegs being much longer than the hinds. From their massive shoulders and broad chests stretched an extremely long neck, which sloped forward, surmounted by a very small head with short horns and tubular ears – giraffes that traveled in groups from five up to a hundred. A big herd of giraffes in the open plain was a sight never to be forgotten: it was as though a forest of trees, inclined in one direction by the strength of the wind, was moving from place to place in the bright sunlight, casting patches of weird shadow as it went.

The giraffes would move at times at a trot, at times they galloped with a peculiar gait, bending their forelegs under them, and stretching their hinds out far behind. The bright yellow network of fine lines on their skins, separated by big irregular black patches, was so much like the shadows cast by the trees that the animals were invisible under them.

Carefully they plucked leaves from the branches with their lips, eating their fill, without any show of greed, their big sensitive ears turning from side to side. A long line of their necks was frequently to be seen above the waving sea of tall grass-they moved slowly, their heads with their flashing black eyes held proudly at the height of ten cubits from the ground. The controlled movements of the giraffes were so beautiful that the harmless animals called forth involuntary admiration.

Through the thick wall of grass, the travelers sometimes heard the malicious snorts of a rhinoceros, but they had already learned how to avoid this shortsighted animal and the possibility of meeting the monster no longer filled the former slaves with fear.

The travelers marched in single file, treading in each other's footsteps, only their spears and the tops of their heads, shielded from the sun by rags and leaves, being visible above the grass on either side of the narrow lane. The monotonous grassy plain stretched away on all sides, seemingly endless. Grass and the burning sky followed the travelers by day, grass came to them in their dreams at night, and they began to feel that they were lost forever in that stifling, rustling, never ending vegetation.

Not until the tenth day, did they see ahead of them a ridge of rocks over which spread a bluish haze. Ascending the rocks, the travelers found themselves on a stony plateau overgrown with bushes and leafless trees whose branches stretched up towards the sky like outstretched arms. (Euphorbia candelabrum - a plant related to the European euphorbia but outwardly resembling a cactus.) Their trunks and branches were of the same venomous green color; the trees looked like round brushes, the bristles trimmed on top, placed on short poles. Growths of these trees gave off a sharp, acrid smell, their fragile branches were easily broken by the wind, and from the places where they snapped off, there flowed abundant sap like thick milk, that congealed quickly into long grey drops.

The guides hurried through these thickets since they believed that if the wind grew fresher, it might blow down these strange trees and crush anybody near them. The plain began again beyond the thickets, but this time it was the undulating country with fresh, green grass.

When the travelers reached the summit of a hill, they were unexpectedly confronted by broad expanses of tilled land stretching right up to a dense forest of high trees. In an opening deep in the forest a large group of conical huts occupied a low hill, surrounded by a massive stockade. Heavy gates built of irregular logs and decorated with garlands of lions' skulls hanging from the top, stared straight at the newcomers.

Tall, stern-looking warriors came out of the gates to meet the group of former slaves slowly climbing the hill. The local inhabitants resembled Nubians except that their skin was of a somewhat lighter bronze color. The warriors carried spears with huge heads like short swords and big shields decorated with a black and white ornament. War clubs of ebony, very hard and heavy, hung from their giraffe-hide girdles.

The view from the hilltop was very picturesque. Out of the golden grass of the plain rose the abundant emerald-green vegetation of the riverbanks between which flashed the blue ribbon of the river. Bushes surmounted by fluffy pink balls were vaguely trembling; bunches of yellow and white flowers hung down from the trees.

Preliminary talks between the natives and the newcomers lasted a long time. The Kemtiu with the broken leg, who had said he belonged to this people, served as interpreter. With the aid of a stick, he hobbled over to the warriors, making a sign to his companions to remain behind. Cavius, the Kemtiu with the broken leg, Kidogo, one of the Nubians and one of the nomad guides were allowed to enter the gates and were taken to the house of the chief. Those who remained without the gates waited with impatience, tormented by uncertainty. Only Pandion was motionless and apathetic as he lay on the litter that had been removed from the pack animals.

It seemed to them all that a long time had elapsed before the Etruscan reappeared in the gateway accompanied by a crowd of men, women, and children. The inhabitants of the village smiled in a welcoming manner, waving broad leaves, and speaking incomprehensible but friendly-sounding words. The gates were opened, and the former slaves passed between rows of big houses whose mud walls, built in the form of a circle, were surmounted by steep conical roofs thatched with coarse grass.

On an open space under two trees, stood an especially big house with the roof extending over the entrance. Here the chiefs had gathered to meet the newcomers. Almost all the inhabitants of the village crowded around them, excited by the unusual events of the day. At the request of the paramount chief, the Kemtiu with the broken leg again told the story of the terrible rhinoceros hunt, frequently pointing to Pandion who still lay motionless on his litter. With appropriate exclamations, the villagers expressed their delight, amazement, and horror at this unbelievable act performed by orders of the terrible Pharaoh of Tha-Quem.

The paramount chief rose and addressed his people in a language unknown to the newcomers. He was answered by shouts of approval. Then the chief walked over to the waiting travelers, waved his hand in a circle embracing the whole village and bowed his head. Through the interpreter, Cavius thanked the chief and his people for their hospitality.

That evening the newcomers were invited to a feast to be held in honor of their arrival. A crowd of villagers surrounded Pandion's litter. The men gazed at him with respect, the women with sympathy.

A girl in a blue mantle walked boldly out of the crowd and bent over the young Hellene. After his lengthy sojourn in the hot, sunny lands of Tha-Quem and Nub, Pandion differed from his companions only in the somewhat lighter shade of his skin that now had a golden tone. His hair, however, had grown long and its tangled and matted curls, together with the clear-cut features of his thin face, betrayed him as a foreigner.

The girl, moved by pity for the handsome, helpless young hero lying on the litter, cautiously stretched out her hand and pushed back a lock of hair that had fallen on Pandion's forehead. The heavy eyelids slowly opened showing eyes of a golden color, such as she had never before seen, and a slight shudder passed over the girl. The eyes of the stranger did not see her, his dull glance was fixed on the branches that waved above him.

"Iruma!" the girl's friends called to her.

Cavius and Kidogo came up, lifted the litter, and carried their wounded friend away, but the girl remained standing; with eyes lowered, she stood as motionless and impassive as the young Hellene who had attracted her attention.

CHAPTER SIX

The Road of Darkness

The tender care of Kidogo and Cavius had its effect, and Pandion's bones mended. His former strength, however, did not return to him. For days on end, he lay, apathetic and listless, in the gloom of the big hut. He answered his friends unwillingly and in monosyllables, and ate without appetite, making no effort to rise. He had grown skinny, his face with its deep-sunken, usually closed eyes, was overgrown with a soft beard.

The time had come to set out on the long road to the sea and home. Kidogo had long since questioned the local inhabitants about the way to the shores of the Southern Horn.

Of the thirty-nine former slaves, who had sought refuge in the village, twelve had gone off in various directions - they had formerly lived in this country and could reach their homes without any great difficulty or danger. Those who remained were urging Kidogo to start out. Now that they were all free and healthy, their distant homes called more strongly to them; every day of inactivity seemed like a crime to them. Since their return home depended on Kidogo, they worried him constantly with requests and reminders. Kidogo got out of the situation by making vague promises - he could not leave Pandion.

After these talks, the Kemtiu would sit for hours beside the bed of his friend, torn with doubts. When would there be a change in the sick man's condition? On Cavius' advice, Pandion was carried out of the house in the cool of the evening. Even this did not bring any noticeable improvement. The only times Pandion brightened up was when it rained. The rolling of the thunder and the roaring downpour of rain made the sick man raise himself on to his elbow and listen, as though in these sounds he heard some call unheard by the others. Cavius called in two local medicine men. They burnt grass with an acrid smoke over the patient, buried a pot with some roots in it in the earth, but still, his condition did not improve.

One evening when Pandion was lying near the hut and Cavius was sitting beside him, lazily keeping off the buzzing flies with a leafy branch, a girl in a blue mantle came up to them. This was Iruma, the daughter of the best hunter in the village. The girl whose attention Pandion had attracted the day the travelers arrived. From under her mantle, the girl extended a slender arm on which the bracelets rattled; in her hand, she held a small bag of plaited grass. Iruma offered the bag to Cavius.

By this time, the Etruscan had learned a few words of the local language. He tried to explain to him that these were magic nuts from the western forests and would cure the sick man. She tried to explain to him how to prepare medicine from them, but Cavius could not understand her. Iruma hung her head in perplexity but immediately brightened up again, told Cavius to give her a flat stone that was used for crushing corn, and to bring her a cup of water. Cavius entered the house, and she looked round in all directions, then dropped to her knees at the sick man's head and peered intently into his face. She laid her tiny hand on Pandion's forehead but hearing Cavius' heavy tread she hurriedly withdrew it.

She tipped some small nuts, something like chestnuts, out of the bag, broke them and crushed the kernels on the stone, rubbing them into a sort of thin porridge that she mixed with some milk that Kidogo had at that moment brought. As soon as the Kemtiu saw the nuts, he gave a mighty yell and began to dance round Cavius in joy.

Kidogo explained to the astonished Cavius that in the western forests and in the forests of his country there is a tree with a straight trunk whose branches grow shorter towards the top so that it looks pointed. These trees bear large numbers of nuts that have incredible healing properties. They give new strength to the exhausted, banish fatigue and bring joy and happiness to the healthy. (Cola nuts, now known the world over for their medicinal properties).

The girl fed Pandion with the porridge made from the magic nuts and then all three of them sat down by his bedside and began patiently awaiting results.

After a few minutes had passed Pandion's feeble breathing became stronger and more regular, the skin on his hollow cheeks took on a rosy hue. All the moroseness suddenly left the Etruscan. As though under a spell, he sat watching the effect of the mysterious medicine. Pandion heaved a deep sigh, opened his eyes widely and sat up. His sun-colored eyes wandered from Cavius to Kidogo and then remained fixed on the girl. Pandion stared in amazement at a face the color of dark bronze with an astonishingly smooth skin that seemed very much alive.

Between the inner corners of her long, slightly slanting eyes, faint wrinkles, full of mischief, ran across the bridge of her nose. The whites of her eyes showed clear and bright through half-closed lids; the nostrils of her broad but well-formed nose twitched nervously, and her thick, vivid lips opened in a sincere but bashful smile, that revealed a row of strong, pearly teeth. The whole of her round face was so filled with boldness and at the same time gentle mischief, with the joyous play of youthful life, that Pandion could not help but smile. And his golden eyes, till then dull and apathetic, flashed and sparkled. Iruma lowered her eyes in confusion and turned away.

The astounded friends were beside themselves with delight - for the first time since that fatal day of the battle, Pandion had smiled. The magic effect of the wonderful nuts was beyond all shadow of a doubt. Pandion sat up and asked his friends about everything that had happened since the day he was injured, interrupting them with rapid questions, like those of a man in a state of inebriation.

Iruma went hurriedly away, promising to make inquiries concerning the progress of the patient that evening. Pandion ate a lot and consumed with great satisfaction, all the time interrogating his comrades. By evening, however, the effect of the medicine had worn off, and he was again overcome by drowsy apathy.

Pandion lay inside the house, and the Etruscan and Kidogo were discussing whether or not to give him another portion of the nuts but before doing so decided to ask Iruma. The girl came, accompanied by her father, a tall athlete with scars on his shoulders and chest where he had been slashed by a lion's claws. Father and daughter talked together for a long time. Several times the hunter waved his daughter disdainfully aside, shaking his head angrily; then he laughed noisily and slapped her on the back. Iruma shrugged her shoulders in annoyance and approached the two friends.

"My father says that he must not be given too many nuts," she explained to the Kemtiu, apparently regarding him as the sick man's closest friend. "You must give him the nuts once at midday to make him eat well."

Kidogo answered that he knew the effect of the nuts and would do as she told him. The girl's father looked at the sick man, shook his head and said something to his daughter that neither Cavius nor Kidogo could understand.

Iruma immediately changed into something like an infuriated cat - so brightly did her eyes flash; her upper lip curled, showing a row of white teeth. The hunter gave her a kindly smile, waved his hand, and went out of the house.

The girl bent over Pandion and looked for a long time into his face, then, seeming to remember herself, also hurried towards the door.

"Tomorrow I'll treat him myself according to the customs of our people," she announced decisively as she stood in the doorway. "There's a way that the women of our tribe have long used to heal the sick and the wounded. The spirit of joy has left your friend - without it, no man wants to live. That spirit must be returned to him!"

Kidogo thought over the girl's words and decided that she was right. After all the suffering he had experienced Pandion had lost his interest in life. Something had given way inside him. Nevertheless, Kidogo could not imagine what sort of treatment the girl was talking about no matter how hard he tried, so he lay down to sleep without having thought of anything.

Next day Kidogo again fed the nuts to Pandion. The latter sat up, talked and, to the joy of his friends, ate with a good appetite. He kept looking from side to side. At last he asked about the girl of yesterday. Kidogo pulled a grimace of pleasure, winked at Cavius, and warned Pandion that on that evening the girl would give him a treatment of a kind unknown to anybody. Pandion was at first interested, then, apparently when the effect of the nuts began to wear off, again fell into his usual apathy.

Still, Kidogo and Cavius were of the opinion that their friend's appearance had greatly improved during those last two days. Their young friend tossed about more on his bed, and his breathing was stronger.

No sooner had the sun sunk in the west than the village was, as usual, filled with the acrid smell of burning brushwood and the monotonous thud of heavy pestles in large mortars in which the women crushed millet for the evening meal. Black porridge from this millet, eaten with milk and butter, was the staple food of the villagers. The short twilight turned rapidly into night.

Suddenly the dull rumble of a tom-tom swept across the village. A noisy crowd of young people approached the house of the three friends. In front of the crowd were four girls bearing torches and surrounding two bent old crones in full dark cloaks. Young men took up the sick Pandion and, accompanied by the deafening shouts of the crowd, carried him to the other side of the village, close to the cleared edge of the forest. Cavius and Kidogo followed the crowd, the former looking from side to side in disapproval as though he wished to say that nothing good was to be expected of the performance.

Pandion was carried into a big empty house. It was no less than thirty cubits across. There they laid him down beside the center pole with his back to the wide door. Some torches made of tinder wood soaked in palm oil and fastened to the pole threw a circle of bright light over the center of the house. The walls under the low eaves were hidden in darkness.

The house was full of women, young and old; they sat along the walls talking in rapid tones. Some dark liquid that an old woman gave Pandion to drink immediately cheered him up. A sharp trembling sound came from a hollow elephant tusk - silence fell on the house, and all the men hurriedly left.

The Etruscan and Kidogo tried to hang back but were unceremoniously thrust out into the darkness. A group of ugly old hags stood around the entrance screening the proceedings from the eyes of the curious. Cavius sat down near the house, determined not to go away until the end of the mysterious rites. Kidogo, who bared his teeth in a smile, joined him. He had faith in the methods of treatment used by the peoples of the south.

Two girls carefully lifted the sick man and sat him with his back propped up against the center pole. Pandion looked around in astonishment, seeing everywhere in the semi-darkness the whites of the eyes and the teeth of smiling women.

Inside, the house was hung with festoons of some aromatic plant. Wide garlands hang around the inner cornice of the roof, and thin branches of the same bush were wound around the pole against which Pandion had been placed. The branches filled the whole house with a sharp, invigorating aroma that worried and alarmed Pandion, reminding him of something infinitely close and alluring, and at the same time irretrievably forgotten.

Several women took up their places immediately in

front of the Hellene. The curved lines of two trumpets made of hollow elephant's tusks shone white in the light of the torches, beside them were fat-bellied tom-toms made of hollowed tree-trunks. Again, the trembling note of the horn sounded. The old women placed before Pandion the wooden statuette of a woman crudely carved in strong lines and worn black with time.

Women's high-pitched voices started a soft song. They poured forth slow modulations of guttural sounds and sorrowful sighs, growing faster and louder, expanding, and rising higher and higher in an impulsive rush. Suddenly a heavy and resonant stroke on the drum made Pandion give an involuntary shudder. The song ceased, at the edge of the circle of light a girl in a blue mantle appeared, a girl with whom Pandion was already acquainted.

She stepped into the circle of torchlight and stopped hesitantly. Again, the horn sounded, and several of the old women added their howls to its furious moans. The girl threw off her mantle and stood there naked except for a girdle of branches from the same aromatic bush.

The light from the torches flickered dully on her shining dark bronze skin. Iruma's eyes had been heavily made up with blue-black paint; polished copper bangles shone on her arms and legs; her tightly curling hair tumbled on to her smooth shoulders.

The tom-toms rumbled dully and rhythmically. In time with the drums the girl, stepping softly on bare feet, drew near to Pandion and with lithe, animal-like movements bowed before the statuette of the unknown goddess, stretching out her hands before her in exhausting and passionate anticipation.

In admiration, Pandion followed Iruma's every

movement. There was no trace of mischief left on the girl's face - serious, stern, her brows raised in a frown, she seemed to be listening to the voice of her own heart. She would relax and then stretch herself to full height, throwing out her arms and standing on the tips of her toes as though every particle of her body were striving upwards. Pandion had never seen anything like it.

The mysterious life of her hands merged with the bursts of soulful inspiration on her upturned face. The ivory horns trumpeted feverishly. A sudden rattling blow stopped Pandion's breath - sheets of copper, beaten one against the other, rattled and rumbled victoriously, joyfully, drowning the broken rhythm of the tom-toms.

The girl threw herself backward in a sharp, gleaming curve. Then her tiny feet began to move over the smoothly beaten floor; the dancer traveled round the circle shyly and hesitantly in her bashful confusion.

In the light of the torches, the girl seemed cast from some dark metal. Drawing back into the darkness, she moved there like a light, almost invisible shadow.

The troubled rattle of the drums grew faster and faster, the copper sheets clattered wildly, and the slow dance became more and more impetuous, following the furious dictates of the music. Strong, slim legs moved in time with the shattering bass notes of the copper sheets, twined together, stopped dead still and again slid along scarcely touching the floor. The shoulders and high bosom remained motionless, and Iruma's tensed arms stretched out towards the idol of the goddess, curved slowly and gracefully in supplication.

The persistent rumble of the drums broke off, the rattle

of copper sheets ceased, and only the occasional sorrowful moans of the horns and the tinkling of Iruma's bracelets and anklets broke the silence that ensued.

The strange movement of the muscles under the girl's skin fascinated Pandion. They did not protrude anywhere, they streamed and undulated like the water on the surface of a river and the lines of Iruma's body flashed before Pandion's eyes in constant, never repeated mutation in which there was the smooth rhythm of the sea and the gusty winds of the golden plain.

The supplication that had filled the girl's every movement at the beginning of the dance had now given place to a compelling urge. It seemed to Pandion that the fire of life itself was flowing before him in the bronze reflection of light and the thunder of the music.

A craving for life flashed up again in the young Hellene's breast, former dreams and desires returned, a wide and mysterious world opened up before him. The horns stopped blowing. The low, threatening rumble of the tom-toms merged with the piercing shrieks of the women. The copper sheets rattled like close thunder; then all of them stopped suddenly. Pandion could hear the beating of his own heart.

The girl plunged forward, then suddenly stopped, dropping her arms helplessly down her sides, trembling and exhausted. Her knees bent under her, the gleam went out of her eyes. Iruma cried out sadly and collapsed before the statuette of the goddess. She lay motionless where she had fallen, only her bosom heaving with her rapid breathing. The tempestuous dance had broken off on a note of sadness, and the astounded Pandion shuddered.

The roar of triumphant voices filled the house. Four

women, whispering incomprehensible words, lifted Iruma and carried her out of the circle of light. The ancient wooden statuette was immediately taken away. The women rose to their feet, all excited, their eyes blazing. They talked loudly amongst themselves, pointing to the stranger.

The old women, guarding the door, made way for Kidogo and Cavius to enter; they rushed to their friend with questions. Pandion, however, could not and did not want to talk. The two friends took him home, and he lay for a long time without sleep under the influence of that unusual dance.

Pandion began to recover. His young body regained its former strength with astonishing rapidity. Three days later he went without anybody's help to the house of the hunter - he wanted to see Iruma. The girl was not at home, but her father received the guest in a friendly and tender manner, gave him a good beer to drink and tried to explain something to him, gesticulating and slapping him on the shoulders and chest. The young Hellene did not understand anything and left the hunter's house with a vague feeling of chagrin.

Pandion's rebirth had not been completed: he was free and convalescent, but the spiritual inhibition had not left him. He realized that the trials and tribulations that had fallen to his lot had somehow shattered him. The terrific shake-up he had received during the tussle with the rhinoceros had proved more than he could stand. He had weakened and for a long time did not return to normality. But he must recover, he must be capable of further struggle on the road home. He made a tremendous effort and began gymnastic exercises to be the equal of his comrades as he formerly was.

Kidogo and Cavius were now quite satisfied with Pandion's recovery. Together with all the other former slaves and most of the local people, they set out on a long hunt to round up giraffes, hoping that this would give them an opportunity to find out something about the road they were to travel and at the same time obtain more meat for their hospitable hosts.

To the amusement and good-natured jokes of his neighbors, Pandion, to strengthen his muscles, took to crushing grain for beer making, despite the sneers of the men who regarded it as women's work. Soon Pandion began to leave the confines of the village, taking with him a thin Egyptian spear. Out in the fields, he practiced running and throwing the spear, feeling that every day his muscles were hardening and that his powerful legs were once more carrying his body with their former ease.

At the same time, he made a strenuous effort to study the native language, never for a moment forgetting Iruma. Time and again, he repeated the unfamiliar but melodious words. His excellent memory helped him, and in a week, he was able to understand what was said to him. Pandion had not seen Iruma for a fortnight but did not venture to visit her in her father's absence, as he did not know the customs of these people.

One day, when he was on his way back from the fields, Pandion saw a figure in a blue mantle and his heart began to beat faster. He quickened his steps, overtook the girl, and stood before her, smiling joyfully. He had made no mistake. It was Iruma. His first glance at the girl's face excited Pandion. Uttering with difficulty words to which his tongue was not accustomed, Pandion started to thank the confused Iruma.

Pandion's stock of words soon ran out, and he continued in his own language, and then realized that he was not understood. He looked embarrassed at the girl's colored headdress that just reached his shoulder. Iruma looked sideways at him with mischievous eyes and suddenly laughed. Pandion smiled too, and then carefully pronounced a phrase that he had long since learned.

"May I come to see you?"

"Come," answered the girl simply, "tomorrow to the edge of the forest, when the sun is behind the trees."

Pandion was overjoyed, but he did not know what else to say to her; he merely held out both hands to Iruma. The blue mantle flew open, and two tiny strong hands lay trustfully in Pandion's palms. He pressed them firmly but tenderly.

At that moment, he was not thinking of his distant Thessa. The girl's hands trembled, her wide nostrils were dilated; with a gentle but firm movement she freed herself, covered her face with her mantle and strode swiftly away, down the slope of the hill. Pandion realized that he must not follow her and remained standing where he was, watching the girl until she disappeared behind the houses. Smiling for no apparent reason, Pandion walked down the street, jauntily swinging his spear.

For the first time, Pandion noticed that the village was situated in a very picturesque spot; the houses were big and convenient, the streets wide. Without realizing it Pandion compared the people here with the poorer inhabitants he had seen in the Land of Nub and with the poor people of Tha-Quem, the Chosen People of the Gods, on whose faces moroseness and indifference had left their stamp. There was something debased in bodies that had become exhausted with heavy toil and constant undernourishment. The people here were different; they walked with a light and easy freedom, even the old people retained their graceful bearing.

Pandion's observations were interrupted by the appearance of a young man, muscular and broad-shouldered, wearing a cap of leopard's skin. He looked at the foreigner in an unfriendly manner, stretched out his hand with an imperious gesture and touched Pandion's breast. Pandion stopped short in amazement, and the young man stood still in front of him, his hand dropped to his belt, in which he carried a broad knife, and took stock of the stranger with a challenging glance.

"I've noticed that you're a good runner," he said at last. "Will you compete with me? I am Fulbo, known as the Leopard," he added as though the name would explain everything to Pandion.

Pandion answered him with a friendly smile and said that he had once been able to run much better and had not yet been able to reach his former standard on account of his illness. In response to this, Fulbo showered him with malicious taunts that made the young Hellene's blood boil. Pandion did not know any reason for the young man's hating him and, with his arms akimbo as a mark of disdain, agreed to the contest. The opponents agreed that the race would take place that evening when it became cooler.

All the young people and a few of the elder ones gathered at the foot of the hill, on which the village stood, to watch the contest between Fulbo and the foreigner. Fulbo pointed to a tree that stood alone in the distance; it was no less than ten thousand cubits from where they stood. The one who first ran to the tree, plucked a branch, and returned with it would be considered the victor.

The signal to start was given by a handclap, and Pandion and Fulbo started out. Fulbo, trembling with impatience, immediately sprang forward in a series of long bounds. The youngster seemed to spread himself out and fly over the ground. The youths present encouraged him with shouts of approval. Pandion had not fully recovered and realized that there was a danger of his being beaten. Still, he was determined not to give way.

He set out to run as his grandfather had taught him in the cool hours of the morning on the narrow strip of the seashore, near their home. He ran on, swaying slightly, making no sudden spurts, and carefully reserving his breath.

Fulbo was soon far ahead, but the young Hellene moved at a regular pace, making no effort to overtake his opponent. His chest gradually expanded, taking in greater quantities of air; his legs pumped faster and the spectators, who had at first been sorry for the stranger, now saw that the distance between him and Fulbo was decreasing. The African looked around, let out a shout of anger and ran still faster. He reached the tree four hundred cubits ahead of Pandion, leaped high into the air, snatched off a branch and immediately turned back.

Pandion passed him near the tree and as he passed, noticed Fulbo's stertorous breathing. Although Pandion's own heart was beating faster than it should, he decided that he could count on victory over his far too hotheaded opponent, who knew little of the rules of running.

Pandion continued to run with his former restraint and only increased his speed when a distance of no more than three thousand cubits was left between him and the spectators. He soon overtook Fulbo but the latter, gasping in huge quantities of air through his wide-open mouth, again leaped forward leaving the Hellene behind. Pandion did not give up. Although there were dark patches before his eyes and his heart beat faster than ever, he again drew ahead of his opponent.

Fulbo was now running wildly, seeing nothing before him; unable to choose his road, he fell. Pandion ran on a few cubits, stopped, and turned back to his fallen opponent to help him to rise. Fulbo pushed him angrily aside, staggered to his feet, looked Pandion straight in the face, and spoke with great difficulty:

"You-won-but-look-out!... Iruma..."

In an instant, Pandion understood everything, and his feeling of triumph at his victory mingled with an uncomfortable feeling of having insinuated himself into something that was not his, and that was forbidden him.

Fulbo walked heavily away, his head hanging morosely, making no effort to run. Pandion returned leisurely to the finish and was greeted by the spectators. But the feeling of awkwardness did not leave him. As soon as Pandion found himself alone in his empty house, he began to long for Iruma. The meeting appointed for the next day seemed very far away.

The hunters returned that evening. Pandion's companions came home tired, loaded with the spoils of the chase and full of their adventures.

Cavius and Kidogo were overjoyed at finding Pandion quite well. Jokingly, Kidogo suggested wrestling with the Hellene, and soon they were lolling in the dust, their bodies firmly locked in each other's iron grip, while Cavius kicked and cursed them to get them apart. The friends took part in the general feasting that had been arranged in honor of the returning hunters. The warriors, intoxicated with beer, tried to outdo each other in boasting of their exploits. Pandion sat apart from his companions, his eyes fixed on the glade in which the young people were dancing, striving to get a glimpse of Iruma in the procession of dancing youths and girls.

One of the chiefs, swaying slightly, rose to his feet to make a speech of congratulation, accompanying it with graceful gesticulations. Pandion could only catch the general sense of what he was saying. He praised the newcomers and regretted their early departure. The chief proposed that they stay and be accepted into the tribe. The feast ended late at night when the hunters had eaten their fill of the tender young giraffe meat, and the supplies of beer had given out.

On the way home, Kidogo announced that the former slaves, of whom twenty-seven were left, would the next day hold a conference on their future plans. Kidogo had found an opportunity to talk to nomad hunters he had met in the forest. They were well acquainted with the region to the west of the village and told him which route to take. A great distance separated them from the sea and Kidogo's home, but he now knew that even if they traveled slowly, they would get there in three months. What could hinder them now, experienced as they were in battle, and secure in their friendship? Each of the twenty-seven was worth five warriors! The Kemtiu threw back his shoulders proudly and lifted his tipsy face to the stars; he threw his arms round Pandion and added:

"Now my heart is quiet. You are well - we must go! To

the road tomorrow, if you like!"

Pandion did not answer. For the first time, he felt that his desires did not coincide with the aspirations of his comrades, but did not know how to be hypocritical.

Since his meeting with Iruma that day, he realized that the sorrow that was eating away at his heart was due to his love for her. The girl in the full bloom of her youthful beauty had come into his life immediately after the cruel years of slavery when he stood on the threshold of liberty! Was this then not enough for him who had but recently lain in a dark hole of a prison, clinging to the faintest hope of liberation? What more could he want, in the world and in life, when love called on him so imperatively to remain in that place, in the midst of the golden plain?

The secret urge, which he tried to hide even from himself, to stay forever with Iruma, grew stronger in his heart of hearts. He struggled against himself to test his love for her. The trustfulness of youth led him unnoticeably into the land of dreams where everything was so easy and straightforward.

The next day he would see Iruma and would tell her everything. And she... she loved him too!

The former slaves had arranged to meet at the opposite end of the village, where most of them lived in two big houses. Cavius, Kidogo, and Pandion occupied a small separate house that had been allotted to them because of Pandion's illness. Pandion, who had been sitting in the house sharpening a spear, got up and went to the door.

"Where are you going?" asked the astonished Etruscan. "Aren't you coming to the conference?"

"I'll come later," answered Pandion, turning away and hurriedly leaving the house.

Cavius looked keenly after the departing Hellene and turned in perplexity to Kidogo, who was sitting near the door working hard on a piece of thick hide he was making into a shield.

Pandion had not told his friends that Iruma was waiting for him at the forest edge. He realized that the return of his friends meant a threat to his newfound love but had not had strength enough to forego the meeting with Iruma. His justification was that he would know the result of the conference from his friends even if he were not present himself.

As he approached the forest, Pandion searched with his eyes for Iruma; the smiling girl suddenly detached herself from the trunk of a tree and stood before him. She had put on her father's hunting cloak of soft, grey bark that made her invisible against the background of the trees. The girl made a sign to Pandion to follow her and walked off along the edge of the forest to a place where the trees jutted out into the fields in a semicircle about three thousand cubits from the village. There she passed under the trees.

This was Pandion's first time in an African forest, so he looked about in curiosity. He had expected it to be very different. The forest stretched in a narrow strip along the valley of the river that flowed around the village and was no more than two thousand cubits in width. It consisted of high trees that met overhead in a huge vault forming a dark gallery over the eternal twilight of the riverbed.

Deeper in the forest the trees were taller, and on the steep bank of the river, they bent downwards so that their branches intertwined overhead. The straight, graceful trunks with white, black, and brown bark stretched upwards for a good hundred cubits, like the colonnade of some huge building. The branches were so intertwined in a thick leafy vault that the sun could not penetrate through them.

The grey twilight streamed down from above and was lost in the deep hollows between strange roots that rose up like walls.

The silence, broken by nothing but the faint gurgling of water, the semi-darkness and the great height of the forest colonnade gave Pandion a feeling of oppression. He seemed like an uninvited guest who had insinuated himself into the forbidden heart of a strange nature that was full of secrets.

Over the water, there were narrow gaps in the foliage through which a perfect cascade of golden fire poured down. The golden sunlight clothed the trees in a hazy brilliance and was split up into vertical strips of light that gradually diminished deeper in the forest. The dark, mysterious temples of Aigyptos came to Pandion's mind. Strings of creeping plants hung in free loops between the trees or hung down loosely forming a wavy curtain.

The ground was covered with fallen leaves, rotten fruits, and branches. It was soft and fluffy to the feet, and here and there, brightly-colored flowers gleamed like stars. Long strips of rustling bark hung from the tree-trunks like skin torn from the body. Huge butterflies fluttered noiselessly over the earth; the marvelous color combinations of their trembling wings - bright velvet black, metallic blue, red, gold and silver - filled Pandion with amazement.

Iruma led the way confidently between the roots towards the river, and brought Pandion to a level piece of ground, right beside the water, covered with a soft carpet of fluffy moss.

Here stood a tree that had been blasted by lightning. In the gaping split in the hard, yellow wood, Pandion could see the outlines of a crudely carved human figure.

The tree was apparently an object of worship - colored rags and the teeth of wild beasts were hung all around it. Three blackened elephant's tusks were stuck in the ground in front of it. Iruma, her head bowed in reverence, approached the tree, and motioned to Pandion to do the same.

"This is the ancestor of our tribe, born of a thunderbolt," said the girl softly. "Give him something so that the ancients will be kind to us."

Pandion looked himself over - he had nothing that he could give to that crude god, the alleged ancestor of Iruma. The smiling youth spread his hands to show that he had nothing, but the girl was implacable.

"Give him this." She touched a belt of plaited giraffe tails that Kidogo had just made for him as a memento of the hunt.

The youth obediently unfastened the strip of leather and gave it to the girl. Iruma threw off her cloak. She was without bracelets and necklace and wore nothing but a wide leather belt that dropped down over her left hip. The girl rose up on tiptoe, reaching up to the splintered wood at the head of the idol where she hung Pandion's tribute. Lower down Iruma fastened a piece of brightly colored leopard skin and a string of dark red berries that looked like beads. She sprinkled some millet at the foot of the idol and stepped back, satisfied.

Leaning back against the trunk of a low tree festooned with hundreds of flowers amongst its leaves, (The tulip tree from the family of Bignoniaceae.) she looked fixedly at Pandion. Hundreds of red lamps seemed to be burning over the girl's head, while the sun's rays played on the bronze of her skin. Pandion stood looking at the girl in silent admiration. Her beauty seemed sacred to him in the silence of that forest of giant trees - the temple of unknown gods, so utterly different from the joyous divinities of his own land. A bright, calm joy suddenly filled Pandion's heart. He was once more the artist, and his former strivings were reawakened within him.

Suddenly an extraordinarily clear vision arose in his memory. Far away, in his distant homeland, to the noise of the sea and the pines, Thessa had stood like this in those far-off days that were never to come again. Iruma placed her hands behind her head, bent slightly from the waist and sighed. Pandion was overwhelmed - Iruma had adopted precisely the pose like that in which he had tried to depict Thessa.

The whole past rose before Pandion's eyes. With even greater strength, he felt the urge to return to Oeniadae; to the road, forward to new battles, away from Iruma! Pandion was tormented by desires that had formerly been so clear but now doubt filled his mind. He discovered contradictions in himself that he had never before known, and they frightened him. Here he felt the call of life - hot like the sun of Africa, youthful like the flowering plains after the rain, powerful like a swollen stream – the power of life. Far away there, in his homeland, were his brightest dreams of great creative art. However, was not beauty itself standing before him, close and joyous? So different were Iruma and Thessa; they were in no way alike, yet in both of them there was a real beauty.

Pandion's alarm was transmitted to the girl. She drew

near to him, and the melodious tones of a strange language broke the silence.

"You are ours, Golden Eyes, I have danced the dance of the great goddess, and our ancestor has accepted your gifts." Iruma's voice broke off, her long lashes covered her eyes.

The girl threw her arms round Pandion's neck and pressed tightly to him. Everything went dark before his eyes. With a desperate effort, he broke out of the girl's embrace. She raised her head. Her mouth was childishly half-open.

"Don't you want to live here? Are you going away with your companions?" asked Iruma in astonishment, and Pandion felt ashamed.

Pandion gently drew the girl towards him and, trying to find suitable words from amongst those of the language of her people that he knew, he told her of his great nostalgic longing for his own country; he talked to her about Thessa.

Iruma turned her head upwards to Pandion's broad chest, her eyes peered into the golden gleam of his eyes, her teeth were bared in a feeble smile. Iruma began to speak, and in the sound of her words, there was that same tenderness, that same caressing love that had intoxicated Pandion when Thessa spoke to him.

"Yes," she said. "If you cannot live here, you must go away." The girl stammered the last words. "But if my people and I seem good to you, stay with us, Golden Eyes. Think, decide, come to me... I shall wait."

The girl straightened up, holding her head proudly. Pandion had seen her similarly serious and severe at the time of the dance. For a whole minute, the young Hellene stood before her; then, making a sudden decision, he held out his hands to the girl. But she was gone beyond the trees, melting into the gloom of the thicket.

Iruma's disappearance struck Pandion like a substantial loss. He stood for a long time in that gloomy forest and then wandered slowly across the golden haze of the glade, going he knew not where, struggling against the desire to run after Iruma, to tell her that he loved her and would stay with her.

Iruma, as soon as she had hidden behind the trees from Pandion's eyes, began to run, jumping lightly over the roots and slipping between the lianas. She went on faster until she became exhausted. Breathing heavily, she stopped on the edge of a calm pond, a silent backwater of the river, which grew much broader here. The bright light blinded her, and her body felt the heat after the darkness and coolness of the forest.

Iruma looked round her sorrowfully, and through her tears, she saw her reflection in the smooth surface of the water; almost involuntarily, she examined her whole self in that mirror. Yes, she was beautiful! But, apparently, beauty was not all if the stranger, Golden Eyes, brave, kind and tender, wanted to leave her. Apparently, something else was needed. But what?

The sun set behind the undulating plain. A blue, slanting shadow lay at the threshold of the house before which Kidogo and Cavius were sitting. The way the two friends were fidgeting, told Pandion they had been waiting for him for a long time. With downcast eyes, Pandion walked up to his two friends. Cavius got up, solemn and stern, and placed his hand on Pandion's shoulder.

"We want to talk to you, he and I." The Etruscan nodded towards Kidogo, who was standing beside them. "You did not attend our council, but everything's been decided - we set out tomorrow."

Pandion staggered back. Too much had been happening in the course of the last three days. Still, he did not think that his comrades would be in such a hurry. He would have hurried just as much himself if not... if not for Iruma! Pandion read condemnation in the looks of his friends. He was now faced with the necessity of coming to a decision, an obligation that had long been tormenting his soul and which he had unconsciously evaded in the naive hope that everything would come right of itself. It was as though a wall cut him off again from that world of liberty, which in actual fact, existed only in Pandion's dreams.

He had to decide whether he would stay there with Iruma or go away with his companions and lose her forever. If he stayed there, it would be forever, too. Only by the combined efforts of twenty-seven men prepared to face anything, even certain death, for the sake of returning to their own homes, would it be possible to cover the distance that held them, prisoners.

If he stayed, therefore, he would forever lose his native land, the sea, Thessa - everything that had succored him and helped him get to that land. Would he be able to live there, submerge himself in that friendly but strange life when his comrades were no longer with him, comrades who had been tested in times of peril and on whose friendship, he had unwittingly become accustomed to depending on at all times?

After long contemplation, Pandion's heart told him the right answer. Would it not, moreover, be treachery to leave those friends who had saved him and thanks to whom, he was well again? No, he must go with them and leave half his heart behind him in this foreign land!

Pandion's will was not strong enough to withstand this trial. He seized the hands of his comrades, who were watching with alarm the mental struggle that was reflected in his face, and began to beseech them not to leave so soon. What did it matter, now that they were free, if they remained there a little longer, rested before undertaking a long journey and got a better knowledge of the country?

Kidogo hesitated, for he was very fond of Pandion. But Cavius frowned still more sternly.

"Come inside, there are other eyes and ears here," he said, pushing Pandion into their house; he went out and returned with a burning brand and lit a small torch. He thought it would be easier to cure Pandion of his indecision if it were light.

"What do you hope for if we stay here?" asked the Etruscan in stern tones, his words cutting right into Pandion's heart. "Especially if you intend to go in the end. Or do you want to take her with you?"

The thought that Iruma should go with them on their long journey had not entered Pandion's mind, and he shook his head.

"Then I don't understand you," said Cavius brusquely. "Do you think that none of the others have found girls here that they like? Still, none of them wavered at the conference when they had to choose between a woman and their native land; not a soul thought of staying here. Iruma's father, the hunter, thinks that you are not coming with us. He likes you, and your bravery is common knowledge amongst the people. He said that he is ready to take you into his house! Surely you will not leave us and forget your own country for the sake of a girl?"

Pandion lowered his head. He could not explain to Cavius why he was wrong. How could Pandion tell him that he had not merely given way to passion? How could he explain how Iruma had affected him as an artist? On the other hand, the brutal truth of the Etruscan's words stung him; he had forgotten that other peoples have different laws and customs. If he remained there, he would have to become a hunter and merge his life with the life of the people. Such was the inevitable price he would have to pay for happiness with Iruma. Then again, Iruma alone was all that was near to him in this land. The calm, hot expanses of the golden plain bore no resemblance to his own country, to the noisy and mobile vastness of the sea, and the girl was a part of that world, while he had not yet ceased to feel himself a temporary guest there.

There, far in the distance, his native land shone like a beacon light. If that light went out, would he be able to live without it?

Cavius made a long pause to give Pandion an opportunity to think, and then began again:

"You will become her husband only to leave her shortly afterward and go away. Do you think her people will let us go in peace and help us? You will be paying them poorly for their hospitality. The punishment that you fully deserve will fall on all of us. Why are you so certain that the others of your party are willing to wait? They will not agree, and I am with them!"

Cavius stopped and then, as though a little ashamed at the brusqueness of his words, added:

"My heart aches, for when I reach the sea, I shall not have a friend who is skilled in the sailing of ships. My Remdus is dead, and all my hopes rested on you - you have sailed the sea, you learned from the Phoenicians."

Cavius lowered his head and sat silent. Kidogo ran over to Pandion and hung a bag on a long leather thong around his neck.

"I looked after that for you while you were ill," said the Kemtiu. "It's your sea amulet. It helped you defeat the rhinoceros, so it will help us find our way to the sea if you come with us."

Pandion remembered the stone that Yakhmos had given him. Until that moment, he had forgotten that gleaming symbol of the sea entirely in the same way as he had forgotten many other things. He heaved a deep sigh. At that moment, a tall man with a long spear in his hand entered the house. It was the father of Iruma. He sat down on the floor with natural ease, tucked his legs up under him, and gave Pandion a friendly smile.

"I've come to you on an important matter," he said, turning to Cavius. "You told us that you have decided to leave for your own country one sun from today."

Cavius nodded his head in affirmation but did not speak, waiting for what was to come next. Pandion looked with disturbed feelings at Iruma's father, who behaved with simple dignity.

"The journey is a long one, and many wild beasts are lying in wait for man in the plains and in the forest," continued the hunter. "You have but poor weapons.

Remember, stranger: you cannot fight against beasts as you do against people. Swords, arrows, and knives are good for use against man, but against beasts, the spear is better. Only the spear can stop an animal and reach its heart from a distance. Your spears are useless in our country." He pointed to the thin Egyptian spear with its bronze head leaning against the wall. "This is the sort you need!"

Iruma's father laid the weapon he had brought on Cavius' knees, and removed the long leather bag that covered it. The heavy spear was more than four cubits long. Its shaft, two fingers thick, was made of hard, firm wood that was polished like bone. The shaft was slightly thickened in the middle where it was covered with the rough skin of the hyena. Instead of the usual spearhead, the blade, three fingers wide and a cubit long, made of light-colored hard material - the rare and precious iron surmounted it.

Cavius touched the sharpened edge of the blade thoughtfully, tested the weight of the weapon and with a sigh returned it to its owner. The latter smiled, studying the impression he had produced, and then said cautiously:

"It takes a lot of hard work to make a spear like this. A neighboring people, who sell it at a high price, obtains the metal for it. But that spear will save you time and again in mortal struggle."

Cavius could not guess what the hunter was driving at, and kept silent.

"You brought strong bows from Tha-Quem with you," continued the hunter. We cannot make such bows and want to exchange spears for them. The chiefs have agreed to give you two spears for each bow, and the spears, in my opinion, will be of more service to you."

Cavius glanced inquiringly at Kidogo, and the Kemtiu nodded his head in support of the hunter's opinion.

"There is plenty of game in the plains," said Kidogo, "and we shall not need any arrows, but it will be worse in the forest. Still, the forest is a long way off, and six spears in place of three bows will be of more use against wild beasts."

Cavius thought for a while, then agreed to the exchange and began to haggle. The hunter, however, was not moved. He pointed to the high value of the weapons he offered. They would never have given two spears for a bow, he said, if they had not wanted to know how the bows of the Black Land were made.

"Good!" said the Etruscan. "We would have given you our bows as a gift in return for your hospitality if we had not been traveling so far. We accept your terms. Tomorrow you will receive the bows."

The hunter's face beamed, he slapped Cavius' hand, raised the spear, examined the red reflection of the torch on the blade and covered it again with the little leather bag, decorated with pieces of different-colored skin. Cavius held out his hand, but the hunter did not give him the weapon.

"Tomorrow you will get six spears as good as this. But this one," Iruma's father made a slight pause, "this one I bring as a gift to your friend, Golden Eyes. Iruma stitched the bag herself. Look how pretty it is!"

The hunter held out the spear to the young Hellene, who took it hesitantly.

"You are not going with them," said Iruma's father, pointing to Cavius and the Kemtiu, "but a good spear is the first thing a hunter needs, and I want you to make my family famous when you become my son!"

Kidogo and Cavius peered into the face of their friend, and the Kemtiu pressed his fingers until they cracked. The decisive moment had come unexpectedly. Pandion turned pale and suddenly, with a sharp gesture of dismissal, returned the spear to the hunter.

"You refuse my gift? How is that to be understood?" shouted the hunter.

"I'm going with my companions," muttered Pandion with difficulty.

Iruma's father stood immobile, staring at Pandion without saying a word; then he hurled the spear down at his feet.

"Let it be so, but don't dare so much as look at my daughter again. I'll send her away today!"

Pandion stared at the hunter with wide-open, unwinking eyes. The genuine grief that distorted his manly face softened the wrath of Iruma's father.

"You found courage enough to make your decision before it was too late," he said. "But if you are going, go immediately." The hunter again gave Pandion a saturnine glare, examined him from head to foot and made an inarticulate sound. As he left the house, Iruma's father turned to Cavius.

"What I have said holds good," he said rudely and disappeared into the darkness.

Kidogo was much troubled at the gleam in Pandion's eyes but realized that he would have no time for his friends at that moment. Pandion stood staring into space as though he were asking the distant expanses how he should act. He turned slowly round, threw himself on his bed and covered his face with his hands. Cavius lit a new torch - he did not want to leave Pandion alone in the darkness with his thoughts. He and Kidogo tried to keep awake without speaking. From time to time they looked at their friend in alarm, but could not do anything to help him.

The time passed slowly, and night fell. Pandion moved on his bed, jumped up, stood to listen, and then rushed towards the door. Cavius' broad shoulders, however, barred the way. Pandion frowned wrathfully as he was brought up short against Cavius' folded arms.

"Let me out!" shouted Pandion impatiently. "I can't help it, I must say farewell to Iruma if she hasn't been sent away yet."

"What do you think you're doing?" answered Cavius. "You'll ruin her, yourself and all of us!"

Pandion did not reply to that and tried to push the Etruscan out of his way, but Cavius stood firm.

"You've made your decision, so that's enough, don't make her father angrier," continued Cavius in an effort to convince his friend. "Just think of what might happen."

Pandion pushed Cavius still harder but received in return a blow in the chest that made him step back. Kidogo, seeing the clash between his friends, did not know what to do. Pandion clenched his teeth, and his eyes gleamed with the fire of wrath. With dilated nostrils, he rushed at Cavius. The Etruscan rapidly pulled out his knife and, holding it with the hilt towards Pandion, said:

"Here you are. Strike!"

Pandion was dumbfounded. Cavius thrust out his chest, placed his left hand on his heart and with his right continued offering the dagger to Pandion.

"Strike, strike here! In any case, I won't let you out of here other than over my dead body! Kill me and then go!" shouted the infuriated Cavius.

This was the first time Pandion had seen his morose and wise friend in such a state. He turned away, groaned helplessly, staggered over to his own bed, fell on it and turned his back on his comrades. Cavius was breathing heavily as he wiped the sweat from his brow and returned the knife to its place.

"We must watch him all night, and leave as quickly as possible," he said to Kidogo, who was quite frightened. "At dawn, you'll warn all the others to make ready."

Pandion heard the Etruscan's words quite clearly and realized that they meant him to have no opportunity of seeing Iruma. As he lay on his bed, he felt that he was being asphyxiated; there was an almost physical sense of being in a confined space. He struggled with himself, mustering all his will power, and gradually the violent despair, that was nearly madness, gave way to calm sorrow.

Once more, the hot plains of Africa opened up before twenty-seven stubborn men who were determined to reach their homes, come what might.

After the rains, the twelve-cubit-high elephant grass had formed ears and stood so dense that even the huge elephant was hidden in its stiflingly hot thickets. Kidogo explained to Pandion why they must hurry; soon the period of the rains would be over, and the plain would begin to burn up and would turn into a lifeless, ash-covered expanse where they would find no food.

Pandion agreed in silence. His sorrow was still too fresh. Once amongst those to whom he owed so much, he felt that the bonds of male friendship were again binding him, that the urge to go forward, the thirst of battle, were growing in him, and that the desire to reach Oeniadae as soon as possible was becoming more powerful.

Despite his great longing for Iruma, it was only now that Pandion felt his former self, stepping out firmly on the chosen path without further alarm. The artist's previous hungry attention to the forms and colors of nature had returned, and he was filled with the wish to create.

The twenty-seven strong men were armed with spears, assegais, knives, and a few shields. The former slaves, tried and tested in battle and misfortunes, constituted a considerable force and need have no fear of the numerous wild beasts. The road through the high elephant grass was beset with dangers. They were forced to march in single file, keeping to the narrow paths made by animals and seeing before them nothing but the back of the man in front.

Danger threatened them every minute in the high walls of rustling grass to the right and left. At any moment, the grass might part and make way for a lurking lion, an infuriated rhinoceros, or the huge towering body of a malicious lone elephant. The grass separated the men; it was worse for those who brought up the rear since they could be attacked by an animal that had been aroused by those in front.

In the mornings, the grass was covered with a cold dew, and a glittering haze of water dust hung over men whose bodies were wet as though from the rain. At the hottest part of the day, the dew disappeared completely and dry dust, falling from the tops of the grass-stalks, irritated their throats. It was stifling in the narrow corridors through which they passed.

On the third day of the march, a leopard pounced on the bold Libyan Takel who brought up the rea. It was only by a lucky chance that the young man escaped with a few scratches. The next day a huge dark-maned lion attacked Pandion and his Kemtiu neighbor. The spear, given him by Iruma's father, stopped the lion; his companion, picking up the shield Pandion had dropped in his surprise at the sudden attack, fell on the lion from behind. The animal turned to face its new attacker and fell, pierced by three spears.

Kidogo came running up, panting with excitement, when all was over and the warriors, breathing heavily, were wiping the already coagulating blood of the lion from their spears. The beast lay almost invisible in the matted brown grass. The others all came running up, and loud shouts rose over the scene of the conflict.

All the former slaves were trying to convince two squat Kemtiues, Dhlomo and Mpafu, who, together with Kidogo, was leading the party, that before much longer the beasts would kill somebody. They had to find a way around the tall grass of the plain. The guides did not think of contradicting them. The party turned due south and by evening approached a long strip of forest that led in the required direction.

Pandion was already acquainted with this type of forest; a green, vaulted corridor over the narrow stream of a plains river. Such forest galleries cut across the plains in various directions, following the course of the rivers.

The travelers were lucky: there were no thorn-bushes under the trees and no lianas to make impenetrable barriers between the trees. The party was able to make good time winding its way amongst the trees to avoid their giant roots. The rustling of the grass in the stifling atmosphere of bright sunlight gave way to profound silence and cool semi-darkness. The forest stretched for a long way.

Day after day, the party marched under trees, going out occasionally into the grass for game or climbing the lower trees on the verge of the forest to check the direction they were taking.

Although it was easier and less dangerous under cover of the trees, Pandion felt oppressed by the darkness and silence of the mysterious forest.

Memories of his meeting with Iruma returned to him. He felt that he had suffered an enormous loss, and his sorrow veiled the whole world in a grey haze; the unknown future was as gloomy, silent, and dark as the forest they were traveling through.

Pandion felt that the dark road through the monotonous colonnade of huge trees, the alternative patches of darkness and sunlight, the other depressions, and hillocks, must be endless. It led into the unknown distance, striking still deeper into the heart of a strange, alien land, where everything was unfamiliar, and only a group of faithful friends saved him from certain death.

The sea, towards which he was hurrying, had seemed near and easily attainable when he had been a captive, but now looked immeasurably far away, separated from him by thousands of obstacles, by months of arduous journeying.

The sea had taken him from Iruma, and it was itself unattainable.

The forest path led the travelers into a swamp that stretched away to the horizon on all sides, hidden in the distance by the green gloom of excessive humidity, and in the mornings encircled by a low blanket of white mist. Flocks of white egrets sailed over the sea of rushes.

Cavius, Pandion and the Libyans, puzzled by this great barrier, gazed in perplexity at the bright green thicket of swamp plants with patches of water that seemed to be burning in the sun. The guides were exchanging satisfied glances - they were on the right road; their fortnight's journey had not been made in vain.

The next day, the whole party set about binding the light, porous ambag rushes, (Ambag-Herminera elaphroxylon, a water reed that grows to well over 20 feet in height) whose angular stalks grew ten cubits high, into rafts. After that they sailed past dense jungles of brush-headed papyrus grass, winding their way between floating islands of grass piled up with reddish-brown masses of dried, broken reeds. There were two or three men on each raft, who cautiously punted them along with long poles, plunging rhythmically into the silt of the swamp.

The stinking, dark water seemed like thick oil. Bubbles of marsh gas rose to the surface where the poles dug into the bottom, and sticky mildew made a rusty-brown, lacy border along the green walls of the reeds.

Not a dry place was to be seen all around them, the humid heat was exhausting, and a merciless sun beat down on their perspiring bodies.

In the evening, myriads of midges came to torment

them. It was a great good fortune to find a hillock that was still above water where they could light a smoking fire to drive off the insects. When the wind began to blow, life was made more comfortable; the wind blew away the insects and enabled the men to sleep after days and nights of toil. The reeds bowed before the wind, and wave after wave passed over that sea of green.

The foul water and rotting vegetation abounded in reptiles of all sorts. Gigantic crocodiles gathered in their hundreds on sandbanks or peeped out from the green wall; their bodies half hidden in the reeds. At night, the monsters gave voice. Their low, rumbling roar filled the people with horror. There was no fury or menace in the roar of the crocodiles - there was something soulless and passionless in those low jerky notes that rolled over the still waters in the darkness of night.

The travelers came across a shallow cove in which were many conical hillocks of silt, half washed away, about a cubit and a half in height. The brown water exuded an unbearably foul smell; the hills were covered with a coating of guano. The Kemtiues told the others that this was one of the nesting places of the flamingo, the big rosy-colored bird that at other times was found in large numbers in the swamps.

Several of the travelers, mostly Libyans, took sick from the foul smells and bad water. They were tormented by a cruel fever and lay helpless on the rafts, at the feet of their companions.

On the fifth day of their journey, they began to meet more frequently, stretches of clear water out of which treetops stuck up. Pandion, in his astonishment, asked Kidogo the meaning of this. His black friend told him with a smile that their troubles would soon be over.

"In the dry season," said the Kemtiu, plunging his pole into the deep water, "everything here is dried up by the sun; these floods come after the rains."

"What river is it?" asked Pandion.

"There are two rivers here, (the Bahr el Arab and the Bahr el Qhazal, that formerly carried more water than they do today) not one, and a long string of swamps between them," answered the Kemtiu. "In the dry season, there's almost no water in the rivers." Kidogo, as was always the case in those last few days, was right.

Soon the rafts struck on the silty bottom of the marsh, and in front of them, the earth sloped upwards, merging into a level plain. This plain was covered by a special kind of grass with silver-white ears, and when the sun shone on it, it looked like a continuation of the level surface of the water.

It was with feelings of great relief that the travelers, waist-deep in mud, scaring the crocodiles with loud shouts, scrambled out of the swamp on to stable, hot land. They were greeted by the wind, fresh and dry, that drove away the heavy smells of the swamplands. The group reached an eminence on which grew bushes with bluish-green leaves and orange-colored fruits the size of an egg.

Here they found fresh water and decided to make camp. Around their encampment, they built a fence of thorn bushes six cubits high.

The Kemtiues gathered a big pile of the orange fruits, that proved to be tasty and tender, and some leaves whose sap they used to treat the people suffering from fever. Those who were healthy slept as much as they needed to recuperate their strength, and the sores that had formed from the bites of swamp insects soon healed up.

For several days in succession, there had been no rain. In the mornings, it was very chilly, and the Kemtiues of the party suffered considerably from the cold. Soon the travelers were able to continue their journey.

For twenty-five days, they marched across the plain. Now there were only nineteen of them left, eight others had left after crossing the swamp and gone away northwards to their homes, which lay no more than ten days march away. No matter how much they tried to persuade the others to go with them, the stubborn nineteen continued their way to the sea.

A grey haze covered the heavens that were still glaringly bright. At night the sky was frequently overcast with heavy clouds, the terrible, unceasing roar of thunder swept over the plains; but not a single flash of lightning cut through the velvety blackness of the night, not a drop of rain fell on the dried-up grass and heat-cracked earth. The plain was dotted with small hillocks, some cone-shaped, others like towers with rounded tops, ten cubits high. These hills of clay, hard as bricks, were inhabited by hordes of big insects, resembling ants, whose powerful jaws made them dangerous.

Pandion had already grown accustomed to the great variety of animal life; he was no longer astonished at the giraffes or at troops of elephants a thousand strong.

Then he saw a herd of strange striped animals, colored black and white. They resembled the horses of Oeniadae, except that they were smaller, had thin legs and wide croups that curved sharply towards the animal's back, a gracefully curved upper lip, short tails, and manes. Pandion watched big herds of them that gathered at the drinking places with interest. He dreamed of catching some of the striped horses and breaking them in for riding.

When he shared his ideas with Kidogo and the other Kemtiues, they laughed loudly and for a long time. The Kemtiues explained to him that the striped animals were strong, bad-tempered, and untamable and that although they might succeed in catching a few of the more willing ones, they would never be able to get the two dozen that was needed for their journey, even if they spent ten years on the task.

Pandion's second disappointment came when they met with the buffaloes. He saw the massive dark bodies of the bulls, with their broad horns, turned up at the ends and crawled up to the nearest to bring it down with his spear. Kidogo hastened to throw himself on Pandion and held him pressed to the ground with all the weight of his body.

The Kemtiu assured his friend that the buffaloes were virtually the most terrible of all animals in the southern countries, and they could only be hunted with bows and arrows or assegais; hunting them with a spear was certain death. Pandion obeyed the Kemtiu and hid in the bushes with the others, although Kidogo's fear of the buffaloes remained incomprehensible to him: he considered the rhinoceros or the elephant far more dangerous.

Rocky ridges, ranges of hills or groups of eroded rocks, often intersected their path. In such places, they came across baboons, repulsive, dog-headed creatures. When the men approached them, these monkeys would gather on the rocks or under the trees, and gaze fearlessly at the strangers, making insolent grimaces at them.

Pandion looked with disgust at those naked, dog-like faces with their distended blue cheeks, framed in stiff thick hair, and at their waggling hindquarters with the red, calloused bare patches. The monkeys were dangerous.

Cavius was incensed once by the behavior of three of them who barred his way and struck one with his spear. A serious battle took place at the foot of the crags. The travelers were lucky to get away without suffering any losses, although they had to retreat with the greatest possible alacrity.

On the twenty-fifth day of their journey across the imperceptibly rising country, a dark line appeared on the horizon. Kidogo gave a shout of joy as he pointed to it; that line was the beginning of the vast forest, the last obstacle they had to overcome. Beyond the densely wooded mountains lay the long-awaited sea, the reliable road home.

By midday, the party reached a grove of palm trees whose strange shape astonished Pandion. These were the first palm trees they had seen in the plains that resembled the date palms of Aigyptos. Each of the tall, straight trunks rose directly out of the middle of a star of the shadow cast by its own crown. The dry soil between the black stars of the shadows looked like white-hot metal.

The disposition of the shadows told Pandion that at midday the sun was precisely over his head. He spoke to Cavius about this. The Etruscan shrugged his shoulders in perplexity, but Kidogo said that it was really so. The farther they went to the south, the higher the sun rose, although nobody knew the reason for it. The old people said that there is a legend to the effect that a lot farther to the south the sun gets lower again. Pandion did not have much time to ponder over this problem - his thirsty companions were hurrying to get to the water.

During their midday bivouac, Kidogo told them that by evening they would reach the trees and that their next road lay through forests and mountains that stretched to the end of the earth.

"Over there," the Kemtiu pointed to the right, "and over there," the Kemtiu's hand swung round to the left, "there are rivers, but we cannot travel along them. The right-hand river turns north to the great fresh sea on the edge of the northern desert. The left-hand river turns south, and would take us far from the place we want to reach. Apart from that, strong tribes who eat human flesh and would kill us all, are living along the rivers. We must go straight as an arrow to the south-west, between the two rivers. The dark forests are deserted and safe; in the mountains, there are no people since they all fear the thunder and the dark thickets. There are few animals here, but we, too, are few and can feed ourselves by hunting and collecting fruits." (The right-hand river - the modern Shari. The left-hand river – the Ubangi, the main tributary of the Congo).

Pandion, Cavius, and the Libyans were troubled by indefinite fears as they looked doubtfully at the dark forest that stretched before them.

CHAPTER SEVEN

The Might of The Forest

The most extraordinary trees (Lobelias) towered above the thick undergrowth. Their thin trunks, with convex transverse ribs, were crowned with flat, fan-like platforms of short branches bearing big leaves above which projected long, straight shoots, like green swords up to ten cubits in length. Four of these trees, two on either side, stood at the forest edge like sentinels, their swords raised threateningly. The travelers passed between them, picking their way through thorn-scrub.

A huge wart hog, with long, curved fangs, and an ugly lumpy head, appeared from under the brush, grunted angrily at the intruders and disappeared.

On the very first day in the forest, Cavius lost the stick on which he had cut forty-nine notches to mark the number of days' journey; after that, they lost count of time. The huge forest, monotonous and unvarying, fixed itself forever in Pandion's memory. The party marched in silence, and whenever they tried to speak, their voices reverberated noisily under the impenetrable green vault overhead.

The wide expanses of the golden plain had never given them such a feeling of the insignificance of man; here they seemed utterly lost in the depths of an alien country.

The large stems of creeping plants, often as thick as a man's body spiraled around the smooth trunks of the trees, hung down from above in huge nets and separate loops, sometimes forming a solid curtain. The trees branched out at a tremendous height above the travelers' heads from trunks that faded away in the grey twilight. Stretches of foul water, covered with green slime, frequently barred their way; at times, they came across streams of dark, noiselessly flowing water.

In the rare glades, the sun blinded eyes, long accustomed to the gloom of the forest, and the density of the undergrowth forced the travelers to avoid such places. Tree-ferns (The Cyathea and Todea (grape fern) reach a height of more than 30 ft.), four times the height of a man, such as they had never seen before, spread their pale-green, feathery leaves like huge wings.

The clean-cut, greyish leaves of mimosa formed a delicate pattern in the sunbeams. Myriads of flowers - blood-red, orange, violet, white - stood out brilliantly against the background of light green leaves of every possible kind: big and broad, long, and narrow, regular-shaped, indented, and serrate. The wild tangle of vegetation was made even more chaotic by the spirals of creeping lianas, while everywhere long thorns stuck out to tear ruthlessly at the flesh of the traveler.

These glades were filled with the constant jabber and chatter of birds so noisy that it seemed as though all the life of the forest was concentrated at these points.

The travelers checked the direction of their journey by the sun and again plunged into the twilight of the forest, finding their way along hollows, washed out by the rain, and along riverbeds, and getting a new orientation from the sun's rays that occasionally slanted down through the dense foliage.

The guides tried to steer clear of the glades for yet another reason: the trees near them gave shelter to terribly dangerous insects, deadly black wasps, and huge ants. Big lichens, leathery grey excrescences, and other growths covered the tree-trunks, while the high ridges of their roots were covered in a green coat of moss. These flat roots, often as much as five or six cubits high, branched out from the ribs of the massive tree-trunk like buttresses. The whole party of nineteen men could easily have bivouacked in the deep pits between roots that crossed over each other, making all movement in the forest difficult. The travelers either had to climb over them or go around them, making their way through narrow corridors.

Their feet sank into the thick carpet of half-rotten branches, leaves and dried shoots that covered the ground. Bunches of whitish toadstools gave off a heavy odor, like that of a corpse.

Their weary legs knew rest only in places where the trees were not so high, the roots did not bar the way, and the ground was covered with soft moss. These places, however, were densely overgrown with thorn-bushes that, to be avoided or a path had to be cut through them, which again caused loss of time and effort. A kind of spotted slug fell from the branches on to the bare shoulders of the travelers and burned their skin with its poisonous slime.

On rare occasions, the shadow of some animal could be discerned in the gloom of the forest, but it disappeared so quickly and silently that the travelers were often unable to say what kind of animal it was.

At night, the same profound silence reigned, only to be broken only by the plaintive howl of some unknown animal and by the raucous cries of some strange bird.

The travelers crossed a large number of low ridges of hills but never once reached open country devoid of trees.

The forest between the ridges was thicker than ever; the humid, heavy air of the valleys, rank with rotting vegetation, made it difficult for the men to breathe.

When the party reached a valley in the bed of a rapidly flowing stream of cold water that flowed between big boulders, they sat down to rest. After that, the long uphill climb began again.

For two days they continued their uphill march, the forest all the time grew denser and darker. There were no longer any glades where food was to be found, and wind-felled trees barred their way. In order to avoid the thorny curtain of thin resilient stems that hung down from above and the impenetrable undergrowth of shrubs and small trees, they were forced to crawl on all fours along the rain gullies covering the hillsides. The hard earth crumbled under their hands and feet, but they crawled on through this labyrinth, taking their direction only from the dry gullies.

Gradually the air grew colder as though the party had penetrated into deep and damp catacombs. It was pitch dark by the time they reached the top of the slope on the edge of a plateau. There were no more rainwater gullies, and the travelers halted for the night in order not to lose direction. Not a star was to be seen through the dense vault of leaves. Somewhere far above them, a wind was raging. Pandion lay sleepless for a long time, listening to the roar of the forest that reminded him of the noise of a nearby sea. The rumble, rustle, and clatter of the branches in the strong gusts of wind merged into one mighty sound resembling the regular beating of the surf on the shore.

Dawn came very late, the sun's rays struggling to pierce

the thick mist. Finally, the invisible sun overcame the twilight of the forest, and before the men's eyes, a gloomy, oppressive scene opened up. The black and white trunks of enormous trees, a hundred and fifty cubits high, disappeared in a thick milky mist that completely hid their mossy branches. Moss and lichens, sodden with water, hung down from the trees in long dark braids and grey beards, at times waving to and fro at a considerable height above the ground. Water that exuded from the spongy network of twisted roots, grass and moss slopped underfoot.

Dense thickets of broad-leafed bushes hindered all progress. Big pale flowers, like honeycombed balls, swayed gently on their long stems in the mist. Black and white columns, four cubits in diameter, stood like an army in serried ranks; the grey mist rolled round them, and thin streams of water trickled down their bark. Some of the trunks were coated with a thick growth of soaking moss.

Nothing could be seen at a distance of more than thirty or forty cubits in that awful forest; to make any progress the travelers had to cut a path for themselves at the foot of those forest giants. The piled-up barriers of fallen giants disheartened even the most hardened travelers. The worst thing of all was the impossibility of judging direction since there was no means of checking up.

The Kemtiues shivered in the cold mist, frightened by the unbelievable might of the forest; the Libyans were utterly discouraged. They all had the feeling that they had entered the domain of the forest gods, a place forbidden to man, from which there was no way out.

Cavius made a sign to Pandion; they armed themselves with heavy knives and began frantically to carve a way through the wet branches. Gradually the others started to take heart, and they worked in shifts, relieving each other; climbing over huge barricades of fallen trees; losing their way in their efforts to find a path through the enormous, and again plunging into green thickets. The hours passed; overhead there was the same white gloom; the water continued to drip slowly and heavily from the trees; the air did not grow any warmer, and it was only by the greyish-red hue of the mist that they realized that evening was drawing nigh.

"There's no way out in any direction!" With these words, Kidogo sat down on a root, pressing his head between his hands in despair. Two other guides had returned earlier with similar information.

For a distance of about a thousand cubits, a narrow glade stretched across the path they had cut. Behind them stood the vast gloomy forest through which they had been hacking their way by superhuman efforts for the past three days.

Before the group was an impenetrable growth of bamboo. The polished, jointed stems rose to a height of twenty cubits, gracefully bowing their thin, feathery heads. The bamboo grew so thick that there was no possibility of penetrating that dense throng of jointed stalks as straight as spear-shafts that stood like a solid wall before the travelers. The polished surface of the bamboo was so hard that the travelers' bronze knives were blunted by the first strokes. Axes or heavy swords would be needed to attack that wall. It seemed that there was no way around the bamboo. The glade was bounded by dense forest thickets, and the stand of bamboo stretched in both directions far into the misty distance of the plateau.

The customary energy of the travelers had been sapped by the cold, by insufficient food, and the struggle against the awful forest; the latter part of their journey had been too much for them. Nevertheless, they could not contemplate the possibility of having to turn back. To get through those awful forests, it was not sufficient to keep their former general direction of the south-west; it was not enough to hack and carve their way through the dense vegetation. They also had to know where the path could be cut. Those who lived in the forest could only indicate the right way. So far, they had not met any people in the jungles, and a search for them might well end up on the gridirons of a cannibal barbecue.

We haven't made it! This was the thought reflected in the faces of all nineteen men, in their knitted brows, in their grimaces of despair and in the mask of mute submission. When Kidogo recovered from his first attack of despair, he threw back his head to look up at the giant branches that stretched over the glade at the height of a hundred cubits. Pandion went quickly over to his friend, guessing at what was in his mind.

"Do you think it's possible to climb them?" he asked, looking at tree-trunks that were perfectly smooth to an incredible height above the ground.

"We must, even if it takes us a whole day," answered Kidogo, despondently. "We must go either forward or back, but there must be no more guesswork because there's nothing left to eat."

"That one," said Pandion, pointing to a white-barked

giant that rose high above the glade, its crooked branches spreading like a star against the background of the sky. "You can see a long way from that tree."

Kidogo shook his head.

"No, the trees with white or with black bark* are no good. (Any of the many African hardwood trees such as ebony, ironwood, Macaranga or Polyscias, all of which have either black or white bark.) The wood is as hard as iron, you can't drive a knife into them let alone a wooden peg. If we can find a tree with red bark and big leaves, we'll climb it."

The men spread along the glade in search of a suitable tree. Soon somebody shouted that he had found one. The tree was lower than the iron giants were, but it stood close against the bamboo wall, rising a good fifty cubits above it.

The travelers, with the greatest difficulty, cut two bamboo stalks, split them into pegs a cubit long and made a point at one end of each of them. Kidogo and Mpafu took heavy clubs and began driving the pegs into the soft wood of the tree-trunk, climbing higher and higher until they reached a liana twining around the tree in a spiral.

Kidogo and his companion belted themselves around with thin lianas, pressed their feet firmly against the tree-trunk and, leaning far back from the tree, and began climbing to a prodigious height. Soon their bodies became tiny dark figures against the background of dense clouds that covered the sky.

Pandion grew jealous of his companions; they were high up above him, they could see the wide world, while he remained below in the shadow, like a reddish-blue worm such as they met in the rainwater gullies in the forest. He made a sudden decision and seized hold of the bamboo pegs hammered into the tree. He merely waved his hand at Cavius' shout of warning, scrambled quickly up the tree, and reached the twining liana.

He cut off the end of a thinner liana that hung over his head, belted it around himself, and followed Kidogo's example. He soon found that this method of climbing was far from easy. The liana cut into his back, and the moment he relaxed the tension in his legs, his feet slipped, and he banged his knees against the coarse bark.

With the greatest difficulty, Pandion climbed halfway up the tree. The tops of the bamboos swayed beneath him in an irregular yellow sea, but it was still a long way to climb to the first huge branches of the tree. He heard Kidogo call from above and a strong liana with a noose at the end fell on to his shoulder. Pandion passed the noose under his arms, and those above pulled gently on the liana, rendering him the greatest possible help. With his legs, all lacerated, tired but joyful, Pandion soon reached the bigger lower branches. Here Kidogo and his companion had seated themselves comfortably between two big boughs.

Pandion, from a height of eighty cubits, looked out towards the distant horizon for the first time in many days. Bamboo thickets formed a belt encircling the forest on the high plateau; it stretched to the left and right as far as the eye could see, although in width it was no more than four or five thousand cubits. Behind the bamboo rose a low ridge of black rocks stretching due west in a chain of sloping crags some distance from each other. Beyond them, again, the ground began to fall gently.

An endless chain of densely wooded hills looked like

solid green clouds separated by the narrow slits of ravines filled with curling, dark mists. In these ravines lay endless days of hungry, arduous marching through gloomy twilight, for that was the direction in which the party had to travel.

Nowhere could they see any gap in the solid green wall over which floated huge ragged clouds of white mist, no glade, and no broad valley.

It was doubtful whether the travelers had sufficient strength left to fight their way forward even to that visible distance. Farther, beyond the twilight gloom of the horizon, they might be faced with the same all over again, and, if so, it spelled certain death.

Kidogo turned away from the countryside that rolled away beneath him, catching Pandion's glance as he did so. The Hellene saw alarm and great weariness in the dilated eyes of his friend; Kidogo's inexhaustible vitality had gone, his face was wrinkled in a bitter grimace.

"We must look back," said Kidogo in a mournful voice; he suddenly straightened up and walked along a branch that stretched horizontally high above the bamboo.

With difficulty, Pandion restrained a cry of fear, but the Kemtiu walked on swaying slightly, as though it were nothing at all, until he reached the end of the branch, making the leaves tremble, and the bough bend downwards under his weight. Pandion sat dead still with fright as Kidogo sat down with his legs astride the branch, held himself firmly by grasping thinner branches and began to study the country beyond the right-hand corner of the glade. Pandion did not dare follow his friend. Holding their breath, he and Mpafu awaited Kidogo's report.

The other sixteen men of the party, almost invisible to those on the tree, were eagerly following all their movements. For a long time, Kidogo sat swaying on the springy branch and then, without a word, returned to the tree-trunk.

"It's a bad thing not to know the way," he said sorrowfully. "We could have got here much more easily. Over there," the Kemtiu waved his hand to the north-west, "the grassy plain isn't far from us. We should have gone farther to the right instead of entering the forest. We must go back to the grasslands. Perhaps there are people there; there are usually more people near the forest edge than there are in the forest itself or out in the plains."

The descent from the tree proved much more difficult and dangerous than the ascent. If it had not been for the help of his companions, Pandion would never have been able to descend so quickly, or, far more likely, he would have fallen and been killed. He had no sooner put his feet on the solid ground than his knees gave way under him and he lay spread-eagled on the ground amidst the shouts and laughter of his companions.

Kidogo told the others what he had seen from the treetop, and proposed setting off at right angles to the path they had mapped out. To Pandion's great surprise not a single word of protest was raised, although everybody realized that they had suffered defeat in their battle with the forest and that they would probably be detained a long time. Even the stubborn Etruscan, Cavius, was silent, apparently because he realized how the men had suffered in that hard, but futile struggle.

Pandion remembered that at the beginning of their

journey Kidogo had said that the way around the forest was a long and dangerous one. Strong, savage tribes, for whom the nineteen travelers did not constitute a serious force, lived along the rivers and on the verge of the forest. Grassland, with low trees growing at regular intervals like a planted orchard, sloped down to a fast river, with black rocks huddled together on its far bank. The river had piled up a long barrier of driftwood against the rocks, tree-trunks, branches, and reeds, dried and whitened in the sun.

The party of former slaves skirted a palm grove that had been smashed by elephants, and made another camp under low tree. The aroma of the resin that seeped out of its trunk, and the monotonous rustling of the rags of silky bark, brought drowsiness to the weary travelers.

Kidogo suddenly rose to his knees; his companions, too, were immediately on the alert. A large elephant was approaching the river. Its appearance might bode no good for them. They watched the loose, sweeping gait of the animal that seemed to be waddling unhurriedly along inside its own thick skin.

The elephant drew nearer, carelessly waving its trunk, and there was something in its behavior that differed significantly from the usual caution of those sensitive beasts. Suddenly human voices rang out, but the elephant did not even raise its huge ears that lay back on its head.

The bewildered travelers looked at each other, and stood up, only to fall down to the ground immediately, as though they had been ordered to do so; alongside the elephant, they noticed some human figures. Only then did Pandion's companions notice a man lying on the elephant's broad neck, his head rested on his crossed arms on top of the animal's head.

The elephant went straight to the river and entered the water, stirring up the mud with its huge tree-trunks of legs. It suddenly spread out its ears, which made its head seem three times the standard size. Its tiny brown eyes stared into the depths of the river.

The man lying on the elephant's back sat up and slapped the animal sharply on its sloping skull. A loud shout "Heya!" resounded up and down the river. The elephant waved its trunk, seized with it a big log from amongst the driftwood, lifted it high over its head and hurled it into the water. The heavy log made a big splash and disappeared under the water to reappear farther downstream a few moments later. The elephant threw a few more logs into the water and then, stepping cautiously, walked out to the middle of the river, turned around with its head against the current and stood still.

The people who had come with the elephant - there were eight of them, brown-skinned youths, and girls - with loud shouts and roars of laughter, plunged into the cold river. They played in the water ducking each other, and their laughter and loud slaps delivered on wet bodies resounded clearly on all sides. The man on the elephant shouted merrily but watched the river unceasingly, from time to time making the elephant throw heavy logs into the water.

The travelers watched what was happening in the greatest astonishment. The friendship between people and the enormous elephant was something unbelievable, an unheard-of miracle; still, at a distance of no more than three hundred cubits from them, stood the huge, grey monster, submitting to the will of man. How could it have happened that an animal without equal in size and strength, the undisputed ruler of field and forest, had become subservient to weak and fragile man, an insignificant creature compared with the mass of the elephant, six cubits high at the shoulders? Who were these people who had tamed the lord of the African plains?

Cavius' eyes were gleaming as he nudged Kidogo. The latter turned from watching the merry play of the young people and whispered in Cavius' ear:

"I heard about this when I was a boy. I was told that somewhere along the line where the forest meets the plain, there are people known as the Elephant People. Now I see for myself that the story was a true one. That elephant is standing there to protect the bathers from crocodiles. I have also heard that these people are related to my tribe and speak a language similar to ours."

"Do you want to go to them?" asked Cavius thoughtfully, never for a moment taking his eyes off the man on the elephant.

"I'd like to, but I don't know..." stammered Kidogo. "If their tongue's mine, they'll understand us, and we'll have a chance to find the road we need. If they speak another tongue, things will go badly with us - they'll destroy us like mice!"

"Do they eat human flesh?" asked Cavius after a pause.

"I have heard that they don't. They're a rich and powerful people," answered the Kemtiu, chewing a blade of grass to hide his indecision.

"I'd try to find out what language they speak while they are here, to avoid going to their village," said Cavius. "These people are only unarmed youngsters, and if the man on the elephant attacks us, we can hide in the grass and bushes. In their village, we'd all be killed if we didn't come to an agreement with the Elephant People."

Kidogo liked Cavius' advice. He stood up, displaying his full height, and sauntered towards the river. A shout from the man on the elephant put a sudden stop to the fun in the water; the bathers stood still, up to their waists in water, looking at the opposite bank. The elephant turned menacingly in the direction of the approaching Kidogo; his trunk made a rustling noise as it waved over the long, white tusks, and its ears, like huge, pendant wings, spread out again.

The man on the elephant's back looked fixedly at the newcomer; in his right hand, he held a broad knife with a hook at the end that trembled slightly as he raised it, ready to use it. Without a word, Kidogo walked almost to the edge of the water, laid his spear on the ground, placed his foot on it, and spread out his weaponless arms.

"Greetings, friend," he said slowly, carefully pronouncing every word. "I am here with my companions. We are lonely fugitives on our way home. We want to ask for help from your tribe."

The man on the elephant remained silent. The travelers, hiding under the tree, waited anxiously to see whether the man would understand Kidogo's speech or not. A crucial turning point in the fate of the fugitives depended on what was to follow.

The man on the elephant slowly lowered his knife. The elephant shifted its weight from one foot to another in the swirling water and lowered its trunk, allowing it to hang between its tusks. Suddenly the man spoke, and a sigh of relief burst from Pandion's breast, while a shudder of joy ran through Kidogo who was standing with his body tensely strained. The speech of the elephant driver contained strong stresses and sibilant sounds that were not to be heard in Kidogo's musical language, but even Pandion recognized some familiar words.

"Where are you from, stranger?" came the question that seemed arrogant from the height of the elephant's back. "And where are your companions?"

Kidogo explained that they had been captives in Tha-Quem and were making their way back home, to the seacoast. The Kemtiu beckoned the others and the whole party of nineteen, downcast and emaciated, came down to the riverbank.

"Tha-Quem?" repeated the man on the elephant, pronouncing the syllables with difficulty. "What's that? Where is that country?"

Kidogo told of the dominant country that stretched along a mighty river in the northeast, and the elephant driver nodded his head understandingly.

"I've heard of it, but it's a terribly long way away. How could you have come so far?"

There was a note of mistrust in the man's words.

"That is a long story," answered Kidogo wearily. "Look at these men."

The Kemtiu pointed to Cavius, Pandion and the group of Libyans. "Have you ever seen anybody like them near here?"

With a look of interest, the man on the elephant examined faces such as he had never before seen. The distrust gradually faded from his face; he slapped the elephant's head with his hand.

"I am too young to decide anything without the elders. Come over to our bank of the river while the elephant is still in the water and wait there. What shall I tell the chiefs about you?"

"Tell them that weary travelers ask permission to rest in your village, and find out the way to the sea. We need nothing more," answered Kidogo laconically.

"Never have we heard such things or seen such people," mused the elephant driver. Turning to his own people, he shouted: "You go ahead, I'll follow!"

The young people, who had been studying the newcomers in silence, hurried obediently to the bank, looking back, and talking amongst themselves. The driver turned his elephant so that it stood sideways across the stream.

The travelers crossed the river, breast high in the water. Then the driver made his animal set out at a smart pace and, following the bathers, soon disappeared amongst the scanty trees. The former slaves sat down on big stones to await their fate with some trepidation. The Libyans were more worried than the others, although Kidogo assured them that the Elephant People would not do them any harm.

Shortly after this, four elephants appeared, coming across the fields, with wide platforms of plaited branches on their backs. Six warriors armed with bows and exceptionally broad spears sat on each of the platforms. Under this escort, the former slaves reached the village that proved to be quite close to the meeting place, on a bend of the same river, some four thousand cubits to the south-west.

There were about three hundred huts dotted amongst green trees on a hilly site. To the left of the village spread an open forest, and some distance to the right of it stood a huge palisade of massive logs with pointed tops, solidly buttressed on the outside with other logs. Around this structure, there was a deep moat fenced with the second palisade of pointed logs.

Pandion expressed surprise at the size of the structure, but Kidogo made a guess that this was the pen for the elephants.

Just as they had done many days ago in the east, the travelers stood before the chiefs and elders of a big village; again, and again, they told their marvelous tale of insurgent slaves, to which the great feat of a long journey through an unknown land was now added. The chiefs questioned the travelers closely, examined their weapons and the brand of Pharaoh on their backs, and made Cavius and Pandion tell them about their countries to the north of the distant sea.

Pandion was astonished at the extensive knowledge of these people; they had not only heard of the Land of Nub, where the travelers had come from, but they also knew many other places in Africa in the north, south, east, and west. Kidogo was delighted. The local inhabitants would show him the way to his home, and the wanderers would soon reach their goal by following the correct road.

A short meeting of the Council of Elders decided the fate of the newcomers: they were to be permitted to rest for a few days in the village and would be given food and shelter in accordance with the sacred laws of hospitality. The former slaves were given a big hut on the outskirts of the village where they could enjoy a good rest. They were still more encouraged by the fact that the Elephant People would show them the right way and that their wanderings were coming to an end.

Pandion, Kidogo, and Cavius wandered about the village, observing the life of the people who had won their admiration by their power over the gigantic animals. Pandion was astounded by long fences made from elephant tusks, where cattle were impounded. (Amongst the Shilluks, on the upper reaches of the Nile, barriers of elephant tusks were still to be met with in the middle of the 19th Century.)

It seemed to Pandion that this was a display of deliberate contempt for the terrible monsters. What number of tusks must these people possess if they could waste the valuable ivory on such things? When Pandion asked this question of one of the villagers, the latter very importantly suggested that he ask the chiefs for permission to see the big storehouse in the center of the village.

"So many tusks are stacked there," said the man, pointing to an open space between two huts, a hundred and fifty cubits in length, and he raised a stick above his head to indicate the height of the stack of tusks.

"How do you make the elephants obey you?" asked Pandion, unable to repress his curiosity.

The man frowned and looked at him with suspicion.

"That's kept secret from strangers," he answered slowly. "Ask the chiefs about it, if you want to know. Those who wear round their necks a gold chain with a red stone in it are the elephant trainers."

Pandion remembered then that they had been forbidden to approach the compound bounded by the moat, and said no more, annoyed with himself for the mistake he had made.

At that moment, Kidogo called him; the Kemtiu was in a long shed where several men were working. Pandion saw that it was a potter's shop, where they were busy making big earthenware pots for grain and beer. Kidogo could not retain himself. He took a big lump of moist, well-kneaded clay, squatted on his heels, lifted his eyes to the reed-thatched roof and then began modeling.

His big strong hands longed to be back at their favorite work, and his movements were full of confidence. Pandion watched his friend at work; the potters laughed amongst themselves but did not cease their work.

The Kemtiu's competent hands slowly cut, squeezed, and smoothed the soft clay until the formless mass began to take on the shape of the wide, sloping back with folds of skin hanging like sacks from the shoulders that are typical of the elephant.

The potters soon ceased their chatter, left their pots and gathered around Kidogo, but the Kemtiu was so engrossed in his work that he did not even notice them. The thick legs stood firmly on the ground, the elephant had raised its head with its trunk extended in front of it.

Kidogo found some twigs which he stuck fanwise into the clay and on this framework molded the elephant's ears, stretched like sails on either side. Exclamations of admiration burst from the lips of the watchers. One of the potters, unobserved, left the shed.

Kidogo was working on the animal's hind-legs and did not notice that one of the chiefs, an old man with a long thin neck, a fleshy, hooked nose, and a small grey beard had joined the throng of watchers. On the chief's breast, Pandion saw the gold chain of one of the chief elephant trainers.

In silence, the old man watched Kidogo finish his work. Kidogo stood back and rubbed the clay off his hands, smiling and critically examining the model of an elephant a cubit high. The potters treated him to cries of admiration. The old chief raised his thick brows, and the noise stopped immediately. He touched the wet clay like one who knew the business and then made a sign to Kidogo to come to him.

"I see you must be a great craftsman," said the chief, giving his words great significance, "if you can do so easily something that not one of our men can do. Tell me, can you make a statue of a man and not only of an elephant?" The chief tapped himself on the breast.

Kidogo shook his head. The chief's face grew dark.

"But there's a craftsman amongst us who is better than I, a craftsman from a distant northern country," said Kidogo. "He can make your statue."

The Kemtiu pointed at Pandion who was standing nearby. The old man repeated his question to Pandion, who, seeing the imploring eyes of his friend, agreed.

"But I must tell you, chief," said Pandion, "that in my country we make statues from soft stone or carve them from wood. I have neither tools nor stone here. I can only make your statue from this clay and up to here." He passed his hand across his chest. "The clay will soon dry up and crack; your picture will last only a few days."

The chief smiled.

"I want to see what the stranger craftsman can do," he said. "And let our potters watch him."

"All right, I'll try," answered Pandion. "But you must sit before me while I work."

"What for?" asked the astonished chief. "Can't you model the clay like he did?" And the old man pointed to Kidogo.

Pandion was put out by this, and tried to find words to answer him.

"I just made an elephant," put in Kidogo. "But you, who is a trainer of elephants, know that one elephant does not resemble another. Only a man who does not know them thinks that all elephants are alike."

"You speak the truth," the chief agreed. "I see the soul of any elephant immediately, and I can forecast his behavior."

"That's just it," Kidogo took him up. "If I want to make a particular elephant, I must see him before my eyes. My friend's the same; he's not going to make just a man, he's going to make you, and he must look at you while he's working."

"I understand," said the old man. "Let your friend come to me during the afternoon siesta, and I'll sit before him."

The chief went away, and the potters placed the clay elephant on a bench where ever-increasing numbers of villagers came to admire it.

"Well, Pandion," said Kidogo to his friend, "our fate is in your hands. If the chief is pleased with your statue, the Elephant People will help us."

The young Hellene nodded his head, and the two friends returned to their house, with a crowd of children close on their heels.

"Can you talk to me?" asked the chief, taking his place on a high and uncomfortable seat while Pandion was hurriedly arranging the clay the potters had brought on a block of wood. "Will it interrupt your work?"

"I can, but I don't know your language very well," answered Pandion. "I shall not understand everything you say and must answer with few words."

"Then call your friend, the man from the seaboard forests; let him stay here with you. I'll soon get tired of sitting silently like an inarticulate monkey!"

Kidogo came and sat with his legs tucked up under him beside the chief's chair, between Pandion and the old man. With the Kemtiu's help, the chief and Pandion were able to converse quite freely.

The chief asked Pandion about his country, and his penetrating glance gave Pandion a feeling of confidence in the elephant trainer, a wise man who had seen much. Pandion told the chief about his life in his own country, about Thessa, about his voyage to Crete, his slavery in Tha-Quem and his intention of returning home.

As he spoke his fingers molded the clay, and Kidogo translated what he said. The sculptor worked with incredible inspiration and persistence. The statue of the chief seemed to him to be a finger post pointing to the haven of his native land. Memories of the past gave rise to impatience, and the enforced stay with the Elephant People already began to pall.

The old man sighed and began to fidget. Apparently, he was tired.

"Say something in your own language," the chief suddenly asked.

"To ellnuiksou ellevthepoy!" exclaimed Pandion.

These were the words that his grandfather loved to repeat when he told the boy stories of famous Greek-heroes; they sounded strange when uttered in the heart of Africa.

"What did you say?" asked the chief.

Pandion explained that those words expressed the dream of all the people of his country. "Whatever it is, Hellenic is free!"

These words apparently gave the chief food for thought. Kidogo mentioned discreetly to Pandion that the chief was tired and that what he had done would be enough for that day.

"Yes, that's enough!" exclaimed the elephant trainer, raising his head.

"Come tomorrow. How many days more will it take?"

"Three days," said Pandion confidently, despite the signs of warning that Kidogo made to him.

"Three days, that's not too much, I can bear that," agreed the old man and rose from his seat.

Pandion and Kidogo covered the clay with a damp cloth and put it into a storeroom close to the chief's house.

On the second day, the two friends told the chief about Tha-Quem, its might, and its colossal buildings. The old chief frowned, he was hurt by the stories of the people of Aigyptos, but still, he listened with interest. When Pandion told him of the narrow, monotonous world of the Egyptians, the chief brightened up.

"Now it's time you learned something about my people," he said importantly. "You'll take the news of them to your own distant countries."

The chief told the friends how they made use of the strength of the elephants to make long journeys throughout the country. The only danger that threatened them was the possibility of meeting herds of wild elephants; a tame elephant might, at any moment, decide to return to its wild brethren. But there were certain ways of preventing even that.

The chief told them that farther to the east and the south of the place where the former slaves lived as the guests of a hospitable people, beyond the swamps and mountains there were big freshwater seas.

The seas were so big that they could only be crossed on

different boats and that the crossing took several days. These freshwater seas (the great freshwater lakes of East Africa) formed a long chain, one after the other, running in a southerly direction, and were surrounded by mountains that belched smoke, flames, and rivers of fire.

Beyond these seas, however, there was dry land, high plateau with numerous wild animals, while the real edge of the earth, the shore of the endless sea, lay still farther to the east, beyond a fringe of swamps.

On the plateau stood two gigantic, blindingly white mountains, not very far from each other, the beauty of which cannot be conceived by a man who has not seen them for himself. (Mounts Kenya and Kilimanjaro, two of the highest peaks on the African continent.) Dense jungles, inhabited by savage peoples and mysterious animals, surrounded these mountains, he said. The animals were ancient types, very rare and quite impossible to describe. The Elephant People had seen canyons filled with the bones of huge animals mixed with the bones of human beings and fragments of their stone weapons.

In the thickets that surround the northernmost white mountain, there were wild boars as big as a rhinoceros, and once they had seen an animal there as big as an elephant and much more massive, with two horns placed side by side at the end of its jowl.

People lived in floating villages (villages built on huge rafts are still to be seen on the great East African lakes) on the freshwater seas where they could not be reached by their enemies; these were savage people who gave no quarter to anybody.

Pandion asked the chief how far to the south the land of Africa ran and whether it was true that there the sun was again lower. The old man livened up at this question. It turned out that he had commanded a big expedition to the south when he had been less than forty years old. They went on twenty selected elephants for gold and for the precious grass of the southern plains, that gives strength to the aged and health to the sick.

Beyond the great river (the Zambezi with the Victoria Falls) that flows from west to east, where there are giant waterfalls, and a permanent rainbow plays in the high columns of spray, there are endless blue grass plains. Along the fringes of these grassy plains, along the seacoast, in the west and in the east, there are mighty trees whose leaves seem to be made from polished metal and glitter in the sun like a million mirrors.

The grass and leaves in the south said the old man, is not green but grey, pale blue and dove-colored, which makes the country look strange and cold. It is true, too, that the farther you go to the south the colder becomes the climate. The period of the rains, he added, which coincides with our dry season, is unbearably cold for northern people.

The old man told Pandion about an extraordinary silver tree that is found in the mountain gorges far to the south. The tree grows to a height of thirty cubits, has thin bark with transverse wrinkles, many branches covered with leaves shine like silver and are as soft as down; the tree, he said, is possessed of a magical beauty that charms all who see it.

Barren stony mountains, he continued, rose up like gigantic purple towers with vertical walls, at the foot of which crouched twisted trees, covered with large bunches of bright red flowers. On the barren parts of the plain and the stony slopes of the hills ugly, twisted bushes and low trees grew. (Various kinds of aloe trees from the Liliaceae family, also dragon trees.) Their fleshy leaves, filled with poisonous sap, were attached like outspread fingers to the ends of twin branches that shot straight up into the air.

Other trees had the same sort of leaves, reddish in color, growing in the form of a cap curving downwards at the end of a curved stem, four cubits high, on which there were no branches.

Near the rivers and on the fringe of the forests, there were the ruins of ancient buildings made of huge dressed stones, apparently the work of a powerful and highly skilled people.

"Today," said the old chief, "nobody is living in the vicinity of these ruins, except the dangerous wild dogs that howl there in the moonlight. Nomad herdsmen and poor hunters wander the plains. Still farther to the south, there are people with light grey skins, who have huge herds of cattle, but the expedition of the Elephant People did not go so far." (Tribes of the Hottentot type were much more widespread in times of antiquity than at present. There is some reason to believe them related to the ancient Egyptians.)

Pandion and Kidogo listened avidly to the old chief's stories. His tale of the blue plains seemed like fancy interwoven with fact, but still the old man's voice sounded convincing; he frequently stared into the distance, his eyes flashing with excitement, and it seemed to Pandion that pictures of the past, retained in his memory, were passing before the old man's eyes.

Suddenly the chief broke off.

"You've stopped working," he said, "and I'll have to sit before you for many more days!"

Pandion hurried, although it did not seem as though haste were essential; he felt that the old chief's bust was more successful than anything he had ever done before. He had acquired his skill gradually and imperceptibly, despite all he had gone through; his tremendous experience and his observations in Aigyptos stood him in good stead.

On the third day, Pandion compared his bust with the face of the chief several times.

"It's ready," he said with a profound sigh.

"Have you finished?" asked the chief and, seeing that Pandion nodded in confirmation, got up and went over to view his portrait.

Kidogo looked in admiration at Pandion's work, scarcely able to restrain words of approval. The clay, despite its uniform color, had taken on all typical features of that stern, wise and imperious face, with its firm, protruding jaws, its broad, sloping forehead, heavy lips and thick nose with distended nostrils.

The old man turned to the house and called out softly. One of his wives answered his call, a young woman, with a large number of tiny plaits cut short like a fringe on her forehead. She gave the chief a mirror of polished silver, obviously northern work that had got into the center of Africa by some unknown ways. The chief held the mirror at arm's length against the cheek of the statue and began to compare his reflection with Pandion's work.

Pandion and Kidogo awaited the old man's judgment.

The chief was silent for a long time, and then he put down the mirror and said:

"Great is the power of man's ability. You, stranger, possess this ability more than anybody in our country. You have made me better than I am - that means that you think well of me. I'll pay you in your own coin. What reward do you want?"

Kidogo gave Pandion a push, but the young Hellene answered the chief with words that seemed to come from his very heart.

"Everything I own you see before you. I have nothing but the spear that was given to me..." Pandion stammered and continued jerkily: "I need nothing here in a strange land. I have my own country; it is far away, but still, it is my greatest treasure. Help me get back home."

The elephant trainer placed his hand on the Hellene's shoulder with a paternal gesture.

"I want to talk with you again, come tomorrow with your friend. Now we'll finish this off. I'll order our potters to dry the clay so that it will never crack. I want to keep this picture of myself. They'll take out the surplus clay from inside and will cover it with a special type of pitch – they know how. The only thing I don't like is the blind eyes. Can you put some stones in them that I'll give you?"

Pandion agreed to this. The old man called to his wife again; this time she brought out a casket covered with a leopard skin. The chief took a reasonably big bag out of the box and shook out on to his hand a heap of big, faceted stones, oval arid as transparent as water. The unusually brilliant glitter of the stones attracted Pandion's attention; each stone seemed to concentrate in itself the full power of the sunlight, at the same time remaining cold, transparent, and pure – diamonds.

"I've always wanted to have such eyes," said the chief, "so that they would concentrate the light of life, but themselves would never change. Select the best of them and put them into the bust."

The young sculptor obeyed him. The portrait of the chief acquired an aspect that defied description. The iridescent stones gleamed in place of eyes in the wet, grey clay; their gleam filled the face with magic life. The contrast had, at first, seemed unnatural to Pandion, but later it filled him with amazement. The more he looked, the more exceptional the harmony he found in the combination of glassy eyes and the dark clay of the sculptured face. The elephant trainer was very pleased.

"Take these stones as a souvenir, stranger craftsman!" exclaimed the chief and poured a number of them into Pandion's hand. Some of them were bigger than a plum stone in size. "These stones come from the southern plains and are found in the rivers there. There's nothing in the world that's harder or purer than these stones. When you're back in your distant land, you can show people the marvels of the south acquired by the Elephant People."

Pandion thanked the old man and went away, hiding the gift in the bag that held Yakhmos' stone.

"Don't forget, come tomorrow!" the chief called after him.

Back in their hut, the former slaves talked excitedly about what would happen as a result of the success that attended Pandion's work. Their hopes in the early continuance of their journey were strengthened. It seemed that there was every reason to expect the Elephant People would let them go and show them the correct road.

At the appointed hour, Pandion and Kidogo appeared at the house of the chief. The old man beckoned to them to come up. They sat at the feet of the elephant trainer, hiding their excitement with difficulty. For some time, the chief sat in silence, and when he spoke, he addressed them both at once.

"I've taken counsel with the other chiefs, and they agree with me. Half a moon from now, after the grand hunt, we shall be sending a big expedition to the west for Coaling nuts and for gold. Six elephants will go through the forest and farther to the upper reaches of a big river, seven days march from here. Give me that stick," said the chief to Pandion.

The old man drew the outlines of a big gulf where the sea cut deep into dry land, and Kidogo gave a faint cry. The chief drew a wavy line to indicate a river with two branches at its head and placed a cross in a junction of the waterways.

"The elephants will go this far, you'll follow them and will pass easily through the forest. From there you'll have to go alone, but it will take you five days more to reach the sea."

"O father and prince!" exclaimed the excited Kidogo, "you are our savior. That river flows within the bounds of my country, and I know the plateau where the gold is found." The Kemtiu jumped up in ecstasy.

"I know," continued the old chief, with a somewhat supercilious smile, "I know your people and your country, and was at one time acquainted with one of your strongest chiefs, Yorumefu."

"Yorumeful!" exclaimed Kidogo. "He's my mother's brother!"

"Good," said the chief, interrupting Kidogo. "You will give him my greetings. Have you understood everything I've told you?" Without waiting for an answer, he finished by saying, "now I want to speak to your friend."

The chief turned to Pandion.

"I feel that you'll become a great man in your own country if you succeed in returning home. Ask me whatever you will, and I will answer you."

"For a long time, I've been thinking of asking you how you subdue the elephants," said Pandion. "Or perhaps it's a secret," he added doubtfully.

"The training of elephants is a secret to fools alone," smiled the old chief, "Any man of wisdom can easily guess how it's done. Apart from the secret, however, it implies hard and dangerous work and unlimited patience. Brains aren't sufficient, there's tough work as well. There are but few tribes in this land that possess the three qualities my people have - intellect, industry, and unbounded courage. You must understand, stranger, that a full-grown elephant cannot be trained. We catch them when they're still quite young. A young elephant is trained for ten years. Ten years of persistent labor are required for the elephant to begin to understand the commands given him by man, and to do the necessary work."

"Ten years!" exclaimed the astounded Pandion.

"Yes, not a moment less, that is, if you have correctly judged the character of the elephant. If you make a mistake, you will not manage the task even in fifteen years. There are stubborn animals and stupid ones amongst the elephants.

Then, you must not forget that the capture of young elephants is a matter of great danger. We have to capture them with our own hands, without the aid of trained elephants because they may go back to join the herd. The trained elephants help us when the herd has been driven off, and the youngsters are made fast. Several of our bravest men are always killed during an elephant hunt."

The old chief's voice took on a note of sorrow.

"Tell me, have you seen the exercises that our young warriors perform? You have. Good. These exercises are also necessary training in the art of elephant hunting."

On several occasions, Pandion had seen the unusual games played by the Elephant People. The warriors planted two high posts on a level open space and fixed a bamboo crosspiece between them at the height of about five cubits from the ground. They would then take a long run, make an irregular sort of sideways leap into the air and fly over the crossbar. The jumper's body would double up, almost in two, and fly into the air with the right side forward in the direction of the jump.

Pandion had never before seen anybody jump so high. Some of the best jumpers could spring to a height of almost six cubits. Pandion was filled with astonishment at the great skill of the Elephant People, but could not understand what use they could put this ability to. The words of the stern old chief did something to explain the significance of these exercises.

After a short pause, the chief continued in a louder voice:

"Now you see how difficult a matter it is. Other tribes hunt elephants. They kill them with heavy spears hurled down from trees, drive them into pits or creep up to them when they are asleep in the forest. I'll do this for you."

The old chief slapped himself on the knee.

"I'll order the elephant hunters to take you with them on; the next hunt. It will be soon before our expedition leaves for the western forests. Do you want to witness the glory and the torment of my people?"

"I do, and I thank you, chief. And may my companions go with me?"

"All of you would be too many. Invite one or two to go with you, more would hamper our hunters."

"Then let my two friends go with me. He can go," Pandion indicated Kidogo, "and one other."

"You mean the morose-looking man with the thick beard?" asked the chief, meaning Cavius. The young Hellene affirmed the correctness of his supposition.

"I also want to have a talk with him, tell him to come to me," said the old man. "I suppose you're in a hurry to tell your companions that we are willing to help them. When we appoint the day of the hunt, you will be informed."

The old chief dismissed the two friends with a gesture.

To the menacing rumble of tom-toms, the tribesmen assembled for the hunt. Some of them were mounted on elephants, loaded with ropes, food, and water, the remainder went on foot. Pandion, Kidogo, and Cavius, armed with their heavy spears, joined the latter party.

Two hundred hunters crossed the river and set out across the plains in a northerly direction, making for a range of bare stony hills faintly visible in the blue haze above the horizon. The hunters moved so fast that even such experienced walkers as our three friends had difficulty in keeping pace with them.

The ground that lay to the south and east of the range of hills was perfectly flat, with huge expanses of the level, burnt-up grassland. The wind raised clouds of dust over the yellow plain, obscuring the dull greenery of the trees and bushes. The nearer cliffs were clearly visible, but the rocks beyond them were almost hidden by a greyish-blue mist. Steep rounded peaks jutted up like the skulls of gigantic, phantom elephants; while the lower rocks were hunched up like the backs of huge crocodiles.

The Elephant People spent the night under the southern end of the chai of rocks and at dawn moved off along their eastern slope. Over the plain ahead of them hung a reddish mirage, in which quivered the diffused silhouettes of trees. An extensive swamp spread away to the north.

A young man left the hunting party and ordered the three strangers to follow him up the rocky ridge. Cavius, Pandion, and Kidogo climbed up to a ledge two hundred cubits higher than the surrounding plain. Over their heads rose a sheer stone precipice that breathed intense heat, its bright yellow surface scored by the zigzags of numerous cracks. The hunter led the friends to another ledge that overlooked the swamp, ordered them to take cover behind tufts of coarse grass and stones, made a sign implying silence and left them.

For a long time, the three friends lay still under the blazing sun, not daring to say a word. Not a sound came from the valley that spread out below them.

Suddenly from the left, faint squelchy noises came

floating towards them, growing louder as they drew nearer. From behind his stone, Pandion looked out cautiously through the scarcely moving grass and held his breath.

The dark grey cloud of thousands of elephants covered the swamp. The huge animals were crossing it diagonally from the side of the rocks and, passing over the boundary between swamp and grassland, were making for the southeast. The bodies of the animals stood cut clearly against the yellowish-grey grass. They were moving in herds with anything from a hundred to five hundred head in each, herd following after herd, with a short interval between them. Each herd formed a solid mass of animals pressed close against each other. Viewed from above, it looked like the movement of a grey island whose surface, undulating with hundreds of backs, was scarred by the white streaks of the tusks.

In the swampy places, the herd stretched out in a thin line. Some of the elephants left the herd ran to one side and stood there spreading their great ears and placing their hind-legs apart in a funny way; they soon, however, rejoined the general stream.

Some of them, mostly the huge bulls, moved unhurriedly. Their heads and ears lowered were lowered. Others advanced gravely, holding the forepart of the body high and crisscrossing their hind-legs. A third kind waddled along sideways, their thin tails jutting up above them; tusks of the most varied shapes and sizes - some short, others so long that they almost reached the ground, some curved upwards and others quite straight - flashed white against the grey background.

Kidogo brought his lips close to Pandion's ear.

"The elephants are moving towards the swamps and rivers," he said. "The grasslands are burnt up."

"Where are the hunters?" Pandion asked. "They are waiting in hiding for a herd that contains a lot of young elephants; such herds are always at the end. You can see there are only full-grown elephants here."

"Why is it some elephants have long tusks and others short?"

"The short ones are broken."

"Fighting amongst themselves?"

"I have been told that elephants rarely fight amongst themselves. They mostly break their tusks when they pull up trees. They use their tusks to overturn trees so that they can eat the fruits, leaves and thin twigs. The forest elephants have much stronger tusks than the plains elephants; that's why hard ivory goes to the markets from the forests and soft ivory from the plains."

"Are these forest or plains elephants?"

"They're plains elephants. Look for yourself." Kidogo pointed to an old elephant that was hanging back not far from the rocks where the friends were hiding.

The grey giant, knee-high in the grass, turned directly towards the watching friends. Its ears were spread out widely on either side, their skin stretched taut like sails. The elephant lowered its head. This movement brought the animal's sloping forehead forward, deep pits appeared between the eyes and the crown of the head, and the whole head took on the appearance of a massive pillar that tapered towards the bottom, unnoticeably changing to the vertical pendant trunk. Deep transverse folds, like dark rings, marked the trunk at regular intervals. At the base of the trunk, two tubes jutted out at a sharp angle on either side, from which very short and thick tusks spread outwards.

"I can't understand how you knew that it was a plains elephant," whispered Pandion after carefully examining the calm old giant.

"Do you see his tusks? They're not broken, they're worn away. They don't grow on an old elephant like they do on one in the prime of his life, and he has worn them away because they are soft. You never see such tusks on a forest elephant. They are mostly long and thin."

The friends conversed softly. Time passed, and the leading elephants disappeared beyond the horizon, the entire herd turning into a dark strip. From the left came still another herd. At its head marched four bull elephants of enormous size, almost eight cubits high. They waved their heads as they walked, their long, slightly curved tusks rising and falling, and at times touching the grass with their sharp points.

There were many cows in the herd distinguished by their sunken backs and the huge folds of skin on their flanks.

Baby elephants, pressing close to the hind-legs of the cows, toddled along uncertainly; while to one side, keeping to themselves, was the merry throng of the elephant youth. Their tiny tusks and ears, their small long heads, their big stomachs and the equal length of their fore and hind-legs distinguished them from the grown-ups.

The friends realized that the decisive moment of the hunt had come. It was difficult for the baby elephants to march through the swamp, and the herd moved farther to the right, on to a strip of hard ground between the bushes and occasional trees.

"Why is it that such a heavy animal as the elephant doesn't get stuck in the swamps?" asked Pandion.

"They have special feet," began Kidogo, "they..."

A thunderous noise, made by the hunters banging on sheets of metal and tom-toms, accompanied by their frenzied howls, spread so suddenly across the plain that the friends gasped in amazement.

The elephant herd, panic-stricken, rushed for the swamp only to find there another line of men with tom-toms and trumpets that rose out of the grass. The leading elephants held back, checking the pressure from those behind them. The shrill trumpeting of the frightened elephants, the thunder of metal sheets, the crackle of breaking branches - through all that hellish noise the thin, plaintive whine of the calves could occasionally be heard.

The animals dashed here and there, at first bunching together, then again spreading out. The figures of the men could be seen in the dust clouds in the midst of that chaos of milling giants. The hunters did not approach the herd but ran from place to place, reformed their ranks, and again beat their metal sheets.

Gradually the friends began to understand what the hunters were doing; they were cutting the young elephants off from the adults and forcing them to the right into the open mouth of a dry watercourse that cut into the stone cliff and protected by a strip of forest.

The grey giants ran after the hunters, trying to trample on enemies that had appeared from they knew not where. The men, however, leaping high into the air, hid in the bushes and behind the trees.

While the infuriated animals were waving their trunks and seeking their hidden enemies, new rows of hunters, screaming wildly and rattling their metal sheets, appeared from the other side. The elephants turned on the newcomers who repeated the same maneuver to cut off the young elephants.

The herd moved farther and farther into the grasslands, grey bodies disappeared behind the trees, and only the deafening noise and the clouds of dust that rose high into the air indicated the hunting ground.

The astounded friends, amazed at the bravery and skill of the hunters in avoiding the maddened monsters who charged down on them, and continuing their dangerous business no matter what happened, gazed in silence at the empty land with its crushed bushes and broken trees.

Kidogo's face wore a worried frown as he listened to what was going on, and he said softly:

"Something's wrong. The hunt isn't going the way it should!"

"How do you know that?" asked the astonished Cavius.

"They brought us here because they expected the herd to move to the east. The herd has moved off to the right, I suppose that must be bad."

"Let's go over there, back along the ledge, the way we came," suggested Pandion.

Kidogo pondered over the suggestion for a moment and then agreed. In the bustle of the hunt, their coming could not make any difference.

Bending low and keeping concealed behind stones and grass, the three friends moved a distance of a thousand cubits back in the direction from which they had come until they were again opposite the open plain. They could see the gully in the rocks where the hunters had driven more than a dozen young elephants. The hunters were darting about amongst the trees, skillfully dropping nooses over the animals, and fastening them to the tree-trunks. A line of warriors armed with broad spears closed the entrance to the gully. The noise and shouting were now at its height some two thousand cubits away; apparently, the larger part of the herd was over there.

Suddenly, the loud trumpeting of elephants came from in front and from the left. Kidogo shuddered.

"The elephants are attacking," he whispered.

A man let out a long moan, the angry cries of another sounded like words of command.

On the far side of the open space in front of them, where two wide-spreading trees cast a huge patch of shadow, the friends could see some movement. A moment later, a huge elephant appeared from there with his ears outspread and his trunk stretched out in front of him like a log. Two other similar giants followed him. Pandion recognized them as the monsters who had led the herd. The fourth, accompanied by several other elephants, was a little distance behind.

From the bushes on the right hunters ran out to cut off the elephants. They ran between them, and as they ran, they threw spears at the elephant that had last appeared. The latter trumpeted furiously and turned on the men who were running as fast as their legs could carry them towards the swamp. The other elephants followed him.

The three leaders paid no attention to the hunters' scheme to separate them from their fellows and continued their race towards the valley between the rocks, most probably attracted by the cries of the young.

"That's bad, that's bad, the leaders have turned in the other direction," whispered Kidogo excitedly, squeezing Pandion's arm till it hurt.

"Look... Look, there's bravery for you," shouted Cavius, forgetting himself.

The hunters that barred the entrance to the valley stood firm and made no attempt to conceal themselves from the infuriated monsters. As they moved forward, strung out in a long chain, the low, burned-out grass offered them no cover. The leading elephant rushed straight at the middle of the line of hunters.

Two men stood stock-still while their neighbors on either side sprang forward towards the approaching giant. The elephant slackened his pace, raised his trunk high into the air, trumpeted maliciously and set out to trample the hunters underfoot. No more than ten cubits separated the brave men from the elephant when they leaped aside like lightning. At that same moment, two men rose out of the grass beside each of the elephant's hind-legs; two of them thrust their broad spears into the animal's belly, and the other two leaned back to strike at the elephant's legs. A high-pitched, whistling note escaped the leader's raised trunk. Lowering it, the elephant turned his head towards the nearest man on the right.

The hunter could not escape him or was too slow in his movements. Blood spurted from his body, and the three friends could see from their vantage point the bare bones of his side and shoulder. The wounded man fell to the ground without a sound, but the elephant also collapsed heavily on to its hindquarters and began slowly crawling away sideways.

The hunters that had stopped the leading elephant then joined their comrades who were engaging the other two. These were either cleverer or had previous experience of man; they dashed from side to side, giving the hunters no opportunity to creep up behind them, and crushed three men underfoot. The clouds of dust that hung over the scene of the hunt turned red in the rays of the setting sun.

The elephants looked like huge black towers at the base of which fearless men were darting to and fro. They leaped into the air to escape the long tusks, met the animals' trunks with spears thrust shaft downwards into the ground, and with loud shouts ran behind the elephants, attracting attention away from other hunters who would otherwise have been trampled to death.

The frenzied animals kept up their incessant trumpeting. When they turned their heads towards the rocks on which the three friends were sitting, they seemed extraordinarily tall, their widespread ears waved high above the hunters. Seen from the side the elephants, their heads lowered, looked smaller, their tusks almost raked the ground, ready to gore their enemies.

Pandion, Cavius, and Kidogo realized that they were looking at only part of the battle; it was going on far away beyond the trees where the herd was concentrated, and away to the left in the swamp where the hunters had drawn off the fourth leader and the elephants that had come with him. The three friends had no idea what was going on there, but they had no time to think about it, for the bloody struggle being enacted before their eyes demanded all their attention.

From behind the trees came the rumble of approaching

tom-toms as several dozen hunters went to the aid of their comrades.

The leaders of the elephant herd halted in indecision, the men shouted and waved their spears, and the elephants retreated. They ran to the third, wounded leader, stood one on either side of him, pushed their tusks under his heavy body and lifted him on to his feet. Squeezing him between their huge bodies, they dragged him behind the trees, dropped him, picked him up again and made off.

Several of the hunters started out to follow up the elephants, but the chief hunter stopped them.

"He won't get away... they'll soon leave him... you'll infuriate them again..." Kidogo translated his words.

The noise away to the right died down. Apparently, the battle had been won. A group of hunters that appeared from the north, from the direction of the swamp, were carrying two inert bodies. Nobody paid any attention to the three friends who made their way cautiously down to the plain to survey the field of battle.

They went towards the place where the main herd was concentrated. As they pressed their way through the bushes, Kidogo suddenly jumped back in fright - a dying elephant, the tip of its trunk still quivering, lay on the crown of a tree that he must have broken down by falling against it. Farther on, where the trees were sparser, a second elephant lay in a grey heap on its belly, with bent legs and its back hunched up. As it scented the approach of men, it raised its head; the thick folds of skin that lay around its dull, sunken eyes gave the animal the expression of the infinite weariness of old age. The giant lowered its head, leaning on its tusks, and then with a dull thud fell on its side. All around, the hunters were calling to each other.

Kidogo waved his hand and turned back - another herd of elephants had appeared from the south. The friends hurried back to the rocks, but this time it was a false alarm. The trained elephants of the Elephant People were approaching.

The young elephants tied to the trees stuck up their tails and made frantic efforts to get at the men, trying to reach them with their trunks. The elephant drivers placed their trained animals one on either side of the captives. They squeezed them between their bodies and led them away to the village.

Precautionary ropes were fixed to the neck and hind-legs of every young elephant; fifteen men in front and behind held the ropes. The tired faces of the hunters, haggard from the terrific strain of the hunt, were filled with gloom. Eleven dead bodies had already been laid out on the wattle platforms on the backs of elephants, and hunters were still beating the bushes in search of another two missing men.

The elephants with the captives were led away, and the hunters sat or lay on the ground resting after the fray. The friends went up to the chief hunter and asked him whether there was anything they could do to help. The chief hunter looked at them angrily and said brusquely:

"Help? What can you do to help, strangers? It's been a hard hunt, and we've lost many brave men. Wait where you were told and don't get in our way!"

The friends went back to the rocks and sat down apart from the hunters, afraid to quarrel with people on whom their entire future depended. Cavius, Pandion, and Kidogo lay down to wait until they were called, and talked softly amongst themselves. The sun was going down, and long shadows from the battlemented rocks stretched out into the plain.

"Still I can't understand why the huge elephants don't kill all the people in battle," said Cavius thoughtfully. "If the elephants were to fight better, they could crush all the hunters to dust."

"You're right," agreed Kidogo. "It's the good luck of man that the elephant is fainthearted."

"How can that be?" asked the astonished Etruscan.

"It's simply because the elephant isn't used to fighting. He's so big and strong that no other animal ever attacks him; he's not threatened with danger since only man is bold enough to hunt him. This is why the grey giant is not a reliable fighter, his will is easily broken, and he can't stand up to a long fight if he doesn't crush his enemy immediately. The buffalo is a different case. If the buffalo possessed the size and intellect of the elephant, all those who hunt him would be killed."

Cavius muttered something indefinite under his breath; he did not know whether to believe the Kemtiu or not; but then he recalled the indecision which he had seen the elephants display at the most decisive moment of the battle, and said no more.

"The spears the Elephant People use are quite different from ours; the blades are eight fingers wide," put in Pandion. "What enormous strength must be needed to strike with such a spear."

Kidogo suddenly stood up and listened. Not a sound came from the side where the hunters had been resting. The sky, golden in the setting sun, was rapidly darkening.

"They have gone away and forgotten us," exclaimed

the Kemtiu and ran out from behind the rocks.

Not a soul was to be seen anywhere. In the distance, scarcely audible voices were calling to one another; the hunters were on their way back to the village without the three friends.

"Let's follow them immediately, the journey is a long one," said Pandion hastily, but the Kemtiu held his friend back.

"It's too late, the sun will disappear soon, and we'll lose our way in the dark," said Kidogo. "Better wait until the moon comes up, it won't be long."

Pandion and Cavius agreed and lay down to rest.

CHAPTER EIGHT

The Sons of The Wind

Hyenas barked, and jackals howled plaintively in the impenetrable darkness. Kidogo was worried. He kept looking towards the east where an ash-grey strip of sky above the treetops heralded the rising moon.

"I don't know if there are any wild dogs here or not," muttered Kidogo.

"If there are, we'll be in trouble. Dogs attack together, the whole pack of them, and overcome even the buffalo."

The sky grew lighter, the grim, black rocks turned to silver, and the trees in the plain showed up as black silhouettes. The moon had risen.

The three friends, their spears grasped firmly in their hands, set out southwards along the chain of rocky hills. They hastened away from the gloomy battlefield where the carrion eaters were feasting on the dead elephants. The howls died away behind them, the plain around them seemed lifeless, and only the swift steps of the three men broke the silence of the night.

Kidogo carefully avoided dense groves of trees and thickets of bushes that formed mysterious black hills towering here and there above the grass. The Kemtiu chose his path through open spaces that gleamed like white lakes in a labyrinth of black islands of vegetation. The chain of rocky hills turned to the west, and a narrow strip of forest kept the friends close to the rocks.

Kidogo turned to the right and led the way across a long, stony open space, which sloped down in a southerly direction. Suddenly the Kemtiu stopped, turned abruptly around, and stood to listen. Pandion and Cavius strained their ears, but not a sound could they hear in any direction. As before, absolute silence reigned supreme.

The Kemtiu went hesitantly forward, increasing his pace, and did not answer the whispered questions of the Etruscan and the Hellene. They had advanced a further thousand cubits when the Kemtiu again stopped. His eyes showed a troubled gleam in the bright moonlight.

"Something's following us," he whispered and lay down with his ear to the ground.

Pandion followed his friend's example, but Cavius remained standing, straining his eyes to see through the silver curtain of moonlight. Pandion lay with his ear pressed to the hot stony earth and at first, could hear nothing but his own breathing.

The silent, menacing uncertainty alarmed him. Suddenly, a weak, scarcely audible sound was transmitted through the earth from a distance. The regularly repeated sounds grew more frequent - click, click, click. Pandion held up his head, and the sounds stopped immediately. Kidogo continued listening for some time, pressing first one, then the other ear to the ground; then he leaped to his feet like a spring released.

"Some big animal is following us, it's a bad thing that I don't know what animal. Its claws are outside, like those of a dog or hyena, so it isn't a lion or a leopard..."

"Buffalo or rhinoceros," suggested Cavius.

Kidogo shook his head energetically.

"No, it's a beast of prey," he snapped with confidence. "We must find cover... no trees near us," he whispered, looking round in alarm.

The country ahead of them was an almost flat stony stretch of open ground with occasional tufts of grass and small bushes.

"Forward, as fast as we can!" Kidogo hurried them on, and the friends ran along carefully, trying to avoid the long thorns on the bushes and the cracks in the dried earth.

Now the scratching of heavy talons on the stony ground could clearly be heard behind them. The increased frequency of the regular clatter of the claws told the friends that the animal had also broken into a run. Click, click, click. The sounds drew nearer and nearer.

Pandion looked over his shoulder and saw a tall swaying silhouette, a grey phantom pursuing them. Kidogo kept turning his head this way and that, trying to pick out a tree somewhere ahead of them and to judge the speed of the unknown animal. He realized that the trees were too far away and that the friends would not be able to reach them in time.

"The animal is gaining on us," said the Kemtiu stopping. "If we keep our backs to it, we shall die a sorry death!" he added excitedly.

"We must fight it," said the saturnine Cavius.

The three friends stood side by side, facing the menacing grey phantom that was bearing down on them in silence. During the whole period of pursuit, the animal had not emitted a single sound, and it was this strange fact, so unusual in the wild beasts of the plains, that disturbed the friends. The diffused grey silhouette grew darker. Its outlines became clearer.

When the animal had reduced the distance between

them to no more than three hundred cubits, it slowed down and approached at a steady walk, confident that its chosen victims would not escape.

The friends had never before seen any such animal. Its massive forelegs were longer than its hinds, the forepart of the body rose high above the spine; the back sloped away towards the croup. The heavy head, with massive jaws and a steep, prominent forehead, sat upright on the thick neck. The animal's short, light fur was speckled with darker patches. Long black hair stuck up on the back of its head and neck.

It bore a distant resemblance to a spotted hyena, but of a monstrous size such as nobody had ever seen before; its head was a good five cubits from the ground. The wide chest, shoulders, and withers were frightening in their massiveness. The muscles stood out like hillocks, and the huge claws clattered maliciously on the ground putting fear into those who heard them. The beast moved with a strange, irregular gait, swinging its low rump, and nodding its heavy head so that the lower jaw almost touched the throat.

"What is it?" asked Pandion in a whisper, licking his dry lips.

"I don't know," answered the perplexed Kidogo. "I've never heard of such an animal as this."

The animal suddenly turned; its huge eyes, directed straight at the waiting men, lit up with flickering flames. The animal sidled round the men to the right, then stopped again, with its eyes fixed on them. Its rounded ears jutted out obliquely from its head.

"The brute is intelligent; it has moved around so that the moonlight is against us," whispered Kidogo, his breath coming in short gasps.

A nervous shiver ran through Pandion's body such as

he always felt before a dangerous fight. The animal drew a deep breath and advanced slowly on the men. In its movements, in its malevolent silence, in the persistent stare of the big eyes under the protruding forehead, there was something that distinguished it from all other animals the friends had ever seen.

The three men realized instinctively that the animal was a relic of an older world with different laws of life.

Shoulder to shoulder, their spears held ready, the three men advanced to meet the nocturnal monster. For an instant it stood still, perplexed, then, uttering a short, hoarse sound, hurled itself at them. The huge jaw opened, the thick teeth flashed in the moonlight as three spears plunged into the broad chest and neck of the monster.

The men could not withstand the pressure of the animal's weight and, furthermore, it possessed enormous strength. The spears struck against bone and were turned aside and pulled out of their hands; the three of them were thrown back. Kidogo and Pandion managed to scramble to their feet, but Cavius found himself lying under the beast. The two friends rushed to his rescue.

The monster sat back on its hind-legs and suddenly swung out its front paws. Blunt claws struck Pandion in the hip with such force that he fell and almost lost consciousness. The animal planted its enormous paw on Pandion's leg, causing him terrific pain, the joints cracked, and the animal's claws tore skin and flesh.

Pandion, his spear in his hand, lifted himself from the ground with both hands and, as he did so, he heard Kidogo's spear-shaft break. Rising to his knees, he saw that the Kemtiu held down by the animal. Its open jowl was drawing near to him. Kidogo, his eyes popping out of his head, was pressing both hands under the lower jaw of the monster to turn its head away. Pandion's trusted friend was perishing before his eyes.

The young Hellene was beside himself and, feeling no pain, jumped up and thrust his spear into the animal's neck. The animal snapped its teeth loudly and turned on Pandion, knocking him off his feet with the movement. The young Hellene did not let go the spear and, holding the spear-shaft on the ground, for a short time held the animal fast, while Kidogo managed to get out his knife.

Neither Pandion nor the Kemtiu noticed Cavius rise up on the other side of the animal. Baring his teeth in a grin, the Etruscan coolly aimed at the animal's flank with his spear and thrust it in behind the shoulder blade with both hands. The long blade went in a cubit deep, a roar escaped the gaping mouth of the monster; it shuddered convulsively and turned left, towards the Etruscan. The latter, hunching his shoulders and pulling his head down between them, staggered but did not fall.

Kidogo, with a piercing yell, drove his knife into the animal's throat, and at that same moment, the Etruscan's spear reached the animal's heart. The great beast collapsed convulsively, and an unbearable stench spread around it. Pandion withdrew his spear and thrust it again into the back of the animal's neck, but this last blow was unnecessary. The animal stretched its neck, stubbed its jowl against Cavius, and stretched out its hind-legs, that were still quivering; the claws scratched the earth, the muscles contracted under the skin, but the stiff hairs on the back of the neck had fallen flat.

Great was the joy of the three friends at their

deliverance from the terrible monster that lay motionless before them in the moonlight.

As soon as they had come to themselves, the three friends examined their wounds. A piece of flesh had been torn out of the Etruscan's shoulder, and the animal's long claws had furrowed his back. Pandion's leg was not broken, but he had a deep wound below the knee, and apparently, the tendons had been strained or torn, so that he could not step on his foot. His side was swollen and black from the blow of the animal's paw, but no ribs were broken. Kidogo had suffered more than the others had. He had several deep wounds and had been badly crushed.

The friends bound each other's wounds with strips torn from their loincloths. Pandion was more worried than the others, for his wounded leg made it impossible for him to walk. Kidogo soothed his friend, assuring him that they were now out of danger and that the body of the monster would be sure protection against all other beasts of prey. The Elephant People would miss them and at dawn would set out to find them.

Bearing with patience and fortitude the pain of their burning wounds, the three friends stretched out on the hard stones but were unable to sleep in their excitement.

Dawn came very suddenly, and the sun drove away the mysterious and ominous shadows of the night.

Pandion, tormented by the pain in his leg, opened his tired eyes at the sound of a loud shout from Kidogo. The Kemtiu was examining their nocturnal pursuer and was explaining to Cavius that he had seen drawings of such animals in Tha-Quem, amongst pictures of other animals in a tomb in the City of the White Walls. Cavius stuck out his lower lip incredulously. Kidogo swore and tried to convince his friend that the inhabitants of Tha-Quem had no doubt met with such animals in the distant past.

The sun rose higher. Thirst tormented the three friends, and they were racked with fever from their wounds.

Kidogo and Cavius had decided to go in search of water when they suddenly heard voices. Three elephants with warriors on their backs were moving across the plain below the stony slope on which the friends had met the terror of the night. The Elephant People, hearing Kidogo's shouts, turned their elephants towards them and set them at a faster pace. The elephants were approaching the three strangers when they suddenly shied and began trumpeting uneasily, raising their trunks, and spreading their ears. The warriors jumped down from their platforms and ran towards the dead monster with cries of "Gishu! Gishu!" Yesterday's chief hunter gave the three friends a look of approval and said with a catch in his hoarse voice:

"You are indeed famous warriors if the three of you alone could overcome the terror of the night, the eater of the thick-skinned animals."

The Elephant People told the three friends about the gishu, a very rare and dangerous animal. Nobody knew where it lay hidden by day, but during the night it wandered about in silence, attacking young elephants, rhinoceroses, and the young of other big animals. The gishu was exceptionally strong and stubborn in battle. Its terrible teeth could bite off the leg of an elephant at one snap, and its powerful forepaws crushed its victims, breaking their bones.

Cavius made signs asking the hunters to help him skin the animal. Four warriors willingly set about the task, paying no attention to the horrible stench. The skin and the head were lifted on to an elephant. The three friends were also lifted by the warriors. The elephants, obedient to light blows of their drivers' hooked knives, set out at a smart trot and in a short time covered the distance to the village, which they reached by midday.

The villagers greeted them with shouts of welcome. From the height of the elephants' backs, the warriors shouted out, announcing the details of the great deed of valor.

Kidogo, his face beaming, sat proudly beside Pandion on the wide swaying elephant platform, five cubits above the earth. The Kemtiu had started singing several times, but each time the Elephant People had stopped him, warning him that the elephants did not like noise, and were accustomed to moving in silence.

Four days journey separated them from the village of the Elephant People. The chief had kept his word, and the party of former slaves was allowed to follow the tribe's expedition to the west. As their wounds had not yet healed, Pandion, Cavius, and Kidogo were given a place on one of the six elephants and their sixteen companions followed behind on foot. The elephants marched only half the day, the remainder of the time being required to feed and rest them. Those who were following on foot, however, could just overtake the elephants by nightfall.

The elephant drivers did not select for their charges the way that the people would have chosen for themselves. They avoided forests with stands of tall trees and crashed their way through the bush country where the undergrowth was so thick that the men would have had to hack their way through. From time to time, the leading elephant was changed and sent to the rear to rest. The elephants left a path behind them along which the liberated slaves marched without a single blow of a knife, full of admiration at the ease with which the impenetrable thickets were crushed underfoot.

The three friends on the elephant were even better off. The platform on which they sat swayed slightly as it floated continuously over the ground with its thorn-bushes, insects, and dangerous snakes, stretches of foul, stinking mud, sharp stones on rocky slopes, grass that cut the feet, and deep, gaping crevices.

Only now did Pandion realize the great care that had to be exercised by a traveler on foot through the African jungles and bushlands. Constant vigilance was necessary for a man to remain uninjured, and preserve his strength and fighting ability for the journey ahead of him.

The elephants strode on through all obstacles with the reliability of granite blocks, and Pandion had ample time to drink in the beauty of this strange country, its color, form, aromas, and the magnificence of its plant and animal life.

In the glaring sunlight of the glades, the pure tones of the flowers attained such extraordinary brilliance that to Pandion's northern eye, there seemed to be something vaguely wrong with them. The glaring color sequences seemed harsh and dissonant when compared with the soft, harmonious colors of his native Hellas. But whenever clouds covered the sky, or the party plunged into the deep twilight of the shady forests, this galaxy of color disappeared.

The party cut across an out jutting spur of the forest and found themselves in open, hilly, red-soil country where they again saw the leafless trees that exuded a milky sap. Their bluish-green branches stretched mournfully into the blinding glare of the sky; the tops looked as if they had been deliberately trimmed straight up, some thirty cubits from the ground. The thick trunks and leafless branches had the appearance of candelabra cast from some green metal. Huge blossoms, glowing red at the tips of the branches, gave one the impression of hundreds of torches burning in a sunless cemetery.

There was neither beast nor bird to disturb the deathlike stillness of the tropical heat in these motionless thickets. Farther on, deep watercourses with dazzling white sand scarred the soil, where the red soil had been washed away.

The travelers entered a labyrinth of narrow gullies whose friable purple walls rose to a height of a hundred cubits on either side. The elephants picked their way carefully through a maze of eroded cliffs, pyramids, turrets, and frail pillars. Now and again, they passed through deep depressions, round like bowls, in which spurs of different soil spread radially across the level floor. These spurs formed steep, sharp walls of friable earth that sometimes collapsed as the party passed by, frightening the elephants, who shied away from them.

The color of the eroded earth was constantly changing; a wall of warm red tones would give way to one of light brown that, in turn, was followed by bright yellow pyramids interspersed with strips and ledges of dazzling white.

It seemed to Pandion that he had entered a fairy kingdom. These deep, dry, and lifeless canyons hid a wealth of color contrasts, the iridescence of inanimate nature. Again, came densely wooded ridges, again the green walls hemmed in the travelers, and the elephant platform was like an island floating slowly over a sea of leaves and branches.

Pandion noticed how carefully the drivers led their

elephants, and how carefully they examined the animals' skin at halts. When he asked one of them why they did this, the Kemtiu placed his hand on a gourd that hung at his belt.

"It's a bad thing for an elephant to graze its skin or injure it in any way," said the driver. "If he does, his blood turns bad, and the animal soon dies. We have medicinal pitch we always keep at hand to treat all injuries without delay."

The young Hellene was astonished to learn that the powerful, long-lived giants were so vulnerable, but then he realized why the wise old animals were so careful. The elephants took a lot of looking after. The sites of the night's bivouac and resting places were selected with great care, after a lengthy examination of the country, and numerous consultations. The tethered elephants were surrounded by keen-eyed watchmen, who kept awake the whole night through. Special reconnaissance parties were sent out far ahead to make sure that there were no wild elephants in the neighborhood, and if any were met with, they were driven off with loud cries.

At the bivouacs, the friends talked with their fellow travelers, who answered all their questions. On one occasion, Pandion asked the caravan leader, an elderly man of short stature, why they went so willingly to the elephant hunts despite the terrible danger. The deep furrows around the leader's mouth grew even more in-depth. He answered unwillingly:

"You talk like a coward, although you do not look like one. The elephants are the strength of our people. Owing to the elephants, we live in ease and plenty, but we pay for that with our lives. If we were afraid, we shouldn't live any better than the tribes that feed on lizards and roots. Those who are afraid of death, live a life of hunger and misery. If you know that your death means life to your family, then you go boldly into any danger! My son, a brave man, in the prime of his life, was killed during an elephant hunt."

The caravan leader screwed up his eyes morosely as he turned them on Pandion.

"Perhaps you think different, stranger? If so, why have you journeyed through many countries, fighting against men and beasts, instead of remaining in slavery?"

Pandion grew ashamed and asked no more questions.

Kidogo, who was sitting by the campfire, suddenly got up and shuffled over to a group of trees standing at a distance of two hundred cubits from the camp. The sinking sun turned the big oval leaves to gold, and the thin branches quivered in the light breeze. Kidogo carefully examined the irregular, lumpy bark of their thin trunks, gave a shout of joy and pulled out his knife.

A little later the Kemtiu came back carrying two bunches of reddish-grey bark. One of the bunches he took to the leader of the caravan.

"Give this to the chief as Kidogo's parting gift," he said. "This medicine is quite as good as the magic grass from the blue plains. When he is sick, tired, or sorrowing, let him crush the bark and make a decoction of it. He must drink only a little if he drinks too much it will not act as medicine but as poison. This bark restores strength to the aged, brings joy to the depressed, and new life to the weak. Take good note of that tree, you will be grateful for it." (Corynanthe yohimbe from the Rubiaceae family to which quinine and coffee trees also belong.)

The caravan leader took the gift with pleasure, and immediately ordered his men to get more of the bark;

Kidogo hid the second bunch in the skin of the gishu which Cavius carried with him.

The next day the elephants climbed on to a stony plateau overgrown with tall bushes so bent by the wind that they bowed down to the earth in green humps scattered about the dry grey grass.

Every breath of the wind that blew in their faces brought a pleasant freshness. Pandion brightened up. The air was filled with a strange fragrance, long forgotten yet still familiar, and infinitely dear; but soon it was lost amongst the strong perfumes the wind-carried from the sun-heated leaves of the forest that lay below them. Wide, easy slopes stretched to a great distance, dark strips, and patches of forest thickets marring the even blue of their bare surface.

Far away on the horizon, a high mountain range loomed purple in the haze.

"Tengrela, my country, is over there!" screamed Kidogo in ecstasies of joy, and the whole party turned to look in that direction. Kidogo waved his arms, sobbed, and laughed, and his mighty shoulders shook with excitement. Pandion could well understand the feelings of his friend, but a vague sense of jealousy embittered him. Kidogo had reached his homeland, but how much had he, Pandion, to overcome before the great hour came when he, like his friend, would be able to say:

"This is my native land!"

Unnoticed by the others, Pandion turned away and his head drooped; at that moment, he could not share his friend's joy.

The elephants descended a bare black slope of volcanic

rock where no vegetation could get a foothold on the solidified lava. Their path crossed a level platform dotted with numerous small lakes. The gleaming stretches of clear, blue water stood out in sharp contrast to the black banks.

Pandion gave a shudder as he suddenly saw before him Thessa's deep blue eyes and black tresses. The blue lakes seemed to be looking at him in reproach, like the eyes of Thessa herself.

Pandion's thoughts carried him back to Oeniadae, a vague but intense feeling of impatience filled his breast, and he moved over to his friend and embraced him. The tanned sinewy hand of Cavius lay in Kidogo's black hand, and the three friends joined their hands in a firm and joyous handshake.

The elephants were continuing the descent; the banks of a broad river-valley spread on both sides of them. A little farther on, it was joined by a similar valley on the right, and the two streams they carried, merging into a single river, raced on, gaining more water the farther they went. For a time, the elephants followed the left bank, marching at the foot of a line of eroded cliffs. Ahead of them, the cliffs dropped back from the river whose pure, clear water gurgled merrily as it rushed on through the shade of tall trees that met in a green arch over the river, which was here some fifteen cubits wide. The elephants halted before they reached the trees.

"This is the place," said the caravan leader. "We don't go any farther."

The three friends descended from their elephant and said farewell to their hosts. The caravan crossed the river, and the three friends stood for a long time watching the great grey beasts climb the slope leading to a flat-topped eminence to the north of the river.

An involuntary sigh of regret broke from the lips of all three as the mighty animals disappeared into the distance. The friends lit signal fires to guide the party that was following behind on foot.

"Let us go and look for reeds and small trees to build rafts with, said Kidogo to the Etruscan. "We can make the rest of the journey quickly by water. You, cripple, wait here by the fire and look after your leg," said the Kemtiu to Pandion with rough tenderness.

Pandion and Cavius left Kidogo on the bank of the river amongst his fellow-tribesmen. The smell of the nearby sea intoxicated the two friends, who had grown up on its shores. They pushed off their raft and floated down the left-hand sleeve of the river. Soon the raft was brought to rest on a sand bar.

The friends climbed up the steep bank, their feet and legs tangling in the tall grass. They made their way over a hilly ridge, and, panting with excitement, hurried to the top, and stood stock-still in silence, unable to speak or even to breathe.

They were overwhelmed by the endless expanse of the ocean; the gentle splashing of the waves sounded like thunder to them.

Cavius and Pandion stood breast-high in the tall grass with the feathery leaves of palm trees waving high over their heads. The line where the green of the foothills joined the burning sunlit sands of the seashore looked almost black. The golden sand was fringed with the silver line of the surf, beyond which transparent green waves rose and fell.

Farther out at sea, a straight line marked the edge of the offshore reefs, dazzlingly white against the blue of the open sea. Light, fluffy patches of cloud dotted the sky.

On the beach, a clump of five palms leaned out over the water, the light even breeze opening their leaves out and then folding them again like the tattered wings of birds with dark-brown and golden feathers. The leaves of the palms, the color of cast bronze, shut out the view of the sea and their sharp edges were tinged with brilliant fire, so great was the strength of the sun that shone through them.

The moist wind, bringing with it the salt smell of the sea, flowed over Pandion's face and bare breast as though it were embracing him after years of separation. Cavius and Pandion sat down on the cool, firm sand that was as level as the floor of a house.

After a short rest, they threw themselves into the gently rolling waves, and the sea welcomed them, tossing them tenderly on her bosom. Pandion and Cavius, their arms cutting through the sparkling crests of the waves, enjoyed to the full the smell of the salt spray until the sea-water began to make their healing wounds burn.

When they left the water, the two friends stood on the beach feasting their eyes on the distant ocean. It spread before them like a blue bridge that somewhere joined the waters of their native sea. At that very moment, similar waves were rolling against the white cliffs of Hellas, and the yellow rocks of Cavius' native Etruria.

The young Hellene felt his eyes fill with tears of joyous excitement; he no longer thought of the tremendous distance that still separated him from his home. Here was the sea, and beyond it, Thessa was waiting for him; there awaited everything that was near and dear to him, abandoned and hidden by years of harsh trials, and the countless stadia of the wearisome journey.

The two friends stood on a narrow strip of beach, their faces to the sea. Behind them rose high mountains covered with ominously dark forests, the fringe of a strange land whose burning deserts, plains, dry plateau, and dark and humid forests had held them captive so long; a land that had taken years of life from them, years that could have been devoted to their families. Their liberation had been bought by a long heroic struggle and titanic effort. If all that effort had been devoted to their native lands, it would have earned them honor and glory.

Cavius placed his heavy hands on Pandion's shoulder.

"Our fate is now in our own hands, Pandion!" he exclaimed. The fires of passion gleamed in his eyes, usually dark and morose. "There are two of us; surely we can reach the waters of the Green Sea now that we have fought our way to the shores of the Great Arc. Yes, we shall return, and on the way, we shall be the mainstay of our Libyan companions, who know little of navigation."

Pandion nodded his head but did not speak. Now that he stood face to face with the sea, he felt absolute confidence in his own strength.

Kidogo's voice rang out over the beach. The worried Kemtiu, followed by a crowd of his excited tribesmen and his fellow- travelers, was seeking the friends. Pandion and Cavius were taken back to the river and were ferried across to the other side, where several oxen awaited them for the transport of the wounded, and their weapons amid other belongings. A short stage would bring their wanderings to an end.

The promise made by Kidogo under the trees on the banks of the Nile, when they stood beside their dying comrades after the terrible battle with the rhinoceros, had been fulfilled. All nineteen of the former slaves were given a hearty welcome and an opportunity to rest in a large village near the sea, on the banks of a wide river that flowed parallel to the one they had floated down after leaving the Elephant People.

As far as Pandion and Cavius were concerned, the best thing of all was the news that the Sons of the Wind, after twenty years, had in the previous year, visited those shores again. "Sons of the Wind" was the name given by Kidogo's tribe to the Sea People who had, from time immemorial, come periodically from the northern seas to the Southern Horn in search of ivory, gold, medicinal herbs, and the skins of wild beasts.

The local people said that the Sons of the Wind were in outward appearance like the Etruscan and the Hellene, only their skin was darker and their hair even more curly. The year before, four black ships had come, following the ancient route of their ancestors. The Sons of the Wind had promised to come again as soon as the period of storms in the Sea of Mists was over. According to the calculations of experienced people, the ships should come in three months. It would take them much longer to build their own ship, quite apart from the fact that the sea route was unknown to them.

Pandion and Cavius doubted whether the Sea People would take them on board their ships, together with ten of their comrades, but Kido-go, winking and chuckling mysteriously, said that he would arrange that. There was nothing left to do but wait, although they were tormented by uncertainty. The Sons of the Wind might not return again for another twenty years. Pandion and Cavius comforted themselves with the thought that if the ships did not appear by the appointed time, they would begin building their own ship.

Kidogo's return was an event that was celebrated by noisy feasting. Pandion soon grew tired of the feasts; he grew tired, too, of hearing his prowess praised and of having to repeat stories about his native land and about the adventures he had been through.

Quite accidentally, it happened that Kidogo, constantly surrounded by his relatives and friends, distracted by the admiration of the women, somehow was separated from Pandion and Cavius, and the friends met less frequently. Kidogo was now journeying into the new life by his own path that did not coincide with that of his friends.

Those of Kidogo's traveling companions who belonged to related tribes soon left for their own homes. The party that was left consisted of Pandion, Cavius and ten Libyans, who considered that their return home depended on the Etruscan and the Hellene.

The twelve strangers were accommodated in a big house of grey-green sun-dried clay, but Kidogo insisted that Cavius and Pandion move to a beautiful dome-shaped house near his own.

After the many years of wandering, Pandion was able at last to sleep on his own bed. These people did not sleep on skins or bundles of grass on the ground; they made bedsteads, wooden frames on legs, which supported a net of plaited, pliable reeds that gave rest to the body, and was especially pleasant for Pandion's wounded leg.

Pandion now had a great deal of spare time which he spent near the sea where he sat for hours, either alone or with Cavius, listening to the regular rumble of the waves. He was in a state of constant alarm. His boundless vitality had been sapped by the vicissitudes of his long journey in a hot debilitating climate.

He had significantly changed and admitted it himself. There had been a time when, given wings by youth and love, he had been able to leave behind the girl he loved, his home and his native land, following the urge to learn more of the art of the ancients, to see foreign lands, and to learn something of life.

Now he knew the meaning of the bitterest nostalgia, he knew the meaning of joyless captivity, the oppressiveness of despair, the stultifying drudgery of the slave. Uneasily Pandion asked himself whether his creative inspiration had left him, whether or not he was capable of becoming a great artist. At the same time, he felt that he had seen and experienced much that had left its mark on him, that had enriched him with a great knowledge of life, with numerous, and unforgettable impressions.

Pandion would often gaze lovingly at the spear presented to him by the father of his lost Iruma, the spear that he had carried through plains and forest, the spear that had so often saved him in moments of mortal danger. He regarded it as a symbol of manly courage, a guarantee of personal fearlessness in the struggle against the Nature that reigns supreme in the hot expanses of Africa. He would carefully stroke the long blade before he returned it to the bag that Iruma had stitched. This piece of leather, brightly embroidered in wool, was all that was left to remind him of the distant, kind, and gentle girl that he had met at the crossroads on his difficult journey home.

With these thoughts in his mind, Pandion turned to look at the dark mountains that stood between the ocean and the country he had passed through. The endless days of that long journey floated slowly before his eyes. Over everything, stood the image of Iruma, full of life, and beckoning him irresistibly. She was the same as he had seen her the last time, standing against the trunk of the tree whose flowers were like red torches.

Pandion's heart began to beat faster. His imagination gave him a perfect picture of the sheen of her dark, and tender skin, her mischievous eyes filled with the fires of passion. Iruma's tiny round face drew close to him, and he heard the endearing notes of her voice.

Pandion gradually became acquainted with the manners and customs of Kidogo's jolly and friendly people. They were tall, their black skins had a coppery hue, and all of them were well built.

Most of them engaged in agricultural pursuits. They cultivated the low palms for their oil-bearing nuts and also bananas, huge herbaceous plants with huge leaves that spread fanwise from a bunch of soft stems. The curved, crescent-shaped fruit of the banana plant grew in large clusters and provided tasty and aromatic food. Bananas were gathered in large numbers and formed the staple diet of the people. Pandion enjoyed them greatly, eating them raw, boiled or fried in oil.

The local inhabitants also engaged in hunting, gathered ivory and skins, and also collected the magic, chestnut-like nuts that had cured Pandion of his strange torpor; they also kept poultry, and herds of cattle.

There were many skilled craftsmen among Kidogo's people - builders, smiths, and potters. Pandion admired the work of many artists; whose skill was no whit less than that of Kidogo. Their huge houses, built of squared stones, sunbaked brick, or hard, rammed clay, were all decorated with intricate and beautiful ornaments carved with great precision on the walls. In some cases, the walls were decorated with highly colored frescoes that reminded Pandion of the ancient frescoes in Crete.

He saw earthenware vessels of beautiful shape and covered with fine drawings, delicately executed. In the buildings devoted to public meetings, and in the houses of the chiefs, there were many colored wooden statues. Pandion greatly admired the carvings of people and animals, in which the faithful recording of the artist's impression portrayed characteristic features.

Pandion, however, considered that the sculptors of Kidogo's tribe lacked a profound understanding of form. The same was true of the masters of Aigyptos. The statues of Tha-Quem were lifeless in their fixed poses, despite the precision with which they were carved, and the brilliant finish that resulted from many centuries of experience. Kidogo's people, on the contrary, recorded in their carvings, the most acute impressions, but only in partial, deliberately stressed details.

When the young Hellene pondered over the work of the local craftsmen, he had a vague feeling that the path to perfection in sculpture must lie in some completely new direction, and not in the blind effort to reproduce nature, nor in attempts to reflect certain partial impressions.

Kidogo's people loved music and played on complex instruments made of rows of little wooden planks fixed on long hollow gourds. Some of the sad and tenderly expansive songs affected Pandion greatly, reminding him of the songs of his homeland.

Cavius was sitting beside the dying fire near their house, chewing stimulating leaves (leaves from any bush of the Sterculiaceae family), and pensively stirring ashes with a stick in which yellow fruits were baking. He had learned to make flour from bananas and bake cakes from it.

Pandion came out of the house, sat down beside his friend, and looked idly over the high rows of the houses, and at passers-by. A soft evening light descended on the dusty paths and was lost in the motionless branches of the shady trees.

Suddenly, Pandion's attention was attracted to a passing woman. He had noticed her when they first arrived at Kidogo's village, but since then had not chanced to meet her. He knew that it was Nyora, the wife of one of Kidogo's relatives.

Even in a tribe whose women were famous for their beauty, Nyora was outstanding. She walked slowly past the friends, with all the dignity of a woman who was conscious of her own beauty. Pandion gazed at her in frank admiration, and the creative urge came back to him in all its former strength.

Nyora wore a piece of greenish-blue cloth tightly bound around her loins; a string of blue beads, heavy heart-shaped earrings, and a narrow gold band on her left wrist were her only ornaments. Her short black braided hair was gathered on the crown of her head in a fantastic style that made her head seem longer. Her big eyes showed calm from under long lashes, and the cheekbones under the eyes formed little round hillocks, like those of healthy and well-fed children amongst the Hellenes. Her smooth black skin was so resilient that her body seemed to be cast from iron; it shone in the rays of the setting sun, its coppery hue turning to gold. Her long neck, inclined slightly forward, gave her head a proud poise.

Pandion admired Nyora's tall and lithe figure, her easy but restrained movements. To him, she seemed like an incarnation of one of the three Graces, goddesses that, according to the belief of his country, had control over living beauty and made its attraction irresistible.

Suddenly, the Etruscan gave Pandion a light tap on the head with his stick.

"Why don't you run after her?" asked Cavius, half in joke and a half in chagrin. "You Hellenes are always ready to fall in love with a woman."

Pandion looked at his friend without anger, but rather as though he were seeing him for the first time, and then threw his arms impetuously round his shoulders.

"Listen, Cavius, you don't like to talk about yourself. Aren't you at all interested in women? Don't you feel how beautiful they are? Don't you feel that they are part of all this," Pandion made a sweeping circle with his arm, "the sea, the sun, the beautiful world?"

"No. Whenever I see anything beautiful, I want to eat it," laughed the Etruscan. "I'm only joking," he added in serious tones. "You must remember that I'm twice as old as you, and behind the bright face of the world, I can see the other side that is dark and ugly. You have already forgotten Tha-Quem." Cavius passed his finger over the red brand on Pandion's back. "I never forget anything. I'm jealous of you. You will create beautiful things, but I can only wreak destruction in the struggle against the forces of darkness."

Cavius was silent for a few moments and then continued in a trembling voice:

"You don't often think of your own people back at home. It is many years since I saw my children; I don't even know whether they are alive, whether my clan still exists. Who knows what may have happened there, in the midst of hostile tribes?"

The sorrow that tinged the voice of the always reticent Etruscan filled Pandion with sympathy. But how could he comfort his friend? Then the Etruscan's words struck home painfully: "You don't often think of your own people back home." *If Cavius could say such things to me, could it be true that Thessa, his grandfather, Agenor, all meant so little to me? If such were not the case, I would have become as morose as Cavius, I would not have absorbed the great variety of life, and how would I have learned to understand beauty?*

Pandion's thoughts were so full of contradiction that he could not understand himself. He jumped up and suggested to the Etruscan that they go to bathe. The latter agreed, and the two friends set out across the hills beyond which, at a distance of five thousand cubits from the village, lay the ocean.

A few days before this, Kidogo had gathered together the young men and youths of the tribe. The Kemtiu told his people that his friends had no property of any kind, except their spears and loincloths, and that the Sons of the Wind would not take them aboard their ships without payment.

"If every one of you helps them just a little," said Kidogo, "the strangers will be able to return home. They helped me escape from captivity and return to you."

Encouraged by the general approval that followed, Kidogo suggested that they all go with him to the plateau where the gold deposits were and that those who could not go should contribute ivory, nuts, hides or a log of valuable wood.

Next day, Kidogo informed his friends that he was going away on a hunt, but refused to take them with him, recommending that they save their strength for the forthcoming journey. Kidogo's traveling companions, therefore, knew nothing of the real object of his expedition.

Although the problem of payment for the journey home worried them, they hoped that the mysterious Sons of the Wind would hire them as rowers. If the worst came to the worst, Pandion knew he would be able to offer the stones that came from the south, the old chief's gift to him.

Cavius, also without a word to Kidogo, gathered the Libyans together two days after his Kemtiu friend had left, and set out up the river in search of blackwood trees; he wanted to fell a few of them and float them downstream on rafts of light wood, as the ebony and other blackwoods were too heavy to float in water.

Pandion was still lame, and Cavius left him in the village despite his protests.

This was the second time that his comrades had left Pandion alone, the first time had been when they went on the giraffe hunt.

Pandion was infuriated, but Cavius, superciliously thrusting out his beard, said that on the first occasion he had not wasted time and could do the same again.

The young Hellene was in such a rage that he could not speak, and he rushed away from his friend, feeling deeply insulted.

Cavius ran after him, slapped him on the back and asked his forgiveness, but, nevertheless, insisted on Pandion remaining behind, to complete his recovery.

After a long argument, Pandion agreed; he regarded himself as a pitiful cripple, and hurriedly hid in the house so as not to be present when his healthy comrades were leaving.

Left alone, Pandion felt a still stronger urge to test his ability – he thought of his success with the statue of the elephant trainer. He had seen so much death and destruction during the past few years that he did not want to have anything to do with such an unenduring medium as clay; he wanted to work with material that is more durable. No such material was at hand, and even if he found it, he still had no tools with which to carve.

Pandion often admired Yakhmos' stone that Kidogo insisted had, in the end, brought them to the sea, for Kidogo naively believed in the magic properties of things.

The clear transparency of the hard stone gave Pandion the idea of carving a cameo. The stone was harder than those normally used for such purposes in Hellas, where they were polished with emery stone from the Island of Naxos, in the Aegean Sea.

Suddenly, he remembered that he had stones that were harder than anything else in the world if the old chief of the Elephant People was to be believed.

Pandion took out the smallest of the stones from the south, and carefully drew its sharp edge along the edge of the bluish-green crystal – a white line appeared on the hard surface of the stone. He pressed harder and cut a deep furrow, such as a chisel of black bronze would cut in soft marble. The unusual hardness of the transparent stones from the south was, in all truth, greater than anything then known to Pandion. He had magic tools in his hands that made his work easy.

Pandion smashed the little stone, and carefully collected all the sharp fragments; with the aid of hard pitch, he fixed them into wooden handles. This gave him a dozen chisels of various thicknesses, suitable both for rough carving and for the cutting of fine lines.

What should he carve on that bluish-green crystal that Yakhmos had obtained from the ruins of a temple thousands of years old, and which he had carried safely to the sea, the sea for which it had served as a symbol during the long years of stifling captivity on land? Pandion's head was filled with vague ideas.

He left the village and wandered about alone until he reached the sea. For a long time, he sat on a rock, staring into the distance or watching the shallow water that ran across the sand at his feet. Evening came, and the short-lived twilight robbed the sea of its sheen; the movement of the waves could no longer be seen. The black velvet of the night became more and more impenetrable, but at the same time big, bright stars lit up in the sky and the celestial beacons, rocked in the waves, brought life to the dead sea.

Pandion threw back his head and traced the outlines of constellations unknown to him. The arc of the Milky Way spread across the sky like a silver bridge, just as it did over his own country, but here it was narrower. One end of it was split up by wide dark stripes and separate dark patches. To one side, and below the Milky Way, two dark star clouds gleamed with a bluish-white light. (The Large and Small Magellanic Clouds, big star clusters and nebulae in the Southern Hemisphere.)

Close beside them, he could see a huge, impenetrable black patch, shaped like a pear, as though a gigantic piece of coal hid all the stars in that part of the sky. (The Coalsack-a concentration of black, dark matter in the sky of the Southern Hemisphere.)

Pandion had never seen anything like it in the sky at home in the north and was astonished at the contrast between the black patch and the white star clouds.

Suddenly, the young Hellene sensed the very essence of Africa in that black and white contrast. In its direct and clear-cut crudity, this was the combination which made up Africa, its whole aspect, as Pandion conceived it:

The black and white stripes of the extraordinary horses...?

The black skin of the natives painted with white color and accentuated by their white teeth and the whites of their eyes...?

Articles made from black and pearl-white wood...?

The black and white columns of the tree-trunks in the forest...?

The brightness of the grasslands and the darkness of the forests...?

Black cliffs with white streaks of quartz...?

All these and many other things passed before Pandion's eyes.

His homeland on the poor rocky shores of the Green Sea was quite different. There the stream of life was not a tempestuous flood; its black and white sides were not in such open conflict.

Pandion stood up. The boundless ocean, on the other side of which was Oeniadae, cut him off from Africa, the country that lay hidden morosely behind the night shadows of the mountains, and that in his heart he had already left. In front of him, the reflections of the stars ran across the waves, and away there in the north, the sea joined his native Oeniadae where Thessa was standing on the shore.

For the sake of returning home, for the sake of Thessa, he had fought and struggled through blood and sand, through heat and darkness, against countless dangers from man and beast. Thessa, distant, loved, and unapproachable, stood like those faint stars above the sea, where the edge of the Great Bear just touched the horizon.

It was then that the solution came to him: on the stone, the enduring symbol of the sea, he would create the image of Thessa standing on the shore.

In a frenzy, Pandion squeezed the chisel in his hand until the strong stick broke. For several days he had been working on Yakhmos' stone with a beating heart, stemming his impatience with difficulty, at times drawing a long line with confidence, at others cutting tiny marks with infinite care. The image was becoming clearer.

Thessa's head was a success - that proud turn of the head stood before him as clearly as it had done in the hour of farewell on the seashore at Cape Achelous. He had carved the head in the transparent depths of the stone, and now the frosted blue face stood out in sharp relief on the mirror-like surface of the stone. Locks of hair lay in easy free lines, where a clear-cut arc marked the curve of the shoulder, but further – further on, Pandion suddenly found that he had lost his inspiration.

The young artist, more confident in himself than he had ever been before, cut in bold, sweeping lines, the fine outlines of the girl's body, and the beauty of the lines told of the success of his undertaking.

Pandion cut away the surrounding surface of the stone to bring his carving into even sharper relief. It was then that he suddenly realized it was not Thessa he had drawn. The lines of the hips, knees, and breast, the body of Iruma came to life, and certain features undoubtedly owed their existence to his last impression of Nyora.

Thessa's figure was not the body of the Hellene girl. Pandion had created an abstract image. He had wanted something else. He had wanted to depict the living Thessa that he loved. He tried hard to get rid of the impressions of recent years by a supreme effort of memory, but it proved impossible. The new was still too fresh.

Pandion felt much worse when he realized that, once again, he had proved unable to breathe life into an image. While the figure was still in outline, there had been life in its lines. As soon as the artist tried to bring the flat figure into relief, however, it turned to stone, it became cold and inert. And so, after all, he had not fathomed the secrets of art. This image, too, would remain lifeless! He would not be able to put his ideas into effect!

After he had broken the chisel in his agitation, Pandion took the stone and examined it at arm's length. No, he could not create the image of Thessa, and the wonderful cameo would remain unfinished. The sun's rays shone through the transparent stone, filling it with the golden tinge of his native seas. Pandion had carved the figure of the girl on the extreme right-hand edge of the biggest surface of the stone, leaving most of it still untouched. The girl with the face of Thessa, but who was not Thessa, stood at the edge of the stone as though she were standing at the edge of the sea.

The enthusiasm that had inspired Pandion to work from dawn to dusk, waiting impatiently for the coming of each new day, had left him. Pandion put the stone away, gathered his chisels and straightened his aching back. The grief of defeat was made lighter by the realization that he could still create a thing of beauty... but, alas, how poor it was in comparison with the living being!

He'd been so immersed in his work, that he ceased awaiting the return of his comrades. A little boy who came running up to him took Pandion's mind away from his dark thoughts.

"The man with the thick beard has come and has sent for you to go to the river," announced Cavius' messenger, proud of the task entrusted to him.

The fact that Cavius had stayed by the river and, sent for him to go there, worried Pandion. He hurried to the river-bank, along a path that wound, its way through thorn-scrub. From a distance he could see a group of his companions on the sandy river-bank, standing around a bunch of reeds on which lay a man's body. He hopped clumsily along, trying not to step on his injured foot, and entered the circle of silent friends. He recognized the man lying on the reeds as Takel, a young Libyan who had taken part in the flight across the desert. The Hellene knelt down and bent over the body of his comrade.

Before Pandion's eyes flashed a picture of the stiflingly hot gorge in the sandstone mountains where he plodded along half-dead from thirst. Takel was one of those followers of Akhini who had brought him water from the well. Only now that he knelt before Takel's body did Pandion realize how near and dear to him was everyone who had taken part in the insurrection and the flight. He had grown used to them and could not imagine life without them.

For weeks, Pandion might not have anything to do with his companions when he knew that they were safe, each going about his own affairs; but this sudden loss crushed him. Still, on his knees, he turned inquiringly to Cavius.

"Takel was bitten by a snake in the undergrowth," said Cavius sadly, "while we were wandering in search of blackwood. We didn't know any cure," he sighed deeply "so we abandoned everything and sailed back down the river. When we carried him ashore, Takel was already dying. I sent for you to say good-bye to him... it was too late." Cavius, his head bowed, clenched his fists, and did not finish what he was saying.

Pandion stood up. Takel's death seemed so senseless and unjust to him - not in a glorious battle, not in the struggle against wild beasts, but here, in a peaceful village where he had the promise of a return home after great deeds of valor, and courageous fortitude on the long journey. This death caused the young Hellene great pain; he felt the tears welling up in his eyes, and to conceal them, stared hard at the river.

On either side of a sandbank rose the green walls of dense thickets of reeds so that the mound of light-colored sand seemed to stand in open green gates. At the fringe of the forest grew gnarled and twisted white trees with tiny leaves. From all the branches of these trees hung luxuriant garlands of bright red flowers, (Combretum purpureum) whose fluffy flat clusters looked like transverse bars of red threaded on thin stems, some of which hung down in garlands, while others pointed upwards to the sky. The flowers gave off a red reflection, and the white trees burned in the green gates like funeral torches at the gates of the nether world, to which the spirit of the dead Takel was on its way.

The dull leaden waters of the river, broken by banks of yellow sand, rolled slowly along.

Hundreds of crocodiles lay on the sand-banks. On a sandy spit near where Pandion was standing, several of the huge reptiles had opened their jaws in their sleep, and in the sun, they looked like black patches surrounded by the white spikes of their terrible teeth. The bodies of the crocodiles sprawled out on the sand as though they were flattened by their own weight. The long folds of the scaly skin of their bellies lapped over flat backs covered with rows of protuberances of a lighter color than the black-green spaces between them. Paws, with their joints, awkwardly turned outwards, stretched on either side in an ugly pose. Now and again one of the reptiles would flick its long-ridged tail against another who, his sleep disturbed, would close his mouth with a snap that resounded loudly down the river.

The wayfarers raised the body of the dead man, and carried it in silence to the village, under the alarmed glances of villagers who came running up. Pandion walked behind, away from Cavius. The Etruscan considered himself guilty of the death of the Libyan since the idea of hunting for ebony had been his. Cavius walked beside the sad procession, biting his lip and running his fingers through his thick beard.

Pandion also felt qualms of conscience. He also felt guilty. What right had he to grow enthusiastic over the carving of the girl he loved, He should have been busying himself with something in memory of the fighting friendship of people of different races. People who had passed through all trials together had remained true in the face of death, hunger, and thirst, in the sorrowful days of their wearisome march.

"Why did this idea not occur to me before?" the young Hellene asked himself. Why had he forgotten the friendship that had grown up in the fight for freedom? Not for nothing had his work been a failure - the gods had punished him for his ingratitude. Let today's sorrow teach him to see better.

Like a herd of buffaloes, the low purple and grey clouds crawled heavily across the sky, bunching together in a solid mass. Dull rumbles of thunder filled the air. A tropical downpour was on its way, and people hurriedly took everything that had been lying about into their houses.

Cavius and Pandion had only just time to take cover in their house when the huge bowl of the heavens tipped over, and the roar of the falling water drowned even the peals of thunder. As usual, the rain soon stopped, the vegetation gave off an acrid smell in the fresh, humid air, and countless streams gurgled faintly as they made their way to the river and the sea.

The wet trees rustled dully in the wind. The noise was grim and sad, nothing like the rapid rustle of leaves on a fine dry day.

Cavius sat listening to the noises of the forest and said suddenly:

"I can't forgive myself Takel's death. It was my fault; we went without an experienced guide, and we are strangers in this land where carelessness means death. The result is that we have no ebony and one of our best comrades lies dead under a heap of stones on the riverbank. A high price to pay for my foolishness. I can't make up my mind to try again, and we have nothing to pay to the Sons of the Wind."

In silence, Pandion took a handful of the sparkling stones out of his bag and laid them before the Etruscan. Cavius nodded his head in approval, but suddenly doubt showed on his face.

"If they don't know the value of these stones, the Sons of the Wind may refuse to take them. Who has heard of such stones in our countries? Who will buy them as valuables? Although..." Cavius paused to think.

Pandion took fright. Cavius' simple explanation of their position had not entered his head before. He had lost sight of the fact that the stones might have no value in the eyes of the merchants. The hand he stretched out towards the stones trembled in consternation and fear for the future.

Seeing the alarm in Pandion's face, Cavius spoke to him again.

"I seem to have heard that clear stones of great hardness, were sometimes brought to Cyprus and Caria from the distant east and had a very high value. Perhaps the Sons of the Wind know that?"

The morning after his talk with Cavius, Pandion set out along a path that led to the foothills where the bananas grew. It was time for Kidogo to return, and his friends were awaiting him in impatience; they wanted his advice on how to obtain something valuable for the Sons of the Wind. Cavius' doubts had shattered Pandion's faith in the stones from the south, and the young Hellene now knew no peace.

Without realizing it, Pandion set out towards the mountains in the hope of meeting the expedition of his Kemtiu friend. Apart from everything else, he wanted to be alone to think out a new work of art that was beginning to take form in his mind.

Pandion walked soundlessly along the hard-trampled earth of the footpath. He was no longer lame, and his former natural gait had returned to him. Local people, loaded with clusters of yellow fruits, whom he met on the way, grinned at him or waved bunches of leaves to him as a sign of friendship.

The path turned to the left. Pandion walked on between solid green walls of succulent vegetation, filled with the golden glow of sunlight.

In the hot glare of the sun, a woman whom Pandion recognized as Nyora, was moving gracefully along the path. From the hanging clusters of bananas, she was selecting the greenest fruits, and packing them in a high basket. Pandion stood back in the shadow of the huge banana leaves, and the feelings of the artist put all other thoughts out of his mind. The young woman went from one bush to another, her figure bent gracefully over the basket, and again she stretched up on tiptoes, straining her entire body to reach the higher fruits. The golden sunlight sparkled on her smooth black skin, accentuated by the bright green background of leaves. Nyora gave a little jump, her body arched into a curve as she plunged her hands into the velvety foliage.

Pandion was so engrossed that he caught against a dry twig, and a loud crackle broke the silence. In an instant, the young woman turned around and stood stock-still. Nyora recognized Pandion, and the body that had been tensed like the string of a musical instrument, immediately became calm as she smiled at the young Hellene. Pandion, however, noticed nothing. A cry of ecstasy broke from his lips, and his wide-open golden eyes stared at Nyora without seeing her, his mouth opened in a faint smile. The astounded woman stepped back from him. The stranger suddenly turned and ran away shouting something in a language she could not understand.

Pandion had suddenly made a great discovery, something he had been groping for unconsciously but persistently, something he had always been very near to in his unceasing mental search. He would never have found it if he had not made comparisons, and had not sought new paths for his own art.

That which has life in it, can never be immobile. In a beautiful living body, there is never dead immobility, there is only repose, the moment when a movement has been completed and is changing to another movement, its opposite. If he could seize that moment, and reproduce it in the inert material, the dead stone would live.

This is what Pandion had seen in the motionless Nyora when she stood still like a statue cast from black metal.

The young Hellene went away alone to a tree in a small glade. If anybody had seen him there, he would have been sure that Pandion was mad: he was making jerky movements, bending, and straightening his arm or his leg, and trying hard to follow the movements, twisting his neck, and straining his eyes till they hurt. He did not return home until evening. He was excited and had a feverish gleam in his eye.

To Cavius' great astonishment, Pandion made him stand up in front of him, march about and halt at his command. At first, the Etruscan was patient with his friend and his antics, but at last, he could stand it no longer and sat down on the ground with an air of determination. Even then Pandion gave him no rest. He stared at him as he sat there, first from the right and then from the left, until Cavius, letting out a stream of profanity, said that Pandion had a touch of fever and threatened to tie him up and lay him down on the bed.

"You can go to the crows!" shouted Pandion in a joyful voice. "I'm not afraid of you; I'll twist you up like the horn of the white antelope."

Cavius had never seen his friend in such a childishly, jolly mood before. He was glad of it, for he had long been aware that Pandion was spiritually depressed. He muttered something about a boy who was making fun of his father and gave Pandion a light blow; Pandion immediately calmed down and announced that he was as hungry as a wolf.

The two friends sat down to supper, and Pandion tried to explain his great discovery to his friend. Contrary to Pandion's expectations, Cavius showed interest in the matter and asked Pandion many questions, trying to understand the nature of the difficulties that faced the sculptor in his efforts to depict real life.

The two friends sat talking for a long time until it was quite dark. Suddenly, something stood in the way of the stars that shone through the open doorway, and Kidogo's voice gave them a pleasant thrill. The Kemtiu had returned unexpectedly and decided to pay an immediate visit to his friends. When they asked him about the results of the hunt, he gave them a vague answer, said he was tired, and promised to show his trophies the next morning.

Cavius and Pandion told him about the expedition in search of ebony, and about Takel's death. Kidogo was infuriated, and in his frenzy, showered curses upon his friends said that their actions were an insult to his hospitality, and even went to the extent of calling Cavius an "old hyena." In the end, the Kemtiu grew calmer - his sorrow at the death of a comrade was greater than his wrath. Then the Etruscan and the Hellene told him that they were worried about finding something to pay the Sons of the Wind with, and asked his advice. Kidogo showed the greatest indifference to their worries and went away without having answered their questions.

The despondent friends blamed Kidogo's strange behavior on to his sorrow at the death of the Libyan, and both of them for a long time tossed sleeplessly on their beds, pondering over the situation.

Late next morning, Kidogo came to them with an expression of shrewd cunning on his kindly face. He was accompanied by all the Libyans, and a crowd of young men of his tribe. Kidogo's people winked at the puzzled strangers, whispered amongst themselves, laughed loudly and shouted snatches of incomprehensible phrases. They hinted at the sorcery that was supposed to be a feature of their people and said that Kidogo was possessed of the ability to turn ordinary sticks into ebony and ivory, and river-sand into gold.

The strangers had to listen to all this nonsense on their way to Kidogo's house. Kidogo led them to a small storeroom, a building that differed from the other simple houses in that it had a door that was closed from the outside by a huge stone.

With the aid of several of his men, Kidogo rolled the stone away, and the young people stood on either side of the wide-open door. Kidogo, bending down, entered the storeroom, beckoning to his friends to follow. Cavius, Pandion, and the Libyans did not know what it was all about and stood for some time in the gloom until their eyes got accustomed to the half-light coming through a narrow gap that encircled the wall under the eaves.

Then they saw many thick black logs, a pile of elephant tusks, and five big baskets filled to the top with medicinal nuts. Kidogo observed the faces of his comrades as he spoke to them.

"All that is yours. My people have gathered it all for you to make your journey pleasant and easy! The Sons of the Wind ought to take a couple of dozen passengers and not one for such a price."

"Your people are making us such a present?" exclaimed Cavius. "What for?"

"Because you are good people because you are brave

men, because you have performed so many deeds of valor, and because you are my friends and helped me return home," chanted Kidogo, trying to appear imperturbable. "But wait a minute, that isn't all!" The Kemtiu stepped to one side, thrust his hand down between the baskets and picked up a bag of sturdy leather as big as a man's head.

"Take this," said Kidogo, handing the bag to Cavius.

The Etruscan held out his hand's palm upwards, and almost dropped the bag as his arms bent under the weight of it. The Kemtiu roared with laughter and danced a few steps as a sign of pleasure. The loud laughter of the youths outside was like an echo.

"What is it?" asked Cavius, clutching the heavy bag to his breast.

"How can you, a wise old soldier, ask such a question?" said Kidogo in the merriest of tones. "As though you don't know that there's only one thing in the world that is as heavy as that."

"Gold!" exclaimed the Etruscan in his own language, but the Kemtiu understood him.

"Yes, gold," he said.

"Where did you get so much?" put in Pandion, pinching the tightly packed bag.

"Instead of hunting, we went to the plateau where gold is found. For eight days we dug the sand there and washed it in water." The Kemtiu paused for a moment and then added: "The Sons of the Wind won't take you to your homes. When you reach your own seas, your roads will be different, and everybody will have to make his own way home. Divide the gold and hide it carefully, so that the Sons of the Wind won't see it."

"Who else went on that 'hunt' with you?" asked Cavius.

"All these people," said Kidogo, pointing to the young men crowding around the door.

Deeply touched and filled with joy, the friends hurried to thank the Kemtiues. The latter, confused by this display of gratitude, shifted from one foot to the other, and one by one, drifted away to their houses.

The friends left the storeroom and pushed the stone back in front of the door. Kidogo had become silent suddenly. His gaiety had gone. Pandion drew his black friend towards him, but Kidogo immediately slipped out of his embrace, placed his hand on the Hellene's shoulder and stared deep into his golden eyes.

"How can I leave you!" exclaimed Pandion.

The Kemtiu's fingers dug into his shoulder.

"The God of Lightning be my witness," said Kidogo in a dull voice, "I would give all the gold on the plateau, I would give everything I have, down to the last spear, if you would remain here with me forever." There was an expression of pain on the Kemtiu's face, and he covered his eyes with his hands. "But I do not even ask that of you." Kidogo's voice trembled and broke off. "I learned the meaning of home when I was in captivity... I realize that you cannot stay... and I, as you see, am doing everything to help you go."

The Kemtiu suddenly released his hold of Pandion and ran away to his own house. The young Hellene stared after his friend, and tears made a haze before his eyes. The Etruscan heaved a heavy sigh behind Pandion's back.

"The time will come when you and I must part," he said softly and sorrowfully. "Our homes are not very far apart, and ships sail between them very often," said Pandion, turning around to him. "But Kidogo... he will remain here on the outer edge of Oecumene."

The Etruscan did not say another word.

Now that Pandion was sure of the future, he gave himself up wholeheartedly to his art. He was in a hurry; the magnificence of friendship, cemented in the struggle for freedom, was a tremendous inspiration that compelled him to hurry. He could already see the details of his cameo. The three men must stand embracing each other against the background of the sea towards which they had struggled, the sea that promised to return them to their homes.

On the larger, flat side of the stone, Pandion had decided to depict the three friends, Kidogo, Cavius, and himself, in the sparkling, transparent light of the expanses of the sea, which the bluish-green stone represented as nothing else could.

The young sculptor made a few sketches on thin pieces of ivory, such as the women of the tribe used to grind and mix some sort of ointment.

The discovery that he had made necessitated his having a living figure constantly before his eyes. This, however, presented no difficulty since the Etruscan was with him the whole time, and Kidogo, feeling that the ships would soon be coming, left his own work to spend as much time as possible with his friends.

Pandion often asked the Etruscan and the Kemtiu to stand in front of him with their arms around each other's shoulders, which they, laughing at him, always did. The friends often sat talking together for a long time, confiding to each other their most secret thoughts, their worries, and their plans, and deep down in each of them the realization that they must part dug into his heart like a thorn.

While Pandion talked, he did not waste time but worked persistently on his hard stone. At times, the sculptor would sit in silence; his glance would become sharp and penetrating - he was trying to catch some detail in the features of his friends that was important to him.

The three embracing figures began to stand out in ever-greater relief, all the time becoming more lifelike. The central figure was that of the huge Kemtiu, Kidogo; to the right, turned slightly towards the blank space on the stone stood Pandion, and on the left, Cavius, both with spears in their hands.

Cavius and Kidogo thought that their images were very lifelike, but insisted that Pandion had drawn his own portrait poorly. The sculptor laughed and said that that was not important.

The figures of the friends, despite their diminutive size, were extremely lifelike and there was real virtuosity in every line of them. There was robust and impetuous movement in their bodies, but at the same time, there was elegant restraint in them. In Kidogo's arms, thrown around the shoulders of the Etruscan and the Hellene, Pandion had managed to express a movement of protection and fraternal tenderness. Cavius and Pandion stood with heads inclined warily, almost menacingly, with the tense vigilance of mighty warriors ready at any moment to repel the attack of any foe. The group as a whole gave this impression of might and confidence, and Pandion made every effort to express in his carving all the best that was in those who had become his dearest friends on the long road from slavery to his native land.

The sculptor realized that at last, he had succeeded in

creating a work of art. Kidogo and Cavius stopped making fun of Pandion.

For hours they sat with bated breath watching the movements of the magic chisel, their new attitude towards Pandion being the expression of a vague sort of adoration. Their young friend, bold, merry, and even childish, at times amusing in his admiration of women, had proved himself a great artist! This was a fact that both pleased and astonished Kidogo and Cavius.

Pandion put all his love for his friends into that burst of creative enthusiasm. His original idea-that of carving Thessa on the stone-did not have any further appeal. Thessa, Iruma, and Nyora, women from different peoples, were sisters in their beauty; in all of them he felt the same power of attraction. Whether they were sisters in all other respects, Pandion did not know. Could Thessa form as firm friendship for Nyora as he had for Kidogo?

In Pandion's friendship with Cavius and Kidogo, in their comradeship with the other fugitive slaves - but, few of whom were left together now-there was a fraternity of identical thoughts and efforts, cemented more firmly than stone by loyalty and courage. They were real brothers even though one of them had been born here under the strange trees of Africa of a mother as black as himself. The second had lain in his cradle in a hut that trembled in the bitter storms of the northern lands at a time when the third was already a warrior fighting against the fierce horsemen of the distant steppes on the shores of a dark sea.

Their hearts, tested hundreds of times in adversity, were joined by strong sinews and... of how little importance now were differences of country, faces, bodies, and religion!

The days passed quickly. Pandion suddenly realized that three months and a half had passed and that the time appointed for the arrival of the Sons of the Wind had also passed.

Pandion experienced mixed feelings of anxiety and relief - anxiety because the Sons of the Wind might never come at all, and relief because the inevitable parting with Kidogo was being postponed.

In his wearying anxiety, Pandion often left his work - it was, incidentally, almost completed. The Hellene again began making frequent trips to the sea, always hurrying back so as not to be long away from his friends.

One day Pandion was making ready to go for his usual bathe in the sea. He got up and called his friends, but they refused; they were engaged in a heated argument on the best way to prepare leaves for chewing. In the distance, they suddenly heard the sounds of numerous voices, shouts, and screams of ecstasy, such as Kidogo's excitable people gave vent to on every occasion of importance. Kidogo jumped up, his face turned ash-grey, the pallor even spreading to his mighty chest. Staggering slightly, Kidogo ran to his own house, shouting over his shoulder to his astonished friends:

"That must be the Sons of the Wind!"

The blood rushed to the heads of the Etruscan and the Hellene, and they, too, set off at a run along a short path to the sea known to Pandion. On the crest of a hill, Pandion and Cavius stood still.

"The Sons of the Wind!"

The dark purple shadow of the huge mountain lay on the shore and stretched far out to sea, dulling the sparkle of the waves, and giving the water the dark tones of the forest thickets.

Black ships, in shape like those of the Hellenes, with curved swanlike breasts and high prows, were already drawn up on the greying sands. There were five of them. With their unstopped masts, they looked like black ducks asleep on the beach. Bearded warriors in rough grey cloaks walked up and down in front of the ships, the bronze of their shields flashing; in their hands, they carried broad battle-axes on long handles.

The chiefs, the merchants and all those who were not on guard duty must have gone to Kidogo's village. The Etruscan and the Hellene turned back. Kidogo awaited them impatiently at their house.

"The Sons of the Wind are with the chiefs," the Kemtiu informed them.

"I've asked my uncle to talk to the big chief, and he will talk to them about you. It will be safer that way. The Sons of the Wind will not dare to quarrel with him, and will bring you safely home." In the Kemtiu's wan smile, there was no joy.

Hundreds of people gathered on the shore to bid farewell to the parting ships. The Sons of the Wind were in a great hurry; the sun was already setting, and for some reason of their own they were determined to set out that day. The loaded ships were slowly rocking on the swell beyond the reefs. Amongst the other goods lay the gift of Kidogo's people - payment for the return of the former slaves to their own countries.

To reach the ships they had to wade breast-high through the water that covered a sandbank. The chiefs of the Sons of the Wind held back to talk with the Kemtiu chiefs, asking them to prepare a greater number of goods for the next year, swearing that they would arrive at the appointed time.

Cavius stood beside Kidogo, holding in one hand the huge bundle that contained the skin and skull of the terrible gishu. As a parting gift, Kidogo gave Cavius and Pandion two big throwing-knives. This implement of war, invented by the Tengrela people, consisted of a large sheet of bronze divided into five fingers, four of them crescent-shaped with sharpened edges and the fifth long and thin with a horn handle on it. This weapon, when hurled by able hands, whistled through the air, and killed its victim at twenty cubits distance.

With a heavy heart, Pandion looked around him, examining his new fellow travelers and masters. Their harsh, wind-burned faces were the color of dark brick; their unclipped beards were tangled on their cheeks; in their heavy gait, in the grim folds of their foreheads and lips, there was none of the kind-heartedness that was typical of Kidogo's people. Nevertheless, Pandion trusted them, perhaps because the Sons of the Wind, like he, were loyal to the sea, lived in accord with it and loved it. Or perhaps it was because he and Cavius met familiar words in their speech.

The Sons of the Wind willingly consented to take the former slaves with them for the payment offered. Kidogo's uncle, Yorumefu, even bargained for a reduction of six tusks and two baskets of medicinal nuts, which were loaded on to the ships as the property of Cavius, Pandion, and the Libyans. The Sons of the Wind separated their passengers against their will - six Libyans on one ship, Pandion, Cavius, and the other three Libyans on another.

The harbor of the Sons of the Wind was near the Gates

of the Mists, a tremendous distance from Kidogo's country, no less than two months sailing in the most favorable weather. Cavius and Pandion were dismayed at this; they had had no conception of the enormous distance and realized that the Sons of the Wind were men as skilled in their battle against the sea as were the Elephant People in their battle against the plains of Africa. Pandion still had to sail almost the whole length of the Green Sea from the harbor of the Sons of the Wind to his own country, but it was a distance a little more than a third of that from Kidogo's village to the harbor of the Sons of the Wind. The Sons of the Wind pacified Pandion and Cavius with the assurance that Phoenician ships often came to them from Tyre, Crete, Cyprus, and the Gulf of Sidra.

As Pandion stood on the shore, however, he was not thinking of that. In his confusion, he stared at the sea as though he were trying to measure the long journey before him, and then turned to Kidogo. The commander of the fleet of ships, a man with a circlet of solid gold in his curly hair, shouted loudly, ordering them to get aboard. Kidogo seized Pandion and Cavius by their hands, making no effort to hide his tears.

"Good-bye forever, Pandion, and you, Cavius," whispered the Kemtiu.

"When you are there, in your distant country, remember Kidogo who truly loves you both. Remember our days of slavery in Tha-Quem, when our friendship was our mainstay; remember the days of the insurrection, the flight and the great march to the sea. I shall always be with you in my thoughts. You are leaving me forever, you who have become dearer to me than life itself." The Kemtiu's voice grew stronger. "I shall believe that the time will come when people will learn not to be afraid of the expanses of the sea. The sea will unite them. But I shall never see you again."

"Oh, great is my grief..." Bitter sobs shook Kidogo's huge body.

The friends joined hands for the last time as the Sons of the Wind called to them from the ships. Pandion's handclasp slackened, Cavius turned away. They stepped into the warm water, and sliding over the slippery stones, hurried to the ships.

Pandion stepped on to the deck of a ship for the first time in many years. He was flooded with memories of the days of happy sailing in times long past - no more than fleeting thoughts, however, for the memories soon disappeared. All his thoughts were concentrated on the tall black figure standing aloof from the others on the seashore at the very edge of the water. The oars splashed, their rhythmic beat grew faster, and the ship passed out beyond the reefs. The seamen raised the huge sail, and the wind carried the vessel before it.

The figures of the people on the shore grew smaller and smaller; and soon Kidogo lost to his friends forever, was no more than a tiny black dot. The deepening twilight hid the coastline, but the dark mountain ridge hung gloomily over the stern of the ships.

Cavius wiped away a big tear, and it was not the first. A huge bat that flew out from the coast, parallel to which the ships were traveling, brushed Pandion's face with its wing. That light, silky touch affected Pandion like the last word of farewell from the land he was leaving. It was with a sense of dismay that Pandion parted from his Kemtiu friend, and from the land in which he had gone through so much, where he was leaving part of his heart behind.

He had a vague feeling that in future days of weariness or sorrow, at home in his own country, Africa would appear before his eyes, beckoning and beautiful and that only because it was lost to him forever, like Iruma.

In abandoning everything that had become part of his very life, in turning his face and his heart towards Hellas, Pandion was stricken with doubt. What awaited him there, after so long an absence? How would he settle down amongst his own people, he who was returning a different man from the one who had left? Whom would he find amongst the living? Thessa? Was she still alive, and did she still love him? Or?

The ships, headed westwards, dived wearily into the troughs of the waves. The Sons of the Wind had told their passengers that they would sail westwards for a whole month before turning north. The mighty breath of the ocean ruffled Pandion's hair. The taciturn sailors were unhurriedly busy at their work beside him. The Sons of the Wind, descendants of the ancient mariners of Crete, seemed more alien to Pandion than the black-skinned inhabitants of Africa.

The Hellene squeezed the bag that hung on his breast - it contained the stone on which was carved the image of Kidogo - and joined his companions huddled together sadly in the corner of a strange ship.

A round, orange-colored moon rose from behind the mountains. In its light, the ocean, the Great Arc that encircled all the lands of the world, was furrowed with black hollows over which the brightly lit caps of the waves glided smoothly on their way. The tiny vessels sailed bravely on, pointing their sharp prows straight up at the star-filled sky amidst showers of silvery spray, then racing downwards into the dull roar of the dark depths.

To Pandion, this seemed like his own life story. Far away ahead of him the opalescent crests of the waves merged into one bright path of light, the stars descended and rocked on the surface of the water just as they did by the shores of his native Hellas. The ocean had accepted these courageous men, had consented to carry them on its bosom over an immeasurable distance-to their homes.

***

"Eupalin, did you see that cameo cut on a stone the color of the sea. It is the most perfect work of art in Oeniadae, or rather if the truth be told, in all Hellas?"

Eupalin did not answer immediately. Listening attentively to the strident neighing of his favorite horse, held by a strong slave, he wrapped himself more closely in a cloak of fine wool. In the shade of the stable, the spring wind had a tinge of cold in it, although the grey slopes of the stony hills were already covered with blossoming trees.

Down below, the almond groves stretched in delicate pink clouds; above them, higher up the slopes, patches of dark rose, almost violet, coloring marked the thickets of dense shrubs. The cold breeze from the hills carried with it the fragrance of almond blossoms, the herald of a new spring in the valleys of Oeniadae.

Eupalin took a deep breath and tapped with his finger on a wooden post.

"I've heard," he began slowly, "that it was carved by the adopted son of Agenor who's been wandering abroad for many years. He was believed dead, but recently returned from some very distant land."

"And Agenor's daughter, the beautiful Thessa. You've heard of her, of course?"

"I've heard that she refused to marry for six years in the firm belief that her lover would return. Her father, the artist, allowed her..."

"I know that he not only consented to her waiting, but himself also awaited the return of his adopted son."

"This is one of those rare occasions when things turn out according to expectations. Pandion did not die but became Thessa's husband and a great artist. It's a pity you did not have an opportunity to see the cameo; you are a connoisseur and would have appreciated it!"

"I'll do as you wish, and go to see Agenor. He lives on Cape Achelous which is no more than twenty stadia from here."

"Unfortunately, you're too late, Eupalin. The artist who carved the cameo made a present of it - just imagine! To a friend of his, some Etruscan vagabond. The man fell sick on the journey home, and he took him to Agenor's house, looked after him until he was well again, and then gave him a jewel that would have made all Oeniadae famous. The Etruscan rewarded him with the skin of a disgusting beast, a horrible thing that has never been heard of before."

"A beggar he left and a beggar he has returned. Didn't he learn anything from his wanderings that he cannot make a valuable gift to anybody he meets?"

"It's hard for you and me to understand a man who has lived so long in strange lands. Still, I'm sorry the cameo has gone from us!"

END

THE HELLENIC SECRET

IVAN EFREMOV

"I am very grateful to all of you," Professor Abramovich Faincimmer, a professor in Israel, spoke softly to the audience, and his huge dark eyes lit up.

"In our difficult days, you have not forgotten about my modest celebration. In gratitude, I will tell you one remarkable story of recent times. We, the scientists, do not really like disclosing facts that have not yet been confirmed by others, so accept this as a sign of my respect and trust in you.

"You know that I dedicated my life to studying the human brain and the workings of the psyche. But not on the one hand, not within the limits of one narrow specialty. I approached this interesting section of science and tried to cover the activity and structure of the brain, in all its complexity, as a thinking apparatus. I was a diligent anatomist, a physiologist, a psychiatrist and so on until I found my own direction - psychophysiology of the brain.

"In recent years, I have worked hard to clarify the nature of memory and, I must confess, have done a little more to clarify the issue: it's a very difficult task. Feeling and groping in the midst of the chaos of inexplicable facts, wandering as in the dark, in the complex interconnections of brain nerve cells, I collected only individual grains that had become clear, trying to create from them a trustworthy foundation of the doctrine of memory.

"But that's not what I want to talk about right now. I want to talk about the fact that I came across some special phenomena that are still very dark, and I haven't even tried to report anything about them in the press.

"I call these phenomena memory of generations or gene memory. I will not give you scientific evidence, but I will only say that by inheritance, some rather complex unconscious, sometimes completely automatic actions of the animal's nervous mechanism are transmitted.

"Instincts and complex reflexes can't, in my opinion, be only in the subcortical, inferior, centers of the brain. The crust necessarily takes part in this - hence, the whole mechanism has been much more complicated than it was supposed to be until now.

"Simplification of the mechanism of instincts is the biggest mistake of modern physiology. But this is not memory. Memory is much higher in the chain of increasingly complex organizations that are aware of the perception and comprehension of the world around them. As is accepted by modern science, memory is not hereditary, that is, those imprints of the external world that the brain stores in itself, and accumulates throughout the lifetime of the individual, disappear forever with his death and do not enrich anything. Nothing transfers to the offspring that emerged from this individual.

"The essence of my discovery is that I found facts proving the transfer of some memory footprints inherited from generation to generation. You really must excuse me for the long introduction, but the question is so complicated that I must bring you to it prepared; otherwise, you will not explain your extraordinary knowledge without mysticism and devilry. Do not grin. This is a common reaction to all or for a lot of the weaknesses of human nature.

"You are not the first, and you are not the last reliable fact, but it is absolutely unexplainable for you to consider it as supernatural.

"I continue. All of you noticed, but nothing was

connected with the fact that, for example, the beauty of the forms, whether architectural, whether it be the terrain of somebody, be it of a human body, etc., is felt and, in general, equally evaluated by all people of the most diverse categories, development and upbringing.

"Let's associate this beauty to the appropriate.

"These are known, but generally deemed inaccurate, facts of a perfectly accurate description of people in places where they have never been; dreams that reproduce the exact situation of past events, never seen or heard, and much the same. All such phenomena, by believing mystics and other eccentrics, are considered proof of the transmigration of souls, and scientists only shrug their shoulders, according to the famous proverb about the monkey that has nothing to say. Probably, there are people with a more acute memory of generations, and, conversely, with its complete absence.

"So, my dear, recently, during the difficult days of the great war, I unexpectedly received new evidence of the real existence of the memory of generations, and even immediately from the field of conscious mind.

"The war forced me to break away from purely scientific work. I could not by my nature, not directly participate in the medical profession of the Soviet Army, and started working in several large hospitals where numerous concussions, shocks, psychoses, and other brain injuries required the application of all my knowledge.

"In my apartment on Sretensky Boulevard, I used to sit for about two hours in an armchair in front of my desk resting and at the same time thinking about ways to cure especially difficult wounded people. Sometimes I wrote down important facts or rummaged in the literature, hunting for descriptions of similar clinical cases.

"This pastime has become a habit for me. I rarely have time for friends and fellow scientists. My late returns did not leave much time, and I do not like telephone conversations and use this device only in the most extreme cases.

"My extraordinary idea came to me quite unnoticeably on a quiet evening. In silence, from time to time disturbed by the usual vile clanking of the tram, rational thoughts followed one after the other.

"I thought about the loss of speech from one senior lieutenant, who was shell-shocked from a mine. When the ultimate conclusion was just beginning to emerge, the phone rang. I did not wait for the call; in the silence and concentration of the evening, he seemed so loud to me that I quickly pulled the receiver away from my ear, wincing with vexation. My doctor's ear noted the agitated tension of the voice, inquiring whether it was Professor Faincimmer's apartment. Then the following dialog occurred."

"Are you Professor Faincimmer?" He asked. "I...Forgive me, please, for the late call. I called five times in the afternoon until they told me that you do not come home before eleven."

"It's nothing, I do not go to bed for an hour yet. How can I help you?" I said.

"You see, Professor Novgorodtsev sent me to you. He said that you are the only one who can help me. He said that I will be an interesting subject for your... consideration..."

"Well, who are you?" I asked.

"I'm a lieutenant, wounded, recently discharged from

the hospital, and I need..."

"You need to see me. Come tomorrow at two o'clock in the first department of the Second Surgical Clinic of the special hospital. And, you know the address... Well, ask for me, and you will be held until I can see you."

The voice, shyly muttering gratitude, faded down the line.

The name of my surgeon friend, who often found fascinating cases of illness, had spoken to me about an unusual patient. I tried to guess what it could be, then lit up a cigarette and resumed the interrupted course of my reflection.

The special hospital occupied excellent premises, and I often used the chief surgeon's office for important consultations.

At two o'clock, I walked along the wide corridor of the clinic, beside the huge windows over a soft path that perfectly drowned out my steps. At the end of the corridor, at the last window, stood a man with a hand in a sling. Approaching closer, I saw a beautiful, tormented young face. The military tunic was very flattering to his slim, slender, athletic figure. The wounded man hastily approached me and said:

"You are Professor Faincimmer. I immediately felt that it was you. And I'm the one who called to you yesterday."

"Very good, let's go."

I unlocked the door and led him into the office.

"Let's get acquainted, young man." I extended my hand as usual.

The wounded lieutenant, embarrassed, gave me his

left hand - the right helplessly hung in a sling - and named himself Viktor Filippovich Leontiev.

I lit a cigarette for myself and offered him one, but he refused and sat bent forward, while the long, flexible fingers on his good hand nervously felt the carved ornaments on the massive table

I carefully studied his appearance with professional thoroughness. Certainly, a beautiful, regular face, with a thin nose, thick, distinct eyebrows, and small ears. Pleasant lip pattern, dark hair and dark brown eyes completed the picture.

Impressive and passionate nature, I thought and noted the guilty confusion on his face, characteristic of very nervous or sick people. While I was looking at him expectantly, he looked twice into my eyes, then immediately took them away and made several throat movements, as if swallowing something.

<u>Vasotonic</u>, flashed in my mind.

The wounded lieutenant spoke in a low voice, visibly agitated, sometimes slightly panting. He smiled, and I was fascinated by this cursory, but particularly joyful and bright smile, which completely removed the tortured frown from his very young face.

"Professor Novgorodtsev told me that you have studied a lot of different, difficult-to-explain brain diseases. He is, you know, a compassionate person. I'll remember him with gratitude all my life. I'm in a bad state now - hallucinations are pursuing me, and some wild tension is growing; it seems that I'm about to lose my mind. Also, I get insomnia and have severe pain in the head - right here," and he pointed at the top of the nape. "Different doctors have tried to treat me differently, but it did not help."

"Tell me the story of your injury," I enquired, and again the charming, fluent smile transformed his face.

"Oh, it can hardly be related to my illness. I was wounded in the joint of my right hand, by a splinter from a mine but there was no concussion. The splinter broke the bone, it was taken out, then the bone was transplanted, and now the hand dangles like a whip."

"So, you did not notice any concussion at the time or after the wound?" I asked.

"No, not at all," he replied

"When did you start to get such a special mental state?"

"Not so long ago, about a month and a half. Yes, perhaps. Back in the hospital where I was recuperating, I had a growing sense of anxiety when recovering, then the feeling passed, and now this is what's happened. I left the hospital two months ago."

"And now tell me why, how do you think your disease has arisen? What sensations and hallucinations do you have?"

The lieutenant struggled with growing embarrassment. I hastened to help him, sternly stating that if he wanted my help, he must give me as much information as possible; I'm not a prophet or a medicine man, but a scientist who needs a specific factual basis to solve any problem. Let him not be embarrassed - I have time today - and will be grateful for all the details.

The wounded man gradually managed his shyness and

began to talk; initially stammering and with an effort to pick up expressions, but then he got used to my quiet attention and laid out his entire history even, I would say, with artistic taste.

Before the war, Lieutenant Leontiev was a sculptor, and I remembered that I had seen some of his works at one of the exhibitions at Kuznetsk. These were mostly small statuettes of athletes, dancers, and children, performed simply, but with such an in-depth knowledge of the nature of movement and body, which are inherent only in genuine talent.

The artist himself was a decent sportsman - a swimmer. At one of the swimming competitions, he met Irina - a girl who overwhelmed the artist with the perfect beauty of her body. Irina, in contrast to many beautiful girls, was sensitive and straightforward. The lieutenant's eyes shone with deep inner ecstasy as he talked about his beloved, and I very vividly, even with some hint of envy, imagined this beautiful young couple. You need to have the heart of the lover and the soul of the artist so that you can live modestly and briefly talk about your girlfriend, conveying all the clarity and power of your love. In short, the lieutenant completely conquered me and at the same time charmed me with his Irina.

With this love, where the enthusiasm of the artist and the joy of the lover were harmoniously combined, an authoritarian desire came to Leontiev, the work bringing to everyone the wonderful feeling that was created by Irina and him. He decided to make a statue of his beloved and to convey in her the whole sparkle of her charm, all the fire being the key of life, and not to just create a cool, refined symbol of the beautiful body, similar to classic patterns.

This first vague desire gradually took shape, becoming stronger, until at last the artist was utterly overwhelmed by his idea.

"You understand, Professor," he said, leaning towards me, "this statue would not only be of service to the world, not only my idea, but also a great tribute to Irina."

And I understood him.

The idea of the artist took shape quickly. His beloved did not part from him, but Leontiev could not decide for a long-time what material to make the statue from. The ghostly whiteness of marble did not fit, just as the sharp swarthiness of bronze did not match his idea. Thoughts of other alloys either died in his imagination or were short-lived. The artist also wanted to preserve for centuries the flourishing beauty of his Irina.

The decision came when the artist became acquainted with the descriptions of ancient Greek authors, in which the statues of ivory that were not extant have been mentioned. Ivory - that's the material he needed; tight, allowing him to create the smallest details - those details that form the impression of a living body with the magic of art. Finally, color, the perfection of the surface and lasting strength — ivory, that's what he looked for.

Knowing that individual pieces of bone can be glued together without any trace of joints, the artist devoted about a year to buying and selecting the right pieces of ivory. It must be said that it was very hard work: in our country ivory is not available. It is possible that all the material would not have been collected if Leontiev had not sought permission to receive ivory from abroad.

After visiting an extensive ivory auction in Africa House in London, he quickly picked up the right amount of excellent material and returned to Moscow, full of the desire to start work immediately. However, a severe illness prevented him from doing it immediately, and then the war broke out.

The war took him away from his beloved, and from the world of his feelings and ideas. He honestly fulfilled his duty, bravely fought for everything dear to him in his native country, but two months later he again found himself in Moscow after a severe wound. Here he was met by the same Irina: nothing had changed in her, only a deeper tenderness for him, and was even brighter in her appearance.

The old dreams enveloped the artist with a new force, but now they were mixed with the bitterness of consciousness that he could not create statues with one hand, and if he could, then probably the whole fire of his creative impulse would dissolve in the difficulties of the technique of execution - the execution of murderous slowness.

Along with the bitterness of this helplessness, there was also fear. The terrible destructive force of modern warfare was only now truly realized. He feared he would not have time to fulfill his plan, not to be able to capture nor stop the moment of the blossoming of Irina's radiant beauty.

In the hospital, he often moved restlessly about in the bed and did not sleep at night because of the chains of endless thoughts. The thoughts rushed about in search of a way out, anxiety continued to penetrate deep into the depths of his soul, and nervous tension grew.

Weeks passed, and mental excitement developed, something arose from the bottom of his soul, causing his brain to strain, and he struggled greatly and unconsciously in search of an exit. Leontiev felt that he had to remember something, and then immediately the door would open for the power beating inside, then the former, clear harmony of the world would return.

He slept little; ate little. It was difficult for him to communicate with people. The dream was not real - the tension strained the brain strings, and there was no abandonment of the artist. More often, instead of a dream in half-forgotten, the line of misty thought-images slid around. It seemed that a little more burst strings, vibrated in the brain, and then comes complete madness.

So, after several unsuccessful attempts with other doctors, Leontiev came to me. I asked, not whether he was having recurring hallucinations or, as he called them, mental images. The lieutenant shook his head and said, that he asked the same question of all the other doctors.

"Well, what of it," I retorted. "The reference points for all of us should be the same since we use the same science. But I will ask you the same question but differently: try to remember, if there is anything there - something in all of your visions of an overall picture, some basic, or binding of your ideas?"

Leontiev, after a moment's hesitation, revived and answered briefly.

"Yes, of course."

"What is this?" I asked.

"It seems to me I see Ancient Hellas."

"So, you want to say that all the pictures passing in front of you, in your thoughts, have in some way something to do with your perception of Hellas?"

"Yes, that's right, Professor."

"Well, concentrate, let your thoughts flow calmly and tell me, for example, two or three of your hallucinations. Try the brightest and most complete."

"There are a lot of bright ones, but there are no finished ones, Professor. In fact, any vision for me gradually dissolves in the mist, slips, and breaks."

"What you said is very important, but more on that later. Now I need examples of your fantasies." I replied.

"Here is one of the most striking: the shore of a calm sea in bright sun. Slow topaz colored waves lapping on greenish sand. The tops of the waves almost reaching the edge of a small grove of dark green trees with thick and broad crowns. To the left, the low coastal plain expands into a bluish distance, in which the contours of many small buildings vaguely appear.

"To the right of the grove, a high rocky slope steeply rises. There is a twisting, rising road, and behind this road are groves of trees, behind that..."

The Lieutenant paused and looked at me with the same guilty expression.

"You see, that's all I can tell you, professor."

"Great, great, but, in the first instance, how do you know, it's Hellas, and secondly, whether the visions are like you just described, or are the pictures by artists, reproducing Hellas and her imaginary life?"

"I cannot say how I know it's Hellas, but I know it's hard. And none of these visions reflect the pictures I have seen on the themes of ancient Greek life. And in detail, there is also a similarity, and not common to all of our representations formed from our favorite artworks," he said.

"Well, today should not bother you anymore. Tell some more of your other fancies, your hallucinations, and more about your pretty lady," I prompted him.

"Again, I see a high rocky slope, sizzling with heat. A narrow road rises along with it, strewn with hot white dust. Dazzling light flickers in the haze of heated air. High on the edge of the slope are trees, and behind them is a white building, covered with a belt of slender columns, as if proudly standing straight over the cliff edge. And nothing more."

The lieutenant's stories did not give me a single crack into the wall of this unknown person, for which one could cling a thought on to. I said goodbye to my new patient without a sense of confidence that I really could help him, and promised two days later to call him, after considering what he had related to me.

The next two days I was swamped, and whether as a result of brain fatigue or because the conclusion had not yet ripened, I had no judgment about Leontiev's disease.

However, the appointed time was over, and in the evening, I picked up the phone with a feeling of guilt. Leontiev was at home, and I was annoyed to hear the tone of hope coming through in his questions. I said I could not even think because of a pile of other things on my mind, and therefore I would call a few days, and asked if he had pictured something else - anything.

"Of course, thank you very much, Professor," answered Leontiev politely.

I asked him to tell me over the phone, the most vivid

vision he had had. What he said was:

"High above the sea is a large white building, and it seems that its portico with six tall columns dangerously lean forward over a cliff. To the side of the portico, white colonnades are scattered, half-hidden by the bright green of the trees. A wide white staircase leads to the portico, framed by a parapet of marble blocks, fitted with geometric precision. The upper edge of the parapet is smoothly rounded, and under it runs clear bas-reliefs of moving naked figures. On each ledge, there is a wide platform, encircled by cypresses, and statues on it. I cannot see these statues: my eyes cut through the glitter of the dazzling sun on the marble steps, the sharp shadows of the trees across the platform," Leontiev told me.

When I finished the conversation, I leaned back in my chair, thinking, and considered for a long time the strange case that appeared in front of me. I do not have to provide you with all my attempts to solve the problem. They just are not interesting, as well as the usual range of the facts of our everyday existence; not interesting, until an exciting event happens then something bright suddenly changes everything.

Current thinking has discounted an instantaneous flash of consciousness, that the vision of this artist in his emotional scenes, represents excerpts or pieces of the whole in its gradual development. If so, what? Have I met with an example of generational memory, preserved, and speaking of the past centuries in this person?

Seized by my assumption, I continued to string the facts I knew about the suddenly appeared thread.

Leontiev complained of pains in the upper part of the

nape, namely, there, according to my ideas, in the posterior regions of the cerebral hemispheres, are the most ancient connections - the memory cells nest.

Obviously, under the influence of tremendous mental stress, ancient imprints began to appear from the depths of the brain, hidden beneath all the richness of the memory of his personal life. And his sense of obsessive effort to remember that, without a doubt, was an echo of innermost thoughts slipping in unformed imprints of memory. As an artist, his visual memory was unusually highly developed. Therefore, the manifested pieces were reflected in thinking in the form of paintings.

Finding a foothold, I continued to reinforce my guess, but I interrupted my reasoning and picked up the phone again with excitement. If my reasoning was correct, then I'd hear from Leontiev exactly what I needed to hear. If I did not understand, everything would be wrong and again the way ahead would be a smooth, impenetrable wall of the unknown. I forgot even about the late time.

Leontiev, as usual, did not sleep and immediately answered the phone.

"Is that you, Professor," I heard him over the phone - the usual tense voice, then, "what are you...? Have you come to a conclusion?"

"Well, my dear, is your pedigree known to you?" I asked him.

"Oh, how many times have I already been asked about this! As far as I know, in our family, there are no crazy and drunkards," he replied abruptly.

"Stop talking crazy. That's not what I'm asking. Do you

know who your ancestors were by nationality, where they lived, in what country? You should be a southerner!" I retorted.

"This is so, Professor, but I cannot understand what..."

"I'll explain later. Do not interrupt me! So, who is a Southerner in your family?" I asked.

"I'm not a distinguished person, and I do not have an exact genealogy. All I know is that the parents of my grandfather were both originally from the island of Cyprus. But that was a long time ago, and my grandfather moved to Greece, and from there to Russia, to the Crimea. I was born in Crimea. But why do you need this, Professor?" he asked.

"You'll see. If my guess is correct." Not hiding my joy, I said that I agreed with his request to meet tomorrow and hung up.

Lying in bed, I pondered for a long time. The task was clear, and the diagnosis correct. Now all that was needed was to strengthen and continue the manifestation of the memory of generations to come. It is important for Leontiev's threshold. But what that was for Leontiev was, of course, I did not know, and now was I able to guess. Nearly asleep, I decided that the future would reveal itself.

The next day Leontiev was sitting in the same office and in his previous position. His pale face was no longer gloomy, and he kept an eye on me, while I was walking around the room and initiated him into my theory. When I finished, I sank into a chair at the table, and he sat in deep thought. I moved, and he flinched, then, stubbornly looking me in the eye, asked:

"And do you not think, Professor, that the very idea of

the ivory statue has arisen precisely from me?"

"Well, maybe," I said shortly, not wanting to be distracted from the way to further elucidate Leontiev's memories.

"And do I have something that I must remember regarding the relationship to my statue?" the artist continued to insist.

"Oh, that's very likely," I said at once, as the artist's words seemed to put the point into my thoughts.

The burning eyes of Leontyev showed how strongly my guess worked on him. Maybe he instinctively felt the correctness of the way to solving the riddle, and he already had helped me in his search.

We agreed that the artist would try to immediately isolate himself from all external influences. Locked in his apartment, he was to try to focus on his visions in the half-darkness, and when the pictures disappeared, he would try to recall them again with thoughts of his statue. I told him not to struggle with the sense of necessity to remember something, but, on the contrary, strengthen it, stirring up memory with some unique techniques according to my instructions. In an effort to remember, nervous excitement can reach a dangerous limit, but this risk would have to be taken. Leontiev agreed to tell me about his visions and his state on the phone in the evening.

This time the lieutenant hurried home. Seeing his slender figure, I once again thought of the rare attractiveness of this man, who, unknown to me, was now dear to me.

In the evening, against expectations, the call did not

follow. Slightly worried, I was about to call myself but changed my mind, determined not to interfere with the lonely concentration of my patient. However, somewhere inside me was a doubt about the safety of the treatment system I had invented, and when the phone rang the next night, I looked at the nasty device with relief.

"Dear Professor, you are probably right... I went in," Leontiev told me without preamble, and his voice did not seem to have unhealthy tension.

"What is it, where did you enter?" I did not understand it.

"Well, this house or palace; that white building on the precipice," the artist said hurriedly. "Of course, all these pictures that I remember so clearly are gradually introduced one into another. Now I saw what's inside this building. It's a large room or rooms. Instead of a door, there is wide-open brass lattice. Copper sheets line the floor. There are no windows; instead, there are wide arcades at the top. A smooth light without shadows flows through them. There are many statues and other things there, but I cannot see them: clearly, they are not visible. At the wall opposite the lattice, in the center of the main axis of the hall is a low, wide arcade, in which the thick tops of the pines and the sky sparkling through them are visible. This arcade still has a white statue, and next to it some tables and vessels. Oh, my God, now I understand – it's a sculptors' workshop! Good-bye, Professor!"

The receiver snapped. I, perhaps no less than the artist himself, was eager to learn more, clearly aware of the extraordinary nature of what I had been told. But as a scientist, I was trained in patience and would continue on with my own thought processes, even though the phone was silent for the next two evenings.

The bell rang out early in the morning when I was just about to start the working day and did not expect any communication from Leontiev. The artist tiredly asked me to come to him immediately if I could.

"I seem to have finished my wanderings around the ancient world. I cannot understand anything, professor, and I'm very scared..." He did not finish his sentence.

"Well, I'll try. Wait. Either I'll come, or I'll call," I hurriedly agreed.

Having provided myself a free morning, I went to Taganka, and not without effort found a beautiful small house with a turret, located on a hill, in a garden, hidden deep in a broken street. I called and was immediately greeted by Leontiev himself.

The artist quickly introduced me to his room. It was very simple, without any deliberate disorder in the tastes and habits, for some reason accepted as normal by artists.

A window hung with a thick carpet gave no light. A small bulb, enclosed by something blue, barely made it possible to distinguish objects. I grinned when I saw how accurately all my instructions were fulfilled.

"Light in the light, you cannot see the devil," I said.

"If you can, you do not need the light, Professor," my patient responded then timidly asked, "I'm afraid suddenly. I'm not the same. I'm afraid of losing my ability to concentrate again, I no longer have the strength."

"Of course," I agreed, and Leontiev, pulling the blue cover

off the light bulb, seated me on a large ottoman, and sat.

Even in limited light, I could see how his cheeks were puffed and pale, and the shining in his eyes increased.

"Well, tell me," I encouraged the artist, pulling out a packet of cigarettes and carefully watching his face. Leontiev slowly reached for the table, took a sheet of paper from it and silently handed it to me.

The large sheet was covered with uneven lines of incomprehensible signs. Some crosses, corners, arcs and eight, not written, but somewhat painstakingly sketched, went in groups, apparently forming separate words. I had a general idea of different alphabets, both ancient and modern, but I had never seen anything like it before. On the top were written two short lines, apparently denoting the title.

I looked at the page of unknown letters for a long time, and a presentiment of unusual and interesting thoughts gradually embraced me, then a pleasant sensation of the threshold of suspense, familiar to anyone who had made any great discovery.

Looking up at the artist, I saw that he was watching me carefully - even his lips were half opened, giving the man a childishly attentive expression.

"Do you understand something, Professor?" Leontiev asked anxiously.

"Of course not, nothing," I said bluntly, "but I hope to understand after your explanations."

"Oh, it's the same chain of visions. Remember, I called you and told you about the interior of the building? During the conversation with you, I realized that this is a sculptor's workshop or an art school. Another extra connection with my dream struck me, and I hurried back to the hallucinations, already understanding in them some definite line, some sense, which I should have probably unraveled.

"Yet, again, I succumbed to my visions, strengthening them, and focused on your instructions, but all the other pictures that had flashed before me, or again disappeared, or somehow faded, became vague. As soon as the moment of the appearance of the most distinct and long visions came, the hall in the white building, the art workshop, invariably returned. I could not see anything else and began to despair. The feeling of being shut out of the memory, about which you spoke, did not come.

"Suddenly, I noticed that one part of the room gradually, with each new vision, became more distinct, and realized the continuation of the mental pictures had to be searched for only inside the sculpture workshop. My images were no longer on. As much as I tried, so to speak, to get into the workshop of the sculptor, I could not see anything else. But the right side of the wall against the grille became more distinct, where there was a wide and low window - an arch. The vision of the bas again appeared, and each time I could see more and more details.

"To the left, through the arcade, a small silhouette was visible against the background of pine trees and the sky. It was a small statue, half the size of a man, made of ivory. I tried very hard to study it, but it did not become gradually clearer, but on the contrary, the vision was extinguished. The new detail also faded away. At first, it became more distinct than the statue, a low and long bath of gray stone filled almost to the brim with some kind of dark liquid. In this bath, I could see the outline of a sculptured figure was vaguely visible. It looked as if a naked body had drowned in the dark liquid.

"But even this detail faded away, and next to the bathroom there was a large table with a thick stone slab on top and a long seat like a bench in front of it made from a yellow, smoothly polished tree. On the table in disorder, lay sticks, bundles, and other objects in which, I can vouch for this, I recognized as some sculptural instruments, similar to those that I used to use.

"Closer to the right corner of the table lay a square slab or a thick sheet of smooth copper without any ornaments, covered with some signs. This sheet became more distinct, and, finally, the entire vision was focused on this sheet of copper. It clearly stood out in front of me, with symbols carved on its greenish surface. I did not understand anything, but after all, I sensed intuitively that in this place, the end of a series of mental pictures, is the closure of a chain of visions, according to your assumption.

"Exhausted by an obscure alarm, I began to paint the signs of the copper plate. You see, Professor," his flexible fingers touched a whole heap of sheets, "it was necessary to start again and again. The vision disappeared and sometimes did not come back for hours, but I patiently waited until I could compose this sheet that you have in your hands.

"My left hand was not yet fully adapted, and things were going slowly. And now I do not see anything more, fatigue, it became all the same... I just cannot fall asleep. I'm afraid of making an unclear and persistent mistake. I do not see any connection to myself in these intricate signs. Earlier I felt it very sharply - sculptures, a statue made of ivory - and now again, I do not understand anything. What is it, Professor?"

"What's what?" I answered, trembling with intense agitation. "Take a dose of the sleeping pills I prepared for you in case you overdid it with your visions. You will fall asleep - this is what you need most of all - and I will take the sheet, and by evening we will get an idea of what all this means. Indeed, your hallucinations have come to an end. I do not understand everything yet, but I think that you have finally remembered what you need to. Here are just unexpected strange letters. Once again, I ask, are you absolutely sure that your visions are Hellas, or perhaps are only somehow connected with it?"

"I told you, Professor, I can't explain why, but I'm sure I saw Hellas, or, more correctly, pieces of it."

"Well, now try to sleep. Down with all these shutter curtains, my darling, and you will return to life! Well, enough, enough!" I interrupted further questions from the artist and quickly left, carrying the mysterious sheet.

A little more patience, I thought, going to the tram, *and everything should be decided. Or is it really torn from the depths of the past record of something important, or ... crazy nonsense. No, the last does not seem right. The same signs are often repeated, groups of an unequal number of signs are separated by intervals, at the top, obviously, the heading. No, you can't write such a thing in delirium.*

So, since the artist is sure that this is Hellas, one must go to the Hellenist. Who of us in Moscow is the principal specialist in this area I wondered? I continued my thinking, but could not remember anyone.

At home, with the help of a directory of scientists, the

Academy calendar, and the despicable phone, I found the person I needed and immediately called him. Luckily, he was at home. Not later than forty minutes, I lit a cigarette in his office, while the scientist glared at the sheet I had submitted with the mysterious signs.

"Where did you copy it, or rather, write it from?" exclaimed the Hellenist, piercing me with narrowed, shining eyes.

"I'll tell you everything in secrecy, only first, for God's sake, explain to me, what is this?"

The scientist sighed impatiently, and again bent over the sheet, and spoke in a measured, unintelligible voice:

"The passage you brought is written in so-called Cypriot script, syllabic alphabet, from right to left, as was written in Hellas. These letters are written in the Aeolian dialect of the ancient Greek language. Therefore, I find it difficult to quickly translate the entire passage. Here is the title line. Yes, it's interesting! It consists of three words: at the top, *'malakter elephantos.'* Below them, *'zitos.'* The first two words mean literally the 'ivory softener,' and in a figurative sense literally: the ivory master. Our name 'master' also comes from this root.

"A special now unknown liquid – is a means for softening ivory. You know that in Ancient Hellas, the artists knew the secret of making the ivory soft like wax, and thanks to this, they molded from it very sophisticated works, that after hardening, again became ordinary ivory. This secret was later irretrievably lost, and no one until now..."

"Oh, damn it, I understand everything!" I cried as I jumped up from my chair.

Seeing the scientist's frightened-bewildered face, I

suddenly remembered him and added hastily:

"Forgive me, for God's sake, but this is very important to me, and most importantly for my patient. Can you at this moment give me, even in the most general terms, the content of the page?"

The Hellenist shrugged his shoulders and did not answer. However, I saw that his eyes were running along the lines of the sheet, and he tried to freeze in his chair, restraining excitement and boiling with frenzied joy.

After several minutes that seemed to be very long, the scientist said:

"As far as I can understand without special references, a chemical recipe is recorded here, but the names of the substances will have to be specially interpreted. It says about sea water, then about the powder of cinnamon and some oil of Poseidon and so on. Probably, this is the recipe of how to soften ivory, about which I have just told you. This is very important," concluded the Hellenist.

The tone of his voice seemed too dry to me for the enormous meaning of his words. But one way or another, everything was clear. On the copper plate, that is here, on the sheet, a prescription for ivory softening was recorded. The artist has finally remembered through dozens of generations, and indeed now he will be able to create a statue of Irina!

The scientist looked at me expectantly.

Full of triumph and excitement, I rose and immediately told him the story of my patient and some of my theory. When I finished, the expression of incredulous astonishment finally disappeared from the face of the Hellenist. His small eyes became very kind and, perhaps, wet too.

As I left his office, I saw the scientist already rummaging

in bookcases, quickly retrieving book after book. Calmly, he had promised that the translation of the sheet would be made as rapidly as is possible. I went away feeling happy joy had come into the world in my normal affairs.

The sense of peace and the happiness of the winning mind did not leave me in the usual silence of my office. I felt impatient to quickly inform the artist that all had become clear, and I immediately called him. He apparently was waiting for my call and at my invitation to come to me directly, quickly answered:

"I'm coming now!"

I vividly remember this evening because of Leontiev's sharp, emaciated face, illuminated by shadows from the table lamp, and his attentive eyes that sparkled with amazement, joy, and triumph.

"So, I've remembered the lost secret of ancient masters?" exclaimed the artist excitedly, still not believing what had happened. "But how could I do this?"

I explained to him that science does not yet have exact data, but it seems that in the previous generations of his ancestors there were masters who knew this secret. The long work and importance of this recipe was because, in the memory of one of his ancestors, some powerful bonds were formed, fixed for transmission in the mechanism of heredity.

These connections, stored under the spell of his personal memory, also arose in his, Leontiev's. Thus, only one thing is wonderful here: a remarkable coincidence of the manifestation of ancient memory, and the importance of the Hellenic secret for him, who also became a sculptor, like his ancestors. A very great desire to create a statue of

Irina, the will and tension of all forces, helped him to evoke from the subconscious, a picture of ancient visual memory. Without knowing it, he felt all the time that he knew exactly what was needed of him.

The painter listened to the end of the clarification absent-mindedly, nodding his head and trying to make me understand that he already understood everything. Hardly had I finished, when a quick question followed:

"So, when the scientist does the translation – will I have a formula for this tool, Professor?"

It is difficult for me to convey the joy and excitement of the artist after my affirmative answer.

"Think of it! Now I, with one hand, will fulfill my dream, my goal." And his long fingers moved as if already processing the magic material of soft ivory. "Now, tomorrow…" His voice quivered. "And it was you, professor, your science that gave me…"

The artist jumped up, grabbed my arm, and reached out to me like a child to his father, but then felt ashamed of his impulse, turned away, sat down, and lowered his head on his good hand, on to the table. His shoulders shook slightly.

I went into another room, very worried to the depth of my soul, and sat down to smoke.

The next day I saw the artist again with the Hellenist, who had made the translation of the record containing the exact recipe for the lost secret. After that, I parted with my patient and began to make up for some of the lost business during this time, trying at the same time to make a full report with all possible explanations for the extraordinary encounter.

The days passed, the spring ones were replaced by

summer ones, the autumn came quietly. I was very tired from the heavy load, the years after all made themselves felt; I felt a little screwed up, and glad to be at home.

Suddenly, two young people appeared. I immediately recognized Leontiev, and the other I guessed to be Irina. The hand of the artist hung in a sling, but he was a completely different person, and I have rarely seen in someone so much clarity and kindness. About Irina I will only say, that she was worth the insane love of the artist and of all of our work in search of the secret of the Hellenic.

Irina kissed me and silently looked into my eyes. I was more moved by this silent gratitude, than being given a thousand praises.

Leontiev, worrying, said that the statue was ready. He dedicated it to me as a scientist and as a tribute to the saved savior's feelings and mind, and wanted to show it to me.

Well, I saw the statue. I cannot describe it - that will be done by specialists. As an anatomist, I saw in it the highest perfection of expediency, that all of you will call beauty, in which the artist's love put in joyous and natural movement.

In a word, the statue did not want to leave. For a long time, this amazingly beautiful woman stood before my eyes as proof of the entire influence of Form's power - the subtle happiness of beauty, familiar to all people.

1942 – 1943

END

About The Author

Ivan Efremov (1908 – 1972) was a Russian writer of science fiction, a renowned scientist in paleontology and geology and known as a progressive social thinker for his time. His last name is sometimes spelled Yefremov.

After a brief military career in the Red Army, he was discharged and went to St Petersburg to study, where he completed his education and went onto the Leningrad State University to study paleontology. He led several expeditions, headed a research laboratory, and received awards and degrees during his career, including a doctorate, in biological sciences.

He wrote his first work of fiction in 1944, 'The Land of Foam' and his most recognized science fiction novel 'Andromeda Nebula' was published in 1957.

In the 1960's he became disillusioned with the communist system, with his subsequent books becoming a rarity, and banned. Eventually, he was interrogated by the KGB, his apartment searched, his manuscripts and writings confiscated, and all his works also confiscated and banned from all public libraries and schools in the Soviet Union. He remained under suspicion, surveillance, and censorship for the remainder of his life, and died in 1972.

About The Publisher

Royal Hawaiian Press is a publishing house located in Honolulu Hawaii. It was established in 2005, primarily to promote the works of author and founder, Maria Cowen. Since then, it has expanded to encompass an assortment of other authors from around the world.

Royal Hawaiian Press specializes in providing books in a variety of languages and genres, including translating, and publishing existing European-language books into English for the English-speaking market.

To learn more about Royal Hawaiian Press and the books it represents, please visit:

www.royalhawaiianpress.com

To receive an alert when new books are released, subscribe to the Royal Hawaiian Press Mailing List:

http://tiny.cc/rhp